Beating for Light

Dedication

For Fiona, whose patience and generosity of spirit made
this book possible.

Beating for Light

The Story of Isaac Rosenberg

Geoff Akers

JUNIPER BOOKS

Copyright © Geoff Akers 2006
First published in 2006 by Juniper Books
16 Foulis Crescent
Edinburgh EH14 5BN

Distributed by Gazelle Book Services Limited
Hightown, White Cross Mills, South Rd, Lancaster, England LA1 4XS

The right of Geoff Akers to be identified as the author of the work has been
asserted herein in accordance with the Copyright, Designs
and Patents Act 1988.

Jacket illustrations – photo of Isaac Rosenberg by kind permission of The
National Portrait Gallery;
Der Krieg by Otto Dix by kind permission of the estate of Otto Dix,
© DACS 2006

British Library Cataloguing in Publication Data
A catalogue record for this book is available from the British Library

ISBN 0-9547428-0-X

Typeset by Amolibros, Milverton, Somerset
This book production has been managed by Amolibros
Printed and bound by T J International Ltd, Padstow, Cornwall, UK

Contents

Prelude: Summer 1917

Dead Man's Dump

The plunging limbers over the shattered track
Racketed with their rusty freight,
Stuck out like many crowns of thorns,
And the rusty stakes like sceptres old
To stay the flood of brutish men
Upon our brothers dear.

The wheels lurched over sprawled dead
But pained them not, though their bones crunched,
Their shut mouths made no moan,
They lie there huddled, friend and foeman,
Man born of man, and born of woman,
And shells go crying over them
From night till night and now.

Earth has waited for them
All the time of their growth
Fretting for their decay:
Now she has them at last!
In the strength of their strength
Suspended-stopped and held.

What fierce imaginings their dark souls lit
Earth! have they gone into you?
Somewhere they must have gone,
And flung on your hard back
Is their souls' sack,
Emptied of God-ancestralled essences.
Who hurled them out? Who hurled?

None saw their spirits' shadow shake the grass,
Or stood aside for the half used life to pass
Out of those doomed nostrils and the doomed mouth,
When the swift iron burning bee
Drained the wild honey of their youth.

What of us, who flung on the shrieking pyre,
Walk, our usual thoughts untouched,
Our lucky limbs as on ichor fed,
Immortal seeming ever?
Perhaps when the flames beat loud on us,
A fear may choke in our veins
And the startled blood may stop.

The air is loud with death,
The dark air spurts with fire
The explosions ceaseless are.
Timelessly now, some minutes past,
These dead strode time with vigorous life,
Till the shrapnel called 'An end!'
But not to all. In bleeding pangs
Some borne on stretchers dreamed of home,
Dear things, war blotted from their hearts.

(Maniac Earth! howling and flying, your bowel
Seared by the jagged fire, the iron love
The impetuous storm of savage love.
Dark Earth! dark heavens swinging in chemic smoke
What dead are born when you kiss each soundless soul
With lightning and thunder from your mined heart,
Which man's self dug, and his blind fingers loosed.)
[Verse missed out in final version.]

A man's brains splattered on
A stretcher-bearer's face;
His shook shoulders slipped their load,
And when they bent to look again
The drowning soul was sunk too deep
For human tenderness.

They left this dead with the older dead,
Stretched at the cross roads.

Burnt black by strange decay,
Their sinister faces lie
The lid over each eye,
The grass and coloured clay
More motion have than they,
Joined to the great sunk silences.

Here is one not long dead;
His dark hearing caught our far wheels,
And the choked soul stretched weak hands
To reach the living word the far wheels said,
The blood-dazed intelligence beating for light,
Crying through the suspense of the far torturing wheels
Swift for the end to break,
Or the wheels to break,
Cried as the tide of the world broke over his sight.

Will they come? Will they ever come?
Even as the mixed hoofs of the mules,
The quivering-bellied mules,
And the rushing wheels all mixed
With his tortured upturned sight
So we crashed round the bend,
We heard his weak scream,
We heard his very last sound,
And our wheels grazed his dead face.

Isaac Rosenberg – 1917

M*y Dear Marsh,*

We are camping in the woods now and are living great. My feet are almost healed and my list of complaints has dwindled down to almost invisibility. I've written some lines suggested by going out wiring or rather carrying wire up the line on limbers and running over dead bodies lying about. I don't think what I've written is very good but I think the substance is, and when I work on it I'll make it fine.

Isaac Rosenberg stopped writing for a moment and eased back against the bole of a large beech tree. He'd left his tent ten minutes ago, tempted outside by the warmth of the early morning sun. Slowly placing pen and paper on the grass, he ran exploratory fingers over the half-healed sores dappling his rib-cage. The problem of lice had eased off recently, perhaps because everything was so much drier now, making it possible to wash clothes and hang them out to dry. An examination of his feet revealed a similar improvement, although discoloured patches round the heels and the dark, swollen appearance of both big toes testified to the pain he'd endured for months on end.

Sending poems to his patron, Edward Marsh, was always a frustrating exercise. Isaac desperately sought the approval he knew from past experience was unlikely to materialise. Fierce criticism generally accompanied any grudging admission that the poem under scrutiny had potential if carefully reworked. Recent praise from a fellow poet had provided some encouragement, but, deep inside, he knew that none of his correspondents could ever possibly understand the difficulties of writing at the front. The gulf between the two worlds was just too wide to bridge. Isaac rarely mentioned the hardships he experienced. What was the point? Since arriving in France, he'd sought to minimise the rigours and maximise the few advantages the situation bestowed.

Only when his health almost gave out at the turn of the year had he asked for help. Despite Marsh contacting the War Office and writing a letter to Isaac's captain, nothing had come of it at first. The battalion doctor insisted on declaring him fit for duty, even though his hands and feet were in a dreadful state and his chest giving cause for concern. Major Alexander prided himself on his ability to detect malingerers, and, as far as he was concerned, Isaac fitted the bill. Nothing could persuade him—not Marsh's efforts nor Captain Normoy's personal intervention—to send the private to the field hospital for a fuller examination. Eventually, he was reassigned to the divisional works battalion and the slightly improved conditions behind the front led to a partial recovery of his strength.

Like most trench fighters, Isaac subscribed to the philosophy of "grin and bear it" as a way of coping with the burden of existence; but an unflinching resolve to reveal the true horror of the war through his poetry, provided the strongest motivation to persist. People must be moved to ponder why nations priding themselves on the extent of their civilised accomplishments were able to tolerate barbarity on such an immense scale. Turning a line over in his mind from his most recent poem, he reflected for a moment on the extremes of life in this terrible place: "*What of us, who flung on the shrieking pyre...*" With a sigh, he resumed his letter:

> *Bottomley told me he had some very old poems in The Annual but, of course, it's too bulky to send out here. Your extract from his 'Atlantis' is real Bottomley-ian. The young Oxford poets you showed my things to, I've never come across yet and I'll soon begin to think myself a poet if my things get admired so...*

Again, he ceased writing and contemplated the rutted track snaking its way through the camp-ground, up over the wooded ridge and down towards the front line. Only a few miles from here thousands of men gazed at each other through their gun-sights, productive farmland lay devastated, and human remains, uprooted from temporary graves, festered in the warm spring sunshine. It was sometimes hard to imagine what Marsh's young Oxford friends, and those back home with no direct experience of conditions at the front, would ever make of his poetry. This sort of speculation was, he realised, self-defeating. He must never succumb to the sense of futility which, of all the forces ranged against him, was by far the most dangerous. The struggle to remain intact had tested his resolve on many occasions but, so far, he'd refused to compromise.

With an effort he returned to the letter; his mind was forever wandering off in different directions, how ever much he tried to focus on specific tasks. He realised it was this failure that got him into so much trouble with his superiors.

I'm writing to my sister to send you the lines as she will type several copies.

Mention of his sister brought fresh guilt flooding back. How his family, especially his mother, was coping constantly troubled him. His decision to join up had hit them all badly. With a pang, he recalled the fateful day he'd packed a few things and sneaked out of the house to join the newly formed Bantams—the only battalion prepared to accept men of his diminutive stature. He tried to dismiss the disturbing thought and added a p.s. asking after his patron's job at the Colonial Office.

Folding the paper, Isaac rose to his feet and slowly stretched his thin body. Suddenly, out of nowhere, a harsh voice broke the back of his reverie.

"Rosenberg, where the fuck do you think you are? This isn't some sort of bleedin' holiday camp, you know! Get your uniform back on now and report to me at nine hundred hours. Maybe some more pack drill will learn you respect for regulations."

With a mixture of anger and trepidation, he watched as Sergeant Jackson disappeared in the direction of the latrine. The army was full of such small-minded bullies who liked nothing better than to put the men through it. Isaac had always taken a lot of flak from NCOs on account of his forgetfulness and "unsoldierly" demeanour. The fact that he was regarded as eccentric and found it hard to mix with the other men also marked him out as an obvious target. Being caught like this was rotten luck but his own fault. Jackson was particularly vigilant, at least where he was concerned, and failing to dress properly before leaving the tent had been foolhardy. The pack drill would break into his quiet time, threatening the only real opportunity he had to write without interruption. The prospect extinguished the warmth of the sun, and his rare sense of well-being popped like an oversize bubble.

The following morning, while most of the wiring company slumbered in their tents, Isaac prepared to work on what he hoped would be the final version of "Dead Man's Dump". He'd already sent a second copy to his Sister Anna for typing before forwarding to Marsh.

Writing the first draft of any poem was, of course, the most traumatic part of the whole business. What followed, although necessary, was thoroughly tame by comparison. In this instance he'd found it particularly hard to contain himself and exert control over the process. Swept along on a fierce riptide of exhilaration, his racing pen barely able to keep up, he'd found himself dumped on an unfamiliar hinterland feeling confused and disorientated.

He recalled a fragment from a letter to Marsh where he'd tried to convey something of the ordeal involved.

If you are not free, you can only, when the ideas come hot, seize them with the skin in tatters raw, crude, in some parts beautiful in others monstrous.

This certainly summed up the latest experience, but, try as he might, he could never make Marsh understand, obsessed as his patron was with inherited tradition and technique. These conventions, however important to the people who championed them, were useless when it came to articulating the horrors of modern warfare. He had no choice but strive for a more powerful means of expressing himself. Throttling his longstanding bitterness, he tried to focus on the job at hand.

Reading through the poem, he recalled the mood of the evening when the first, stark images had broken through.

Dusk had been gathering beneath the trees when the limbers were finally loaded up and ready to move. His mind, unusually restless, lent a heightened awareness to everything. With a shiver of excitement he sensed his muse hovering close by. Resting a quivering arm against one of the thick wheel spokes, Isaac began to perceive the piled-up mass of rough cut stakes and rusting screeds of barbed wire in a completely new way. The flicking tails of the tethered mules, the clouds of flies swarming round their bowed heads and gaunt rumps, the impatient stamp of hooves, all assumed an added significance. His mind was soon struggling to contain the swirl of images.

On the command from Sergeant Jackson, he and a fellow private climbed aboard the rear-most cart and, as usual, perched themselves in the narrow space between the stacked-up freight and the tall, rickety wheels. Amidst a cacophony of hoarse yells and lashing whips, they lurched forward, bumping slowly along the track. Soon, the first clear pictures began to emerge: the rusty iron stakes were transformed into sceptres of power and the cruel, twisting wire, innumerable crowns of thorns. The scourging of Christ and his death on the cross struck him as tame in comparison to the terrible things now accepted as normal in the waging of war. In Isaac's waking vision, an ancient tyrant— the image of the hopelessly corrupt God he'd reviled so many times in the past—shook his sceptre menacingly as armies tramped past, en route to distant battlefields.

The cart suddenly dipped in and lurched out of an unusually large pothole. Isaac, immersed in another world, was almost thrown off. His companion grabbed his arm, pulling him upright.

"For fuck-sakes, 'old on. If the sarge sees ya, you'll be for the 'igh jump."

He muttered his thanks, but already another harrowing image was unfurling in his mind's eye: corpses, hurtling through the air, crashed into the scorched earth and smashed into dozens of shard-like pieces. Then, slowly, terrifyingly, fiery holes began to open in the ground like mouths flicking tongues of red flame. The human fragments slid inside and the apertures snapped shut leaving a blasted landscape devoid of life.

By now the limbers were over the ridge and trundling down a long slope towards an area recently laid waste by the retreating German army. Gradually the surface began to widen and flatten out as other tracks flowed in like tributaries feeding a major river system. The marching feet of countless soldiers had compressed the soil and the convoy gained speed. The crashing hooves of the mules and the creaking of boards and harness added a frenzied accompaniment to his racing thoughts. Lines from an earlier poem flashed across his consciousness: *But a subtler brain beats iron/ To shoe the hoofs of death./ (Who paws dynamic air now.)* This was all becoming too much to bear. He made a desperate attempt to regroup by focusing on practical aspects of the night's work ahead.

Barbed wire barriers, erected to hinder movement across no-man's-land, sustained considerable damage each day and had to be restored during the hours of darkness. Although much less hazardous than manning front line trenches, or even labouring with the divisional works battalion behind the front line, the job was by no means free from danger. At any moment, soldiers could be torn apart by exploding shells or targeted by enemy snipers. The prospect sobered him and his muse retreated for a while. Despite this temporary assuagement, however, he knew the process was continuing, albeit on a subliminal level.

Staring around him, Isaac realised that even though the horrors of this place were virtually impossible to describe, many of the sights had become so commonplace he and his companions hardly reacted to them at all. In the lurid glare of the lanterns, he could see bodies, or parts of bodies, rotting at the side of the track. A detached head, lying face down in the centre of an arid shell hole, looking for all the world like a tattered football, barely merited a glance. Often the wheels lurched over these gruesome remains, and, despite his apathy, Isaac winced at the sound of crunching bone.

Almost all of the corpses were German in origin. Many enemy soldiers cut down during their strategic withdrawal to the heavily fortified Hindenburg line back in February, and hastily interred in temporary graves, had been thrown up by the pitiless shells. No one now seemed particularly interested in reburying them. Perhaps the task was viewed as a dangerous waste of effort, although the stench of rotting flesh and the bloated flies and rats attracted to the feast must, Isaac suspected, be creating problems for the infantry battalions manning adjacent trenches.

As they threaded their way through the network of reserve trenches, a green flare arced into the sky, lending a sinister lustre to the surrounding landscape throughout its long descent. Without warning the convoy ground to a halt and Jackson's voice erupted out of the darkness.

"Right lads, look lively. Start unloading and no skiving about or you'll feel the toe of my boot up your arse. Do you hear me, Rosenberg?"

Things went well that particular night. Nobody was killed or even injured. Only a few shells dropped despite the continual rise and fall of the flares. Immediately on returning to camp, while the others stretched out to sleep after the exhausting night's work, Isaac began to write, striving to shape and sequence the torrent of words.

Now, studying the first draft and subsequent alterations, he wondered how the thing as a whole might be improved. The prospect of Marsh's inevitable censure spurred him on. Were there any words or lines in the poem which could be amended or dropped altogether? Was there anything obscuring or interfering with the clarity of the whole? Maybe he shouldn't have sent off the amended copy so quickly to his sister, but always felt he had to in case something happened. His own fate seemed somehow less important than preserving the lines he dashed off.

He was immediately faced with the agonising dilemma side-stepped during his first revisitation. What to do with stanza eight? A decision would have to be made; there could be no more putting it off. With a pang of regret, he realised few would understand his agonised appeal to "Maniac Earth!" Even he felt somewhat bewildered reading over the lines, and Marsh would doubtless dub them grotesque. There was certainly no denying the verse was intrusive, breaking up the *stretcher bearer* sequence, but, then again, it powerfully expressed something of the savage extremes of war. With a long sigh, Isaac finally scribbled it out and began to carefully copy out the remainder of the poem, pausing now and again to make amendments to the original holograph.

Several minutes later, the sound of heavy boots clumping up the track returned him to reality. Remembering his recent clash with Jackson, he slowly sunk down into the grass, unwilling to be seen or interrupted at such a crucial stage. Whoever it was passed by, unaware of his presence. Anger and frustration swept through his mind like storm clouds blotting out the sun; it was utterly intolerable he was forced to write under these conditions. As a means of dispelling the darkness, he reread the verse just copied out:

> *None saw their spirits' shadow shake the grass,*
> *Or stood aside for the half used life to pass*
> *Out of these doomed nostrils and the doomed mouth,*
> *When the swift iron bee*
> *Drained the wild honey of their youth.*

To his surprise, warm tears welled up and spilled down his cheeks. Dashing them impatiently aside, he inwardly cursed this dangerous overflow of sentiment. Objectivity must be maintained at all costs; emotional involvement, he knew, would irretrievably mar the process.

Finishing, he read through the poem once more in order to satisfy himself that the alterations had resulted in the desired improvement. Several lines in the ninth stanza caught his eye and drew him down into their ominous core:

Their sinister faces lie
The lid over each eye
The grass and coloured clay
More motion have than they,
Joined to the great sunk silences.

With a shudder, he felt the immunity of the seasoned soldier stripped away. Not for the first time, he wondered whether he would soon be one of these *sinister* corpses stiffening at the side of a track, ignored by the jaundiced eyes of those still endowed with *vigorous* life. As usual, his reaction was ambivalent—dread and allurement grappling on the battlefield of his tortured imagination. For the moment, however, the allure was eclipsed by a potent vision of the soul *beating for light*, like an injured bird striving to regain its former grace and mastery.

Carefully signing and dating what he hoped would be the final copy, Isaac folded the sheets away and crept back to his tent. His two companions were still fast asleep, their breathing deep and regular. He was amazed how peaceful they looked, as if they'd found a haven in their dreams far removed from the rumour of war. He, on the other hand, was unable to free himself from the fear the poem had released. His chest was tightening up, and the irregular beat of his heart worried him. Praying the condition would ease, he forced himself to breath slowly and deeply. He must snatch some sleep. In less than five hours he'd be back on his feet loading up the limbers all over again, and, after that, Jackson would be enforcing his latest round of punishment drills. Most days were the same, but, in comparison to the trenches last winter, he felt his lot to be wonderfully improved. This sustained him, as did the satisfaction of finally completing a piece which, he believed, conveyed something profound and important.

Falling asleep, he was immediately caught up in the loop of a recurring nightmare sparked off by an incident that had taken place a few days after he first joined the wiring company.

In the cold light of dawn, as the men return to the assembly point ready for transportation back to their billets, Isaac, already mounted on an empty cart, watches as one of the work team stoops to pick something off the ground. As if in slow motion, he begins to rise and turn. Knowing what's going to happen, Isaac is desperate to scream a warning, but cannot. Suddenly, the air fills with a strange whirring sound as if some gigantic insect is hovering directly overhead, followed almost instantaneously by a shattering explosion. When he looks again, the man's head is gone. Bizarrely, the body remains upright for a moment, its arms waving in the air as if searching for the missing part, before toppling over. The legs paddle convulsively for a few seconds longer. As usual, it's the image of the headless body standing upright in the mud that fills him with most horror.

Part One

1897–1915

Chapter One

1897–1902

*One conceives one's lot to be terribly tragic.... . You are the victim
of a horrible conspiracy; everything is unfair. The gods have either
forgotten you or made you a sort of scapegoat to bear all the
punishment...*

*You mustn't forget the circumstances I have been brought up in,
the little education I have had. Nobody ever told me what to read,
or ever put poetry in my way.*

*I can't say I have ever experienced the power of one spirit over
another except in books, of course, at least in any intense way
that you mean. Unless you mean the interest one awakes in us,
and we long to know more, and none other. I suppose we are all
influenced by everybody we come in contact with, in a subconscious
way, if not direct, and everything that happens to us is experience;
but only the few know it...*

Extracts from letters to Miss Winifreda Seaton—1911

...And my soul thought,
'What fearful land have my steps wandered to?
God's love is everywhere, but here is naught
Save love His anger slew...'

                    From "A Ballad of Whitechapel".

...The world rustles by me—let me heed.
Clutched in its madness till I bleed.

For the rose of my heart glows deep afar.
If I stretch my hand, I may clasp a star.

                    From "The World Rumbles By Me"

No one in possession of their sanity, or the most modest of incomes, would have chosen to live in Cable Street. Piles of evil-smelling rubbish spilled out of alleyways onto the cobbles where noisy urchins splashed in puddles of foul water. The remains of a dog lay in the gutter, its skull and rib cage picked clean. Barnett Rosenberg, immigrant Jew and peddler by trade, stared in disbelief at number forty-seven fronted by a dilapidated rag and bone shop. It was hard to believe that this miserable hovel contained the room he was here to rent. Habitually short of money, this was apparently the best he could do to house his wife and five children. He knew little yet of the area's unsavoury reputation for vermin, crime and prostitution; being so close to the docks guaranteed lawlessness and moral laxness in equal proportion.

Perhaps his friends, the Levines, had exaggerated the good living to be found in London. He fervently hoped this was not the case. He'd prayed for months that the move might be the first step in achieving the success which had eluded him in Lithuania and continued to elude him in Bristol ten years after his flight to England. The opportunity to expand his religious horizons, improve his economic status and secure Isaac's education was of the utmost importance to him, and could all now be within his grasp. The thriving East End Jewish community with its numerous synagogues and chevras would surely benefit himself and his family; and, of course, the reputation of the Jews Free School was legendary. Maybe it was just a matter of getting his foot in the door, then they'd be out of this slum and moving up in the world in no time at all. An unshakeable belief that God was guiding him along the path to good fortune and prosperity helped sustain him. Stroking his beard and adjusting his hat, Barnet crossed the road and entered through the shop door.

It was gloomy inside and he could feel the dust catching in his throat. Detritus littered the floor and lay strewn across various shelves and counters. He found it hard to imagine what use anyone could find for the motley collection of rags, broken bottles and rusty metal items apparently for sale. Even the goods he carried in his cases, so useless that often all he wanted to do was tip the lot into the nearest ditch, were infinitely more appealing than such junk. Hacha would be horrified by the squalor, and the musty smell saturating everything. She'd been unconvinced by his reasons for moving to London, accusing him of placing selfish motives before the welfare of his family. A sense of long-standing bitterness flooded his mind —nothing he ever said or did was right in her eyes.

He suddenly sneezed three times in quick succession. Pulling out a white handkerchief from an inside pocket and pressing it hard against his nose, he managed partially to suppress a fourth. The effort almost choked him however, triggering an intense bout of coughing. Wiping the tears away, he noticed a man standing beside the dusty remains of an ancient grandfather clock rubbing the palms of his hands on a soiled leather apron. Despite a marked stoop, he was at least six inches taller than Barnett and, judging by appearances, must surely be half-starved or the victim of some wasting disease.

"You must be Mr Rosenberg unless I'm much mistaken. Adam told me you was coming. The name's Eli Bernstein."

He grinned and stuck out a grimy paw. Barnett could not help noticing that his prospective landlord's cheekbones looked ready to burst through the tight, waxy skin at any moment.

"Things is pretty quiet just now so I can show you around. If you follow me through the back I'll let you see the accommodation. The privy's down 'ere an' all." Eli grimaced over his bony shoulder. "I'm afraid the wife and me 'as to come through the room to get upstairs. It's not so bad when you gets used to it; we try to respect our lodgers' privacy like. Any'ow, I'm in the shop all day and Miriam 'ardly ever goes out wiv the twins, so it's all right most of the time."

At the end of a narrow, ill-lit corridor, he pushed open a battered door and invited Barnett to enter. The blackened stubs of teeth, fronting the depths of Eli's cadaverous smile, did little to reassure him.

"So, 'ere we are then. Quite roomy for a family. Adam said you 'ave a wife an' five young children. Is that right?"

Staring round in disbelief, he found himself unable to answer for a moment. This was worse than anything he'd imagined. The place had only one tiny window, so grimy, little light managed to trickle through. A closed door over to the right obviously led to the Bernsteins' home directly above. And in one corner he could just make out a greasy stove and an attached blackened metal pipe snaking its way up through the ceiling. The air in the room felt cold and clammy.

The sudden wail of a baby was so loud that Barnett glanced around the room wondering where it might be hidden. A woman's harsh voice, followed by a reverberating thump directly overhead, brought an uneasy smile to Eli's lips.

"That's Miriam. She's a wonder wiv the twins; 'ardly ever a peep out of 'em."

The baby's screaming intensified and both men had to shout to make themselves heard.

"So, Mr Rosenberg, will you be wantin' the room then? Someone else was asking if it was available yesterday like, but when Adam said a friend of 'is was interested, I said I'd give you first shot. Only seemed fair at the time."

Although quailing inside, Barnett realised this was the best he was going to do in the short term. Besides, Hacha and the children were already on their way here. Overriding his wife's fears, he'd promised to meet the family at Paddington Station and convey them to their new home. He tried not to think about her inevitable wrath when she found herself deposited in this cramped slum.

"Yes, I'll take it. Where did you say the lavatory was situated?"

Leading the way back out, Eli pulled open another door. The putrid stench, flooding out into the dark corridor, took the peddler's breath away; the tiny compartment was pitch black but he knew the hole was overflowing and the contents slopping around the floor.

"Sorry about the mess, I'll unblock it later on. There's been a lot of the customers in and out today. I can 'elp you wiv items of furniture if you like. Somebody brought in a fold-up table, two chairs and a cradle the other day—part of a job lot. Some of it's a bit damaged like, but I can fix it up, no bother."

In a daze, Barnett heard himself reply. "Yes, thank you—that would be much appreciated."

"Adam was tellin' me you're a religious man. There's a chevra just up the street. It's a bit small but friendly like. Me and the wife go along; give you a chance to chat wiv some of the locals. Maybe not quite what you're used to but you can try it out, eh? We'll see you later on then?"

"Yes. I've got some more furniture to sort out. I'm hiring a horse and cart to collect it and bring my family up from the station. We should be here by six o'clock."

"Perfick. And don't worry, I'll get the place cleaned up a bit. We don't want your wife getting the wrong idea, do we?"

Barnett smiled wryly. Bernstein was obviously trying to be helpful but whatever he did would change nothing. Hacha would never be placated.

Emerging into the street, he took a deep breath before walking swiftly away. A filthy creature lifted her skirts at the corner of the street and grinned toothlessly at him.

"Three pence a go, mister, what you say?"

He said nothing, contriving to blot out her existence.

"Fuckin' Jews, think they're better than the rest of us."

She spat on the cobbles and retreated into a dark alleyway.

Barnett and Hacha Rosenberg's first born son, Isaac, stood at the door watching a gaunt mongrel urinating against the wall of the cobbler's workshop across the street. Although small for his age, his unusually melancholic disposition made him appear older than his seven years. Normally, he wasn't allowed outside by himself—his mother's nervousness compounded by the strange mixture of misfits and foul-mouthed stevedores who wandered the street at all times of the day and night—but today she was busy spring-cleaning the corridor leading to the shop and the tiny privy which served her family and anyone deemed a client or agent of the landlord. She was so involved in the task that her son, normally the apple of her eye, had managed to slip past her undetected. As far as she knew he was still inside sketching his sister Annie.

A little under a month since they'd moved here, Hacha was striving to create a home fit for her young family to live in. Barnett was off peddling his wares somewhere in Kent, and she hadn't seen him for a fortnight now, which suited her well enough. Apart from anything else, there was more space when he wasn't around. Incredibly, she'd managed to create three separate areas in the cramped room, each affording a measure of privacy: the largest of these doubled as a master bedroom and dining space; the smallest was reserved for their eldest daughter Minnie, who'd reached the age where it was preferable she sleep alone, while the remaining section was used as a kitchen and bedroom for Isaac, Annie and Rachel. The baby, David, slept in a cradle beside his parents' bed. Hacha insisted they all eat together at the ancient foldaway table, brought out at mealtimes and set up next to the stove. After a few weeks, she'd become a little more accustomed to existing in the limited space. However, the constant reek in the corridor and the comings and goings of the Bernstein family tested her patience to its limits. Every time there was a tap on the door and the slatternly Miriam waddled through, a baby clasped in each plump arm, Hacha ground her teeth and tried to fill her mind with positive thoughts.

Stepping out onto the broken cobbles, Isaac began to cross the street. By this time the dog had disappeared, but the boy noticed something else was moving along the edge of the dank wall forming the outer limit of a tiny courtyard piled high with refuse from a workshop and adjoining houses. It was hard to see anything properly in the deep shadows, but curiosity, coupled with a compelling desire to explore the limits of the strange new world, drew him on. The movement had stopped now but Isaac instinctively knew something was still there, crouched close to the dark, dripping stones. Despite growing trepidation, the boy continued to advance. Without warning, a large, grey shape streaked towards him. Isaac fell over backwards screaming in fear. Swerving aside at the last moment, the rat leapt over his outstretched arm and disappeared through the grill of a drain a few feet to his right. Although the entire incident was over in less than three seconds, every detail was imprinted on the boy's brain: the matted fur, the sinuous, leaping body, the long, naked tail; he even registered the beady eyes, tiny ears and numerous whiskers sprouting obscenely from the creature's snout.

"What the matter, boy? Ain't you never seen a bleedin' rat afore?"

A huge figure in a long, ragged coat towered over Isaac. Half of the face staring down at him, including the nose, was almost entirely eaten away, while the remaining skin and flesh looked like grey wax trowelled on in rough layers. The words were forced out in a series of gasping growls punctuated by wheezing in-breaths. Two gnarled hands hoisted him to his feet, and rough fingers began to feel their way through his trouser pockets.

"Now, what 'ave you got in 'ere for old Tom then?"

Overcome with terror, but unable to call out, the boy tried to wriggle free but was held tight as the search continued.

Suddenly, a loud, clanging thump reverberated above his head and he was instantly released. With a deep grunt of pain, the derelict hirpled off down the street. Eli Bernstein, grasping a greasy frying pan with a jagged hole in its centre, stood grimly watching the retreat.

"Now then, Isaac, what's you doing outside? The street's no place for a young lad. We better get you back inside in a 'urry; your mother'll be scared out of 'er mind when she finds out what's 'appened."

Noticing the boy was trembling with fear, he made an effort to speak more kindly.

"Maybe we'd better keep it our little secret, eh? There's no 'arm done, far as I can see. What you think?"

Although Isaac's thought processes were barely functioning, he made an enormous effort to pull himself together, knowing from past experience that telling his mother would only make matters worse.

Leading him back into the shop, Elie tried to sound cheerful, as if nothing out of the ordinary had happened.

"Maybe you'd like to 'elp me go through some of this stock." He leaned over the counter, his nose almost touching a grubby sheet of paper. "Let's start wiv this stuff over 'ere. All right?"

At that moment, Hacha appeared from the corridor, her large, matronly body filling the entrance way.

"Isaac, where have you been? I hope you're not bothering Mr Bernstein."

Elie shook his head and smiled ingratiatingly.

"Not at all, Mrs Rosenberg. Isaac's been 'elping me go through some of the stock. Haven't you, son?"

"Yes. Can I stay and help Mr Bernstein, Mother?' To Elie's amazement, the lad somehow managed to control the wobble in his voice. Fighting back the overwhelming urge to cry and throw himself into his mother's plump arms, he produced a rare smile to reassure her.

"Well, if Mr Bernstein says it's all right, but what about the drawing of your sister? Did you finish it?"

"I'll finish it later. But she won't sit still for more than a minute; I got fed up."

"All right then, but send him back through if he starts to make a nuisance of himself, Mr Bernstein."

Hacha disappeared down the corridor. Eli smiled.

"You're a very brave boy. I don't think she twigged anything 'appened."

"I saw a rat, Mr Bernstein. I thought it was going to bite me."

Starting to recover a little, Isaac felt the urge to talk about his nerve-wracking experience.

"You take care, boy. These brutes'll 'ave a go at almost anything. They come up from the docks you know. Big as blasted cats an' all. Only last week one of 'em ete the toes of Jenny Spence's new baby. She'd just left the little thing for a few minutes and…"

He suddenly pulled himself up short and stared guiltily at Isaac.

"What I meant to say is keep clear of 'em at all costs. They're dirty, filthy creatures that knows no fear."

" Y…yes, Mr Bernstein."

There was little doubt that the landlord's advice would be taken very seriously indeed.

"Who was that man? Wh…wh…what was wrong with his face?"

Relieved that the boy appeared not to have been upset by his horrific story, but on his guard now, Eli responded cautiously.

"Don't you worry about 'im; 'e's pretty 'armless really. Looks more scary than 'e actually is. 'E'll not bother you no more; sometimes 'e just needs a lesson to keep 'im in line."

"You batted him over the head with that frying pan, didn't you?"

"Well, we couldn't 'ave 'im man-'andling you now, could we?" Eli was beginning to enjoy the boy's obvious hero worship. It had been a long time since anyone had seen him in that light. "I gave 'im a right old whack, didn't I?

Isaac's solemn face broke into another smile. He looked up with wide eyes.

"You gave him what for, Mr Bernstein."

"I surely did, boy. Now, let's get on with this stock-taking. We'll never get it done if we just keeps rabbitin' on for ever, will we now?"

"No, sir."

Less than a week later, Barnett led his eldest son through the streets of Whitechapel on their way to the Jews Free School in Spitalfields. He felt guilty that he hadn't tried to gain admission for the boy as soon as the family arrived in London, but Hacha's fury at the time had driven everything else out of his mind. Now, though, things having calmed a little during his two-week absence, he intended to put matters right. This was, after all, the main reason why he'd insisted they move to London. He hoped his son would ultimately grasp the opportunity to enter the Judaic priesthood, fulfilling the destiny so cruelly denied him. Besides which, he believed his wife would see the sense of relocating after their boy was enrolled in one of the finest schools in England.

At first, Isaac kept a tight grip on his father's hand and stared down at his feet, trying to make himself as inconspicuous as possible. After his encounter with the rat, the week before, he'd temporarily lost the impulse to explore the surrounding area and gain a measure of freedom from Hacha's smothering affection. Indeed, he'd been shadowing her so closely for the last few days that even she was becoming a little disturbed by her son's clinging need. Now, tucked in close to his father's leg, his natural curiosity began to return, and he was soon staring around him at the strange new sights unfolding as they passed through the extensive dockland. Most of these streets were so narrow that the sun rarely managed to find its way through the crowded buildings. Even on the warmest days, moisture oozed blackly from the stonework. Isaac noticed many beggars and cripples propped up against the damp walls, or lying stretched out on the pavements. Some shouted aggressively at passers-by, while others remained passive, their heads bowed over strange caps. Glancing down, he saw they usually contained the odd farthing or two.

A man without legs, sitting on a filthy wheeled contraption, caught his roving eye and grinned at him. Isaac stared at the trouser ends, cut at the knees and roughly knotted up at the top of each stunted thigh.

"Go on, son, get an eyeful. The bleedin' fuzzy wuzzies cut off me legs wiv their spears. 'Elp out a crippled veteran of Ondurman, won't you?"

The appeal, aimed at Barnett, fell on deaf ears. Judging by the look on the peddler's face, he and his son were walking through empty streets devoid of human life.

An old hag suddenly thrust a handless stump in Isaac's face, cackling with laughter as he reeled back. His father's grip tightened as they thrust past. A little further on, a rag-taggle band of urchins appeared out of nowhere and began to torment them. Pulling at Isaac's jacket and his father's coat tails, they harried the pair relentlessly until Barnett had no choice but to throw two or three coins onto the cobbles.

A few minutes later, without any warning whatsoever, Barnett pulled his son across the road, accelerating his already fast pace. Isaac puffed along, his small legs hurting from the effort. Out of the corner of his eye he caught sight of a group of men with dark faces, and dressed in flowing, colourful robes, swaggering along the opposite pavement. All appeared to be staring over at them with great interest. One, with a strip of bright red cloth wrapped round his head, pointed and laughed. Isaac caught the flash of white teeth against thick, black lips, then they turned up a side road and the vision was blotted out.

"Why are these men mocking us, Father?"

At first Barnett didn't reply, until the boy repeated the question.

"They are heathen sailors, thieves and whoremongers all of them."

"What's a whoremonger, Father?"

"Don't ask any more questions, Isaac. Save your breath for walking."

Soon they left the docks behind and the streets began to broaden out. The filthy, run-down slums were gradually replaced by cleaner, more respectable buildings with wide entrance doors and curtained windows. For the first time, Isaac noticed trees, hedges and tiny railed-in gardens. At last, his father began to slow down and appeared to be taking some interest in his surroundings.

"Does the Queen live in one of these houses, Father?"

Barnett smiled down at his son.

"No, Isaac. But one day perhaps we will live in such a fine house— if God blesses us with good fortune. When you become a rabbi all my wishes will be fulfilled. That is why we are here today—to start you on the road to enlightenment, which only a true scholar of the Torah can attain. Do you understand?"

"Does God love all his people, Father?"

"Of course, Isaac. Why do you ask?"

"Does he love the man with no legs, and the bad boys who shouted at us?"

"These people are not like us; they have no faith and no understanding. The God of our fathers looks after his own."

"Did God cut off the man's legs as a punishment?"

"That is a foolish question. All important questions will be answered when you are able to understand properly. Until then be content."

Isaac, however, couldn't stop thinking about all the people God seemed to be punishing. He hoped that he would remain in favour and decided to take his father's admonitions seriously.

Eventually, they stopped next to a tall, red-bricked building surrounded by a high, ornate railings. It was a beautiful day now, and the sunlight, slanting through nearby trees, created a chequered theatre of light and shadow. The boy, fascinated by the ever-changing display, was unaware of anything else as they approached a massive wrought-iron entrance gate. Barnett's voice suddenly broke into his reverie.

"Now remember what I told you, Isaac. Let me do the talking. Say nothing unless you are asked a direct question. Do you understand?"

"Yes, Father."

Isaac spotted a man in a dark jacket and peaked hat sitting on a chair on the other side of the railings. He appeared not to have noticed them. With his arms clasped behind his neck and his eyes closed, he was obviously enjoying the warm sun on his face. Staring at the school he'd barely noticed before, the boy suddenly shivered. There was something forbidding about the rows of windows, and the angular shadows cast far out over neat flowerbeds and closely cropped lawns. Barnett coughed to attract the gatekeeper's attention. The latter slowly pulled himself up, adjusting his uniform in the process. He was unusually tall and broad with muscular shoulders. His thick, bull neck was chapped where the hard, starched collar cut into it. Isaac tried to hide behind his father, afraid of attracting the man's attention.

"What can I do for you?"

The guttural voice was unfriendly, and Barnett couldn't help feeling intimidated. The man's looks were also off-putting—the aggressive slant of the jaw, receding forehead and broken nose reminding him of a Russian official back in Lithuania who'd tirelessly pursued him for months, attempting to enforce an army conscription order. He struggled to keep his voice level and business-like."

"I'm here to speak to the headmaster. We have an appointment at two-thirty."

The keeper said nothing, but unhooked a huge set of jangling keys from his belt, unlocked a small side gate and waved them through.

"Will the headmaster be there to meet us?"

Again, the belligerent glance and a new mocking quality in the voice:

"No. The headmaster is a very busy man. You will have to wait! Go straight up the steps and into the entrance hall, take a right turn along the corridor and another right up the first set of stairs. At the top, turn left and the headmaster's office is the first door you'll see. There are seats outside; sit there until you are called."

Barnett screwed up his face up in an effort to remember the instructions and set off up the long drive with Isaac trailing behind him. The boy inwardly quailed as the hallway loomed like the entrance to a dark cave. Only his father's insistent, tugging hand prevented him from bolting back the way he'd come.

Inside, it was surprisingly peaceful. Barnett had somehow expected the school to be full of noisy, playful children, but, instead, the main corridor was entirely deserted. Standing there, overawed for a moment, father and son were aware of the rise and fall of many voices, but found it impossible to pinpoint their exact location. Isaac pushed in closer, scared by the uncanny intonation echoing around the polished walls.

"There's nothing to be afraid of, son." For the sake of the boy, he tried to sound confident. "Your voice will soon be added to those pupils eager to learn and make their parents proud."

After sitting in the first-floor corridor for almost three-quarters of an hour, Barnett began to wonder if they'd been directed to the right spot. There was nothing on the large oak panelled door to suggest that this was the headmaster's office. He recalled the ugly sneer on the gatekeeper's face as they'd turned away. Just when he was considering whether or not to knock, the door opened and a thin, owlish man, wearing a dusty gown, stepped out. He peered through his glasses at the pair.

"Good afternoon, Mr...?"

"Mr Rosenberg, sir, and my son Isaac."

"Ah yes. Come in."

Making no apology for the delay, and failing to introduce himself, he waved them inside. The room seemed vast. Shelves, lining the walls, groaned under the weight of dusty, leather-bound tomes; the floor was littered with thick brown envelopes and what looked like official report sheets. The man crossed over to an expansive desk, buried under more books, masses of class registers and a collection of sundry items. Barnett was singularly unimpressed; this mess was not what he'd expected of the headmaster of the renowned Jews Free School. Without asking them to sit down, the man fiddled with some papers, speaking over his shoulder:

"Now, Mr er..."

"Rosenberg."

"Yes, Mr Rosenberg, I'm afraid the headmaster is unavailable this afternoon, and has asked me to deputise, so what can I do for you?"

"I have brought my son Isaac to the school to be enrolled."

The master, turning round to face them, looked puzzled for a moment and then smiled.

"Quite out of the question, I'm afraid. The school is completely full. There have been no enrolments here for almost a year now. You'll have to find some other school willing to take your boy."

"I don't understand. I was told there would be a place for Isaac here. We moved to London a few weeks ago in order to secure his education. He is a very able pupil and will, I am sure, meet your entry requirements."

"As I said, the school is full. If there's nothing else, I have a great deal to do."

"But...I only came here for the sake of the boy. I wish to speak to the headmaster; I don't even know who you are!"

"My name is Mr Black, assistant head teacher, and I speak for my colleague. Now, I must ask you to leave. There are other people to see."

Black opened the door and ushered them out. Dismayed by the summary dismissal and unsure how to proceed, Barnett hesitated. At that moment a hand bell began to clang loudly. Isaac, who'd been glad to escape the depressing study, almost leapt out of his skin. Doors were suddenly flung open and an avalanche of jostling bodies filled the available space in the corridor. The pair found themselves jammed against the wall until the flow in both directions subsided. In a daze, they made their way back down the stairs, deserted and quiet once again.

The keeper was now standing in the dark hall. Barnett wondered why he'd deserted his post at the gate. Without a nod or a smile, he opened the door and slammed it shut behind them. The day was transformed. Thick, dark clouds, massing overhead, were disgorging torrents of rain; streams raced down the gutters bordering the long drive, and waterfalls streamed off the roof where drainpipes overflowed.

Standing in the shelter of the porch, holding his son's hand and staring out at the downpour, Barnett felt utterly dismayed. Within a few minutes his most precious dream had been shattered and he'd failed to object or remonstrate in any meaningful way. The prospect of Isaac's education was one of the few things that kept him going. He desperately wanted the boy to succeed where he'd so markedly failed. Convincing himself that what had just happened must have been the result of a simple misunderstanding, he decided to return and speak to the headmaster personally. Surely the deputy, or whoever he was, must have got it wrong. Pushing the door back open, he pulled Isaac inside. The doorman turned with a scowl on his face.

"What do you want now? You've had your interview. Didn't Mr Black tell you there was no room here for your son?"

"How…how do you know that?"

"How do I know?" The man laughed nastily. "If I got a penny for every one of you people who come here looking to get their children signed up, I'd be a rich man by now. Maybe you should go back to Russia or wherever it was you came from."

Placing a massive hand on Barnett's chest, he propelled him back out onto the porch and slammed the door shut.

"Can we go home now, Father?"

Trembling with fear and rage, he gazed down at his son. He'd actually forgotten about the boy for a few moments.

"Don't worry, Isaac. I'm sure when I speak to the headmaster we'll clear up this misunderstanding."

"I don't think I…I like it here m…much."

"Nonsense! I've told you how important your education is. Try to remember what I tell you."

"Yes, Father."

A moment or so later they set off out into the deluge. The small side-gate swung open at Barnett's touch and he clicked it shut behind them with customary assiduity. Even though he was rapidly becoming soaked and his legs hurt, Isaac was glad to be leaving. He'd understood little of what had actually been said, but the impatient, unfriendly tone of the man in the office, and the derisive hostility of the porter continued to reverberate inside his head as they splashed through the flooded streets.

Entering the school, Isaac was immediately confronted by the tall figure of Mr Jacobs staring furiously down at him through small, round glasses. The teacher's head was slightly raised and the hooked nose, poised like an eagle's bill, looked ready to tear flesh.

"Ah Rosenberg, kind of you to join us this morning! Would you care to divulge why you missed Mr Hart's Hebrew classes on Tuesday and Wednesday? Scott! Yes, you boy, join us for a moment if you please."

Isaac's friend and fellow truant, Sidney Scott, should have known better than to try and sneak past the head of religious instruction, even when it appeared he was wholly preoccupied with another pupil. It was a well-known fact that Mr Jacobs had eyes in the back of his head.

Having almost reached the sanctuary of his form room, he reluctantly returned to face the music.

"Perhaps you could throw some light on Mr Rosenberg's absences this week. It appears that you also failed to turn up to the same classes. Could the two cases be connected, I wonder?"

The heavy sarcasm highlighted the genuine anger Jacobs felt when Jewish pupils skipped the classes he and his colleagues organised and supervised in their own time. It was incredible, given all the hard work which went into preserving their common heritage, that these brats should show so little gratitude. Their blatant lack of discipline and scant regard for tradition appalled him. Most of the blame, in Jacobs' view, however, lay in the head teacher's unwillingness to sanction proper punishment for truancy. Usherwood's view that after-school activities were, in fact, voluntary, did little to boost his popularity in a school where the majority of pupils and teachers were Jewish. Many of the staff believed it was scandalous that the headmaster was a gentile, but while Baker Street School remained a state institution, there was little they could do. The fact that the authorities were trying to discourage separate Jewish schools, by promoting a liberal interpretation of the Education Act, simply added to the fury felt by passionate supporters of segregation. Since there was little chance of engaging with the representatives of an iniquitous system, Jacobs and like-minded colleagues had to be content with punishing those who dared challenge them directly. On this occasion, given Isaac's consistent level of truancy, he was out to exact a severe penalty.

"Nothing to say? Well, there's a surprise. We'll discuss this further during the morning break. You will both report to me then. Now get along to registration."

Jacobs turned on his heel and stalked off in the direction of the staff room.

"'E's going to cane us, ain't he?"

Sidney's face was white, and tears were already shining in eyes.

"Probably, but I don't care if he does. It won't make any difference; I hate Hebrew and I hate Jacobs too."

Although Isaac feared the beating as much as his friend, his antipathy to after-school classes ran deeper. Why should he sacrifice the free time he enjoyed playing with his friends in the park, and sketching passers-by outside his home in Jubilee Street, on something so utterly tedious?

It was over three years since his father had failed to enrol him in the Jews Free School, and three months since the family finally moved out of the Cable Street slum. Although the new flat was still somewhat cramped for such a large family, it contained several rooms and a toilet. Now, entering his fourth year as a pupil at Baker's Street School, Isaac was beginning to rebel against the authoritarian regime instituted by the Jewish masters.

Leaving school later that afternoon, Isaac felt even less inclined to compromise. The fact that Jacobs had thrashed them both and then sent for them five minutes before regular classes ended to ensure their attendance after school, deeply rankled. He recalled the savage swish of the cane and the searing agony in his right hand which refused to subside however much he spat and blew on it. At least he'd not cringed like Sidney, who, after the first cut, begged Jacobs not to administer further punishment. The teacher's unbearably smug voice remained in his head long after the pain in his hand had gone.

"You may not believe this, Scott, but the beating pains me much more than it does you. I only hope it will serve to show you the error of your ways."

Afterwards, he'd lectured them in his usual haughty manner.

"My only motive, my quest if you will, is to engender respect for our common Jewish heritage; I'm truly sorry that in both your cases there has been no choice but to resort to corporal punishment in order to achieve this end."

Isaac vowed to resist. Already, he was planning in his mind how to evade classes next week. Whether Sidney could be persuaded to join him was, of course, another matter. Perhaps after the memory of the beating had diminished, it wouldn't be so hard. The prospect of running wild and playing in the sunny, green stretches of Greenwich Park was something his friend would find hard to resist if past experience was anything to go by.

✳

John Usherwood glanced up for a moment and studied the small figure hunched over a sketching block next to the window. He'd rarely encountered a child of eleven years old with so much raw talent in the arts. Not only were his drawings skilful, but the little poems and stories he wrote from time to time gave pause for thought.

It was only due to good fortune that Isaac's skills were first brought to his attention. Mr Hart had confiscated a piece of paper his young charge was doodling on and passed it to Usherwood along with a despairing note complaining about the boy's lack of concentration. Gazing at the rough drawing, he'd been amazed to see a remarkable likeness of Sidney Scott, his head turned slightly to the right, chewing on the end of a pencil. There was no mistaking the subject; he'd had too many dealings with this errant pupil not to make the connection.

Although enquiries revealed that Isaac was regarded as a pest by the majority of his teachers, who felt he lacked commitment and showed little interest in most aspects of the curriculum, a few viewed him as unusually creative. The greatest criticism came from Mr Jacobs, which merely whetted Usherwood's curiosity. According to him, the boy was unresponsive and sullen, often skipping after-school classes. The headmaster had never been able to understand how pupils could be accused of truanting from classes which were, after all, supposed to be voluntary. He knew only too well, however, the single-minded and obsessive approach adopted by his colleague. Any deviation from study of the Torah and the assimilation of Hebrew was, at best, frivolous and, at worst, blasphemous. He often thanked God that Jacobs was not in charge at Baker Street or boys like Isaac would never be granted the opportunity to break through the rigid barriers of orthodoxy.

Eventually, he sent for Isaac and welcomed him into his study. Usherwood could see he was apprehensive and expecting some sort of punishment. For a moment, the headmaster struggled to find a way of putting the boy at his ease. Then, in a sudden flash of inspiration, he handed him a sketching pad and pencil and requested a portrait. Although at first somewhat taken aback, the boy quickly got down to work.

Fifteen minutes later, the result convinced Usherwood that his remarkable talent must be nurtured. In the context of the school's rigid curriculum, and the less than flexible attitude displayed by his colleagues, this meant that Isaac would have to be taken directly under his wing. It was thus arranged he would be excused from a number of classes each day to work on his drawings in the sanctuary of the headmaster's office. He was also granted the rare opportunity to remain there after school, if he so wished, providing him for the first time with the perfect excuse to avoid extra Hebrew lessons. Jacobs raged against the decision but there was nothing he could do.

Usherwood wrote home, informing Bennett and Hacha of his interest in the boy. The family were delighted and Hacha felt it might be the beginning of something extra-ordinary. They knew that Isaac was endowed with special gifts, but, given their impoverished circumstances, had not known how to properly encourage him. The intervention seemed like an act of providence.

The fact that this turn of events seemed at odds with his son's Jewish studies, didn't appear to bother Barnett unduly. Despite a single-minded approach to the Torah, he accepted Isaac as an individual in his own right, and was happy to leave the matter in the hands of God. Believing that Isaac's gifts had been granted him for reasons surpassing the comprehension of mere mortals, he displayed a wisdom far beyond the scope of Jacobs and his ilk. Recently, he'd been greatly taken by the boy's obvious fascination with the ancient stories contained within the Pentateuch.

Observing Isaac's total concentration on the task at hand, Usherwood hoped he'd made the right decision. As far as he was concerned, fostering talent was the true calling of a teacher; the satisfaction he derived from setting a youngster on a voyage of self-discovery was what had attracted him to the profession in the first place. He knew, of course, there would be many problems. The boy's racial background and social circumstances were certainly against him; shedding a skin, home grown in the slums of Whitechapel, was never going to be easy. Even at this early stage, he wondered how Isaac's natural abilities could be put to a more practical use. Perhaps he should already be making an effort to encourage the boy to look realistically at the options available to him. For instance, a career as a commercial artist was possible; the borough council ran classes in art metal work aimed at introducing youngsters to the skills required for such a profession.

A loud rap at the door put an end to these musings.

"Come in." He sighed impatiently as Joe Rose entered. "For goodness sake, Rose, does a day ever pass without you being sent up here? What is it this time?

"Mr Goldstein sent me, sir. 'E said I was being uncooperative."

"Are you ever anything else?"

Glancing round, Joe noticed Isaac was holding a picture up to the sunlight flooding through the window. Amazed, he saw an elegant young lady clad in a long, flowing dress gazing at herself in a mirror. Even to Joe's unsophisticated eye, the double image was impressive—the lines bold and the figures symmetrical. Isaac smiled round at his friend and near-neighbour and opened his mouth to speak.

Usherwood rapidly intervened.

"Fine, Isaac, leave the drawing in the corner and return to the class now. At first glance, it looks fine—very fine indeed as a matter of fact. We'll discuss it after school."

"Yes, sir, thank you, sir."

As Isaac left the office, Joe tried desperately to play for time. "That was a great drawin', wasn't it, sir? Isaac's really good wiv a pencil, ain't he? 'E's always out on the street drawin' cats and dogs. The ovver day a toff stopped and bought one of 'is portraits for threepence. 'E's a marvel, 'e really is, sir, no doubt about it 'Is movver woo sayin' that..."

"There's no doubt he is very talented, Rose but, the question at the moment is, what have you to offer? Mr Goldstein obviously thinks you could work a great deal harder, doesn't he?"

With a sigh, Joe resigned himself to his fate.

Chapter Two

1911

He was an artist and a dreamer—one whose delight in the beauty of life was an effective obstacle to the achievement of the joy of living; whose desire to refine and elevate mankind seemed to breed in mankind a reciprocal desire to elevate him to a higher and still higher—garret.

When one has to think of responsibilities, when one has to think strenuously how to manage to subsist, so much thought, so much energy is necessarily taken from creative work.

Brought up as he had been: socially isolated, but living in spiritual communion with the great minds of all ages, he had developed a morbid introspection in all that related to himself....

Extracts from "Rudolph"—an autobiographical short story

...In my great loneliness,
This haunted desolation's dire distress,
I strove with April buds my thoughts to dress,
Therewith to reach joy through gay attire;
But as I plucked came one of these pale griefs
With mouth of parched desire
And breathed upon the buds and charred the leaves.

Lines from "Spiritual Isolation": 1911...

The birds that sang in summer
Were silent till the spring;
For hidden were the flowers,
The flowers to whom they sing.
December's jewelled bosom—
Closed mouth-hill-hidden vale—
Held seed full soon to blossom;
Held song that would not fail...

From "Lines Written In An Album to J.L."
(Joseph Lefkovitz): 1911...

J oseph Lefkowitz opened his new, leather-bound diary and stared for a moment at the blank page headed 2nd of January 1911. The day had proved interesting and he wanted to record his impressions of the young man he'd met for the first time a few hours earlier. He was beginning to realise that the unexpected Christmas gift from his father, might, despite his initial scepticism, prove beneficial.

Like most other days in Joseph's life, this one had begun at the end of a gruelling twelve-hour shift in the furrier's sweatshop where he and four colleagues laboured for a pittance. He'd quickly grown to despise the stink and claustrophobic feel of the two dark, low-ceilinged rooms where he spent the bulk of his daylight hours.

Spilling out onto the street in the early evening, he stretched his cramped limbs, thankful for the release. Apart from the burning ambition to become a writer and translator, the only thing that sustained him was the prospect of meeting up with his friends. As usual, Simon Weinstein was waiting for him, stamping his feet impatiently and bemoaning the cold. His new career in teaching left him with considerably more free time than the others, although he frequently complained about the heap of tatty jotters he carried home each evening. Joseph's mood quickly improved. When they met up with John Rodker, half an hour later, he was in high spirits and ready for anything.

As part of a fresh initiative for the new year, they were considering extending their literary circle to include two other boys whose background and ambitions were similar to their own. After a heated argument, it was decided that the candidates in question were, in fact, unsuitable and likely to cause friction. John, or "Jimmy", as he liked to be known, although forced to agree with his friends, had been particularly keen on the recruitment. Of the three he was the most obviously flamboyant; his hat set at a rakish angle and the large gold ring stuck in his left ear afforded him a reckless air which he fully exploited. His self-confidence also separated him out from the others— their efforts to match his devil-may-care approach to life generally falling short of the mark. Like an actor reaching the climax of an impassioned speech, he suddenly dropped to his knees and raised his eyes heavenward.

"My friends, my friends, without an infusion of new blood, I fear we are doomed to fester in the foothills of mediocrity, seeking in vain for that which would lift us up onto the highest mountain tops."

Joseph laughed raucously.

"There's not much chance of anything like that happening with you around, Rodker."

Turning to address the handful of curious passers-by who had paused to witness the human drama unfolding on the pavement, he spoke in the style of a street orator, determined to match Jimmy's vivacity.

"Please forgive my friend's uncharacteristic outburst. He has been under considerable pressure of late. We trust, however, in the fullness of time, he will recover his former *joie de vivre* and attain that which he most fervently desires in life."

Enjoying the high jinks, the good-natured audience cheered and applauded. Even Simy, generally more serious and moody than the others, began to relax. Eventually, they ran off down the street whooping with laughter.

Later that evening, completely out of the blue, they'd encountered someone who deeply impressed them. Joseph, struggling now to recall his first impressions, began to write, slowly at first, but with increasing confidence.

In Leadenhall Street, we met a fellow who Simy introduces to me as Isaac Rosenberg. He talks to us about poetry. Simy is very silent the whole of the time. Rosenberg has a great opinion of Shakespeare. He thinks the sonnets are the greatest poetry in the language. When we get to the corner of Jamaica Street and Oxford Street, Rosenberg pulls a bundle of odd scraps of paper from

his pocket, and reads us his poems under a lamp-post. The fellow
really writes good poetry.

Pausing for a moment, he pulled out the crumpled sheet Isaac had thrust into his hand as they parted at the corner of Whitechapel Road, and read through the scrawled-out poem, savouring once again its extraordinary power.

Death waits for me-ah! who shall kiss me first?
No lips of love glow red from out the gloom
That life spreads darkly like a living tomb
Around my path. Death's gift is best not worst.
For even the honey on life's lips is curst.
And the worm cankers in the ripest bloom.
Yea, from Birth's gates to Death's, Life's travailed womb
Is big with Rest, for Death, her life, athirst...

This piece, as well as others he'd shown them, generated the impression of an artist beset by a melancholy verging on hopelessness. After the meeting, Simy had told them that Isaac was stuck in a job he hated and believed was damaging his health. He also apparently despaired of ever finding anyone interested enough to publish his poems, convinced that fate was conspiring against him. Joseph immediately sensed that Isaac might be just the sort of companion they needed to boost the integrity of the group, and provide them with the stimulus they agreed was vital to their future. When he brought the matter up the debate was intense. Simy, although admitting he'd been impressed by the gravitas and beauty of some of the poems, remained unconvinced.

"There just doesn't appear to be anybody in there. It's hard to imagine someone like that is capable of writing poetry at all. You must have noticed he hardly spoke, and kept staring down at his feet all the time."

Jimmy shook his head fiercely.

"I think you're being damned unfair, Weinstein. He was obviously a bit overawed by us. You'd very likely be the same under similar circumstances. I say we give him a chance."

"I didn't say we shouldn't give him a chance. You're getting hold of the wrong end of the stick as usual, Rodker. It's always the same…"

"I see what you're getting at, Simy." Joseph moved quickly to quell discord. "But I agree with Rodker. It's fairly obvious that Rosenberg needs some encouragement, and having a real poet among us could make all the difference."

Now he wondered if he'd been wise to push so hard. Perhaps Isaac's presence would make a difference, but Simy's objections were valid. Returning to his diary, Joseph attempted to articulate his doubts.

I wonder whether Rosenberg will be a friend. He seems to be hardly capable of friendship. He is very self-absorbed and there is no lightness in him. He did not smile once the whole evening. I think he rather awed Simy, awed him and depressed him, like something heavy and solemn. He is short and awkward; his features are very plain—he has no personality. Yet he talks interestingly of Poetry. He has evidently read a good deal and it is his passion. He stutters and his voice is monotonous. He has certainly, however, impressed us. Or am I impressed by the fact that he writes real poetry? I hope I am wrong in thinking him incapable of friendship.

Sitting back, chewing on the end of his pencil, Joseph felt more confused than ever. These were exciting times; one rarely knew what was waiting around the next corner. In a sense, their meeting with Isaac seemed somehow fated; it was hard to believe otherwise. The young poet had certainly inspired a new sense of optimism, while simultaneously provoking a degree of perplexity. There was something fascinating and incomprehensible about how the muse could possibly have alighted on such an uncouth individual. During their first, stilted conversation, Isaac had made it clear his artistic ambitions extended beyond poetry, and shared with them his keen desire to enter art school.

Joseph sighed, wondering how it would all work out. It was wonderful to be on the edge of something new. He had little doubt they'd all eventually make their mark on the world.

A few nights later, Joseph and Simy met up with Isaac. They could tell he was agitated by the stutter which rendered him almost inarticulate at times. Simy, frustrated beyond measure, finally intervened:

"For pity's sake, Rosenberg, slow down, will you. Take a deep breath and explain to us what's been going on."

I've m…m…managed to…to…to…finish off a new p…poem, to thank…thank Am…Am…mshewitz for all…all his help. His p…portrait of…of me is…wonderful. I also met someone who seems interested in… . He introduced m…me to Arthur Lewis."

"What? You mean Arthur D Lewis, the writer?" Joseph stared hard at Isaac.

"Y…yes, the writer. He said my new…new poem was very g…good."

"Have you got it with you?"

"Y…yes, as a matter of fact."

"Well, let's have a look then. Why does it always take you so long to get to the point?"

Joseph caught Simy's eye and shook his head in despair while Isaac rummaged in his coat pocket for a few moments before finally pulling out a soiled fragment of paper.

"I hope you didn't show Lewis that disgusting mess!"

"It wasn't so…so bad earlier. It's…it's j…j…just that…"

"Never mind, show us the poem."

Simy wrenched the paper out of Isaac's hand. Stopping under a lamp-post, he peered at the untidy writing and began to read out loud. His voice, mocking at first, quickly changed as the words took hold.

In the wide darkness of the shade of days
Twixt days that were, and days that yet will be,

Making the days that are, gloom'd mystery,
What starshine glimmers through the nighted ways
Uplifting? And through all vain hope's delays
What is it brings far joy's foretaste to me?
A savour of a ship-unsullied sea,
A glimpse of golden lands too high for praise.

Life holds the glass but gives as tears for wine.
But if at times he changes in his hand
The bitter goblet for the drink divine,
I stand upon the shore of a strange land.
And when mine eyes unblinded of the brine
See clear, lo! where he stood before, you stand.

The two young men stood transfixed for a few moments. When Simy spoke his tone was completely altered—derision replaced by awe.

"That must be the best thing you've ever written. It's...it's...wonderful. The imagery of the *ship-unsullied sea* and *the shore of a strange land* is...is..."

"Sublime." Joseph smiled at Isaac. "I particularly like the line, *And when mine eyes unblinded by the brine see clear.* But...the overall shape of the thing, and the...the rhythm is perfect. John Amschewitz is a lucky man to receive such a tribute."

Isaac flushed with pleasure; it was good to be praised by his new friends. Having people of his own age to interact with was a dream come true. Even their frequent criticism failed to diminish his enthusiasm. He knew well enough how difficult his manner must seem to others. Their censure was, after all, an effort to improve his deficiencies.

"He's...he's always tried to h...help me when he could. You must see his p...portrait of me; it's...it's marvellous...really."

"I'm sure, but what we want to see right now is your own collection." Joseph grabbed his arm and began pulling him along the street. "Let's get a move on. Did Rodker say he was going to meet us outside your house?"

A few minutes later they arrived at a large tenement block on Oxford Street where Isaac lived with his family. Staring up at the squalid six-storey brick building with its tiny, square windows, Joseph experienced a sudden dampening of his spirits. How could aspiring artists be expected to flourish in such an environment? Jimmy was luckier than the rest of them. His parents being considerably more affluent, he had the luxury of his own bedroom. Joseph wondered if he'd ever be able to escape the shabby confines of Whitechapel and realise his ambitions. And would Isaac receive the attention his poems undoubtedly merited? The odds against either of them achieving success were formidable. With considerable bitterness, he pondered how wonderful life must be for those wealthy dabblers who had only to worry about degree of talent in their struggle for recognition. Perhaps even talent wasn't an issue where money and influence could be brought to bear.

Jimmy suddenly appeared out of a dark doorway.

"Where the hell have you been? I've been hanging around for ages."

Joseph smiled. "We've been reading Rosenberg's latest poem. Honestly, Rodker, you'll love it. It's his best yet, believe me."

"That's all very well but you could have waited till you got here. Cooling my heels outside this dump isn't my idea of fun it has to be said! No offence, Rosenberg."

The latter managed an unhappy, little grimace.

Entering a dripping passageway, they were forced to crush into the right wall to avoid a huge puddle covering most of the floor in and around the narrow stairwell. Jimmy swore beneath his breath as he tried in vain to brush off the filthy ooze adhering to the shoulder of his new jacket. The musty smell of wet rot assailed their nostrils as they started to climb the twisting steps leading to the flats above. Four floors up, Isaac knocked loudly on an ancient door. The boys couldn't help noticing that the upper hinge was almost wholly detached from the rotting frame. The door suddenly swung open and a girl in a bright, blue dress stood blinking shyly at them. Given the surrounding squalor, she appeared surprisingly clean and presentable. Placing his arm round her narrow shoulders, Isaac produced one of his rare smiles.

"This is my sister Annie. Annie, these are my f...friends, Joseph, Simon and John."

Blushing pink, she smiled fleetingly before bolting back into the flat.

"C...come in and I'll...I'll show you where I...I work."

Inside, the cramped rooms were dimly lit and Joseph had difficulty breathing the heavy, moisture-laden air. In what he took to be the sitting room, a bulky woman rose stiffly, wiping her hands on a large apron. Joseph could see a piece of half-finished embroidery strung over the side of the recently vacated armchair, and endeavoured to assess the quality of the workmanship. Isaac had told them how wonderful a seamstress his mother was, and he wished to judge the veracity of these claims for himself. Offered in conjunction with hints regarding Mr Rosenberg's literary background, they suggested to Joseph an over-eagerness to establish artistic credentials. It was perfectly possible the claims were just another manifestation of the poet's low self-esteem. Whatever her degree of skill, however, his mother's work undoubtedly provided a much-needed boost to the meagre income generated by her recondite husband.

When she spoke, although the English was formal and correct, her voice was heavily accented, betraying the fact she was not from these shores.

"Unfortunately, my husband is not here at the moment to welcome you. If you care to go through to the kitchen, you'll find chairs to sit on. Isaac, please see to our guests' needs."

Smiling, she resumed her seat and picked up the abandoned embroidery in her thick fingers. Isaac ushered them into a room almost filled by an ancient foldaway table and a stove radiating intense heat. A battered, black kettle stood steaming on the hob. Again, the atmosphere was unbearably stuffy.

"You work here?" Simy sounded amazed.

"Yes. It's not so...so b...b...bad at the moment. On washdays you can hardly get in. P...please sit down."

Joseph looked doubtfully at the rickety chairs lying folded up against the wall.

"How many brothers and sisters did you say you have?"

"There's Annie who you already met. Then there's my older sister Minnie, Ray, D…David and Elkon."

"It must get a bit over overcrowded at times."

Isaac merely shrugged in reply, pulled out a thick portfolio wrapped in an old bed sheet and hoisted it onto the table. In the process, he smashed it into a set of burnt pans hanging from the stove, and sent them flying. Mrs. Rosenberg's voice, emanating from the adjacent room, sounded irritated.

"Be careful, Isaac! I hope you didn't break anything."

"No, Mother. It was just the p…p…pans. The crockery is fine."

"Be sure to pick everything up, won't you?"

"Yes, Mother; d…don't worry."

"So this is your studio!" Jimmy gave a low whistle. "My God, man, how do you manage to paint anything here?"

"I manage b…because I have to. Where else can I go?"

Jimmy smiled, to cover his embarrassment.

"Are you going to show us these drawings or not?"

One by one, Isaac pulled out the sheets and laid them on the table for perusal. Joseph stared at each with a growing sense of dismay. The subjects were mainly large, plain-featured females, strongly reminiscent of the artist's mother. Simy picked one up and examined it closely.

"Have you ever considered varying the models you use? These are a bit too…samey for my taste."

"I c…can't afford to use models, and my siblings usually refuse to sit still long enough for me to…to draw them. Anyway, I'm not sure where they would p…pose. My mother probably wouldn't p…put up with having a nude woman sitting around while she prepared dinner."

They all burst out laughing; even Isaac couldn't help grinning at the thought of his mother bustling around while a naked, female model lounged in the corner.

Later on that evening, unable to sleep, Joseph began to consider Isaac's obvious inadequacies. Maybe he was being unfair, but the enigma remained. In a sense, the paintings reflected the cruder aspects of Isaac's personality, while the poetry suggested something else entirely. He wondered again, how such prodigious talent could reside in someone so awkward and unfavoured in background or character. His friends, he knew, shared the same keen interest in understanding Isaac's true nature. The quest was rapidly developing into an obsession. Foremost in their minds was the desire to improve the young poet's social skills thereby increasing his chances of success. Joseph experienced a nagging doubt that all such efforts were doomed to failure. So far, despite encouragement, entreaties and calculated insults, Isaac remained detached, and apparently immune to change.

Turning over, Joseph tried to ease himself into a more comfortable position on his lumpy, old mattress. Thoughts of Isaac's failings were replaced by the wearying prospect of work in the morning. In little under seven hours, he'd be breathing the fetid air of the sweatshop all over again. He tried to imagine the ecstasy of emerging from the depths of that pit for the final time.

"Of course, of course! How could anyone think otherwise? The East End sweatshops represent some of the worst aspects of the capitalist system. To their employers, or owners might be a better way of putting it, workers are simply a means to an end; few of them would treat animals with such callous disregard."

Determined to hold his own, Simy countered:

"That's all very well and good, Rodker, but what are we supposed to do about it? Most of the people you want to liberate are frankly incapable of seeing beyond their immediate needs."

"For God's sakes, try to think like a socialist and grasp the concept of historical inevitability. No one said it would be easy, but we can't afford to fudge the issue. You were at the lecture on dialectical materialism last Tuesday. Did none of it rub off? We've got to stop dancing to the capitalist tune. The revolutionary agenda is clear."

Joseph nodded vigorously.

"I agree with Rodker. We mustn't lose sight of the wood for the trees."

"So you'll be breaking off with Fannie then, I take it! Surely collaboration with a daughter of a petty bourgeois who just happens to be your employer isn't part of the proletarian vision of the future, or am I missing something?"

Simy sneered, relieved that Joseph's intervention had provided him with the opportunity to avoid locking horns with Jimmy whose caustic tongue he secretly feared. His best friend's "understanding" with Fannie Blanket was an easy target.

"What has Fannie got to do with anything?" Joseph's face twisted in indignation. "You have a bad habit of reducing everything to the personal."

Isaac who'd been shuffling behind the others and, so far, contributed nothing to the debate, suddenly intervened.

"While m...much of what you say is undoubtedly true, where does p...p...poetry fit into things? Will the revolutionary authorities tolerate the work of bourgeois poets? What about Byron and B...Blake?"

Jimmy glanced round, as if newly aware of Isaac's presence.

"Art will, of course, remain an integral part of everything the revolution is striving to attain. The world requires men of vision. The task of poets will be to revitalise the spirits of those dulled by years of abuse. Things must change of course. Poetry will have to reflect the seriousness and fervour of the times. Self-indulgent naval-gazing will not be tolerated."

"But...but much in p...poetry is beautiful and...eternal. There is a great deal more to it than the merely functional and...p...political. Keats could be interpreted as self...self-indulgent b...by...by those who fail to understand the...underlying..."

"Don't worry, Rosenberg, we'll have you to keep us on our toes." Jimmy smiled indulgently. "Now, Weinstein, surely you must realise that..."

"What I realise is that you two revolutionaries are walking around the streets of the world's greatest city, hatless. Do you really expect anyone to pay attention when you fail to look the part. Some of us, on the other hand, try to maintain standards of dress appropriate to our position in life."

He smiled and tipped his worn, old bowler hat.

"What the hell are you talking about? What have hats got to do with any...?"

Simy grinned, cutting across Joseph's incredulous response.

"I'm sorry, Lefkovitz, but that's typical of the irresponsible attitude undermining everything we believe and strive for in life."

"Is this just another way of evading the real issues or have you finally taken leave of your senses?"

Despite an impulse to laugh, Jimmy was genuinely annoyed he'd forgotten to bring along the rakish hat that he believed gave him a distinct sartorial advantage over his friends. Undoubtedly, Simy was out to take full advantage of his absent-mindedness.

"Think what you like, but I stand by what I've said."

Joseph suddenly snatched Simy's hat and threw it to Jimmy who leapt up and caught it in mid-air. Evading the owner's frantic efforts to recover his property, he examined the soiled bowler with exaggerated interest.

"So, you actually think this, thing is going to earn you the respect of our comrades engaged in the class struggle? Do you really, Weinstein? I think not."

Again the hat twirled through the air over Simy's head. Neatly catching it by the rim, Joseph was about to throw it on to Isaac when he noticed the latter was still walking along, head down, mumbling something about Keats. Winking at the others, he drew their attention to the poet, who seemed to have completely missed the fun and immersed himself in a world of his own.

"Keats tried to reach out to p...people, you know. He saw his p...p...poetry as a way of changing their p...perceptions. Only when confronted with the ills of life could they aspire to...to...an awareness of…of the…infinite. Shelley on the other h…hand was more interested in…."

Shaking his head, Jimmy stepped back and tapped Isaac on the shoulder. Startled out of his monologue, the poet stared at them blankly for a moment.

"Who are you talking to, Rosenberg? Are you in touch with the spirit world? They say the dead are all around us."

Keen to avoid a discussion on a subject so dear to Jimmy's heart—Joseph attempted to lighten the mood.

"We've been having fun with Weinstein's silly hat. He thinks it gives him…gravitas. Hatless mortals, he feels, are at a serious social disadvantage. What do you think about that, Rosenberg?"

Isaac stared at his feet, reluctant to establish eye contact with his friends.

"I'm…I'm afraid I have no…no opinion on that matter."

Joseph raised his eyes imploringly. Jimmy merely laughed while Simy grabbed back his hat, dusted it down and feigned annoyance for a moment.

Returning home a little earlier than usual, Joseph, determined to keep his diary up to date, spent an hour or so writing at his desk. Later, reading through the completed entry, he alighted on a reference to Isaac's eccentric behaviour. The poet never failed to intrigue him.

It is strange that Rosenberg took no part at all in our little dispute tonight. He shuffled along, very taciturn at one side, talking about Rossetti's letters and Keats and Shelley. He mumbles his words very curiously. Poor Rosenberg. His people are very unsympathetic to him. They insist on treating him as a little out of his mind. They consider him as an invalid, somewhat affected mentally. But he goes on his own way, running away to the libraries whenever he can, to read poetry and the lives of poets, their letters, their essays on how to write poetry, their essays on what poetry should be and do…. His strange earnestness and single-mindedness have had their effect on us. I wish though it did not affect Jimmy with the love of the macabre.

*

Trailing behind his friends, Isaac felt closer to them than he had since being admitted to their inner circle a few months previously. Events earlier in the evening, stimulated by youthful high spirits and pent-up energy, had marked a sea change in the relationship, at least as far as he was concerned. For the first time he'd joined in the fun instead of sitting on the sidelines feeling awkward and left out.

He knew very well, of course, why he'd originally been invited to join the group; they'd decided to put up with his debilitating shyness and defective manner because of respect for his poetry. Naturally, he was flattered by their praise at the time, but his social inadequacies were another matter. The fact that he was incapable of articulate speech and fell to pieces when required to explain the simplest of ideas, filled him with embarrassment and frustration. His reputation as a pathetic, rambling idiot was hard to shake off. The others knew where his talents lay but never ceased to criticise what they regarded as major flaws in his personality. Knowing they were trying to shame him into amending his behaviour didn't make him feel much better, nor did it result in any marked improvement. Despite a strong desire to gain their sympathy, he'd found it impossible, at least until tonight, to relate to them in the way he wanted.

Although a new chapter had opened in his life, it was strange to be an insider while still experiencing the isolation and loneliness of the outsider. Most of the time Isaac felt as though he was standing alone on a cold street corner staring through the window of a room crowded with people. While everyone laughed and chatted in the warm glow, he shivered outside, feeling icy fingers probe his heart. Desperate to enter and join in, something always held him back. Perhaps his self-conceived role as victim, coiled like a snake around the inner core of his being, was the main inhibiting factor. Inexplicably, he gained perverse pleasure in seeing himself as the recipient of a great gift, who, due to the exigencies of a harsh fate, struggles in vain to attain recognition. His poetry was full of such notions. Like a tragic character in a play, his course seemed set, his ultimate demise inevitable. This ability to detach himself and spectate on his own life, although strangely intoxicating, frightened him. While experiencing an extraordinary sense of destiny, he suspected that God's malice might well be undermining his best endeavours.

Earlier in the evening, the boys had met in Jimmy's room to listen to the prose compositions each had agreed to write for the delectation of the group. Only Isaac and Joseph, however, managed to meet the deadline. Sitting on the bed, the others seemed ill at ease as the poet read his satirical commentary on the door knocker as fitting symbol of social and religious trends, past, present and future. There was a long silence after he'd finished, then Jimmy rolled over on his side and patted him on the shoulder.

"That was excellent, Rosenberg; the work of a man who has gauged the idiosyncratic nature of existence. I foresee a bright future for you, my friend."

"Why thank…thank you, Jimmy. I appreciate…"

"Anyway, it suddenly struck me as Rosenberg was reading his piece, that we might all collaborate on the writing of a novel. Something that will set a fire beneath the establishment and burn a few over plump derrières! What do you think?"

"I think that's the best idea I've heard in a long time." Joseph leapt to his feet and spun round to face his friends. "Imagine the stir! The Whitechapel boys—literary giants; their first novel, a revolutionary tour de force. I can hear the plaudits now."

Simy laughed, grabbed a pillow and threw it high in the air. Bouncing off the ceiling, it burst directly over Joseph's head, covering him in a drift of white goose feathers.

Coughing and spitting, he grabbed at the remains of the pillow and threw it at Simy who ducked just in time. Isaac received the projectile full in the face with its flurry of attendant flakes. Forgetting his studied role as outsider for a moment, he reached for the cushion propping him against the headboard of Jimmy's bed and hurled it with uncharacteristic abandon. Missing Joseph, it smashed into the opposite wall disintegrating in a renewed blizzard of flying feathers. Jimmy leapt to his feet, upsetting a heap of peanut shells they'd all been devouring for the last hour or so.

"You're destroying my room, you barbarians. Take that."

Gathering up two handfuls of shells, he launched them over the room endeavouring to catch everyone in the wide spray. Soon they were rolling and wrestling on the floor, laughing hysterically all the while. This was the first time Isaac had joined in the fun and he felt as if he'd successfully passed some sort of initiation test.

Wrapped in these warm thoughts, Isaac was suddenly jerked back to reality by a loud voice hailing them from across the street. He recognised Morris Goldstein and David Bomberg, standing beside a thin, elfin girl he'd never seen before. Goldstein shouted again.

"Rosenberg, Rodker! Join us for a moment will you; I've got someone here I'd like you all to meet."

Crossing over, they stood huddled on the pavement as the flow of pedestrians parted round them and swept past. Morris made the introductions.

"This is Sonia Cohen who writes quite excellent poetry." He winked at Isaac. "I was telling Sonia about your poetic aspirations. Perhaps you could help each other explore the inner workings of the muse."

Glancing up, after his usual squirm of embarrassment, Isaac beheld the slim body and pretty face of the girl who appeared quite unabashed by Morris's comments. Her smile lit up a countenance that Isaac felt was the most beautiful he'd ever seen; her high cheekbones, delicate, slightly upturned nose and sensuous lips fascinated him. What a model Sonia would be. He yearned for the opportunity to sketch her. Beyond these purely artistic feelings, he was aware of a quickening of the pulse, a hot flush on his cheeks and a stiffening in the crotch of his trousers. He wondered if she was romantically attached to Morris or David, and experienced a sudden, unexpected stab of jealousy.

David also elicited strong feelings. The fact that he was now a first-year student at the Slade, simultaneously filled Isaac with renewed hope and stomach-churning despair. Being accepted by London's most inspiring and revolutionary art school was something he deeply yearned for. But, so far, the opportunity had eluded him. His recent decision to quit Carl Hentschel's photographic engraving works had been largely influenced by a burning ambition to become an art student. While poetry was his first love, he knew that the necessary task of earning a living as an artist could only be fulfilled if he learned to hone and develop his drawing skills. John Amshevitz had told him that painting portraits was the way forward. Financing the enterprise, though, would not be easy.

Morris was now boasting on David's behalf. Isaac noted that the latter showed no signs of modesty; his dark eyes, glaring out from under a mop of red hair, seemed to dare contradiction.

"Bomberg was talented enough to receive a grant from the Jewish Educational Aid Society. Quite frankly, there was no luck in it; they saw what he could do and were properly impressed."

Isaac had twice tried to gain financial support from the Society, and been refused on both occasions. Stifling a long-standing sense of bitterness, he listened attentively to David's account of his enrolment and initial experiences at the Slade.

A few minutes later, as they all strolled together up Whitechapel Road, he found himself deep in conversation with Sonia who seemed little troubled by his stuttering and hesitations. She was delighted when he promised to show her some of his recent work; he, in turn, experienced elation at the prospect of meeting up with her again. Apart from his sisters, he'd mixed with very few girls of his own age, and felt an aching need to conquer his shyness in this regard. By the time she left with Morris and David, Isaac felt thoroughly aroused, the tumult inside refusing to subside. For the first time in his life he had some sort of focus for the inchoate sexual fantasies which daily tortured him.

Jimmy obviously couldn't get her out of his head either. As soon as the trio disappeared he started to scoff.

"A poet Goldstein called her! That's a joke. I knew I'd heard her name before. Paul Levi used to hang about with her although we were never introduced. She's apparently been in an orphanage most of her life. You know what that means, don't you?" He paused and looked around, receiving blank stares in return. "Come on, wake up! Goldstein obviously thinks he's onto a good thing, and he's probably right. She's ripe for prostitution if you ask me."

"You're obsessed with prostitution, Rodker. Don't you think you're over-reacting a little?"

"What would you know about it, Weinstein? Leave sex to those of us who have some experience in the field."

"As with most other things, you're all talk, Rodker. Unfortunately for you, nobody's fooled for a moment."

Joseph quickly stepped in to prevent matters getting out of hand.

"Sonia was obviously impressed by you, Isaac. What were you talking about?"

"Not much really. Just...just about p...p...poetry. She said she...she wanted to see some...some of my stuff so I said I'd show her some time."

"I'm sure it wasn't your poetry she was interested in, Rosenberg. Maybe she wants to see something else."

"Give it a rest, Rodker. There are other things in life besides sex, you know. Perhaps we should consider the moral implications of being brought up in an orphanage without parental guidance." Joseph shook his head, despairing of ever breaking Jimmy's fixation.

"Of course we should, Lefkowitz, but morality and sex are interesting bed-fellows, are they not? The bourgeoisie worship the family and pray at the altar of Christian morality, but who do you think frequent the East End brothels, eh? The same faithful husbands and holier-than-thou fathers, of course. Girls like Sonia are grist to their mill; that's surely obvious enough even for you."

"That's got nothing to do with the point I was trying to make. Your problem, Rodker, is that you always use the worst examples of human behaviour to justify your absurd over-generalisations. Most people are not so obsessed and hypocritical as you make out. My father, and yours for that matter, live decent, upstanding lives."

"You're forgetting one thing. Our families are Jewish, not Christian."

"I fail to..."

"I'm off h...home now. I'll be continuing with my copy of

Velasquez's *Philip IV* in the National Gallery tomorrow. I'm still hoping the Society will change their minds about fun...funding me when they see the work I've p...p...put into it."

The others stopped bickering for a moment, knowing how important this matter was to Isaac.

"It's just that I can't continue living off my p...people for ever. Thanks again for all...all your help. I'd never have left Hentschel's without your support."

"I'm sure everything will work out, Rosenberg."

Joseph hoped his optimistic tone would inspire confidence but somehow doubted it. The others grinned and nodded encouragingly.

"Good...goodnight then. I really enjoyed this evening. I'll see you...you all on Friday."

They gazed at Isaac's retreating figure, hunched in his shabby, black coat. Simy broke the uneasy silence.

"Sometimes I don't know what will become of Rosenberg. He just doesn't inspire confidence. That's probably why Solomon and Rothenstein won't support his bid for funding."

"Not to mention the fact he's so damned careless." Joseph frowned. "Imagine ruining that self-portrait he put so much work into. It could easily have been accepted by the Academy, you know."

"I couldn't believe it when he told us about that." Jimmy shook his head.

"You saw it. Didn't you think it was the best thing he'd ever done?"

"It's a bloody shame..." Jimmy tailed off, his voice sounding unusually dismal. "He is making some progress though, isn't he? He really got into that pillow fight earlier on. It was good to see him joining in a bit."

"It was, but we'd better get a move on now or we'll be late for the meeting." Joseph sounded a little panicky.

"Who's speaking tonight?"

"A German Zionist, Abraham...something or other; I can't remember his last name. It should be really interesting. Apparently, he has new insights into the Torah. He claims there's a clear link between Zionism and modern socialist thinking.... I thought Rosenberg wanted to hear him speak. He was making a big thing of it earlier on."

"When it comes to a choice between art and politics—or religion for that matter—there's no contest as far as he's concerned."

"That's true enough, but he does claim that Zionism is bound up with his writing."

"I can't say I've seen much sign of it, except in one poem he wrote when he was fifteen. Anyway, come on, let's go. You just said you didn't want to be late."

Rodker broke into a run quickly followed by the other two who sprinted after him down the street.

Reuben Cohen and Isaac Rosenberg, deep in conversation, were oblivious to the amused glances of passers-by. The physical contrast between the pair was enough to elicit laughter: Isaac, small and shabby, shuffling a step or so behind Cohen whose considerable height, bolting blue eyes and long red beard gave him the looks of an old testament prophet beset by visions. Regarded as highly eccentric, if not downright crazy, by people who knew him, Cohen, a printer by trade, inhabited a world far removed from the humdrum of daily existence. In a sense, it was inevitable they'd come together; a mutual passion for poetry above all things coupled with the desire to change the world, had created a strong bond between the two men.

"It would be an honour to help get your book of poetry into print, Isaac. As soon as you have put everything together, come and see me. I'm sure my employer, Israel Narodiczky, would look favourably on the publication of such a pamphlet. He is a good man who will charge you only for the cost of printing."

"Thank you for...reading the p...poems I gave you, Reuben. I appreciate your help and advice."

Cohen shook his head.

"No thanks are needed. One day we will set up in partnership. You will write great poems and I will print and review them. We will achieve fame and fortune together. It is only a matter of time, my friend. Only a matter of time."

As they walked, Cohen muttered a great deal Isaac couldn't make out. When the printer stopped abruptly and grasped him by the shoulders, his heart skipped a beat.

"Have you considered our Jewish heroes as possible subjects for your future poems? What about a verse play on the prophet Elijah, for instance? He stared at the poet for a moment with unblinking, blue eyes. "Think about it, Isaac —the power of your poetic vision enriching our great heritage."

He released Isaac and strode on with renewed vigour. Trying to keep pace, the poet looked like a deferential servant hurrying along in the wake of a demanding master. Cohen's voice suddenly rose in bitter acrimony.

"For far too long we have been at the mercy of those who would corrupt us. London is full of Jews who have betrayed our once proud culture; who have put mammon and their own selfish interests before God."

Isaac began to feel uneasy. His own commitment to things Jewish was tentative to say the least. Perhaps Cohen knew this, and was building up to a personal attack.

When he halted once again and spun round, Isaac flinched as the massive, red beard pushed to within an inch of his face.

"Our people have suffered much, Isaac, but this gives us a truly unique perspective on things. Imagine the poetry which could express the travail of centuries; the tragedy of a people dispersed and humiliated but not defeated; the vitality of our heroes; and, of course, the passion of redemption. This is our destiny—our calling. Will you consider writing such poetry?"

"Of...of course, but..." While not wishing to offend his friend, Isaac felt the need to back away from a definite commitment. "But you must remember that my p...p...poetry owes much to...to the English tradition. I'm not certain if..."

"Yes, yes, but you speak much of God." Cohen craned his head skywards as if searching for a sign. When, at last, he glanced down, Isaac felt like a child addressed by an indulgent parent. "It is the blending of two great traditions that will mark the crowning glory of your genius. You have a unique opportunity, Isaac; we have a unique opportunity! I would deem it an honour to help you fulfil your great destiny."

"I've certainly always c…considered Moses as a p…possible subject for…"

Cohen appeared to be having a seizure. He leapt in the air, clasping his head in both hands and shouting at the top of his voice.

"My God, my God, Isaac, there you have it! I knew our nation's blood beat strongly in your veins. Moses, yes, of course, Moses! Possibly the greatest hero of them all. A man destined to lead his people out of bondage into freedom. More than anything else we need to regain the incorruptibility of our greatest leader."

A few people stopped to gape at the patriarchal figure beating his head and plucking at his massive beard.

"Moses—virtuous and passionate. An inspired choice, Isaac, an inspired choice."

"It's only a p…p…possibility, but…but…"

With a sinking feeling, Isaac realised any backtracking was now hopeless. Cohen seemed to have sunk back into himself once more. His voice lowered to an incoherent mumble as they continued along the Mile End Waste. Soon, it was as if he'd forgotten that Isaac was there at all.

Isaac sat on an ancient foldaway chair, his easel propped up in front of him. Gazing intently at the interplay of light on water as the Thames flowed swiftly beneath the curving span of Blackfriar's Bridge, he experienced a strange mix of emotions. Being out here on the embankment free to paint and enjoy the cool air on his face was a dream come true. In comparison to the heat and corrosive atmosphere of Hentschel's workshop, it was blissful. On the other hand, he couldn't stop thinking about his continuing failure to persuade the Jewish Society to fund his bid to enter the Slade. For the past three months he'd brought in no money at all; and the prospect of remaining a burden on his family weighed heavily on his spirits. Thoughts of Bomberg's success merely added salt to the wound.

His meeting with Mrs Lily Joseph at the National Gallery back in March had been the only spark of light in the prevailing darkness. The wealthy Jewess, a painter and artist in her own right, seemed to have taken a shine to him, and he'd been invited to her home and offered the position of art and poetry tutor to her young son.

He strove now to banish all such worries and concentrate on recreating the choppy motion of the water, aggravated by the fitful breeze and passing boat traffic. Reflections of the changing sky, with its transitory splashes of bright sunlight and fast moving shadows, fascinated him. He wanted to incorporate everything in the strokes of colour he constantly mixed and remixed in an effort to keep up.

"I thought I might find you down here. The painting's progressing well, I see; you must be pleased."

Joseph Lefkowitz had been standing behind his friend for several minutes watching him work. The half-finished painting, he felt, had already captured the complex interplay of motion and light; the bridge seemed poised between two constantly shifting elements, shattering the illusion of solidity and permanence.

"Oh hello, Joseph. Have you b...been spying on me for long?"

"Only a few minutes. How are you feeling?"

"Oh, not so...so bad when I'm working. It's easier when you...you paint or write. That's why I've been coming down here for the last few days actually. I just...just d...d...don't want to think about the way things are at the moment."

"It's not so awful, surely? At least you've got some freedom to work. Think about me shut up inside that sweatshop all day."

"Shouldn't you b...be there now?"

"Oh, I couldn't stand it! I skipped off for an hour. If Blanket wants to sack me he can, for all I care."

"That's what I thought when I cleared out of Hentschel's, b...but, it's not as simple as that, unfortunately. You c...can't expect your family to support you indefinitely."

"I suppose that's true but I get so fed up! I know things'll get better, but on days like this I just feel so...so restless. When will our time come? Life is rushing by like that bloody river! You can't stop it, or get back what you've squandered. Maybe I need to try harder somehow." Joseph halted for a moment, the old, familiar sense of frustration welling up inside. "I can do better than that damned sweatshop—I know I can! Did I tell you I've been working on some Hebrew translations recently? I'll make a go of it if only... . It's all just a matter of getting a proper crack of the whip, you know. As for you...you belong in art school. Life is just so unfair at times."

"Unfair! You're right about that. Unfair and unlucky. Just when you think you might have made a b...breakthrough—maybe impressed someone with... with the power to change your life, the whole thing falls through. Like Adolf Tuck back in March."

"That was a pity! Especially after he granted you an interview and offered to consider some of your poems for publication."

"Yes. And what happened?" Isaac got up from the tattered stool, stretched his arms in the air then bent forward to ease the dull ache in his shoulders and the small of his back. "He rejects the lot while telling me how much p...potential I have and how important it is to persevere. The story of m...my life, I'm afraid."

"Come on, Rosenberg, it's not all bad. You've written some great stuff recently and your paintings are better than ever... . You've obviously impressed Lily Joseph. She's done a lot to help; that's true, isn't it? In some ways she's become your unofficial patron." Joseph searched for other things to cheer his friend up. "And there's the election coming up. You must be looking forward to the campaign; the Party's bound to do well this time."

"To be honest, I don't care much about the...the election. All I want is...is to make my mark "

"Frankly, that's a selfish way to look at it. Things will change for the better if people like Chesterton and Grayson are elected. You must see that!"

"Will they g…get me into art school or publish my poems?"

"Come on! It's not as simple as that."

"As far as I'm concerned it is. Maybe I need to get out of this country altogether. Why don't we both…emigrate to America or South Africa maybe? A fresh start; people might recognise our talents out there."

"It's worth considering I suppose." Joseph sounded somewhat doubtful. "But if things didn't work out, we'd probably be in a worse position than before. Life might change for the better here, and at least there's some leeway if it doesn't." His face creased in thought. "Maybe the best thing is just to keep working away and hope for an improvement in our fortunes. Anything's possible—you've really got to believe that. I know I'm going to get out of that bloody sweatshop one day; it's only a matter of time."

"You're right, but imagine escaping from all this. Anyway, when the p…picture's finished, I've got some notions for a set of new p…p…poems. Reuben Cohen said he might be able to arrange for another pamphlet of my stuff to…to be published. But…I'm not really holding out much hope."

"I wouldn't rely on crazy Cohen if I were you. He's a weird character. Someone told me recently that he'd…"

"Oh R…Reuben's all right. His heart's in the right p…place and he's got a lot of good ideas. You've just got to understand the way his mind works, that's all."

"You'll know best about that. I'd better get back to work now before old Blanket has a fit. I'll see you tomorrow night at the library as usual!"

"I'll be th…there." Isaac sat down and gazed at the river. The sun had disappeared behind a thick bank of clouds and the water looked grey and sullen. He quickly turned away and watched his friend trotting back along the embankment.

Later that evening, Joseph reread the entry he'd written in his diary.

His father's gift had certainly proved its worth. As well as helping him put things in perspective and see beyond the obvious, it had provided a focus for his writing. He now felt that he had gained a deeper understanding of his friends, which would otherwise have been lacking.

Skimming the paragraphs, he eventually alighted on the section he'd written concerning Isaac's catalogue of woes. His own problems always seemed suitably scaled down by comparison. Would his friend ever be able to surmount the difficulties ranged against him? Perhaps more importantly, would he ever manage to ameliorate his gloomy outlook and cultivate the confidence that might just make the difference to his future prospects? There was little doubt that Isaac was his own worst enemy.

Rosenberg told me about his plans and about his ideas for future poems. But he spoke in a very melancholy and dispirited way about them. He is very disappointed. He seems able to do nothing about his work. No one will give him any real encouragement. He can't get anything printed anywhere.

Chapter Three

1911-13

*...I am studying at the Slade, the finest school drawing in
England. I do nothing but draw-draw...*
From letter to Miss Seaton: September 1912.

*...I feel very grateful for your interest in me—going to the
Slade has shown possibilities—has taught me to see more
accurately—but one especial thing it has shown to me-—Art is
not a plaything, it is blood and tears, it must grow up with one;
and I believe I have begun too late...*
From letter to Mrs Cohen: October 1912.

...O that the tortured spirit could amass
All the world's pains,
How I would cheat you, leaving none for life,
You would recount
All you have piled on me, self-tortured count
Through all eternity.
Lines from "Invisible Ancient Enemy Of Mine": 1914.

The fog pressed close in around Isaac. He'd been walking for hours and was tired and soaked. Worse perhaps, he felt disorientated and hoped to find a clue soon which would put him back on track.

Earlier, Venus, shining like a cut diamond below the silver sickle of the new moon, had held him spellbound; but within minutes the stars dimmed and blanked out, and in less than half an hour the dark streets with their tiny reservoirs of light were shrouded in mist so thick the poet's world shrank to a yard or so in circumference. The swirling vapour, like a grey curtain parting in front and drawing in noiselessly behind, made him feel as though he was trapped in an opaque dream where the victim, trying to escape his confinement, always finds himself back where he started. Although a veteran of many such "pea-soupers", Isaac could never shake the fear they provoked.

Twice he stumbled and almost fell on the uneven cobbles. Once he walked into a barrow being pushed along the pavement by a cursing vendor. Limping on, his shins scraped and bruised, he tried to escape the present by concentrating on the recent transformation in his fortunes.

When Lily Joseph told him his hopes of entering the foremost school of drawing in England were about to be fulfilled, he could hardly believe his good luck. She, and two friends, had decided to sponsor him on condition he worked hard and produced a body of work commensurate with their faith in his talent. Mrs Herbert Cohen, one of the three patrons involved, was to be his first line of contact. From the beginning her gimlet eyes and cut and dried manner disconcerted Isaac, although the joy of being afforded the opportunity to realise his ambitions easily overrode the vague unease created by the arrangement.

As well as exhilaration, he experienced dread as the day of his interview with Professor Brown grew closer. Bomberg delighted in reminding him how much the Prof's lieutenants, Henry Tonks and Wilson Steer, enjoyed bating prospective students. No one, according to his friend, emerged from the gruelling session unscathed.

As it turned out, his encounter with the dreaded trio in Brown's massive, barn-like room was not so bad. Despite feeling like an invading cockroach pinned to the floor by Brown's steely eyes, and intimidated by Tonks' angry pacing, he was at least spared the derision dolled out to those tempted to lighten the atmosphere with superfluous talk. When, in response to a question from Steer, he mentioned his interest in poetry, Tonks began to pay more attention to the shabby and unimpressive little man fidgeting nervously in his seat.

"Well, Mr Rosenberg, that's certainly in your favour. In order to write good poetry one must sweat blood. Every serious painter should be a practising poet; it encourages good habits, don't you think?" Isaac opened his mouth but quickly closed it again as Tonks ploughed on obviously uninterested in any response he might be tempted to offer. "Many students make the mistake of underestimating the need for sustained effort in the creative process. They believe that the muse will seek them out and spark the latent genius within." The teacher smiled mirthlessly. "The Slade is no place for such esoterics. There is no substitute for mental rigour, no substitute at all."

He turned and frowned over at his colleagues. Brown merely nodded, but Steer, smiling grimly, fixed the young Jew in his sights.

"My esteemed colleague is, of course, correct when he emphasises the importance of hard work and commitment. These qualities, alongside the will to succeed, are vital in achieving success and getting the most out of one's time here. If you feel unable to rise to such a challenge, or doubt you possess the skills necessary to progress your studies, it would be best to admit your mistake now and get out before further damage is done. There are many who would gladly fill your place. Do I make myself clear, sir?"

"Y...yes, perfectly."

"On arrival, you will proceed directly to the men's life class. Having studied your portfolio, we feel you would gain little by spending time in the Antique Room."

Isaac's heart quickened; he'd prayed this would happen. In Bomberg's view, months spent sketching the dismal collection of classical casts amassed by the college would most likely engender despair and cripple inspiration, while the men's life class provided the new student with an opportunity to engage with the real thing right away.

Brown noisily cleared his throat and spoke for the first time.

"Well then, Mr Rosenberg, we will meet again—no doubt— in drawing class. Welcome to the Slade. I hope your time here will prove both beneficial to the school and yourself."

"Thank…thank you, sir."

Leaving the room, Isaac experienced an extraordinary sense of destiny. He would show these great men, and everyone else who mattered, how serious he was; there could be no question of allowing this chance to slip through his fingers.

Isaac was shaken out of his reverie by a volley of oaths erupting close by. This, followed by shrill screaming and sounds of a violent scuffle, brought him to an abrupt halt. Thoughts of Jack the Ripper making a triumphant return to the streets of Whitechapel after a twenty-year absence evoked a numbing fear. Moving cautiously forward through the murk, he was almost knocked off his feet by a pair of struggling women intent on tearing each other's hair out by the roots. The fight, enacted beneath the dull yellow rays of a street lamp, lent the scene a vaguely theatrical air, heightened by the diffused backdrop of railings and alleyways. The combatants suddenly fell apart, panting hoarsely. One of them took to her heels, drawing up thick skirts as she disappeared into the mist. Isaac could hear her clogs, hammering on the wet cobbles, grow fainter by the second. The other muttered angrily to herself, while endeavouring to rearrange her dishevelled clothing.

"Who the fuck does she think she is any'ow, moving into my patch? She'll not be back in an 'urry, that's for sure."

Noticing Isaac for the first time, she smiled in an effort to appear more alluring despite her rumpled hair and dirty, tear-stained cheeks.

"Hello, ducky. You lookin' for a bit of company then?"

With a lurch of recognition, he realised he'd seen this pretty face before, albeit a little less grimy and upset. He struggled to remember where.

"No. I...I'm a little lost actually. I was wondering if...if you c...could tell me where I am."

"That's easy enough; you're at the end of 'Oundsditch near Bishopsgate."

The information amazed him; he wasn't so far from home at all.

"Oh well, in that case I'm not lost then. Thank you very much for your help."

"It's a pleasure." Are you sure there's nothing else I can do for you?"

At that moment, Isaac recalled where he'd previously encountered her. She was one of the models in the men's life class. It was hard now to imagine the exquisite beauty hidden beneath the folds of that tattered dress: the curving slope of the hips, the pink, soft flesh, the winsome smile as her eyes roved from one student to the next, each thinking himself the recipient of a secret invitation. If only they could see her now!

"No, no thanks."

As he backed away, part of him wished he had the courage, or the cash, to accept her offer and explore the fantasies which had tantalised him for months.

Turning back down Houndsditch, he walked as rapidly as his stiff legs would allow towards Aldgate and Whitechapel High Street. His thoughts soon returned to the Slade, and he recalled, with a swell of pride, the moment he'd first entered the vast room containing the men's life class. Awestruck, he'd stood for a while watching the ranks of students perched behind their drawing boards all busily sketching with rough sticks of charcoal. Apart from the harsh rasp of the pencils, the only other discernible sounds were the creaking of rickety stools and the hiss and crackle of heating conduits running the entire length of the left wall like the pipes of an upended church organ. Setting up his own board, he gazed at the platform, half of which was taken up by a blackened iron stove, and began to carefully study the naked model draped provocatively along a red-plush *chaise longue*.

Just as he began to draw the first long curving line, a chorus of voices shouted change and the model assumed an entirely different position. Less than a quarter of an hour later the call was repeated and so it continued until the morning break. At first, Isaac was dismayed by the rapidity of these movements; he'd never experienced the need to sketch under such pressure before. But, a few hours later, he'd become more accustomed to the procedure and once or twice actually found himself waiting for the next pose.

The fog was undoubtedly less dense than it had been. Striding up Whitechapel Road, he felt considerable relief. It was amazing how one's senses could be so easily fooled. Perhaps the landscape he strove to uncover in words, and on canvas, lay obscured behind a veil as thick as any "pea-souper". He desperately wanted his work to reveal the otherness of things. The feeling that God had somehow forsaken humankind, and corrupted the nobility of His creation, magnified the importance of the artist in his mind. As far as he was concerned, his calling embodied the deepest spiritual significance.

It was fortunate he'd managed to make a few friends during his first weeks at the Slade. The place contained its fair share of bullies who loved nothing better than to pick on vulnerable newcomers. He knew Bomberg of course. While they disagreed on almost everything, the pugnacious artist could be relied upon to pitch in and defend against calculated anti-Semitic insults. Smiling to himself, Isaac recalled a recent incident where Bomberg had pushed Alvara Guevara to the floor following a particularly nasty racist comment. He would never have been able to respond in such an aggressive manner but, despite certain pacifist reservations, felt the Chilean artist had got what he deserved.

Mark Gertler, another penniless Jew from the East End, had also befriended him. This young man's verve and dazzling good looks, although at such variance with Isaac's plain appearance and stumbling ineptness, belied a sympathy which had rapidly developed between the two students. Gertler was already getting noticed by important people, and, despite his unpromising background, appeared to be grasping the coat-tails of success. Isaac felt fortunate to be associated with such a charismatic individual, but sometimes wondered why he attracted any interest at all. Given such low self-esteem, he underestimated the fascination his strangely ambivalent personality evoked in others. His reputation as a poet, strengthened by Bomberg's assertion that he was truly a writer in painter's clothing, had, in fact, generated a lively degree of curiosity and interest.

Isaac knew very well that, if it wasn't for Gertler, Bomberg and a few others who could be relied upon to intervene on his behalf, life would be very much harder for him. He recalled Stanley Spencer, a painfully shy, working class boy from Cookham, mocked by those who envied his talent and despised his lowly background. This wasn't helped by the fact that Spencer returned home to the bosom of his family every night and rarely mixed with fellow students. Unfortunately, his eccentric behaviour made him an easy target.

Sometimes, Isaac despaired of mankind when supposedly enlightened people treated others in such a despicable fashion.

The vein of prejudice seemed to run deepest in those who had least reason to behave intolerantly. Again, he tried to make sense of the contradictions plaguing his life and society in general. He always had trouble accepting the goodness of a deity who not only tolerated cruelty, injustice and alienation in man, but appeared to embody these negative traits Himself. On the other hand, he desperately wished to believe in a world where perfection existed and lay within the grasp of the true artist. It was sometimes all too easy to view his own protracted struggle to achieve recognition as proof of God's essential spite.

By now, the thick blanket had lifted from the dripping streets. His sense of disorientation vanished and he felt a new resolve emerging. Despite everything, he would avoid the numerous pitfalls—his entry into the Slade at least proving that the odds could be rearranged in one's favour. Who could tell what might be possible in the future? Glancing up, he smiled as the stars began to repopulate the clearing skies.

✻

"I've written a poem I'd like to show you. It s…sums up how I…I feel. I just wanted to…to let you know."

"I love your poetry, Isaac…I'm only sorry I can't…"

"Please read it b…before you say anything else."

"Very well."

Sonia reached across the table and lifted the sheet of paper from her friend's slightly trembling hand.

The pair were seated in Isaac's cramped kitchen after returning from a three-hour walk along the Thames embankment. The February night was bitterly cold and they were still thawing out in the warm, steamy backroom. At last, he'd summoned up the courage to show her the poem which he felt best expressed his aching need. He hoped the sentiments might stir sympathy for his suit.

Unfolding the sheet she began to read. Paradoxically, while feeling compassion for Isaac's plight, she savoured the power his infatuation afforded her.

The Cage

Air knows as you know that I sing in my cage of earth,
And my mouth dry with longing for your winsome mouth of mirth,
That passes ever my prison bars which will not fall apart,
Wearied unweariedly so long with the fretful music of my heart.

If you were a rose, and I, the wandering invisible air
To feed your scent and live, glad though you knew me not there,
Or the green of your stem that your proud petals could never meet,
I yet would feel the caresses of your shadow's ruby feet.

O splendour of radiant flesh, Oh your heavy hair uncurled,
Binding all that my hopes have fashioned to crown me king of
*   the world,*
I sing to life to befriend me; she sends me your mouth of mirth,
And you only laugh as you pass me, and I weep in my cage of
*   earth.*

"Oh Isaac, that's so beautiful." She laid the poem down and gazed over the table into her suitor's green eyes. She was baffled, and a little exasperated, at how quickly they disengaged themselves and stared down at the table's heavily scratched surface. Eager to relieve the tension, Sonia searched for something illuminating to say.

"I love the flower imagery, especially the lines: *Or the green of your stem that your proud petals could never meet/ I yet would feel the caresses of your shadow's ruby feet.* It's a work of genius, it really is!"

"It's only how…how I feel." He spoke slowly without looking up. "The inspiration is yours."

"It's a wonderful tribute but—" She paused for a moment before continuing: "—I hope you don't think I'm laughing at you. And…I don't much like the idea of anyone weeping in *a cage of earth* either." Without thinking, Sonia giggled nervously. "I…I'm not sure what to…"

At that moment Hacha entered the room, her arms loaded with wet sheets and towels.

"I hope I'm not interrupting, but I need to get the washing hung up and dried."

"No, not at all. How are you and the family?"

Sonia was relieved she'd been spared the necessity of explaining, yet again, her inability to return Isaac's affections. Things were not, of course, quite so straightforward as they seemed. Protestations of love, while problematic, went a long way towards satisfying her craving for attention and affirmation. Years in an orphanage had done little for her self-esteem.

Hacha smiled, appreciating the polite inquiry.

"Oh, we get by. Elkon's not been so well recently. We haven't had

78

to call the doctor in yet, which is a blessing—the expense you understand. And there's Isaac's cough." Glancing at her eldest son, she smiled wearily for a moment. "We're hoping that he might be able to sell a few of his paintings soon. Has Mrs Amshewitz offered to buy anything yet, Isaac?"

"No, Mother. I've not…"

"A lovely family, the Amshewitzs'. Did you know that one of her sons, John, befriended Isaac many years ago and encouraged him to paint?"

"Yes, I think Isaac's mentioned…"

"Mother, we're talking…"

"Of course. I'm sorry to disturb you. Just give me a minute and I'll be out of your way. I know how much you young people love to talk." She turned, smiling again at Sonia. "Isaac's always got somebody or other round."

Hacha released the pulley, which swooped down on the old table forcing Sonia to duck.

"Mother!"

"I'm sorry, but could you move back a little—just for a few minutes—while I hang the sheets."

Isaac, red with impatience and bursting to resume the interrupted dialogue, pushed his chair back, his nervous eyes flitting between Sonia, Hacha and the rather severe portrait of his father, hanging over the old fireplace. He could feel the moment slipping away. The hope that the poem might move her to reconsider their relationship was rapidly evaporating.

Even when his mother at last vacated the kitchen, the wet sheets, dangling absurdly an inch or so above their heads, made it difficult to resume the previous conversation. In any case, Sonia was eager to change the subject.

"Did I tell you that David tried to seduce me again? I couldn't believe it after what I said to him last week. He just won't take no for an answer!"

Isaac knew the feeling but said nothing. At least Sonia was confiding in him, and, despite some unease, he preferred to believe she was not placing his own efforts in the same league. Perhaps she appreciated his somewhat more ascetic approach, so different from the blatant sexual methods employed by Bomberg. Naturally, he experienced moments of doubt. It had occurred to him on a number of occasions that he should adopt more direct tactics but had finally rejected the idea, believing he was irrevocably committed to the romantic route to his heart's desire.

From time to time Bomberg also appeared to doubt the wisdom of his adopted strategy. Once he'd even persuaded Isaac to write a poem to Sonia expressing his undying devotion. It was, however, becoming clear that their respective suits were doomed to failure, although each seemed unwilling to face this fundamental truth. If anything, Sonia appeared to be developing feelings for Rodker, despite the fact that he had shown little interest in her so far. Knowing Jimmy's obsession with sex, Isaac imagined it must only be a matter of time before he responded in some way. The prospect of a liaison between the two tormented him. How Bomberg would react if they ever had an affair was anybody's guess.

He now wondered whether he should return to the subject of the poem, but decided against it for the time being. Perhaps if he listened patiently to Sonia's account of Bomberg's clumsy attempts at seduction instead of pushing his own case, he might appear more enlightened in her eyes.

"It was just after he kicked you out, which I thought was unnecessarily rude!"

At the time Isaac had thought little of it. He accepted that Bomberg viewed him as a rival, and would inevitably expel him from his tiny studio as soon as Sonia appeared on the scene. It was good each was able to tolerate the other in her absence. Aware, though, of the possible advantage to be wrung out of acquiescence, he assumed a deeply hurt expression.

"After you'd gone, he just sat staring at me. When I asked about his paintings, he smiled and told me to get undressed. I know he's always direct—Morris says it's one of his endearing qualities—but that was just too much! I mean, what was I supposed to say?"

Isaac feigned shock while at the same time wishing he could be more assertive in his own dealings with her.

"I just got up and left; there was nothing else I could think to do. Do you think I was too hard on him?"

"N...no, not at all. Bomberg can be...overpowering. He says things without thinking most of the t...time, I'm afraid."

"Well, thank goodness you're not like that, Isaac." Sonia felt she had at last succeeded in steering the conversation away from dangerous rocks. "At least we can talk about things, can't we? It's good when you can rely on friends to be so...understanding. I really value our friendship, you know. Being in love can spoil things, don't you think?"

Anxious to avoid being trapped by the friends-are-better-than-lovers argument, Isaac made a last desperate attempt to latch onto the central theme of his poem.

"Yes, but I believe...that...that falling in love and being loved in...in return is like being released from a prison. Sometimes one f...feels trapped and...and sad when..."

"I really must be getting home now. It's late and I've got an early start tomorrow. You know what they're like at the wash-house when you're late for work."

Standing up, she pulled on her thin coat. Although realising this was a crude way of avoiding the issue, there simply seemed to be no choice; Isaac was obviously not going to be diverted. For a moment her head was lost in the canopy of sheets, hanging like main sails from the straining pulley.

"It's always good to talk to you, Isaac." Her voice was muffled as she tried to pull herself clear of the wet, clingy material. "It's so reassuring when someone understands. I just wish David could be as sensitive as you. I really loved your poem. Will you be at the library tomorrow night? Jimmy's going to be there; and Morris, I think."

"Yes, yes...I'll probably be..."

"That's wonderful. I just can't wait for tomorrow to pass. It's so hot and tedious in the wash-house. You've no idea how awful these women can be."

"Can I w…walk you home?"

"No, Isaac, I'll be fine, thank you."

He escorted her to the front door. His sister, Annie, was sitting on the couch deeply engrossed in one of the cheap novels he sometimes enjoyed reading when she'd finished with them.

"Where's Mother?"

Annie barely looked up.

"She's got a headache and gone to lie down."

"Ah."

"Well, good night, Isaac."

Sonia squeezed his thin wrist as he opened the door. For a moment he contemplated grabbing her in his arms and kissing her passionately, but, instead, smiled bleakly and muttered something incoherent. She was walking swiftly down the street when he realised that a peck on the cheek might have been an alternative to shuffling back and forth staring at his feet. If only he had Gertler's ineffable charm. Combined with Bomberg's honesty and Rodker's humorous detachment, Sonia might then embrace him as her lover. Poetry, however poignant, was just not enough to win a woman's heart.

Feeling empty, he closed the door and wondered where he might go from here. More than ever before, he realised he must somehow get out of his parents' house and acquire a proper studio. Perhaps then his luck would change. He tried to imagine personal space to work, entertain friends, and, most important of all, pursue uninterrupted his quest for Sonia's affections. The prospect raised his spirits a little as he crawled into bed and tried to relieve the aching lust inside.

Isaac sat back, gazing helplessly at the huge canvas. Having blanked out a large part of it earlier in the morning, he wondered if he'd done the right thing. Initial enthusiasm at the outset had quickly been replaced by disappointment as efforts to manifest his complex vision failed to satisfy him. Every time he added or removed something, the result was the same, further soul-searching and inevitable frustration. Somehow, he'd lost control of the piece.

The most recent change made it unlikely he'd be able to meet the deadline for the Slade summer competition, and the knowledge depressed him further. On top of this, Mrs Cohen was arriving at the studio in less than half an hour to inspect his progress. Their relationship had deteriorated to the point where Isaac could only envisage another unpleasant stand-off.

Until a fortnight ago, things couldn't have been better. Escaping the narrow confines of his mother's kitchen, and acquiring a proper studio, had released a creative wellspring. In the wake of his move, ideas for new projects piled up in his mind. As well as his inspired conception for the Slade competition, he'd managed, with the help of Reuben Cohen, to print a pamphlet of his latest poems. "Night and Day", he believed, could very well launch his career as a poet.

In the event, the first run of fifty copies was quickly disposed off without even covering the modest publishing costs. After having been forced to borrow the two pounds fee from Mrs Cohen on the understanding he would repay her from sales of the copies, this was not exactly the outcome he'd hoped for. On the other hand, the joy of seeing something of his in print at last temporarily eclipsed the sense of despair arising from being unable to make ends meet.

The failure of his latest painting reminded him that poetry was the medium he felt most comfortable with these days. Bomberg was right—he seemed capable of expressing things so much more clearly in verse. Unable to suppress a growing unease, he rose, walked over to his desk and opened his personal copy of the thin, grey booklet. Leafing through the pages, he arrived at the verse which expressed one of the many ideas he'd striven unsuccessfully to reproduce on the canvas.

Lo! She braideth her hair
Of dim soft purple and thread of satin.

Lo! She flasheth her hand—
Her hand of pearl and silver in shadow.
Slowly she braideth her hair
Over her glimmering eyes,
Floating her ambient robes
Over the trees and the skies,
Over the wind-footing grass.
Softly she braideth her hair
With shadow deeper than thought.

A sharp knock interrupted his musings. Wearily, he turned towards the door, reluctant to justify himself to a haughty benefactress who would undoubtedly demand a full explanation for his tardiness. Why oh why had Mrs Joseph and Mrs Lowy left him in the hands of this pompous harridan?

Without waiting for an invitation, Mrs Cohen strode into the room.

"Good morning, Isaac. I've come to see how you're getting along. The ladies were interested to know if you'd finished the painting yet."

If that was really the case, Isaac gloomily reflected, why hadn't they bothered to come and see for themselves. He gazed with dislike at the woman who'd made his life a misery for the past few weeks with her carping, impatient letters. Her plump, self-satisfied face and the expensive, but gaudy jewellery, bedecking her pudgy forearms and fingers, merely added to his antipathy. The imperious flash of dark eyes and the contemptuous sneer, which always seemed to be curling around the edges of her mouth, were magnified today as she examined the painting.

"So, is this finished then? I must say I find it difficult to tell."

"N...no. I've had to change a number of things. Firstly the..."

"How long will it take? The last day for entering pieces is next Monday is it not? Ruth said so."

"Yes...but..."

"Will it be ready or not? I'm disappointed that the painting has not already been submitted. You've been working on it for weeks now."

"I thought it was finished, but there were a number of things I...wasn't really s...satisfied with. So I..."

"I'm not really interested in your excuses, Isaac. We've all invested a great deal of time and money providing you with the opportunity to develop your talent, but now I wonder if we made a mistake. To be quite frank, I'm not sure what to make of this..this..." A contemptuous, dismissive gesture seemed to consign Isaac's work to oblivion. "It isn't what I expected when..."

"Please, Mrs Cohen, do not pre...presume to tell me how to p...p...paint."

"Your manners are as bad as ever, I see. Your recent letters have been impudent and presumptuous—not to mention sloppy. I'm not used to being treated in this way, you know! A little more gratitude would be in order."

"I never meant to insult, or disappoint you. I just w...wanted to explain that..."

"Well, that's by the by. I'll have to talk to the other ladies, of course, but I think it unlikely we will be prepared to sponsor your studies beyond the autumn term this year. I'm afraid you've failed to live up to expectations, young man. Perhaps you might be able to convince others that you merit their assistance, but, as far as I'm concerned, you've reached the end of the road."

"I'm s...sorry you feel that way."

"And what about the two pounds you promised to pay back a month ago? I'm afraid you just cannot be taken at your word."

"You will be repaid. In fact I want you to...to view all the money advanced to me as a l...loan which I will repay as soon as I can."

"I think I've listened to enough of your ingratitude for one day."

With a derisory shake of her head, Mrs Cohen turned and swept out of the studio, slamming the flimsy door behind her.

Isaac immediately felt sick to his heart; he hated confrontations. And what on earth was he going to do now? In the midst of remorse, a sudden whirlwind of anger swept through him. How dare this Philistine, whose knowledge and appreciation of art was so severely circumscribed, burst in here and presume to criticise his efforts. She could never even begin to comprehend the enormous pressure he was under. The effort he'd made to finish the cursed painting, not to mention the self-doubts which plagued him, were factors beyond her capacity to imagine. Money was nothing to her and her wealthy friends, yet its absence haunted his dreams and dogged every aspect of his miserable life. Most artists, apart from a privileged minority, had always been dependent on their patrons but he wondered how many were obliged to put up with this kind of sustained abuse. There was little choice but to throw them over and find some other source of income.

Filled with despair, it struck him he should give up his doomed artistic odyssey and return to Hentschel's. He was becoming a burden to everyone he knew; most of all, his mother bore the brunt of his overweening ambitions. With so many worries clamouring at her door, his selfish behaviour was increasingly hard to justify. At least he'd been able to help her financially while employed at the photographic engravers. He suddenly experienced an overwhelming urge to ram his fist through the large area of the painting he'd blanked out a few hours earlier. Why had he called the thing "Joy"? The work begun with such earnest devotion and high hopes had turned into a nightmare. It was hard to see where he went from here. Slumping into the only chair in the room, he rocked back and forth, clasping his head between both hands.

Slowly, he returned to a more balanced view of his situation. He had to get a grip of himself; the alternative was just too awful to contemplate. One moment he was on top of the world, anticipating imminent success and recognition, while the very next he was railing against everything and assigning blame to everyone but himself. In many ways he had been very lucky and had gained a great deal from his time at the Slade. Even the painting itself had afforded him insights and greater understanding of what he was trying to achieve in life. Why couldn't he see this? He must stop regarding himself as the underdog constantly beaten down by a merciless master or a hapless victim buffeted by capricious fate. The self-indulgence he had wrapped around himself like an overcoat was creating more problems for him than anything else. While his friends desperately tried to bolster his flagging ego, he perversely ignored or rejected their efforts. Where would this pathetic response to life eventually lead him? It was time to grow up and take life's various setbacks and disappointments squarely on the chin.

He recalled his time at Baker Street School where he'd refused to be browbeaten by his old Hebrew teacher, Mr Jacobs. He'd taken all the punishment doled out then but had remained uncowed. Although only a small boy, he had displayed qualities that he needed right now: the strength to stand up for himself, the wisdom to accept help when needed—as he had from the school's enlightened head teacher, Mr Usherwood—and, finally, the determination never to succumb to self-pity or self-doubt. Despite all the angst and self-centred behaviour exhibited over the last few months, he knew he had the courage to pull back from the edge. The thought sustained him as he finally rose to put the kettle on.

"I really want to introduce you to Hulme; he should be in tonight. I think you'll find him worthwhile."

"Thank...thank you, Gertler; I'm looking forward to it."

"And it's possible Eddie Marsh might drop by after the theatre. He could be of great help if he takes a shine to you."

Hurrying round Regent's Street towards Piccadilly Circus, Isaac felt excitement welling up inside him at the prospect of an evening in such distinguished company. The loss of his patrons several months ago, and the fact that he'd been forced for financial reasons to give up his studio and return home, didn't seem quite so important now. It was encouraging how he was able to rally even when things appeared hopeless. London was, in many ways, such a great place to be at the moment. With the artistic world in ferment, the Café Royal, according to reputation, was the very hub of revolutionary ideas and stimulating debate. It was good of Gertler to take such pains on his behalf; he was lucky to have such devoted friends.

They entered through large double doors and stood for a moment in an expansive hallway.

"The Domino Room's on the first floor, and there's a restaurant down there and two others upstairs."

Isaac stared into a large, dimly lit room crowded with diners. An immaculately dressed waiter, standing just beyond the open doorway, stared coldly at them for a moment before turning away to bid goodnight to a departing guest.

"Never mind him. Let's go."

Following Gertler up the stairs, he noted the thickness of the blue plush carpet and the exquisitely carved banisters. The place reeked of money. He wondered how it could possibly be the haunt of penniless artists and revolutionaries.

"Bomberg told me he passed Lloyd George strolling down these stairs last week. He tried to speak to him apparently, but 'the Welsh bastard', as he put it, declined to acknowledge his existence." Although smiling briefly at the thought of his friend's inevitable frustration at being so pointedly ignored, the story failed to put Isaac at his ease.

On the first floor, Gertler pulled him into a huge room humming with conversation occasionally punctuated by bursts of raucous laughter. Gazing round in wonder, the poet took in the distinctive white marble-topped tables littered with half-empty bottles of wine and sparkling glasses. The walls, hung with innumerable mirrors reflecting crimson velvet and multiplying elaborately carved pillars, were thick with intricate gilding. Again, Isaac felt intimidated; with only two pennies and a farthing jingling around in his pocket, he was keen to avoid the embarrassment arising from his conspicuous poverty. How could he possibly fit in here?

He quickly noticed, however, that many of the people crowding the room could hardly be described as affluent. There appeared to be plenty of young artistic types like himself, shabbily dressed and sipping carefully from half-empty coffee cups. He also recognised a gregarious crowd of painters from the Camden Town group, noisily slurping wine and cavorting with a bevy of young girls he reckoned must be their models. The hurrying waiters, dressed in distinctive white aprons, took no notice whatsoever of this boisterous behaviour, or the large numbers of people obviously eking out their drinks. There was little doubt that the Domino Room, despite first impressions, lived up to its reputation as a haven for artists and those espousing art, whatever their financial or social status.

"Over this way. That's Hulme sitting in the corner. Luckily, there's room for us to sit down."

Approaching the table, Isaac noticed a subtle change in Gertler's body movements and facial expression. This was not the first time he'd witnessed his friend assume a mask appropriate for the occasion.

"Gentlemen! Good evening."

His voice exuded a suave charm that caught and held the attention of the seated company. Isaac experienced a twinge of envy, wishing he were capable of projecting such a winning persona.

"Allow me to introduce you all to my friend, Isaac Rosenberg, who has the good fortune to be both talented poet and painter."

People nodded and smiled before returning to their conversations. Almost overcome by the glowing compliment, Isaac smiled lamely and hastily sat down. He hated being in the limelight. A large man with thick black hair flecked with grey and strongly chiselled features, whom Isaac correctly assumed to be the philosopher and man of letters, T E Hulme, leaned forward and stared at him across the marble table.

"Well, well, Gertler. You appear to know everyone of note in London. A poet and a painter, you say!" The deep voice was self-assured without a hint of irony.

"Yes, although Rosenberg does claim poetry as his first love. Isaac, this is Mr Hulme whom I mentioned to you earlier this evening."

"I'm honoured to meet you, sir."

"Likewise I'm sure. I only hope that Gertler has not been over-zealous in his criticism of me. I like to think he has an open mind; I would not want you to get the wrong idea Mr...er...Rosenberg."

"No...no, sir. He speaks very highly of you."

"Well, that at least is encouraging, though I fear you may be slightly exaggerating his ardour." Hulme laughed good-naturedly. "So, Gertler," the great man clasped his large hands together and pushed his chin forwards on to the tips of his thumbs, "are you still on the fence, or has Eddie Marsh been corrupting you recently? Eh?"

The question was left hanging by the arrival of a waiter. Gertler smiled and turned to order.

"A glass of the house red for me and…Rosenberg, what is your pleasure this evening?"

"A c…coffee will be fine."

"Thank you, sir." Without noting anything down, the man hurried off towards another table.

Unwilling to let go, Hulme continued to gaze at Gertler, a wry smile playing around the edges of his lips.

"Bomberg dropped by last night. Now, there is a man who understands the power of form; the desirability of utilising art to express the real—the concrete—instead of flirting with notions of the infinite and other such romantic tosh."

Gertler, unabashed, responded with typical aplomb.

"You are, of course, correct, sir. Many poets and painters appear to have eschewed clarity, choosing instead to embrace obscurity. The language of art needs to be harder and less equivocal. Naturally, this does not necessarily require that one rejects all things which cannot immediately be perceived or pinned down. The challenge for the serious artist is to find a way of expressing himself more…precisely"

"Ah ha, Gertler, I see that our debates have not been totally in vain. There may be hope for you yet. The first step is to stop gazing dreamily at the stars and see what is all around us. What do you think, Mr Rosenberg? Do you hanker after the infinite?"

Put on the spot, Isaac turned red and struggled to gather his wits. Despite the pressure of Hulme's narrowed, assessing eyes, he suddenly found his voice.

"I…I…agree that language must be clear, and more…p…precise. But surely poetry and all other art forms exist to reveal the truth and beauty at the heart of creation. Otherwise, we merely restate what is obvious and...and ultimately...mundane."

"Another romantic, I see. Don't you understand that striving after this mystery of yours necessarily enervates language. Nothing can be described without being wreathed in a mist obscuring what actually is!"

"So...so, as Gertler says, the p...priority must be to use words as explicitly as...as possible. We need to work harder to express the...the otherness of things."

"A poet after my own heart, I see."

Turning quickly to discover the owner of the clipped aristocratic voice, Isaac beheld a tall man immaculately adorned in tails and top hat, gazing benignly down on the company. His grey eyes, flicking from face to face, were alight with enthusiasm.

"Good evening, Eddie." Hulme sat back in his chair, draining a last mouthful of wine from his glass. "Just in the nick of time to save your young acolytes from further embarrassment." He chuckled, without the slightest hint of sarcasm or ill-feeling.

"I'm sure everyone was managing very well without assistance from me. How are you, Gertler? I thought you were joining me for breakfast yesterday morning."

"Yes, I'm sorry, Eddie. Something came up I'm afraid."

"Think nothing off it; next Saturday morning perhaps. Anyway, who is the young man who was speaking so eloquently a few moments ago?"

"Ah yes, Eddie. This is my friend Isaac Rosenberg, whom I've mentioned to you on more than one occasion."

"It's very good to...to make your acquaintance at last, sir."

Marsh smiled broadly, his thin eyebrows lifting quizzically.

"The honour is mine. It's always a pleasure to meet Mark's friends. You are a writer if I'm not mistaken?"

"I...I..."

Gertler swiftly intervened.

"Rosenberg is both gifted poet and painter. But Bomberg feels that it is through poetry he will ultimately make his mark."

"Perhaps, but Bomberg can be a little too sure of himself at times. Is that not right, Hulme?"

"If you mean that he sees a thing for what it is and is not afraid to express himself in a refreshingly original and forthright manner, I couldn't agree more. Bomberg certainly calls a spade a spade and thank God for people like him!"

"That's certainly true. I've always been a champion of clear thinking and articulation as you know."

"Of course, of course. Now, I'm afraid I must take my leave. There are a number of friends gathering at Frith Street as we speak; it would be terribly bad manners to keep them waiting. I hope to meet you again, Mr Rosenberg. You are welcome to join our discussion groups at my digs any time. Gertler will fill you in. Eddie, give my regards to Rupert when you see him next. Goodnight all."

Hulme strode quickly out of the Domino Room, enthusiastically acknowledging the chorus of goodnights thrown at him from various tables. Most of the young men seated nearby hastily gathered up coats and hats, presumably bound for Frith Street. Isaac wished he was going too, but simultaneously experienced intense curiosity regarding Gertler's patron.

At that moment the waiter returned with their order.

"Please let me get this."

"That's all right, Eddie, we..."

"No, I insist. Mr Rosenberg, would you like something a little stronger?"

"No thank you, sir, I'm fine."

"Very well. Could you bring me the bottle of the eighty-eight we started last night? I think there was a glass or two remaining."

The waiter nodded. "Certainly sir, right away."

"So, what did you make of our resident philosopher, and critic?" He smiled at Isaac. "Quite a remarkable man, is he not?"

"Yes. He has some v...very interesting things to say about art."

"He has, he certainly has." Marsh smiled.

"He only touched on things tonight, Eddie."

"Ah well, perhaps you should take him up on his invitation then. The Firth Street gatherings can be very…stimulating. As you probably already concluded, Mr Rosenberg, Hulme and I do not always agree. I feel he rather misses the point at times. Romanticism cannot be dismissed so easily. What Hulme fails to acknowledge is the emergence of an entirely new generation of artists, who, despite having developed their own distinctive styles, are not afraid to admit their debt to past masters." Marsh paused and gazed into space for a moment. "These are new and exciting times, but everything that went before cannot simply be ditched! Too many of those clamouring for change are reluctant to acknowledge that past, present and future are indissolubly linked. What we were informs what we are and what we will become. Through art we aspire to something beyond the here and now. Just as you were saying when I arrived, Mr Rosenberg—or perhaps you will allow me to call you Isaac?"

"Yes, p…please do…I think I…I was saying something of the sort."

Marsh was, as Gertler had suggested, a man worth meeting. To have encountered two great minds in the course of one evening was extremely fortunate. Who could tell how this might aid his struggle for recognition? Perhaps Marsh, who obviously relished his role as mentor to young, aspiring artists, might be persuaded to look at his latest poetry, and ultimately help him publish it. As a well-known collector of modern paintings, there was also a chance he would buy some of the pieces Isaac was currently working on. The need to generate some sort of income remained vital.

Sipping at his coffee, he felt as though things might really be looking up at last. He must strive to put the problems and failures of the last twelve months well and truly behind him, and concentrate on making the most of new opportunities.

News that Sonia had finally moved in with Rodker broke Isaac's heart, nudging him into a terrible depression. At first, he found it hard to concentrate, suffered from acute insomnia, and took little interest in anything beyond the withering of his hopes. Eventually, he managed to draw a somewhat shaky line beneath the affair, and, unlike Bomberg, decided to maintain close links with both parties. Out of the original circle of literary comrades, Jimmy was his closest friend and sacrificing their relationship would in any case change nothing.

Brooding in his new studio one wet Sunday afternoon, Isaac sat staring out of the window as droplets of rain, coursing down the glass panes, blurred the hard outlines of the buildings across the street, making it seem as if as they were melting away or completely reconstituting themselves. The pages of his latest poem lay scattered on the desk in front of him. The act of writing had undoubtedly helped reconcile him to the loss, but something inside had altered. He felt brittle— uncharacteristically fragile—as if a blow or even a loud noise might shatter him in pieces. Picking up a sheet, he read listlessly, wondering if he'd ever recover from the wounds recent events had inflicted.

Mist-like its dusky panic creeps in the end to your proud heart:
O you will feel its kisses cold while it rends your limbs apart.
Have you not seen the withering rose and watched the lovely moon's
*   decay,*
And more than mortal loveliness fade like the fainting stars away?

I have seen lovely thoughts forgot in wind, effacing dreams;
And dreams like roses wither leaving perfume not nor scent:
And I have tried to hold in net like silver fish the sweet starbeams,
But all these things are shadowed gleams of things beyond the
*   firmament.*

In an effort to ease the pain, Isaac reflected on the unexpected burgeoning of a relationship with a woman he'd known for years, but never considered as anything more than a friend. Until recently, he'd turned up at Annetta Raphael's small flat only when in need of distraction. As a singer and accomplished piano player, her music served to relax him and provided a ready source of inspiration. He'd always

94

been impressed by her quiet, unassuming manner; she seemed pleased when he called and never pressed him to stay or come more often.

Sitting in Annetta's untidy lounge one evening, a few days after Sonia's shocking disclosure, he was unable to hold back his tears. Annetta stopped playing, crossed over the room and knelt down in front of him, wrapping her arms around his shaking body. She then took his hand and drew him through the door of her bedroom, gently removed his clothes and laid him on the bed. Stretching out beside him, she ran her hands slowly up his legs, using the tips of her fingers to softly caress his inner thighs. He'd never been touched in this way before, and, for the first time in his life, eagerly responded to a powerful physical stimulus induced by someone other than himself. The entire situation seemed unreal as if he was spying on Annetta with a secret lover; but the knowledge that he was the focus of her lust quickly engulfed him.

To his amazement, she began to rub her thumb and forefinger back and forth over his erection. She then sat on top of him, and pushed down hard until he was settled deep inside her.

Later, lying quietly under Annetta's warm, collapsed body, he tried to come to terms with what had just happened. At the moment of orgasm, he'd envisaged Sonia and almost screamed out her name. Although feeling a little ashamed, he recalled with wonder the sheer ecstasy; even now, he didn't want to move, afraid to consign the transcendent experience to dull memory.

Annetta broke the spell. Sitting up, she pulled gently away from him and ran her hands through her hair. As she rose and moved towards the bathroom, he knew with certainty that this had not been her first time. Whether with the man she'd been engaged to a number of years ago, or others since, was impossible to tell, but her experience was undeniable. Not that he minded. If they'd both been as green as he was, things would have quickly fallen to pieces.

Since then they'd met a few times and made love on the large bed with its lumpy old mattress and iron head rail. Many of the poems he'd been working on recently could hardly have been written, he realised, without this carnal awakening. While deeply injured by his failure to win Sonia, the affair with Annetta had, at least, partially reconciled him to the loss, and he felt satisfied his work was gaining in depth and maturity. Perhaps he should send some of the latest stuff to Marsh. According to Gertler, he was more than willing to assess pieces, whether poetry or paintings, produced by his circle of young artist friends.

Isaac noticed that the rain had finally ceased and patches of blue sky were splitting up the dense cloud continents into shrinking islands. Sunlight, kissing a distant factory stack, illuminated the vertical funnel a fiery red. For a moment it seemed as though the bricks had caught alight and were blazing from top to bottom. It suddenly struck him how desperate he was to burn so brightly. Like a meteor cutting a swath of light through the universe, his greatest desire was to irradiate the lives of those obscured in darkness. He would persist. He must persist.

Chapter Four

1913-15

...I am not going to refute your criticisms; in literature I have no judgement—at least for style. If in reading, a thought has expressed itself to me, in beautiful words; my ignorance of grammar etc, makes me accept that...

> *Extract from letter to Edward Marsh, June 1914*

...There's a lot of splendid stuff to paint. We are walled in by the sharp upright mountain and the bay. Across the bay the piled up mountains of Africa look lovely and dangerous. It makes one think of savagery and earthquakes—the elemental lawlessness. You are lucky to be in comfortable London and its armchair culture...

> *Extract from letter to Edward Marsh from South Africa,*
> *July 1914*

...By the time you get this, things will only have just begun I'm afraid; Europe will have just stepped into its bath of blood. I will be waiting with beautiful drying towels of painted canvas, and precious ointments to smear and heal the soul; the lovely music and poems. But I really hope to have a nice lot of pictures and poems by the time all is settled again; and Europe is repenting of her savageries...

> *Extract from letter to Edward Marsh from South Africa,*
> *November 1914*

Dear Marsh,

I am very sorry to have had to disturb you at such a time with pictures. [Ref to Rupert Brooke's death April 23rd, 1915.) But when one's only choice is between horrible things, you choose the least horrible. First I think of enlisting and trying to get my head blown off, then of getting some manual labour to do— anything—but it seems I'm not fit for anything. Then I took these things to you. You would forgive me if you knew how wretched I was. I am sorry I can give you no more comfort in your own trial but I am going through it too.

Extract from letter to Edward Marsh, May 1915

...All July walks her floors that roof this ice,
My frozen heart the summer cannot reach,
Hidden as a root from air, or star from day.
A frozen pool whereon mirth dances
Where the shining boys would fish...

Lines from "Midsummer Frost, (First version) 1914-15

On Receiving News Of War

Snow is a strange white word;
No ice or frost
Have asked of bud or bird
For winter's cost.

Yet ice and frost and snow
From earth to sky
This Summer land doth know,
No man knows why.

In all men's hearts it is.
Some spirit old
Hath turned with malign kiss
Our lives to mould.

Red fangs have torn His face
God's blood is shed.
He mourns from His lone place
His children dead.

O! ancient crimson curse!
Corrode, consume.
Give back this universe
Its pristine bloom.

Capetown: 1914

99

A h, good morning, Isaac. Come in, come in!"
Marsh shook the young poet's hand warmly, ushering him into a room familiar to aspiring artists and academics throughout the south of England, and beyond. The heavy oak table was being laid for breakfast and Marsh's plump housekeeper bustled around arranging china plates, cups and saucers. Both side walls were hung with paintings—a significant selection from the civil servant's much vaunted "modern" collection, Isaac guessed. He also noticed a number of framed photographs, featuring wealthy, upper-class gentlemen in top hats posing impressively for the camera. Marsh was in most of them, but, apart from his mentor, only Winston Churchill's cherubic features and Rupert Brooke's blonde good looks were familiar to him.

"It seems we still have a moment or two to spare. There are some people I'd like you to meet before we sit down to breakfast. They arrived yesterday evening as a matter of fact, and stayed over. Come through."

Two men rose as they entered the spacious lounge. One of them, although only in his early twenties, was completely bald apart from thick pockets of dark hair sprouting untidily from the back and sides of his head; the crown, reflecting light shed by an overhanging candelabra, looked as though it had been recently polished. Tall and disdainful with a slight stoop, he appeared to have embraced cynical middle age with relish. His companion, much shorter with a prominent waistline, appeared at first glance to be more affable although the agreeable impression was belied by sharp, supercilious eyes set too close together.

"Gentlemen, it is my pleasure to introduce you to Isaac Rosenberg, a painter and poet of considerable promise. Isaac, these are my young friends, David Warren and Jonathan Longbotham, both of whom are completing their undergraduate studies at Cambridge. David has already been offered a position with *The Times* when he graduates next year."

Warren, inclined his bald pate slightly. "Thanks largely to your efforts, Eddie."

"The least I could do, my boy, the very least. I see you've brought a few paintings along with you this morning, Isaac. I hope you've included *Sacred Love*. We're looking forward to viewing that piece in particular."

"Yes, I…"

Marsh's housekeeper suddenly entered the room cutting the poet's response short.

"Breakfast is served, sir."

"Excellent. The viewing will have to wait a little while longer."

Chatting amiably, Marsh ushered his guests back through into the dining room.

"Did you bring some poems along as well, Isaac?"

"Y…yes. I was going to leave them with you. I'd…I'd be grateful for your…"

"Of course, of course. Take the seat beside David. That's splendid. Now gentlemen, tuck in, please. Enjoy."

A little under an hour later, Isaac unwrapped one of his canvasses and laid it upright on a high-backed chair for perusal. The three men gazed impassively at the piece for a few moments. Finally, Warren grimaced and turned to Marsh.

"Impressive in a derivative sort of a way. It obviously owes a great deal to Gauguin in style. More muted of course, but instantly recognisable. I'm sure Rupert would be impressed; it's his sort of thing."

"Yes, I suppose it is really. What do you think, Jonathan?"

Isaac felt suddenly invisible as if the others had forgotten he was in the room.

"Mmm, yes." The plump undergraduate nodded reflectively. "The colours are pleasant enough, perhaps a little…underdone for my taste. However, the piece is not without merit; the theme is clear at any rate." Marsh stared more closely, pursing his lips and nodding vigorously.

"Yes, yes. An interesting reaction from both of you, but, while Gauguin is undoubtedly influential, it would be wrong to ignore the boldness of the style. One would obviously wish to acknowledge the influences while praising the diversity and deftness of touch."

Isaac made a desperate attempt to involve himself in the discussion of his work.

"I agree G...Gauguin did have an..."

"Yes, first class, Isaac, first class. Can we agree a price later? Now, what about the poems you've been working on? What was the name of the one you mentioned in your letter?"

" 'A Midsummer Frost.' "

"Ah yes. An intriguing title, eh?" He smiled round while simultaneously pulling a large watch from the pocket of his tweed waistcoat. "Unfortunately, time is running short. What if I read your poem later in the week Isaac, and post my comments on before your departure? Would that suffice?"

"Thank you, Marsh, that would b...be very helpful."

He felt greatly relieved that these haughty young men were going to be denied the opportunity of picking over his poetry.

During breakfast, he'd felt increasingly apprehensive as his fellow guests discussed the strengths and weaknesses of the various paintings decorating Marsh's walls. Unease quickly converted to exasperation when they turned their attentions to his own work. Although intimidated by the all-knowing confidence exhibited by the trio, he was not deceived for a moment. As far as Isaac was concerned they were little more than parasites, who, despite being convinced of their absolute right to determine quality, were utterly dependent on the host, their urbanity a pale reflection of the passion firing the true artist. It was perhaps unfair to categorise Marsh in such a crude way, providing, as he did, much needed encouragement to his group of young artist friends and throwing them a life-line when times were hard; but Isaac instinctively knew where the civil servant's deepest allegiances lay. Preserving the "tradition" was a position he rarely veered from. As members of an elite club, Marsh and his friends measured new work against the rigid yardstick of accepted practice, and Oxbridge orthodoxy remained closest to their hearts. The poet raged impotently against the implicit condescension.

"Will I need my brolly, I wonder? Was it raining when you arrived, Isaac?"

"Just a little."

Marsh strode over to the large multi-paned window and stared down onto the street.

"I believe things have deteriorated since then. Now please, all of you, feel free to remain and further peruse the collection. David and Jonathan may be able to provide some interesting insights." Marsh smiled over at Isaac. "You'd be surprised how well informed they are about such things."

Smiling, he offered no reply. He was now only too well aware of their intellectual perspicacity.

The housekeeper suddenly appeared carrying her employer's coat, hat and umbrella.

"Are you sure you don't want me to call you a carriage, sir? The weather's turned so bad!"

"Thank you. I'll be fine. Oh yes, before I forget, Isaac, I'm considering putting together a set of drawings to complement the book of Georgian poetry Brooke and I are publishing. We would obviously wish to include a number of your own pieces, including *Sacred Love*. How do you feel about the proposal?"

"I'm flattered you c...consider..."

"The enterprise is naturally contingent on obtaining enough advance subscriptions."

"I...I see. Perhaps I could help find some people who might..."

"Excellent. Now, gentlemen, I really must take my leave of you."

"I'll walk with you. There's someone else I have to d...drop in on this morning."

"Are you sure?"

"Yes. I really must be g…getting along."

The prospect of being left alone with the smug undergraduates drove Isaac to uncharacteristic dishonesty.

"Right then. I'll see you two gentlemen this evening. Enjoy the exhibition at the Tate. I'm sure it will prove worthy of your time."

Warren smiled ambiguously.

"I'm sure it will, Eddie."

Minutes later, striding towards Whitehall in the pouring rain, Marsh attempted conversation with his diffident protégé.

"So what did you make of Warren, then? That young fellow has a very promising career ahead of him or I'm no judge of character."

"He certainly seemed very well informed. Did you manage to…?"

"Longbotham too, of course, but Warren is the brightest of the two, don't you think."

"Yes, I…"

"When are you leaving for South Africa? The weather will be a tonic I'm sure. I envy you, Isaac; it's a beautiful country or, at least, so I've heard."

"That's what I was going to ask you about. Did…did you manage to contact the Emigration Office about the…the…?"

"Yes, as a matter of fact. I've not received anything back yet, but I'm sure there will be no problem expediting the matter—no problem at all. Your sister is living out there in comfortable circumstances after all. Just because your own funds are a little…compromised at the moment should make no difference."

"It's just that…"

Don't worry about a thing! I'll make sure you're on the boat, and do call by for that cheque next week. In fact, come for breakfast again, if you like. Maybe I'll have had time to read some of your poems by then."

"Thank you, Marsh."

By now, Isaac was panting and half-running to keep up. His lungs had been very poor recently. He fervently hoped the equable South African climate would improve his health. The winter, with its constant rain and cold winds, had affected him badly, resurrecting fears of tuberculosis.

"I do appreciate the time and trouble you t...take over my work and the...the help you provide."

"Always a pleasure, my dear fellow, always a pleasure. Now, here's where we must part company. Please do drop by again before you sail, and work hard while you're over there. I look forward to seeing a bulging portfolio on your return."

During the walk home, the rain eased off and the skies began to clear. Isaac felt less depressed than he had of late. Despite the mix of emotions arising from breakfast at Gray's Inn, things were looking up. Marsh had admired his paintings and agreed to buy *Sacred Love*. As usual, the money was much needed. Thoughts of the approaching voyage made his heart beat faster and his palms sweat. This could be the start of something big. If he managed to establish himself as a teacher and artist in Cape Town, his life might easily be transformed. He desperately craved recognition and the means of earning a decent living. Selling enough paintings would enable him to devote more precious time to writing and then he'd show these jumped-up Cambridge prigs a thing or two. Or would he? Their innate superiority remained a high wall against which an artist could batter himself for years without making the slightest impression; recognition could never alter the facts of one's birth and upbringing. He tried to dismiss the depressing thought as he entered Whitchapel Library, and hurried up the stairs to spend the remainder of the morning reading Blake and Coleridge.

Grasping the metal safety rail, Isaac stared in awe at the wild elements jostling for his attention. High above the Cape's jagged peaks, a further range of cumulus mountains extended far out into the azure sky. The waves, splashing against the hull of the ship, sparkled and danced in the bright sunlight.

"That's Robben Island. Not much to look at really. But what about

Lion's Head and Table Mountain? Definitely a sight for sore eyes, eh?"

Robert Johnston, successful engineer and socialite, smiled warmly, noting with pleasure his young friend's lively interest. Having lived in Cape Town many years before, he'd been looking forward to airing his local knowledge.

The pair had shared a cabin for the past few weeks and become quite friendly. Despite having little in common, they'd come to rely on each other in small ways throughout the voyage. Johnston had proved to be a fount of knowledge on the shifting balance of power in Europe, as well as recent German incursions into Africa. His predictions that war was inevitable, intrigued and alarmed Isaac in equal measure. While not really interested in poetry or the arts in general, the older man found his companion's stories about the goings-on at the Slade, and the often bizarre behaviour of his various artist friends, extremely entertaining. They generally ate together, and often strode the heaving decks trying to stave off bouts of sea-sickness.

Without a family to worry about, Johnston, at the age of forty-five, had decided to return to Cape Town on a permanent basis. During his last assignment, he'd enjoyed the status accorded a mining engineer in a country desperately requiring his skills. Apart from that, the weather was agreeable, and his earnings went much further than they did at home; he could never have afforded two servants to cater for his needs back in England.

"You can see the docks now. See, there." Isaac, following the line of Johnston's extended arm, failed to make out anything distinct in the jumble of buildings hugging the shoreline. "Your people will no doubt be meeting you."

"I'm not sure if they know which...which boat I'll be on."

"Oh don't worry about that—they'll know all right. Not too many passenger ships arrive from England. Anyway, judging by what you've told me about your sister, she'll probably have been down to meet every boat for the last fortnight!"

Isaac smiled. That was most likely true. Minnie always had had a soft spot for him; in some ways he was lucky to have such an attentive family, even though things could become a little too cloying at times. None of them really understood that an artist required space to work, and had to be left in peace most of the time. His mother, in particular, could never be persuaded that her beloved son needed to stay anywhere else than at home.

"Will anyone be m…meeting you?"

"No. But that doesn't matter; I know my way around. If for some reason your sister doesn't turn up, I'll take you up to De Villiers Street myself. It's not so far away from where I'll be staying until I get fixed up." Johnston suddenly laughed out loud. "My God, Isaac, look at Devil's Peak! Do you appreciate now how untamed this country really is?"

Isaac gazed towards the distant pinnacle soaring high above the bay, then allowed his eyes to run the full length of the rugged plateau bounded in the east by the rearing Lion's Head. His friend was correct. This was civilisation at its most vulnerable, clinging, it seemed, by its fingernails to a land which might suddenly shrug it back into the sea. Nothing could be more different from the city and country he'd left so far behind. Experiencing a sudden jab of homesickness, he recalled, with an effort, how eager he'd been to escape London's claustrophobic atmosphere and bitter disappointments—its cold winds and unrelenting poverty. South Africa promised a fresh start. Maybe here, where people struggled to assert their humanity against a backdrop of encroaching wilderness, he'd at last be judged on his merits. Earning a living as a portrait painter would surely not be so hard! And then, his future assured, who could tell what might or might not be possible. Again, he tried to imagine being able to write without money worries constantly nagging him. How wonderful after years of being denied a fair show. And, to recover one's health and vitality!

As the ship nosed into dock, Isaac noticed a large crowd was gathered on the quay below but couldn't see any familiar faces among the throng of excited people. Then Johnston, whose eyes were particularly sharp, noticed someone pushing her way forward, waving furiously up at the ship.

"Isaac, I think that lady is trying to get your attention. Besides which, I'd be blind not to notice a certain…family resemblance."

"Where is she?"

"Just there. She's managed to reach the front and is looking straight up at us. You see—just down there."

His eyes suddenly clamped on a familiar face wreathed in smiles. With an upsurge of delight, he studied the features of his older sister, realising just how much he'd missed her benevolence and wise counsel over the past two years.

Before disembarking, Johnston shook him warmly by the hand.

"I hope you settle in quickly. Let's get together some time and I'll show you around. There's a lot to discover here, in every sense, if you take my meaning." He winked and tapped his nose. "Cape Town's full of bored young people who appreciate—how can I put it—a little diversion."

Isaac wasn't quite sure what his companion was getting at but guessed it was to do with meeting women. During their time together Johnston had hinted at more than a passing interest in the sins of the body. Sexual gratification, minus the inconvenience of becoming embroiled in a serious relationship, appeared to be the desired outcome of any new affair he embarked upon. For Isaac, the opposite was true. His failure to establish a permanent bond with the woman he idolised was one of the principal reasons for his self-imposed exile. While he hoped to shed the past and bid a final farewell to his unrequited love for Sonia, he certainly didn't feel up to a fling with a stranger, however attractive. His recent dalliance with Annetta, while revelational, had largely failed to assuage the pain of rejection. There could never be anything light-hearted in his approach to the opposite sex; his yearnings were too great for that. The few poems he'd written on the long voyage reflected the struggle still raging inside. Not only had he fallen victim to a jealous God who never tired of inflicting punishment, but was now in thrall to a merciless Goddess determined to assert her dominance.

Walking down the gangway behind a slow moving queue, he recalled the last two verses of a short poem completed while steaming down the West African coast. Under a sea and sky united in dazzling brilliance—the land a mere smudge on the eastern horizon—he'd given vent to his frustrations.

> …Gone who yet never came.
> There is the breathing sea,
> And the shining skies are the same,
> But they lie—they lie to me.
>
> For she stood with the sea below,
> Between the sky and the sea,
> She flew ere my soul was aware,
> But left this thirst in me.

There were tears in his eyes as he rushed forward to embrace his sister.

✳

A week later, Johnston called by De Villiers Street to pay his respects and find out how his young friend was settling in.

"So, what do you think of Cape Town so far?"

"I've…I've not really managed to see very much of it yet, to tell you the truth. I've been so busy, the t…time seems to have rushed by."

The two were sitting in the small lounge used by the Horvitch family to entertain guests. Wolf was still out at work and Minnie was busy supervising preparations for the evening meal. They could hear the impatient rise and fall of her voice as she chivvied on a somewhat reluctant native cook. By South African standards the house was relatively small, but Isaac felt he was living in the lap of luxury. In comparison to the family home in Dempsey Street, the place was a mansion with all the trappings of high living. His own room was delightful, with a view over the bay, but, as he'd suspected, there was little chance of escaping the attentions of his over-solicitous sister.

She was always dropping in with his baby niece to see how her "favourite" brother was getting along. The infant's squalling at night tended to disturb his sleep, and he was already wondering how soon he could move out without offending her.

"I saw Sir Herbert Stanley yesterday. Remember I t... told you that my friend Edward Marsh had given me a letter of introduction."

"Yes, I think so."

"Well, he's commissioned me to paint his t...two young children— only babies apparently, but it's a start."

"Excellent."

"And I've met so many people—most of them relatives who've settled out here. My Uncle Peretz is actually a rabbi in Johannesburg. He's been over visiting some colleagues in Cape Town this week. My father would have loved to see him again.... . The place is so...ideal for...for painting, I've dropped poetry altogether for the time being."

"You've certainly been lucky with the weather. Winter in Cape Town is not always so benevolent."

"It's been marvellous! My chest feels better than it has for years."

Johnston smiled indulgently.

"I'm glad you've taken to the place so quickly. By the way, what are you doing tonight? I thought you and I could go out and enjoy ourselves a little. Remember what I told you. There are plenty opportunities for...for recreation in Cape Town if you know where to find it."

"Thank you for asking, but Wolfie, my brother-in-law, is entertaining some guests this evening. He asked m...me to join them."

"Some of his clients at the post office?"

"B...business men, I'm told."

"Sounds dull, but you'd better show willing, I suppose. What about a week on Saturday then? I've been invited to a do over at the British Embassy. Why not come along with me; there'll be lots of interesting people for you to meet? Just the sort of place to make contacts."

Isaac instinctively knew this was a bad idea. Johnston's concept of enjoyment was unlikely to hold much appeal for him, but it was high time he got out from under his sister's petticoats. It was possible he might encounter a few young artists seeking enlightenment, although, so far, he'd seen little evidence of cultural activity. No one he'd met appeared to have the slightest notion that a revolution in the arts was sweeping Europe, pummelling reactionary elements at every turn. The bright comet lighting up skies in the northern hemisphere had gone quite unnoticed in this southern backwater. If he were going to stay, things would have to change.

"Yes, all right then. Why not?"

Minnie's voice suddenly rose high and impatient from the kitchen, while, simultaneously, the baby began to scream as if in sympathy with her frustrated mother. Johnston rose to his feet and nodded in the direction of the row.

"Preparations for this evening's meal are obviously not going well. These kaffirs can be hard to deal with at times; they seem unable to grasp the simplest ideas. Until next Saturday then. I'll call around at seven-thirty prompt. We don't want to keep the ambassador waiting do we?"

Later that evening, after a pleasant meal which had gone to plan despite Minnie's earlier crisis, the male guests sat sipping brandy and smoking cigars in the cramped lounge. Isaac, who'd declined a cigar, felt his lungs tighten as the thick smoke coiled around the room in blue-grey wreaths. He felt uncomfortable in the company of these men who'd talked of nothing but mining all evening. Even Wolf and his father were obsessed with gold and diamonds to the extent that no other topics of conversation seemed possible. At the moment, Otto Stein, one of the most disagreeable and ignorant men Isaac had ever met, was holding forth.

"You just can't trust these bloody kaffirs, I tell you! Do you know that last week my foreman found three diamonds stuffed up one of their arses, and that's not the only place..."

"Yes, petty theft is a problem in the mines at the moment. How is the price of diamonds holding up? I heard there was a slight rise on the stock market."

Wolf Horvitch moved quickly to steer the conversation in a less risky direction. Even though there were no ladies present, he felt distinctly uncomfortable at the use of such profane language. Stein was not so easily diverted, however.

"I had him flogged, of course. That's the only language these black scum understand."

He inhaled noisily, releasing a lungful of smoke which completely obscured his florid face for a few seconds. When it cleared, his tiny pig eyes, sunk in wrinkled pouches, were still glaring belligerently around the room.

"Thank God we're not so spineless as these bleeding-heart liberals back in England is all I can say."

He suddenly glowered at Isaac.

"Do you think we treat our kaffirs badly, boy? When a dog defies its master should he not thrash it?"

A husky and heavily accented voice cut through the uncomfortable silence.

"Isaac's only been here for a week! How could he be expected to answer a question like that?"

Having effectively silenced Stein, the speaker, a thickset Boer with a trailing moustache and massive side-whiskers, smiled over at his host.

"Unfortunately, Horvitch, prices are dropping at the moment despite that small rise last week. The kaffirs will be the least of our problems if this trend continues for much longer."

The poet breathed an internal sigh of relief. The intervention had saved him a great deal of embarrassment. He'd have felt bound to challenge the bullying oaf, and God knows where that might have led!

When the conversation became as thick and impenetrable as the smoke filling the room, Isaac made his excuses and slipped outside for a breath of fresh air. The night was cold, and he gazed up in wonder at the strange constellations pricking the night sky. Their sparkling lustre was in direct contrast to the murk he'd left inside. It was depressingly apparent that these people had sold their souls to mammon, embracing a threadbare, materialist philosophy. Despite its natural beauty and favourable climate, Cape Town was not somewhere an artist could exist for long without going completely mad. London, for all its shortcomings, contained so many people whose passion and commitment to the arts were undeniable, and the lights of the Café Royal burned brightly enough to illuminate the vital passages to the soul.

If he was to stay here, he'd have to find a way of encouraging these people to lift their eyes from the dust and perceive the wonders shining out like the southern stars wheeling overhead. Maybe this was the sort of challenge he needed in order to hone his creative powers. Life could never be easy for the true artist; he, of all people understood that. His existence had comprised a constant struggle to cut away the hubris separating man from his ultimate destiny.

Walking down towards the harbour, an idea suddenly struck him, bringing him to an abrupt halt. What about a series of lectures designed to reveal the progress of the visual arts through the ages with special emphasis on recent revolutionary developments. Since there seemed to be no way of obtaining useful copies of contemporary paintings here in Cape Town, perhaps he could ask Marsh to send him out some slides that he could use to illustrate advances in European art. As usual, in the wake of a novel idea, Isaac experienced a rush of excitement and an urgent need to get started as quickly as possible. If by lighting a lamp he could reveal a new, vibrant world for those stumbling in darkness, the status of artist as champion of spiritual enlightenment would be fully vindicated. With something akin to religious zeal, he hurried home to begin his quest.

Waiting for Johnston to arrive, Isaac attempted to quell the bout of nerves that every social event he attended inevitably engendered. He'd hired an outfit befitting the occasion and felt a little overdressed. What made matters worse was that he wouldn't know a soul at the party.

On their way to the Embassy, Isaac voiced his misgivings. Johnston assured him there was nothing to worry about.

"You must understand that things like class don't count as much over here as they do back home. I wouldn't be going tonight if they did. The only real split is between white and black, although I suppose there is the problem of the coloureds. And, of course, the English view the Boer as inferior and vice-versa. But, apart from that, everything's pretty straightforward." Johnston frowned for a moment, then laughed out loud. "Anyway, as far as I know, there'll be no kaffirs, Indians or Dutchmen present tonight—at least not as guests—so we should be all right. Just try to avoid the old buffers with grey hair and long beards and you should be fine. And don't worry. There's a crowd of people who turn up to all these functions who you'll enjoy meeting—that I guarantee."

Isaac was worried, of course. He felt awkward in any sort of company. Although his manner had definitely improved over the last few years—friends like Gertler and Goldstein having helped him smooth out the rough edges—he still remained vulnerable, especially among strangers.

Emerging from the cloakroom, the two men entered a large hall with polished wooden floorboards and dark panelled walls. In one corner a string quintet was playing a selection of tunes that sounded vaguely familiar, even to Isaac's untutored ear. Long tables, decked out with spotless linen tablecloths and laden with food, lined one wall, while opposite, bowls of punch and an array of bottles sparkled under bright chandeliers. Crowds of people were already lining up to receive plates and glasses from taciturn black waiters dressed in an immaculate livery.

"Let's get some drinks. Forget about the food for the moment—it just gets in the way."

That was all right for Johnston perhaps, but the sight of pink-fleshed fish, whole ducks roasted to a crisp, and thick cutlets of lamb swimming in gravy, posed an irresistible temptation to a young man raised in the slums of London. His companion's impatient, tugging hand would brook no delay, however.

"Nothing has changed at all since I've been away. The same set-up—the same people. Ah yes, over here, Isaac." He moved swiftly towards a large group clasping charged glasses.

A rather portly young man with waxed moustaches and flushed cheeks turned round as they arrived.

"My God, Johnston, it's you! When did you get back?"

"Almost two weeks ago. Are you seriously suggesting you hadn't heard?"

"Not a word, my dear fellow, not a word, I swear!"

"From the man who claims that if a kaffir farts in Durban, he'll be the first to hear about it, this is certainly a poor state of affairs. What's been happening since I left these shores?"

"That's a long story."

"I look forward to hearing it later. In the meantime, allow me to introduce my friend Isaac Rosenberg, who prevented me from succumbing to ennui during the outward voyage. Isaac, this is Henry Smythe, one of Cape Town's most notorious *bon viveurs*. If you want to enjoy the good life while you're here, or find out anything about anybody, he is definitely the man to speak to—or, at least, he used to be!"

"You flatter me, Johnston, I'm sure. Pleased to meet you, Mr ah…Rosenberg."

"Isaac is an artist who will gladly accept commissions from those vain folk who wish their likenesses preserved in perpetuity. Speaking of vanity, are Miss Vanne and Miss Ffrangcon-Davies attending this evening?"

"Yes indeed. You'll be interested to hear that Marda's divorce is finally absolute. She is a free woman from tomorrow."

"Well, well, interesting news indeed! That young lady may wish to avail herself of your services, Isaac"

Smythe's face twisted into a lascivious grin.

"That's true, my dear fellow. She will undoubtedly welcome the attentions of an artist fresh from England."

This time it was Johnston's turn to leer. Isaac, aware that some private joke was being shared by the two men, felt even more uncomfortable.

Johnston, who was staring hard around the crowded room, suddenly grasped his shoulder.

"Over there, Isaac. These are the two ladies in question. Worth a commission, or two, if I'm not mistaken. We'll see if we can attract their attention."

In response to smiles, nods and beckoning hand gestures, the pair finally broke away from a large group of chattering guests and strolled over. Isaac, feeling desperately shy, tried hard to pull himself together. How would anyone ever think he was worth talking to if this was the way he reacted? Smythe stepped forward—a simpering smile playing on his lips.

"Good evening, ladies. Look who has returned to grace our shores."

The absurd little man stepped aside with an exaggerated flourish of his hand. One of the duo, dressed in a long blue silk gown, offered Johnston her hand which he dully accepted and kissed.

"My dear Miss Vanne. How are you this evening?"

"Very well, thank you. It's good to see you again. You remember my friend and fellow actress, Miss Ffrangcon-Davies?"

"Of course, how could I forget such beauty? Memories of you both sustained me through many a long, hard English winter."

Again, he leaned forward and kissed the proffered hand. Both women smiled, obviously flattered by Johnston's easy charm. Isaac, despite his acute self-consciousness, couldn't help admiring Marda Vanne's striking features. The penetrating blue eyes, full, sensuous lips and slightly upturned nose fascinated him.

"Allow me to introduce you ladies to my friend, Isaac Rosenberg. I see that Isaac is already sizing you up for his next portrait, Miss Vanne."

Isaac squirmed with embarrassment. His friend's sales pitch was too direct for comfort.

"No...not really...I was just..."

"So, you're a painter, Mr Rosenberg?"

Marda stared hard at him, her mouth crinkling at the edges. He was drawn once more to these incredibly blue irises, flecked black around the edges, and now succumbing to the rapid dilation of dark pupils.

The bright red lips suddenly parted, and a small, pink tongue skimmed the glossy surface before vanishing from sight. He stared down at the floor, hoping it might open and swallow him up.

"I...I..." He made a desperate effort to control his stutter. "I paint and...write p...poetry."

"My goodness, I don't think I've ever met a real poet before. What sort of things do you write about, Mr Rosenberg? Love perhaps?"

The voice contained a whimsical, mocking quality which, although disconcerting, fired his desire.

"Ah well, Miss Vanne, that is for him to know, and you to find out."

Johnston winked and smiled. Isaac's cheeks turned fiery red and he suddenly found himself incapable of further speech.

The evening passed slowly. After the initial contact, Marda appeared to show no further interest in him. To someone with such poise and self-confidence, he guessed his awkwardness must be hard to endure. Johnston also drifted away. With pressing matters to attend to, there was only so much time he was willing to expend on integrating Isaac into the company. He'd made the initial introductions and it was now up to his young friend to make his own way. Unsurprisingly, Isaac soon found himself alone. After tucking into the elaborate buffet, and satisfying himself there were no fellow artists, young or old, among the guests crowding the hall, he felt ready to leave. The quintet was now playing a waltz medley inspired by the Strauss family, and Johnston, deeply engrossed with a girl half his age, was cavorting on the dance floor. Judging by the position of his hands, groping below her pinched waist, and the way he kept trying to nuzzle into her exposed neck, there was only one way he hoped the evening would end. Many people seemed to have paired off and Isaac expected to slip away unobserved. He felt depressed and more convinced than ever that Cape Town was a spiritual wasteland.

Just as he was about to enter the cloakroom to retrieve his coat, Marda emerged from the door opposite. Her hypnotic eyes rooted him to the spot.

"Ah, Mr Rosenberg, you're not leaving us so soon, are you?"

"I have to g…get home. My sister is expecting me b…back before midnight."

"I see. I hope you enjoyed the party."

"Yes… it was… interesting."

"Only interesting." Marda laughed suddenly. "It seems that we're a great disappointment to you."

The mock challenging quality had returned to her voice. Isaac was intrigued by the smile which, on this occasion, broadened out a little, revealing a set of perfect, white teeth.

"No… no, I…"

"That's all right, Isaac—may I call you Isaac? Mr Rosenberg seems a little too formal."

"Yes…please do."

"Without wanting to sound disloyal, people here can be somewhat…predictable at times. However, beggars cannot be choosers as they say, and living in Cape Town does have its advantages."

"Yes, the weather is very agreeable and the…"

"I wondered whether you'd like to call on me some time. Mr Johnston said you were a painter and I'd very much like to commission a portrait, if you have the time."

"I'd…I'd be delighted, of course, to…"

"That's settled then. How about tomorrow afternoon? Would that be suitable, or maybe you've made other arrangements?"

"No…I mean yes…that's f…fine."

"Splendid. I'll expect you at five o'clock then. It's been a pleasure talking to you. Goodnight, Isaac." Turning, she walked back down the long hall towards the crowded room. He watched, fascinated by the alluring sway of her dress and rhythmic click of heels.

This was certainly an unexpected end to the evening. In a strange sense he no longer felt so shy of her. Maybe she did want her portrait painted or…no, it was hardly possible that someone so sophisticated could find him remotely interesting. She might, of course, be thoroughly bored by Cape Town and, after the recent divorce alluded to by Smythe, intent on finding something or someone new in her life. Although the prospect excited him, Isaac hardly imagined he fitted the bill. It would be a mistake to get too worked up. But these eyes, that beautifully sculpted face and shapely body! To merely draw her would be a sensual pleasure.

Walking home, he struggled to keep things in perspective. Despite the prospect of the terrible heartache that would inevitably follow, he was already beginning to idealise Marda Vanne. He must strive to shed the image of her beauty burgeoning in his mind. Such an obsession was absurd given the brevity of the meeting and the fact there was so little to base it on. Perhaps this was the greatest danger of being an artist where the world of imagination tirelessly strove to create an ideal, inevitably heightening vulnerability to the wiles of the *femme fatale*. In light of his recent efforts to draw a line beneath the unhappy events of the past three years, the situation was all the more preposterous. It had only taken a casual introduction and two minutes of superficial conversation to sweep that angst away and fill him with a host of inchoate longings. By ironic coincidence, he'd been working only yesterday on a new poem expressing the bitter resentment he felt as victim of a merciless female god. Some of the lines, running through his mind, seemed more apposite than ever:

> *We curl into your eyes.*
> *They drink our fires and have never drained.*
> *In the fierce forest of your hair*
> *Our desires beat blindly for their treasure.*
>
> *In your eyes' subtle pit*
> *Far down, glimmer our souls.*
> *And your hair like massive forest trees*
> *Shadows our pulses, overtired and dumb.*
>
> *Like a candle lost in an electric glare*
> *Our spirits tread your eyes' infinities.*
> *In the wrecking waves of your tumultuous locks*
> *Do you not hear the moaning of our pulses?...*

Why must he always be in thrall? Always on the receiving end of fate—someone's dupe! He suddenly resolved to fight back. He would attend Miss Vanne, but only as an artist interested in procuring a commission, which was probably the only reason she wanted him to call on her. The rest of it, he told himself, was self-generated illusion, bubbling in the magma chamber of his imagination and must be expelled for the sake of his psychological well-being.

On arriving home, he went straight to bed, strengthened by the determination not to be shaken from the tree so easily. But in his dreams, he gazed into Marda's fathomless eyes and burrowed his face deep into her soft, fragrant hair.

Rising from his desk, Isaac crossed over to the window and stared out into the extensive gardens encircling the mansion. The lawns, exquisitely manicured, were surrounded by beds of glowing flowers, their vibrant colours filling the broad canvas of his mind. Above the waving trees, he could see tiny puffs of white cloud herded along by a brisk south-westerly breeze.

His lectures on the development of modern art had gone surprisingly well. The audience, although relatively few in number, at least proved that the Cape contained a small but vigorous colony of committed artists and art lovers. Distinct in most respects from the flighty clique of socialites Isaac had encountered during his first weeks in South Africa, they projected an exciting aura nonetheless.

He had assumed the status of a minor celebrity in their midst, and the editor of a local arts magazine agreed to publish a number of his poems, as well as the text of his lectures in full. Never before had he been the subject of such intense interest; his ego, shrunk by years of rejection, began to unfurl its first, tentative green leaves. He was also introduced to Betty Molteno whose invitation to stay at her beautiful family home in Rondebosch provided a timely escape from the increasingly claustrophobic Horvitch household. The last thing he wanted, of course, was to hurt his sister's feelings, but she seemed delighted by his newfound success. Now, here he was, living in style, and granted the opportunity to work without interruption or constraint.

Picking up a letter recently penned to his family and about to be posted home, he read it over one last time, reminding himself in the process just how uncharacteristically lucky he'd been of late.

Dear Mother—Father—and everybody,

I have not read your letters this week as I've been staying out at a pretty suburb with a very pretty name, Rondebosch, with very nice people. It was through my lecture and poems being printed. I went out one day to see the lady who is the editor of the paper it was printed in, and there I met a Miss Molteno—who told me how delighted she was with my poems. She asked me to come to Rondebosch where she lives; and there she took me to see some beautiful places, and then asked me whether I'd like to be her guest there for a week or two. She is the sister of the speaker to the House of Parliament here. Her father was famous out here—Sir John Molteno, and she has crowds of relations. Anyway, I'm here at Rondebosch having a happy time, you will be glad to hear—I'm anxious to know how you all are and will run down to town about the letters tomorrow, today being Sunday. I'm living like a toff here. Early in the morning coffee is brought to me in bed. My shoes (my only pair) are polished so brightly that the world is pleasantly deceived as to the tragedy the polish covers. I don't know whether there are snakes or wild animals in my room, but in the morning when I get up and look at the soles of my shoes, I see another hole. I shan't make your mouths water by describing my wonderful breakfasts—the unimaginable lunches—delicious teas, and colossal dinners. You would say all fibs. I won't tell you of the wonderful flowers that look into my window and the magnificent park that surrounds my room. Of the mountain climbing right to the sheerest top until the town, the sea and fields were like little picture postcards lying on the pavement to one looking from the top of the Monument. In a few months I hope to be back in England—I should like to get there for the warm weather—about March or so.

Isaac

He reread the last sentence several times. Despite the unaccustomed luxury and the success he'd found here, he was determined to return home soon. The unreality of this life had begun to impinge on the sense of who he was. He was certainly no toff and never would be. A wealthy Bohemian existence, although novel and undoubtedly pleasurable, could not last forever. Isaac, reluctantly aware that his best poetry had been fashioned in adversity, knew where his future lay. Besides which, he had recently begun to realise just how much he missed London's cultural ferment, the familiar streets, and the company of fellow artists.

And, of course, there was the war. Since hearing the news his mind had filled with conflicting thoughts. The concept of a regenerated society, rising from the ashes of the old, kindled his imagination. He'd always yearned to see the dross burned away, revealing the rich vein of pure ore he believed lay at the heart of humanity. The demise of the traditional, in his view, hopelessly corrupt God, followed by the elevation of the poet, was the only way forward for a civilisation grown sick at heart. On the other hand, the prospect of unleashed violence depressed him terribly. The impulse to self-destruct was a powerful force in the human psyche, and the prospect of men dying, and the world rent to pieces in the process, cut him to the core. Whichever way he looked at it, he needed to be back in the thick of things.

At that moment there was a discreet tap on the door. Thankful for the diversion, Isaac leapt up from his desk to answer. A young, black woman dressed in a neat maid's uniform stood in the hallway.

"Lunch will be served in half an hour, sir."

"Thank you, Sarah. I'll not be late."

He smiled, trying not to look uncomfortable. The idea of servants, black or otherwise, was not something he found easy to accept. The Moltenos employed at least ten native people to look after their domestic needs. He was again struck by the artificiality of his present situation. One could get flabby here, in every sense. The girl gave an almost imperceptible nod before turning away, her impassive expression revealing nothing of the secret life inside. What she really felt about things was impossible to gauge. The indigenous population might labour for their white masters and thole the various injustices heaped upon them, but somewhere, beyond all that, he felt their spiritual life remained inviolate—untainted by servitude. Isaac desperately wanted to draw these faces—to reveal that inner life.

Shutting the door, he walked slowly over to the magnificent four-poster bed and threw himself face down on the immaculate top cover. With his face squashed into the scented material, he deliberately summoned memories of his extraordinary encounter with Marda Vanne, the day after the embassy party. Despite the passage of several months, they gleamed like precious gems in the recesses of his mind.

The trepidation had been enormous when, arriving at her door, he'd finally plucked up the courage to knock. A sense of unreality gripped him as he was ushered into a beautifully furnished room by a young white girl, offered a drink and informed that Ms Vanne would be down directly. Half an hour later he was nervously fumbling with his drawing block and pencils when Marda entered and sat down on a chair next to the window.

"Sorry I've taken so long, Isaac," her voice sounded husky and subtly provocative, at least in his fevered imagination, "but I had to change into something more…appropriate for the sitting. You will forgive me, I hope."

Overcome by the vision of loveliness clad in a light, cream-coloured gown, he could only nod in reply. Her perfume, although faint, acted as a powerful aphrodisiac and he was glad the large pad was set solidly on his lap.

"I'll g…get started then."

"Which way do you want me to face for the portrait?"

"Of course. I'm sorry I forgot to…"

"Don't worry, Isaac." Her lips momentarily parted to reveal the smile that had so aroused him the previous evening.

"Perhaps you c…could look towards the p…painting over there."

He pointed to a large, rather pedestrian landscape on the wall adjacent to the French windows.

"Very well." She pulled her chair round and positioned herself carefully. "Will that do?"

"Yes, that's f…fine. Thank you."

He settled down to work, struggling to quell the turmoil inside. Why had she really asked him to her home? Was it the portrait or had that merely been an excuse to ensnare him? The question continued to torture him.

She proved a good sitter and barely moved in the hour it took Isaac to complete the initial drawing. It was obvious his fantasies had been groundless; he wasn't sure whether to be relieved or disappointed.

"I think I've finished the first version, if you'd like to see it now."

Marda slowly rose and stretched. He noticed the contours of her rounded breasts pressed tight against the thin cotton material of the dress. Stepping behind him, she studied the drawing for a moment or two.

"I think you've caught something of the real me, Isaac. I'm impressed." He suddenly felt her fingers running through his hair. "Now, I want you to study me a little closer up."

The seductive tone of her voice took his breath away, and, for a few moments, he sat gulping like a fish out of water.

She moved back round, knelt down, and wrapped her arms around his neck, pulling his face deep into her soft breasts. When he felt as though he might soon be smothered, she released him and deftly unbuttoned his trousers. Without further preliminaries, she pushed her hand inside and began massaging his genitals. The vigorous action brought him close to premature ejaculation.

"Oh, I'm sorry, Isaac. Am I going too quickly?"

The enquiry merely added to his mounting excitement and he struggled to hold onto the remaining threads of self-control. As if aware of his perilous state, she suddenly gripped him much more tightly, providing just enough pressure to contain his orgasm but maintain a high degree of pleasure. Catching hold of his right hand, she pushed it deep into her crotch and thrust against it with surprising force. A few moments later, they climaxed in a duet of gasps and groans.

Releasing him, Marda stepped over to a large mirror set above the fireplace and adjusted her crumpled dress. She then turned round to face him, smiling warmly as if he'd just dropped by to pay his respects.

"I'm afraid I'll have to take my leave, Isaac. Some friends are arriving for dinner within the hour and there are still a few preparations to complete. It was nice meeting you again. Keep the portrait if you like— to remember me by. The place is full of them; I don't really need any others." Isaac wondered if she was teasing him; her voice sounded impossibly matter-of-fact and detached given what had just occurred. For the moment, however, he felt satiated, and the fact that he'd been used for her pleasure merely added to his delicious sense of satisfaction. Whatever the future held, he felt profoundly grateful to her for arousing an intensity of sensual delight he'd never experienced till now.

"Perhaps you'd like to tidy yourself up before leaving."

"Yes I would. Thank you for…"

"Goodbye, Isaac."

As it turned out, this was the first and last time they met in private. On the one other occasion they encountered each other socially she virtually ignored him, making no attempt to engage in conversation. Johnston's revelation that many others, similarly lured, had been just as quickly discarded, provided little comfort at the time, although he'd now come to accept her as a force of nature —his time with her, however brief, thrilling beyond anything previously imagined, and hoarded in his memory. The strange thing was that love—or the painful emotions harboured for Sonia over the past few years—hadn't really come into it. What he'd felt was immediate—in some ways akin to his sensual awakening with Annetta—but fuller, more potent. For the first time in his life he'd truly revelled in the moment and been central to someone else's powerful sexual craving. A scrap of poetry, written a day or two after the affair, swam back into his consciousness:

…Our lithe limbs
Frenzied exult till vision swims
In fierce delicious agonies;
And the crushed life bruised through and through,
Ebbs out, trophy no spirit slew,
While molten sweetest pains enmesh
The life sucked by dissolving flesh.

All that had occurred before his lectures and the warm welcome extended by prominent members of Cape Town's artistic community. Nevertheless, it now seemed to him that his encounter with Marda Vanne was the true highlight of his visit to South Africa. At times he found it difficult to convince himself the entire incident hadn't been some kind of alluring dream. Like many of his experiences in this strange country, it represented a distraction from the harsh realities of his life in England. The sooner he got back to the real world the easier it would be to make the necessary readjustments. Even the thought of returning to a city containing Sonia and Rodker was preferable to remaining here. Minnie would be distraught, of course, but he'd find some way of justifying his decision.

In the meantime, he'd better get down to dinner before Betty Moltena was forced to dispatch her enigmatic servant to provide another reminder. Rising from the bed, he sighed, wondering what delightful cuisine would be on offer tonight.

"Well, well, Isaac, this is a pleasant surprise. I had quite resigned myself to an evening alone. How are you?"

"Fine." Unequal to the task of looking the part, however, he decided to come clean. "Somewhat under the weather to tell you the truth, Mark."

Isaac was standing at the door of Mark Gertler's Hampstead studio where his friend now lived and worked. Earlier in the evening, he'd been driven out of his home in Dempsey Street by a severe bout of depression. Although buoyed up on his return from South Africa, initial good spirits had proved to be short-lived and his mood often dipped to such a serious extent, he found the company of his family insufferable. Walking the streets sometimes proved beneficial, but tonight, unable to shake the despondency that had settled on him like a black cloud, he'd felt in desperate need of a shoulder to cry on.

"My health's not been so good since my return f…from… warmer climes, I'm afraid."

"Come in, come in. I've quite forgotten my manners. Let me take your coat."

Gertler, who'd been working obsessively on a painting to be exhibited in less than a week's time, experienced intense irritation when first interrupted by the tentative knock. Seeing Isaac so stricken, he quickly cast this initial anger aside.

"Come through. I've been putting the finishing touches to a piece for the New English Exhibition. I thought you might be entering something yourself."

"No. I've b…been a little busy to manage anything of that sort. I'm…I'm sorry if I've… interrupted your work."

"No, not at all. I was beginning to lose concentration," Gertler lied. "A break will do me good. Can I get you anything?"

"Some tea would be fine. I've been walking around for hours."

Brushing down a chair, Gertler motioned for his friend to sit down.

"If you feel up to it, have a look around. I'm sure you wouldn't object to some bread and cheese with your tea?" Isaac's weary smile affirmed his need for nourishment. "I'd be interested to hear what you think about the stuff I've been working on lately."

Returning some minutes later, carrying a laden tray, he found Isaac closely examining his latest painting.

"This is excellent, Gertler. One of the b…best things you've ever done, in my view. Is this the piece you're going to exhibit? I certainly hope so."

"It is, as a matter of fact. I'm glad you like it."

"'Like' doesn't begin to describe my feelings. There's something here that goes to the heart of things. Words are…inadequate."

Shoving the tray onto a table cluttered with old brushes and charcoal sticks, the painter experienced a keen stab of pleasure. He was pleased with what he'd achieved so far and was glad to hear this confirmed by a fellow artist, even if he really was a poet by inclination.

"It's very kind of you to say so. But sit down and have a bite to eat. You look all in."

"Yes. I do feel a bit tired out." Isaac eased himself into the chair, stretched out his stiff legs, and watched as his friend poured tea into two chipped enamel cups.

"Help yourself to some cheese, Isaac."

"Thank you, I will."

"So, what's been keeping you so occupied lately? I haven't seen you since May."

"I've been writing a few p…poems and trying to drum up interest in *Youth*. Did I tell you Schiff bought three copies? Meeting him was the best thing that's happened since I came home, and I've got you to thank for it."

"Think nothing of it."

"He's promised to show my poems around. Apparently, some critic friend of his, a chap by the name of Clutton-Brock, might be interested. If so, this could be the b…break I've been waiting for. I certainly need some form of regular income; things are pretty tight at home at the moment."

"How are your family?"

"Everyone's fine, although Elkon's been causing my mother a lot of worry recently. He's going through some sort of rebellious phase;

nothing to worry about in my view, but she's very concerned. As usual, she blames our father's laxness, and wants me to speak to the boy…I'm convinced that would only cause more p…problems. He's not going to listen to his jobless elder brother—an unwelcome d…drain on family resources."

"I think you're being a little hard on yourself, Isaac. It's surely only a matter of time before…"

"Let's face facts, Gertler. I'm never going to make an adequate living from painting. My patrons are b…becoming, shall we say, a little…weary."

"If you mean that spat you had with Marsh a few weeks ago, I wouldn't worry. After Brooks' death, and Churchill's resignation, he was in a bad way. None of us came out unscathed. He wouldn't speak to anyone for a fortnight."

"Yes, but I made the mistake of intruding on his…his private grief with yet another appeal to his charitable nature. I hadn't the…the…d…decency to wait for a more appropriate moment."

Gertler was surprised at the bitterness in Isaac's voice. He had evidently been badly affected by Marsh's ill-concealed anger.

"What he doesn't realise is the extent to which I…I d…depend on him! Does he think it gives me any pleasure tramping the streets trying to peddle d…drawings that I know aren't up to the mark?"

"There's nothing inferior about the work you do!"

"That's not really the p…point, is it? Once upon a time, the artist, or a poet, could earn an honest living, but now, unless he…he…has the money or…the contacts, he's d…doomed to a life of…of penury—living hand to mouth."

"Maybe to some extent, but…"

"You and I are in the same boat—dependent on a rich p…patron who thinks he understands the nature of what we do so much better than we do ourselves. It's always been that way. You know how bad it can be. What about the time you stormed out of his dinner party when some Cambridge p…pup tried to tell you where you were going wrong. We've all b…been through that, haven't we?"

Isaac's anger was now threatening to shatter the fragile walls of his self-control. For the life of him, Gertler could not seriously dispute his friend's assertions or, for that matter, come to his abused patron's defence. Everything Isaac said was true; his own patience had often been tested to its limits. He nodded sympathetically, wondering, at the same time, how he could calm things down a little.

As it turned out, there was no need. Isaac's anger dissipated as quickly as it had arisen, and he flopped back in his seat, apparently too exhausted to continue.

"I know I'm being hard on him. It's only that…he doesn't begin to understand the pressures, or the…the f…frustration arising from such…condescension. If…if it wasn't for Marsh though, I don't know where we'd be…" he finished lamely and lowered his head.

Gertler suddenly experienced a powerful urge to express his own frustration at the recent turn of events. Given Isaac's state of mind, he knew he shouldn't but couldn't help himself. The matter had been smouldering under the surface for too long and he needed to tell someone how he felt.

"To be perfectly honest, Isaac, I agree with you. Marsh is kind, and…considerate, at least in some ways. But I have to tell you…I've almost decided to break with him for good."

Isaac stared over the table in disbelief. Gertler rose and started to noisily clear the plates and cups back onto the wooden tray, his handsome face dark and moody.

"I didn't know, Mark. I'm sorry if…"

"No, no, Isaac, this has been coming for a long time now. In some ways Marsh is blind to the needs of other people—especially those who you rightly say are most dependent on him. And all this nonsense about Brooke! His death was tragic, of course, but his poetry! You've told me often enough yourself that he only ever wrote one decent piece. What was it you said about his work? It reminded you too much of…of flag days. But that doesn't seem to matter. To Marsh, he represented everything that a poet should be: looks, background, wealth, education—all impeccable. The fact that the reality didn't match up to the ideal made not a whit of difference. Do you see? They've turned him into a national hero, and his mediocre, sententious lines into some sort of shining…paragon to which all art should aspire. This may sound like terrible ingratitude after all Marsh has done for me but…I can't bear it any longer; the hypocrisy is becoming just too much."

"I'm not sure I follow. I thought you were…close to him."

"We were—are—in some ways, that's true—although never in the way he and Brooke were. I've been able to put up with things for a long time now, but since the war started I…" Gertler swallowed hard and seemed unable to continue for a moment. His eyes blinked and his mouth quivered as he struggled to control his emotions—his normal insouciance completely evaporated. This was a new Gertler, one Isaac had never encountered before.

Pulling himself together with a visible effort, he resumed, although haltingly at first.

"After all, he's been paying for all of this," —raising both hands, he gestured round the studio—"since I moved out of his digs…. Ten pounds a month is more than enough to get by on. You of all people understood that. But…you know my attitude to this bloody war. So, I've more or less decided to go it alone. As a conscientious objector I can hardly carry on accepting money from someone as…committed to the war as Marsh, can I?"

"I understand the problem, and I agree with you, but…"

"But what?"

"I've…I've been considering joining up myself."

Gertler stared at Isaac in disbelief, unable to reply for a moment. The poet experienced a surge of pure relief. At last he'd managed to blurt out the predicament that had been occupying his thoughts all day.

"Surely not! I know the way you and your family feel about the army! I'm surprised that…"

"Yes, but I can't make ends meet, however hard I t…try." Isaac's anguish burst through the words. "My…my circumstances are just b...becoming too...too much to bear. Army pay is at least...regular. The fact that I'm a b...burden on everyone is driving me mad. I don't want to fight; I hate the idea, and I'm not sure I could kill anyone...but..."

Suddenly, all his confused notions about the war, and the guilt turning round and round in his head for the past few weeks tumbled out.

"The Germans represent oppression but...I've always b...believed in...in diplomacy as a way of solving problems. At first, I thought this war might...ultimately change things for...for the...better, but now...now it's turning into a bloody slaughter! We'll be lucky if there's anything left to...rebuild at the end. Maybe if I join up, I might be able to use my poetry to...to convince people that...that... . There must be a chance that public opinion could end this madness."

"You're making a grave mistake, Isaac." Gertler's voice assumed a flinty quality. "The war will swallow you up. There's nothing that can stop it now. Your poetry will be blown away like so many dead leaves in the path of a hurricane. Surely you understand the necessity of resisting such madness?"

"Yes, but it's just sometimes...I don't think I can take any more. That's why I had to get out this evening. I feel so...useless, so inadequate. My mother sits there apparently contented b...but I can somehow...feel her resentment."

"You're imagining that! Try to understand how she would feel if you were ever to join up. It's not hard to envisage your father's reaction either, given all he went through to avoid conscription back in his old country."

"That's true, but...but the two situations are hardly c...compatible."

"Maybe not, but all war is wrong! Hold onto that central tenet, for God's sake, Isaac! Too many good people are being sucked in. You've heard that Hulme, Nevinson and Bomberg have decided to join the fight?"

"I heard Bomberg was turned down, but I'm not sure why."

"Even Spencer for God's sake! Although, at least he's in the Medical Corps. There was a rumour running round the Café Royal last week that Montague had dyed his hair in order to fool the recruiting board.

Can you imagine it? The bloody fool! Think before you do anything you'll live to regret, or not, as the case may be. Please, for everybody's sake!"

"Yes, M...Mark, I...I will. I haven't come to any c...clear-cut decision yet. There's a chance I may return to my old trade, although I'd have to go to evening classes. Hentschel's—you remember the printing firm I worked for—told me I'd require additional training if they were to take me back. Naturally, I'd have to pay the fees, which I can't afford. I was thinking of writing to Schiff for help. He's been very generous in the past. What do you think?"

"If that's the only alternative to joining the army then I'm for it."

"I'm worried about my health though. I'm convinced the vapours from the chemical vats they used in the print room damaged my chest in the past."

"I don't suppose that basic training, followed by mortal combat, is going to be particularly good for you either. I've heard that life in the camps is awful although the press would have you think otherwise. You can't believe anything you read these days. Along with the politicians, they're driving this bloody hysteria." Gertler sighed. "Just don't make any hasty decisions, that's all I have to say, Isaac.... . It's strange you know, but after our talk, I feel fully resolved to write to Marsh tomorrow, first thing, and tell him how I feel. We all need to make sacrifices now. This farce can't be allowed to continue."

"He'll be upset. I think after Rupert, you've always been his favourite."

"Do you really think so?" There was a catch in his voice. "Well, that can't be helped now. A man without convictions or conscience is no man at all."

With a deep intake of breath, Gertler changed the subject.

Tell me more about your poetry, since you've obviously not been doing any painting recently. Did the editor of *Colours* accept any of the poems you sent him?"

"Yes, as a matter of fact. He's already printed three and has asked me for more."

"Well, there you are then! Things are beginning to happen."

"I won't p...pretend I'm not pleased, but it's hardly the breakthrough I envisaged. I've only sold ten copies of *Youth* so far and..."

"Yes, but you've managed to get something into print. That's important!"

"Let's be honest, Gertler. C...*Colours* is a... lightweight magazine. The pieces I wrote were...t...toned down, shall we say? The tragedy is that my real hopes lie in the p...poems Marsh and Schiff claim are...obscure, and...and *Colours* would never dream of publishing. I want to produce larger works like Lascelles Abercrombie. Have you read his 'Hymn to Love'?"

"No, although Marsh told me it's outstanding."

"That's no exaggeration. He's the best poet of our time!"

"What, even better than Brook?" Gertler's attempt at irony fell flat.

"These two shouldn't be mentioned in the same sentence. Brooke may be fashionable at the moment b...but will be completely forgotten when Abercrombie's work is still revered."

"You've missed the point. I didn't mean that..."

"I've also been reading some excellent poems by Gordon Bottomley. Have you heard of him?"

"I think Marsh has mentioned him once or twice."

"These two have fired my ambition. Some day, d...despite the odds, I may write something which will catch their attention."

"You will, Isaac. I don't doubt that for a second."

"Thank you, Gertler. Your support has always meant a g...great deal to me."

Feeling somewhat embarrassed, Gertler again changed tack.

"Have you seen Rodker recently?"

"Yes, last week. Why do you ask?"

"Oh, I just wondered what he had to say about the war."

"If anything, he's even more against it than you. He says he'd rather languish—his word not mine—in p...prison than have anything to do with it."

"People like Rodker and myself may have to do just that before all this is over."

135

"I sincerely hope it doesn't come to that! It'll surely be finished before they consider conscription."

"Perhaps, but—forgive my scepticism—the whole thing was supposed to be sown up by last Christmas; now they're all sitting in the trenches waiting for the *coup-de-grace* that never comes. This bloody stalemate could go on for years."

He stopped suddenly, unwilling to go over old ground.

"So, how is Sonia these days?"

"She seems well. I painted her p...portrait last week." Knowing Gertler was probably trying to gauge his state of mind regarding Sonia, he tried to sound unconcerned. "They b...both seem very happy." It struck him that his friend was unlikely to be fooled by this half-hearted attempt to conceal his true feelings. He continued rather lamely. "It's reassuring to know a few p...people have found some measure of...happiness. I never expect to be so favoured myself, so, at least I might still be surprised in life."

Isaac gazed down at his feet, experiencing a powerful resurgence of the bitterness that had dogged him for so many years. Deep down, he believed that his twin, dead at birth, was the one best chanced for life. His survival was an error God seemed determined to rectify.

Noting the reaction, Gertler felt sorry he'd raised the subject. Isaac rose to his feet.

"Well, I must really b...be going now. It's a long walk home."

"You're welcome to stay. There's room if you..."

"No thanks. My mother would worry. I've enjoyed our talk...I hope things work out between you and Marsh..." He finished lamely. "It's a pity friendship has to..."

"Sometimes there's no choice. One has to retain a degree of integrity."

After the poet had disappeared into the night, Gertler returned to his painting. Gazing at the canvas for a few minutes, he couldn't help thinking that it looked subtly different. Maybe the unexpected encounter with Isaac had helped him see a number of things more clearly. He sincerely hoped his friend would emerge from the darkness encircling him. Joining up, he sincerely believed, would be the worst disaster in a life already beset by farce and misfortune. Now, though, he had his own demons to face down. He wondered where he'd be a year from now.

Part Two

1915–1918

Chapter One

1915-16

*I could not get the work I thought I might so I have joined this
Bantam Battalion (as I was too short for any other) which
seems to be the most rascally affair in the world. I have to eat
out of a basin together with some horribly smelling scavenger
who spits and sneezes into it. It is most revolting, at least up to
now—I don't mind the hard sleeping, the stiff marches, etc.
but this is unbearable. Besides my being a Jew makes it bad
among these wretches. I am looking forward to having a bad
time altogether...*

Extract from letter to Sydney Schiff: October 1915

*...I can only give you my personal and if you like selfish point
of view that I, feeling myself in the prime and vigour of my
powers (whatever they may be) have no more free will than a
tree... It is true I have not been killed or crippled, been a loser
in the stocks, or had to forswear my fatherland, but I have not
quite gone free and have a right to say something...*

Extract from letter to Sydney Schiff: Late October 1915

*...I know my faults are legion; a good many must be put down
to the rotten conditions I wrote it in—the whole thing was
written in barracks, and I suppose you know what an ordinary
soldier's life is like. Moses symbolises the fierce desire for
virility, and original action in contrast to slavery of the most
abject kind.*

Extract from letter to R C Trevelyan: June 1916

*...And suddenly
We are lifted of all we know
And hang from implacable boughs.*

From Chagrin: 1915

Marching (As Seen From The Left File)

*My eyes catch ruddy necks
Sturdily pressed back—
All a red brick moving glint.
Like flaming pendulums, hands
Swing across khaki—
Mustard coloured khaki—
To the automatic feet.*

*We husband the ancient glory
In these bared necks and hands.
Not broke is the forge of Mars;
But a subtler brain beats iron
To shoe the hoofs of death,
(Who paws dynamic earth now).
Blind fingers loose an iron cloud
To rain immortal darkness
On strong eyes.*

Entering the training depot, Isaac walked along a broad white track towards an array of wooden huts laid out in identical clusters of six. Four of these formed the base of each unit, while the remaining two, side on, stared at each other across bleak parade grounds. Squadrons of soldiers, drilling nearby, caught his attention. He admired the unity of swinging arms and marching feet moving with the precision of a single organism.

He wasn't sure what to do next. Having been instructed by a recruiting officer back in London to report here, exactly where and to whom was as yet unclear. Spotting what he assumed to be an officer marching smartly along an adjacent path, swagger cane neatly tucked beneath his arm, he hurried to intercept.

"Ex...excuse me, sir, excuse me!"

At first the man ignored him, then swivelled with an impatient snap of heels.

"Who the hell are you?" The voice was inexplicably harsh.

"Rosenberg, sir; Private Rosenberg reporting for duty, sir."

"Firstly sonny, you do not call me sir; you address non-commissioned officers by their rank. These three stripes denote the rank of sergeant; you therefore address me as sergeant. Do I make myself clear?"

"Yes, sir...I mean Sergeant."

Isaac felt intimidated and foolish at the same time; for the life of him he couldn't work out what he'd done to deserve such an attack. The attitude of the soldiers at the recruiting office had been very different. In the meantime, the man gazed at him as though he was a piece of refuse abandoned at the roadside.

"Which regiment? No, don't tell me. You're one of these damned bantams aren't you, assigned to the 12th Suffolks!"

"Yes, Sergeant."

"Well blow me! I knew they were taking them small but not that small. The bloody Hun'll run right over the top of you lot without even noticing you're there. I've never seen such a rag, tag group of scarecrows in my life. The quicker you start training the quicker they can throw you out I suppose. Did they bother to give you a medical?"

"Yes, Sergeant."

"Well, that's something at any rate. Report to the third set of barracks on the left." The NCO continued to stare at him. "Didn't you bring any kit then, or did you manage to lose that on the train?"

"I left in a bit of a hurry, Sergeant; I thought the authorities would provide…"

"You bloody idiot! Don't think, boy! That's the first thing you need to learn here."

Shaking his head in disgust, he strutted off. Isaac stood motionless for several seconds, staring after the retreating figure. What had he got himself into?

He arrived at a hut, identical to every other one he'd seen so far except for a board nailed to the door chalked with the name of his new regiment. He knocked and entered. A single officer, seated behind a desk at the far end of the room, was interviewing recruits who'd formed themselves into a queue straggling all the way back to where he stood. One man, half way up the line, seemed in a bad way. Bent double, he swore feebly between intense bouts of coughing. His filthy jacket looked as though it had been slept in for a month.

The door opened behind him and shut with a slam. Several people glanced round. It struck Isaac that the majority of his fellow recruits had been sleeping rough until very recently. Their matted hair, ragged garments and dulled eyes suggested a brutish existence scavenging on the streets. Perhaps they'd been tempted to join up at the prospect of a square meal and a roof over their heads, although it was hard to believe that any of them had been declared fit for active service.

Three-quarters of an hour later, feeling a little headachy and sick, he found himself at the head of the queue which by now extended beyond the door and out into the parade ground. The lieutenant barely glanced up.

"Name?"

"Rosenberg."

"Date of birth?"

"November the 25th, 1890."

"Place of birth?"

"Bristol."

"Recruiting office?"

"Sorry?"

"Where you signed up." The voice sounded flat and uninterested.

"Ah yes. Whitehall, London."

"Right. You're assigned to hut three, straight over the square. There are no beds at the moment so you'll be sleeping on the floor. Until a proper mess hut has been designated, rations will be served in the barracks. Uniforms should be available some time next month; until that time you'll be in civvies. Pay will not be issued until you are in uniform. Is that clear?" The words, reeled off quickly, betrayed no emotion whatsoever.

Choking back anger, Isaac fought to remain calm.

"But… but I was told uniform and k…kit would be available on arrival. I've not brought anything with…"

"Next."

"But sir, surely we get paid from…"

"Is there anything else, Private?"

The deliberate emphasis on the last word suggested that any further appeal against the iniquitous arrangement would be unwise.

He turned away with a growing sense of despair. For months he'd struggled to find an alternative to joining up, even considering a return to his old trade in printing despite its adverse affect on his health. The final humiliation occurred when his previous employers refused to have him back. His first thought in the wake of this latest setback had been to join the Medical Corps where at least he would be preserving lives not destroying them. But, after screwing up the courage to try, he was rejected on height grounds.

Eventually, he tried for the regular army, convincing himself that the more who heeded the call the quicker the war would be over. This allowed him to conceal the much more practical and ultimately mundane motives behind the decision to push ahead. The fact that he would not be able to send money home for the foreseeable future tormented him, but there was nothing he could do. The decision by the army authorities to make pay contingent on the wearing of a uniform they had failed to provide, afforded him an early insight into the oppressive nature of the system. And how he'd manage without towels or even a change of clothing was something he didn't care to think about— his fastidious nature quailed at the prospect.

On his way across the parade ground, Isaac passed the wretched invalid who'd been ahead of him in the queue. Although no longer coughing, the man was swaying on his feet and breathing heavily. Again, he wondered how this physical wreck could possibly have been passed fit by the army recruitment board. The situation must be much more desperate than he thought.

Inside the barracks, the heavy, moisture-laden air and the sharp reek of sweat almost took his breath away. He noticed the grimy windows were nailed shut and that the entire space appeared to be crammed with men, some jealously guarding tiny spaces and glaring at anyone who came too close, while others, like himself, shuffled from foot to foot unsure how to proceed. The sense of despair, growing steadily since his arrival, threatened to overwhelm him now. What was he supposed to do here? Sleep, wash, eat? Despite the fact that his family was poor, Hacha had always kept the house scrupulously clean. Admittedly, he'd often been forced to share his room with lodgers— a state of affairs which never failed to frustrate him—but that had been nothing to the hardship likely to be experienced in this foul-smelling, overcrowded den.

He noticed two soldiers handing out blankets and trying to create walkways through the lines of recruits already ensconced on the rough floorboards. One of them, a corporal, repeatedly prodded at the men with the toe of his boot.

"Come on, you bastards; move yer 'ides. You can't sit 'ere. Move in towards the walls, will ya."

Isaac approached the pair and asked where he might sleep. The corporal thrust a coarse blanket into his hands.

"Anywhere you can find a bit of space, mate. It don't pay to be too fussy in 'ere. Just make sure you don't block the passageway through to the wash room and latrines, that's all."

"Latrines!"

"Yeh, that's what I said, wasn't it? At the other side of the 'ut. There's extra buckets if they get full during the night."

"What about washing?"

"There's a couple of taps and pails. No fuckin' problem at all. You come down from Buckingham Palace or somethin'?"

"No, from...from Whitechapel."

"Ah, I see. You a Jew boy then? Thought you was. You'll just 'ave to muck in wiv the rest—there's no special treatment for Jews 'ere, I'm sorry to say." He laughed unpleasantly and moved on through the crush. "Come on, Dave, 'e don't want to talk to the likes of us. The place is full of four by twos, so 'e shouldn't be lonely for long."

"He can fuckin' 'ave 'em, corp."

Spotting a small space beside the wall at the opposite side of the hut, Isaac pushed his way through the throng, brushed half-heartedly at the floor with his hands and sat down. He'd expected a degree of anti-Semitism, but was taken aback by the vehemence of the reaction. Was this going to be the way of things? Surely the officers would rise above such petty prejudice! Pulling out a large pocket handkerchief—all he had to dry himself with—he dabbed at the sweat beading his forehead. Sleeping, he knew, would be virtually impossible.

Isaac suddenly woke in the small hours of the morning and sat bolt upright, unsure where he was for a moment. The knowledge, returning with a rush, merely served to heighten his feeling of anguish and disorientation. His neck ached as he lay down and tried to stretch into a more comfortable position. The sweltering darkness resonated with gasps, snores and intermittent coughing. Immediately to the right, his neighbour, packed in beside him, turned over and farted loudly. The stench, reaching him a few moments later, was overpowering. Burying his face in the rough material of his blanket, he found the stink of sweat-saturated wool equally repugnant. His own bowels were clamouring, and he knew he'd soon be forced to find his way to the latrines at the other side of the barracks hut. Isaac suspected that the foul slop spooned out of a communal basin earlier, in the company of the five other recruits, had something to do with his present discomfort. With a shiver of disgust, he recalled the diseased wretch, who'd dogged him since his arrival at camp, sneezing violently into the communal tub before eating. Desperate enough to consume anything by this stage, he'd been forced to gulp down his share.

He held out until the effort became unbearable then rose to his feet—careful to avoid trampling on his immediate neighbours—tiptoed through the lines of sleeping bodies, and reached the latrines without mishap. A single bulb, glaring harshly from the ceiling, revealed crudely nailed boards blocking access. Instead, a row of buckets next to the wall had obviously been installed as a temporary measure. With a sinking heart, Isaac recalled the corporal's reference to full tanks. The fact that they were all occupied deepened his sense of despair. Struggling to control the fierce spasms of pain in his abdomen, he sat, doubled up, on the filthy floor.

A friendly voice suddenly cut through his misery:

"You all right, mate? You can 'ave this one in just a sec. The tanks is full so there's nothin' for it. I don't fink anyone emptied them this morning—that's the problem. It's fuckin' disgraceful—that's what I say."

Peering round, Isaac noticed a tiny, dark-haired man crouched over a bucket, grinning down at him through a mouthful of rotting teeth. He tore a page from the newspaper he was clutching and wiped between his legs.

"Found this on the train on the way 'ere; thought it might come in useful. The name's 'Arry Jacobs. I'll not shake 'ands. 'Ere you go." He ripped another page from the broadsheet and handed it over to Isaac. "A bit 'ard maybe, but better than the back of your hand, eh? What you called then?"

"Rosenberg...er...Isaac."

Harry's was the first friendly face he'd encountered since arriving at the depot. A deep voice sounded from the shadows behind them.

"Are you two going to rabbit on all night? Some of us needs to take a crap, you know."

Harry laughed. "Better get on wiv it, Isaac, before that bastard gets in first. Watch not tip it over, mind; these things are not meant for shittin' in really. See you later on then."

Surrendering himself to the churn of his stomach in such a public place wasn't as awful as he'd imagined. Poised over the pail, he tried to shut out the stink and anal eruptions. The relief when he finally arrived safely back at his blanket was palpable; he even summoned up enough courage to shove a sleeping body back into its own space.

Exhausted, and drifting towards sleep, he considered for the first time that the privations he was now suffering might actually work in his favour. This journey into the unknown with its attendant hardships and dangers could very well transform his writing. The thought was a comfort and he felt the urge to endure no matter what. He owed it to his calling as an artist. Great poetry could never be written by someone afraid to meet life head on. Perhaps the process demanded a crucible hot enough to burn away the dross of his old life. The prospect somewhat unnerved him, but he experienced a brief swell of excitement nonetheless. He was on the brink of a great adventure and although the future remained daunting and largely uncertain, it marked a significant break with the ennui of the past few months.

Captain Graeme Philips twisted the ends of his moustaches impatiently as he watched the platoon form itself into four untidy lines. Many of the recruits, he noticed, could barely stand up straight and stood shivering in the cold wind sweeping the parade ground. To make matters worse, they were either clad in filthy rags or garments totally inappropriate for drilling purposes. Philips' contempt for the miserable collection of "sub-humans", who'd clearly not joined up to serve King and Country in its hour of need but to secure free accommodation and regular meals, was absolute. Well, by God, he'd make them regret their decision to quit scavenging for the delights of His Majesty's armed forces.

As a serving officer in the regular army, he felt innately superior to the hundreds of thousands who'd responded to Kitchener's call to arms. None of these people, including the new generation of officers, could ever begin to appreciate the pride and sense of duty experienced by the professional soldier. His indignation, normally simmering close to the surface, suddenly spilled over.

"For God's sake, Sergeant, get these men into line and make them stand up straight, will you?" He took a step forward, and shook his cane at the rabble. "I've never seen anything like this in my life. You, man!" He rapped Isaac on the shoulder twice. "What the hell do you think you're doing? Face the front and stand to attention. Did you not hear the command?"

"I…I'm s…sorry, sir. Someone stepped on my…"

"I'm not interested in your miserable excuses. Sergeant, put this man on latrine duty for the next week. It may encourage him to listen more carefully to orders issued by his officer."

"But sir, I…"

"Give him two weeks for answering back. Is there anything else you wish to say, Private?"

"N…no, sir."

"Well, g…g… get in l…l…line then."

The sergeant, smiling at his officer's parody of the little Jew's stutter, roughly shoved Isaac back into the crowded ranks.

Minutes later—the men now quiet and in position—Philips cleared his throat and began to speak.

"Never have I had the misfortune to witness such a disgrace to His Majesty's Armed Forces. Why you misfits were ever allowed to take the King's oath is beyond me. It is my unfortunate duty to transform you into fighting men. I have no idea how this will ever be achieved but…"

A sudden outburst of coughing interrupted his flow. He tried to shout over the racket but the effort was useless; the tension had been broken and attention redirected. Straining his eyes to the left without turning his head, Isaac could see the victim on his knees, his back heaving with the effort of breathing. Unable to make out who it was, but suspecting his wretched dining companion, he managed a brief smile. The captain's frustration was obvious—a suitable come-uppance for his earlier vindictiveness.

"Get that man out of here. Come on quickly, get on with it!"

Two corporals wrestled the invalid to his feet and dragged him away, his limp feet gouging two tram-lines in the loose gravel.

Thrown off his guard, Philips struggled to regain the initiative.

"So, hem…basic training will begin today. You will be issued with sticks for drilling purposes as rifles are not, hem…available at the moment. Uniforms should arrive in the next week or two. Right, Sergeant, start with four circuits of the square in formation, then issue the…gu…er…sticks. Is that understood?"

His face was congested with fury; one of the few high points of his week had been ruined, and he'd been made to look foolish into the bargain. The bastards would suffer for this.

"Yessir. Right, you lot. By the left, quick march. Left, right, left, right. Keep in line with the man beside you; swing your arms in time with your legs."

After a while, Isaac felt he was getting the hang of it. The precision of the marching and the sharp turns kept his mind busy, so much so that he temporarily forgot how much he hated his new life and the petty regime which so dehumanised the recruits.

Earlier that morning—his fourth since arriving at the depot—Isaac received a rude reminder of just how appalling his life had become in a relatively short space of time. Slower than usual in reaching the area assigned for washing purposes, he found the surface of each bucket and the surrounding area covered in a thick, grey scum. With a shiver of revulsion, he reached down into the depths of the first pail and recovered the oozing remainder of three bars of carbolic soap squashed together. Realising that trying to clean himself was a lost cause, he returned with heavy heart to discover that one of the two books he'd brought with him—a tattered copy of Donne's collected poems—had disappeared. This was the last straw and for several appalling moments he felt his resistance buckle like the hull of a sinking ship. He only just managed to pull himself together.

After breakfast the book was mysteriously back. The thief had most likely found there was no market for such an item. Apart from anything else, Isaac doubted whether many of his fellow recruits could actually read. At least, whoever it was had shown a little decency in returning the worthless article. He could have thrown it away or used it as toilet paper, depriving Isaac of one of his few consolations.

Following three hours of drilling and a four-mile route march, Isaac reported to Sergeant Denholm for latrine duty. The senior NCO was drinking a cup of stewed tea when the private entered the mess. He noticed the corporal he'd spoken to on the day of his arrival, lounging nearby.

"So this is the Jew you was tellin' me about, Nick. The one that wanted a room to 'imself with private facilities."

"Yeh, that's 'im, Sarge."

"Well, Private, as you can see, we're a little full up, so maybe you wouldn't mind sharing with the other lads for the time being. Oh, and by the way, the maid can't make it in today; apparently down with the clap." The corporal sniggered. "Nothing to laugh about, Nick. Apparently, she caught it off a yid with no foreskin—or so she said. Anyway, we can't 'ave the men catchin' diseases off the lavatory seats, now can we?" The sergeant's mocking tone suddenly changed. "Get yerself a mop and make sure the place is cleaned up. I want these buckets emptied and scrubbed out, properly mind, or you'll be doing 'em all over again. Corporal Jones'll be over to inspect your work later."

✳

Despite his hatred for the authorities, which grew steadily with each passing day, Isaac felt he was finally adjusting to the circumstances of his new life. When the recruits finally received their regulation footwear, no one offered any advice regarding the softening process the iron hard leather required. Isaac certainly noticed the rigidity of the boots but, like most of his mates, ignored the obvious and got on with the day's activities. Less than two miles into a six-mile march, the pain in his feet had become unbearable; gritting his teeth, he hobbled on.

Later, examining the damage, he wondered how he could have been so foolish. He was not alone; many members of the platoon could barely walk for days. Philips said it would act as a lesson encouraging common sense and self-reliance, but Isaac knew it had been another act of petty cruelty designed to tighten the yoke.

Even at this early stage, the army epitomised the arbitrary and unjust forces which he believed had plagued him all his life. For years he'd laboured to express the misery of spiritual subjugation and the difficulty of breaking free. Now, resentment fanned his creativity into an extravagant blaze. His new verse play, "Moses", begun a few weeks earlier, was beginning to write itself. Instead of being beaten down, he was actually flourishing in adversity—his poetry infused with an extraordinary energy. The constant round of punishments, fatigues, drills and route marches only seemed to encourage the process. However tired and over-burdened he might appear; however much he might complain and rail against army life, the melting pot filled and refilled with material fashioning itself in his mind.

Consigned to hospital after a nasty fall while being inspected by the battalion CO, he was finally granted the time to ponder the full extent of his remarkable transition. The incident, occurring little more than a month after his arrival at the depot, had left both hands badly cut and his self-respect in tatters. The sneering faces of officers and fellow recruits, as he'd pulled himself to his feet and limped off the parade ground, remained etched on his mind. Although a great improvement on the barracks, the military hospital was far from ideal. The tiny windows were permanently shut, letting in precious little light or the clean, fresh air he craved. After half an hour's writing, he always experienced considerable difficulty keeping his eyes open.

In addition, Isaac lived in constant dread of contracting the diseases afflicting a sizeable number of his fellow patients. The wheeze and rattle of infected lungs added a frightening backdrop to the clamour of the ward. Although due to be shipped out, these incurables, for some obscure bureaucratic reason, remained "on hold".

Sitting up in bed, penning a letter to his friend and patron, Sydney Schiff, he paused as the need to express something more profound took hold. The first section contained the usual mixture of complaints and requests he felt no guilt in burdening his correspondents with. It was still hard to write with the heavy bandaging round his right hand, but his fingers had largely escaped injury and were free from restraint. After a minute or so, he resumed the task:

> *I hope you are happy with your work. Any kind of work if one can only be doing something is what one wants now. I feel very grateful at your appreciation of my position, it keeps the clockwork going. To me this is not a result but one motion of the intricate series of activities that all combine to make a result. One might succumb, be destroyed—but one might also (and the chances are even greater for it) be renewed, made larger, healthier. It is not very easy for me to write here as you can imagine and you must not expect any proper continuity or even coherence. But I thought you might like to hear how I am placed exactly and write as I can.*

Strangely enough, in spite of everything, he did feel more in touch with himself; his life somehow fuller, more fulfilled than it ever had been. His experiences were undoubtedly having an unexpected but profound effect.

Pushing the letter aside, he pulled out a sheet of tattered paper from beneath his pillow and gazed avidly at the lines he'd written in the wake of Major Devoral's rounds earlier that morning. Not for the first time he considered just how much he identified the sardonic chief medical officer with the oppressive regime that so circumscribed the lives of ordinary soldiers. Isaac constantly fantasised about ending the reign of the despots who controlled every aspect of life in the training camp. Vanquishing the likes of Devoral, Philips and Denholme had become a consuming inner passion. Whenever he conjured the characters of Pharaoh and his overseer, Abinoah, Devoral's florid face, with its bolting blue eyes, was never far away. The poet yearned for the strength to strike back; to crush and destroy.

> *Till my hands ache to grip*
> *The hammer—the lone hammer*
> *That breaks lives into a road*
> *Through which my genius drives.*
> *Pharaoh well peruked and oiled,*
> *And your admirable pyramids,*
> *And your interminable procession*
> *Of crowded kings...*
>
> *I am rough now, and new, and will have no tailor.*
> *Startlingly,*
> *As a mountain side*
> *Wakes aware of its other side,*
> *When from a cave a leopard comes,*
> *On its heels the same red sand,*
> *Springing with acquainted air,*
> *Sprang an intelligence*
> *Coloured as a whim of mine,*
> *Showed to my dull outer eyes*

The living eyes underneath.
Did I not shrivel up and take the place of air,
Secret as those eyes were,
And those strong eyes call up a giant frame?
And I am that now.

It was clear that his antipathy for the doctor, and everything he represented, had tightened the structure of the text and expanded the power of his imagery. Instead of gratitude, however, he experienced only rage recalling word for word the belittling sarcasm he'd endured that very morning.

"Matron tells me you've been writing poems. Is that correct?"

Isaac, noticing the jeering expressions of Devoral's sycophants crowded expectantly round his metal bedstead, was reluctant to be drawn.

"Yes, sir."

"So you're a poet then?"

A spatter of sniggering.

"And an artist, I hear! Is there any end to your talents? I'm sure we all feel privileged to be in the presence of such an…inspiring sort of a chappy. Lieutenant Philips and his NCOs must be missing you terribly. "Gentlemen," he turned to address his eager audience. "I fear we must not hold this patient back any longer. The morale of our brave recruits demand that he be released as soon as possible. I want this man out of hospital and returned to his unit by the end of the week. His malingering has gone on quite long enough. If he can write, he can fight."

The matron, her abdomen bulging obscenely beneath the tight confines of her starched, white uniform, merely nodded, betraying no emotion whatsoever. But Isaac knew the dictate met with her approval. Like Devoral, she'd used every opportunity to make his time in hospital as unpleasant as possible.

Anger quickly superseded by ennui, he turned over and closed his eyes. The letter would have to wait, his energy levels had to be carefully nursed. Three more nights on the ward and then back to the barracks.

The prospect depressed him, though in some ways the move would be welcome despite the fact that his feet remained unhealed and his hands, sore and stiff. Whether he was up to the demands of training and the inevitable punishment fatigues, remained unclear, but, somehow, he would prevail. One day he would prise loose the *rotting God's* strangling grip on every aspect of his life.

*

In early December, the weather turned decidedly wintry. The barracks, formerly stuffy, now seemed to concentrate the freezing air. The men shivered in their blankets, and wore all the clothes available to them, but nothing could keep the bitter cold at bay.

Apart from the icy conditions, life suddenly improved in the camp. Philips and Denholme were transferred to France, and their bullying regime came to an end. Deprived of the sergeant's support, Corporal Jones was forced to give ground and tended to leave Isaac and the more vulnerable recruits alone. The new senior NCO, older and much less antagonistic than his predecessor, appeared even mildly impressed by the private's reputation as a poet and man of letters.

Out of the blue, hundreds of uniforms arrived in the camp, inundating the quartermaster's store. Although the tunics were generally too big for the undersized bantams, they began to look and feel like soldiers at long last. The heavy great coats and thick woollen socks helped keep them warm, and morale crept up in contrast to the plunging temperatures.

Begging letters from Isaac to his patrons also paid off. An influx of chocolates and cigarettes guaranteed increased popularity for the man who, until recently, had been mocked and largely ostracised by fellow recruits. He even managed to buy new boots with money sent by Schiff, leading to a marked decrease in the suffering of his blistered feet. The cold seemed to exacerbate the hand wounds, however; his fingers swelled up, and the half-healed wounds turning dark and blotchy. Devoral would have none of it, refusing point-blank to excuse him heavy duties.

One bitterly cold morning the men were ordered to clear snow from the square and spent several hours removing the thick, white layer with spades. On their break, drinking stewed tea and chain-smoking cigarettes, they felt appreciably cheerier than of late. Warmed up by the heavy work, Harry Jacobs, barracks wit and anti-authoritarian, was in full flow.

"It's a bloody disgrace that Rosie should be workin' with 'is 'ands in that state. Devoral should be in charge of a slaughter 'ouse, not a bleedin' 'ospital. These army doctors is all the same: everyone's a bleedin' malingerer as far as they're concerned. Fuckin' bedside manner! Jack the Ripper 'ad more concern for 'is victims than they 'ave for their patients."

Most of the other men nodded; the major's tarnished reputation was universal.

"What the hell are you moaning about now, Jacobs?"

Slapping vigorously at his body with outstretched arms and hands, Sergeant Grey made his way across the crowded room. Unlike Denholme, he enjoyed a spat with the men. He could take a joke against himself, as well as dish it out.

"It's just the state of Rosie's 'ands, Sarge. The doc declared 'im fit for active duty but 'e can hardly 'old a spade, never mind dig wiv it."

Gray sat back, lit a cigarette and pulled in a lungful of smoke. Exhaling slowly, he sighed.

"Let's have a look, Private."

Isaac drew back the rags he'd wrapped round his palms and fingers. Peering closely at the discoloured flesh, the sergeant nodded slowly.

"They're a mess, right enough. You'd better lay off digging for the rest of the day. Maybe I can find you something else to do."

"Thank you, Sergeant."

"Oh, by the way, I'd like a word later on. Five o'clock all right?"

"Yes, Sarge, that…that's fine." He hoped he was not going to receive further punishment fatigues. Yet there was something about his superior's tone of voice which suggested this was not the case.

"Good. Okay, lads, the rest of that snow'll not shift itself. Let's get going. Captain Thornhill wants the parade ground clear by three o'clock at the latest."

"What's he want it for? A bleedin' march past!"

Harry's muttered imprecations were audible throughout the room. The men laughed as they struggled to their feet.

✳

"Have a chocolate, Sergeant."

"That's very kind of you, Rosenberg. Don't mind if I do."

The two men were sitting at an old table weighed down by a mass of paper threatening a landslide at any moment. Gray had cleared a small space for the two tin cups of coffee now steaming in the chilly room.

"Not to beat around the bush, lad, I've asked you in here to offer you a stripe."

The private's eyes widened in amazement. This was almost the last thing he'd expected to hear. Until recently, the idea would have been utterly absurd; even now it was hard to take seriously.

"Captain Thornhill felt it was a good idea, given your…educational advantages. We could do with a capable man. You know, signing things in and out, keeping account of various army issue and other light duties. It would certainly allow your hands and feet a proper chance to heal up and give you a bit of…authority with the men. What do you think?"

"Thank you for c…considering me, Sergeant. Can I have time to think about it?"

"Of course, of course. Take a few days. There's no hurry at all."

Leaving Gray's office a little later, he felt more than tempted by the offer. He'd noticed the sergeant's interest in his writing activities, but had put that down to simple curiosity. The piled-up desk, of course, told its own story. The promotion would certainly give him a chance to recover his health, and distance him from the rough and tumble of life in the crowded barracks. He knew once the chocolates and cigarettes ran out, his newfound popularity would quickly melt away. He'd recently been exposed to a level of intimidation that left him acutely apprehensive most of the time. Being free from fear was no small matter in a place like this. On the other hand, accepting the offer would pull him into the system, establishing a link with the regime he abhorred, and inevitably undermine his moral stand.

Back in the barracks, he climbed up into his bunk bed, and pulled a wad of paper from his tunic pocket. It had been more than a month since the rough hewn, two-levelled structure, running round the walls of the hut, had been installed, but Isaac still savoured the increased comfort and privacy the new arrangement afforded. Leafing through the sheets, he came to the lines particularly apposite to his current dilemma.

> *There shall not be a void or calm*
> *But a fury fill the veins of time*
> *Whose limbs had begun to rot.*
>
> *Who had flattered my stupid torpor*
> *With an easy and mimic energy,*
> *And drained my veins with a paltry marvel*
> *More monstrous than battle,*
> *For the soul ached and went out dead in pleasure.*

Being here at all sullied his dignity, but to cosy up to the authorities for selfish purposes would surely destroy any remaining self-respect. Deep inside, although he'd tried to convince himself otherwise, he instinctively knew now how much he hated the war and the destructive forces it represented. Everything about killing ran contrary to his most cherished principles. From the little he'd heard about life at the front, previous wars paled into insignificance when compared to the present conflict. Casualty statistics, filtering back to those at home, appeared to bear out the worst of the rumours. Again, he questioned the motives that had brought him into the army in the first place. Even though his poetry had much improved over the past few months, the fact that his mother had received not a penny piece yet, aggravated the inner misery he felt.

Despite the enticing nature of the offer, he realised that refusal was his only option. The alternative was too awful to contemplate. His conscience could never endorse such a betrayal for short-term gain. Besides which, he'd been in this situation before. The temptation to jettison his self-imposed search for perfection had been whispering and cajoling as long as he could remember. Over the years, his iconoclastic leanings had served to isolate him—his stubborn refusal to identify with any movement, or embrace popular trends in art, effectively sundering him from the artistic mainstream. As an outsider, exiled from both the inner sanctum of orthodoxy and the hotbed of modernistic dogma, his poetry often proved unacceptable to traditionalists and revolutionaries alike.

He hoped his application for Christmas leave would prove successful. He desired time away from this place to regroup and consider his future. He also desperately needed to put things right with his mother, by trying to make her understand why he'd joined up in the first place.

Later, crossing the deserted square, now virtually cleared of snow, he wondered how long he could hold out. His resolution, like a piece of elastic, could only be stretched so far; safeguarding purity of purpose was no easy task. The contradictions plaguing his life had never been more to the fore than at present—hatred and fear constantly striving against a perverse fascination to see how much abuse he could withstand and how his artistic life would develop as a result.

He entered the mess, to an uproarious greeting. The basins of disgusting slop were being distributed and Isaac sat down beside the eager diners. Afterwards, he offered round the remainder of his bounty, ensuring at least one more threat-free evening in the company of his peers.

Chapter Two

1916

I am known as a poet and artist, as our second in command is a Jewish officer who knows of me from his people...
> *Extract from letter to Sydney Schiff: January 1916.*

Believe me the army is the most detestable invention on this earth and nobody but a private in the army knows what it is to be a slave...
> *Extract from letter to Lascelles Abercrombie: March 1916.*

I have food sent up from home and that keeps me alive, but as for the others, there is talk of mutiny every day. One reg close by did break out and some men got bayoneted...
> *Extract from letter to Sydney Schiff: March 1916.*

Spring 1916

Slow, rigid, is the masquerade
That passes as through a difficult air;
Heavily-heavily passes.
What has she fed on? Who her table laid
Through the three seasons? What forbidden fare
Ruined her as a mortal lass is?

I played with her two years ago,
Who might be now her own sister in stone,
So altered from her May mien,
When round vague pink a necklace of warm snow
Laughed to her throat where my mouth's touch had gone.
How is this, ruined Queen?

Who lured her vivid beauty so
To be that strained chilled thing that moves
So ghastly midst her young brood
Of pregnant shoots that she for men did grow?
Where are the strong men who made these their loves?
Spring! God pity your mood.

Isaac woke up in freezing blackness unable to breathe. Someone was seated on his head, and sharp knees dug painfully into his arms. The stink of greasy sweat almost made him gag. He could feel rough hands rummaging through the empty pockets of his tunic, and, nearby, someone was ransacking his kit bag. Struggling to breathe, he tried to free his mouth. A voice hissed out above him:

"Keep still or I'll cut your fuckin' throat."

Another distinctly nervous voice intervened:

"It's all right. I've found three bob and a 'alf a box of chocolates. Let's get out of 'ere before somebody wakes up."

"Right yid, keep your mouth shut or I'll come back and shut it permanent."

The crushing weight on the side of his face was suddenly removed, the bunk creaked loudly, and he heard a scrape and rustle below as the men moved off. Straining to see, the private could make out nothing in the grainy darkness. He could hear the usual heavy breathing and restless movement as men turned in their sleep. Perhaps they really had slept through it all.

Tension was running high in the barracks. Food was in such short supply that, for those not fortunate enough to be receiving help from the outside, life was becoming increasingly desperate. Isaac was among the few recruits to receive regular parcels from home and as the identity of this elite was well known among the men, attempts were often made to persuade or compel them to share their bounty. His relative good fortune was thus a double-edged sword, threatening both personal safety and peace of mind. Acts of violence were now so commonplace it was hard to know where it all might end. Fear stalked the camp and the authorities seemed unable or unwilling to deal with the problem. Isaac knew it was quite possible that the thief might return to make good his threat. He could count himself lucky to have avoided the thrust of cold steel in the first place. Life was so cheap here, anything was possible. His ears strained to detect the slightest creak of a floorboard beneath stealthy feet. Hearing nothing beyond the stir of near neighbours, he turned the hopeless situation round in his mind for the umpteenth time, desperate to find some cause for optimism.

The latest rumour that mutiny had flared up in a regiment billeted close by was hard to verify, and the fact that most of the gossip centred round its bloody repression led Isaac to wonder if the whole affair might have been concocted by the authorities in the vain hope of warning off would-be conspirators and trouble-makers. If true, however, something of the sort could yet happen here. Part of him hoped it would. He guessed it must only be a matter of time before the army was forced to root out its more lawless elements. On the other hand, it had also occurred to him that the dehumanising process might well be a calculated attempt to goad the men into violence in preparation for war. If this was the case, the plan was working only too well. He prayed for a transfer to a regular unit where conditions were better and life less stressful. Living under constant threat, day after day, was a dreadful strain and beginning to take its toll.

The substandard physical fitness of the majority of bantams also posed a serious problem, exacerbated by the meagre rations and unhygienic conditions prevailing in camp. Isaac doubted sometimes whether he would pull through in the end. Although his health was better than most, the troublesome cough, which had so badly affected him last winter, had returned and his feet were still playing up. He found it difficult to determine how he'd feel if discharged on health grounds. There would certainly be an overwhelming sense of relief; but the ignominy of having failed yet again to live up to expectation—of falling short of the mark—would be hard to bear. His mother's delight at having him safe back home might well be short-lived if he failed to secure a proper job and make a meaningful contribution to struggling family finances. Based on past experience, there was no reason to imagine matters would improve in this respect. The situation prior to his joining up had been hopeless. The sudden realisation hit him that being in the army solved a number of pressing problems that would have to be faced the moment he returned to civilian life.

There were other factors in the complex equation. In a strange sense, despite his continuing hatred of almost every aspect of army life and the constant fear he lived with, something had shifted inside. The future, for better or worse, seemed to him inextricably linked to this new existence.

In the meantime, his remaining money and food were gone. Complaints to the authorities were a waste of time and would only place him in further danger. He had no idea who the thieves were, and it was unlikely anyone would co-operate in the event of an investigation; few were willing to place themselves in the firing line.

Unable to sleep, he alighted on the one good thing that had happened since his transfer to Blackdown Camp in early January: the fortuitous meeting with Major Abrahams—second in command of the 12th South Lancashires. It turned out the major's uncle had known his father back in Lithuania. Both had been intent on entering the Judaic priesthood, and both had fled the threat of conscription into the Russian Army. Meeting again in London, many years later, they vowed to keep in touch. Incredibly, Abrahams had heard all about Isaac's aspirations to become a poet and painter.

"So, have you continued writing since...taking the King's oath? I imagine it must be somewhat difficult for you."

The two men were sitting in Abraham's little office where Isaac had reported two days after his arrival at Blackdown. Instead of the usual lecture about dress and deportment, he'd been delighted by the warm reception afforded him. The major was a large athletic man, ten years older and at least six inches taller than Isaac. His candid blue eyes and ready smile suggested humour and intelligence in equal measure. Isaac felt immediately at ease in his company.

"I've been mainly w...working things out in my head, sir. Sometimes you...you get the opportunity to jot down a verse or two, but it isn't easy."

"Yes, I can imagine. The men would be less than...sympathetic, shall we say. I'd be pleased to offer you pen and paper if that would help."

"That's very kind of you, sir. A friend in London sent me down brushes and p...paints while I was in hospital a few months ago. I enjoyed getting back to my old work again and sketched a few of the p...patients but, naturally, they wanted what I did."

Abrahams nodded and looked thoughtful for a moment.

"Did it ever occur to you that your drawing talents might be of value to the army? Good war artists are few and far between, you know. Perhaps you might consider that as a way forward. I could certainly look into it for you."

Isaac dropped his eyes and stared at the discoloured floorboards for a few moments. Another lifeline was being thrown to him and, though quite different from the promotion offered two months earlier, the temptation to grab it was equally powerful. With a sigh, he tried to express the feeling that had been growing in him lately, hoping the major would understand his need to refuse.

"Thank you, sir, but...I'm committed to it now...the war I mean. It's hard to explain...but it seems as if my destiny is, is to somehow see things through.... I believe that the true artist mustn't shrink from d...danger, or take the easy way out, but...meet things head on. Only...only then might his work ever be considered...worthy. Some of what I've written since joining up is...so much better.... Maybe...I can do my bit to uncover the...the truth about things. I want to p...pull through, of course, but..."

He finished lamely, feeling rather foolish. Abrahams slowly nodded and stared into space for a few moments as if trying to gauge the significance of what had been said.

"I'd like to see something you've written. Are you working on anything special at the moment?"

Isaac felt grateful his superior had made an effort to appreciate his eccentric stance.

"I'm attempting a reworking of the Moses theme. I suppose what interests me is that he stuck to his principles…re…refusing to live the life of a slave—however luxurious."

Abrahams smiled. Despite the difficulties the young poet encountered in trying to express himself, his passion and commitment were undeniable.

Encouraged, Isaac gave voice to his ambition for the work. "Maybe his moral struggle reminds us of the need to resist corruption at whatever cost to ourselves, in order to…to hold on to what is…is…best in human nature. That, I believe, remains the key to our salvation."

"You do not lack insight, or integrity, I see. Your father would be proud of such a worthy inspiration, I'm sure. I wish you luck in the enterprise. You mentioned earlier that you'd finished a shorter poem recently."

"Yes. I think I may have a c…copy of it with me somewhere. I'd be interested in your…your thoughts." Groping awkwardly in the pockets of his tunic, he pulled out several sheaves of crumpled paper. "Here it is. I c…called it 'Spring 1916'."

Taking the poem, the major opened the top drawer of his desk and placed it inside. Rising, he smiled down at the private fidgeting uncomfortably in his seat.

"Unfortunately, Isaac, I have to go and check a new consignment of rifles which arrived this morning. We'll meet again…after I've read your poem perhaps."

"I look forward to it, sir. I'll…I'll write to my father and tell him I've met you. He'll be d…delighted you've taken an interest in me."

Turning restlessly on the hard, unforgiving mattress, he now realised that being in the company of an intelligent and humane member of his own race, even for a short time, had made the task of coping with the depressing realities of life in the barracks all the more daunting. The fact that he'd rejected another avenue of escape gave him little cause for complaint, however. What had happened tonight was just the latest example of the danger he faced every day. Thank God his family were unaware of how bad things actually were. He wondered how his mother would cope if something happened to him in this place. He tried to blot out images of her overwhelming grief.

Two hours before reveille, Isaac fell into a sound sleep. For a short period, he was granted respite from the fear and guilt tormenting him.

✱

Isaac was taken unawares when two burly corporals dragged him out of the barracks and hauled him in front of the duty officer.

The week before, in the wake of sweeping changes reducing the strength of his old battalion from a thousand strong to just over two hundred, Isaac was transferred to the Eleventh Kings own Royal Lancasters—the regular unit he'd prayed for. Buoyed up by the much sought-after change in his fortunes, he relaxed for the first time in many months and promptly forgot to turn out for sentry duty.

The gangly lieutenant, long legs thrust under his desk and hands clasped behind head, stared at him across the cramped office. He smiled wearily.

"So you're Rosenberg, the private who couldn't be bothered turning out. Perhaps you had something more interesting to do with your time. I don't suppose the Suffolks ever bothered enforcing duty rosters or anything else for that matter, eh?"

The last syllable, assumed a high, mocking edge.

"No...no, sir. I mean yes, sir. I'm very s...sorry but the...the duty slipped my...my mind... . I've been quite ill recently and... felt a little...t...tired."

"Of course, you were tired. How obtuse of me. I'm sorry if we seem rather unsympathetic. Maybe it's because we're trying to win a war or something silly like that."

"No, sir... . It's only that I..."

"Well, Private Rosenberg, I'm afraid you'll have to learn that such dereliction will not be tolerated in the Lancasters. You do realise that failure to turn out for any duty is a court martial offence?"

For a moment, he felt as though his trembling knees would give way. Fortunately for him, the captain was merely going through the motions.

"On active duty, you would most likely be shot, but on this occasion I will be more lenient. Further laxness on your part, however, will meet with a much harsher punishment. Do I make myself clear?"

"Yes, sir. Th…th…thank you, sir."

"Right then—three days in the lockup with double punishment fatigues on release. Dismissed."

As usual, in these situations, Isaac found himself incapable of meaningful resistance. Like a rabbit caught in the beam of a poacher's night lamp, he could only passively accept his fate. However much he might wish to challenge military authority and its host of petty regulations, his dread of the consequences always proved too powerful a deterrent. The irony of the situation was not lost on him. The most important motivation for writing "Moses" was, after all, his desire to re-establish control and counter tyranny. Inwardly, he cursed his weakness.

Outside, the corporals gloated. One of them seemed to find the whole affair particularly amusing.

"Jesus Christ, imagine forgetting to report for duty. No wonder most of you got kicked out!" He grinned over at his mate. "Christ only knows how this little fucker got through the net."

"He'll wish 'e 'adn't after three days in clink."

Later on, wrapped in the one thin, army-issue blanket provided in the lock-up, Isaac tried to make sense of the latest turn of events. It was hard to believe that he'd ended up in this tiny cell with its peeling walls and overflowing slop bucket reeking in the opposite corner. Just when he felt things were improving, calamity had struck once again. The realisation sunk his spirits to a new low. The whole situation was absurd. For years he'd struggled to gain some measure of personal freedom, but his aspirations had been cruelly thwarted at every turn. It seemed that all his long-term ambitions were destined to come to nothing. He would most likely finish up like his father—a victim of world weariness and perverse circumstance. It was hard to imagine how things could get any worse. As if in answer, the single light bulb, hanging above his head, flickered out. He calculated that it couldn't be more than seven-thirty. Sleep was out of the question.

Conjuring Barnett's face in the darkness, he pondered the high cheekbones, the greying beard and the dulled eyes of a man who'd fought all his life to retain some personal dignity and failed. It seemed they were both casualties of the same sardonic forces plaguing the poor and downtrodden throughout the world. The only difference was that, while his father clung tenaciously to the idea of God as redeemer, he had long since rejected the notion. Isaac knew that if the old man had had any inkling of the depths of his son's loathing for the God he unswervingly revered, the knowledge would have been almost too much to bear.

The more he considered his fate, the more hopeless he felt. Abrahams had warned him that unorthodox behaviour in the present climate could seriously backfire. Artistic endeavour, the major insisted, was never going to accord special rights or evoke respect in the minds of his superiors. The army authorities were intent on building an efficient fighting machine, and were not inclined to consider the evils underlying the waging of war itself. Isaac had agreed, but, seated once more in the haven of Abrahams' office, he argued passionately for poetry as a necessary precursor of change.

"P…poetry is not a…a…balm as so many think…but a way of…expressing our deepest spiritual aspirations." Struggling desperately to find the right words, he inwardly cursed the hesitations and stutter that so often rendered him semi-articulate in conversation. "At its best, it's like a…a knife cutting away dead and dying tissue. In 'Spring 1916' I wanted to show how this war has…blighted so…so many lives. The perversion of spring was…was an attempt to provide a…an effective means of conveying this."

"I understand that." Abrahams leaned forward, fixing Isaac with his penetrating, blue eyes. "The poem has great power, but will change nothing in the short term, don't you see?" Abrahams' squinted at the sheet for a moment. *To be that strained chilled thing…*—is undoubtedly accurate, but you have to understand we're embroiled in this war and there's no going back. How did Shakespeare put it?" He sat back again, screwing up his forehead in the effort to remember the exact quotation. "*I am in blood/stepped in so far that, should I wade no more, /Returning was as tedious as go o'er.* A little out of context, granted, but close to the mark. The war will continue, Isaac, and prove costly in ways we cannot yet imagine; but in the long run it may be crucial in stamping out future wars. Your poems could be part of the reckoning; a coming to terms, if you will."

"Yes, I see that, but…"

"That is why you must learn to live by the rules and be a good soldier. In persevering, you triumph. Look to the future, Isaac. If there is any hope, it lies there."

Abrahams was right. Perseverance was vital; he'd said so himself many times. Perhaps the role of the poet in wartime was more important for posterity than for those locked into the present conflict. He struggled to apprehend the true meaning of immortality. In spite of all the great works of art, little had actually changed in the world. Ignorance, violence, greed and envy still held sway—the agonised striving of great visionaries over the centuries somehow futile in light of the present madness.

His thoughts had come full circle, providing him with precious little comfort. If only he could sleep now, things might seem less onerous in the morning. The prospect failed to fortify him as he lay shivering on the narrow bunk.

Harry Jacobs passed on the information as they returned from a gruelling two-hour stint on the firing range. Isaac despaired of ever managing to load and discharge his rifle in the time required by the infuriated instructors, or clean the barrel without leaving traces of dust and grease.

"It's true. We're being shipped out end of next week."

"Where to?"

"Beats me but we're entitled to a week's leave."

Isaac experienced a ripple of nervous excitement. At last, a break from the mindless army routine, but then what? He pushed the thought out of his mind, concentrating instead on the delights of pre-embarkation leave. The only break he'd had since joining up more than seven months ago was four days last Christmas. He might even be able to arrange to have his latest work printed. Reuben Cohen could probably be persuaded to help him out again. If the costs were kept low enough and his friends persuaded to buy a few copies, he might cover his expenses with a little left over. It was a gamble, but he felt confident that "Moses" and his *barracks* poems were the best things he'd written so far.

Only half listening as Harry babbled on, he tried to assess the full impact of the past few weeks. After being released from lock-up, he'd been forced into a harsh regime which effectively stripped his physical reserves; endless trench digging, coal shovelling, cookhouse duties and forced pack drill had taken their toll, leaving him close to collapse. Seeing his family and friends again, and walking the streets of Whitechapel was the tonic he craved. A week at home might even lead to a partial recovery of his strength. And then to France or the coloured countries. Events were gathering pace.

"So, where are you going to spend your leave then?"

Isaac stared blankly at his friend.

"Sorry, what d…did you say?"

"Your leave. For fuck sakes, Rosie! 'Aven't you 'eard a bleedin word I've said? I was askin' about your leave."

"Ah yes. I'll probably s…spend it with my family."

"Ain't you going to get yourself a woman then? It might be your last chance."

Sonia flitted, unbidden, into his mind. If there was anybody he wanted to be with it was Sonia; but that, of course, was out of the question.

Perhaps Annetta could be persuaded to take him back, but, recalling the circumstances of their last encounter, he deemed it highly unlikely.

His treatment of her had been scurrilous and he deserved nothing more than her contempt. Memories of their affair seemed distant now, although he recalled closing his eyes and visualising Sonia beneath him while making love to her.

"So, are you?"

Harry's impatient voice intruded into his thoughts once again.

"What?...No...er...yes, probably."

"You're a strange cove, right enough. You'll most likely be writin' more poetry. You've got to try and enjoy yourself, Rosie. God knows 'ow long any of us 'as got, now we're being shipped out."

Harry was right, but he didn't want to think about the dangers they would soon be facing. Instead, he focused on what he might actually do during his leave.

"Maybe I'll try to sell a few of my sketches, but there won't be enough time to write much p...poetry I'm afraid. There are a few people I want to meet up with. What with that and...and trying to get some of my stuff published, there won't be time for much else."

With a sinking heart, he realised that this was the truth of the matter. Before joining the army he'd had time in abundance but largely frittered it away. Now there was so much to do in such a short period. After that, God alone knew when he'd ever get back to London. A strange, weak sensation suddenly engulfed him as the knowledge he might never return hammered itself home. He had naturally considered the possibility before, but only in the abstract. At this moment, the feeling was so powerful it was as if he was staring down the black throat of personal extinction. He was gambling with his life in the hope of producing better poetry! Nothing would come of it if he was killed in action before being allowed to assimilate the true nature of the experience. This time the sound of Harry's cheery voice was a distraction he readily embraced.

"Everybody to their own, I suppose. But try and get 'old of a woman if you can. Most of them foreign tarts 'ave the pox or so I'm told. Best to keep your old todger inside your trousers when you're abroad."

"Maybe you're right, Harry. I'll bear it in mind."

"You do that, Rosie. You do that."

✳

Isaac watched with distaste as the colonel slowly pulled himself up onto a hastily erected rostrum. Turning towards the assembled battalion, he noisily cleared his throat in readiness for a speech designed to inspire the soldiers about to be shipped out. The redness of his face and the swell of his stomach, pushing uncomfortably against his tightly buttoned uniform, suggested a profligacy at odds with the lives of those he commanded. Clearly he would not be grappling personally with the enemy.

"Basic training over, you now go to support our gallant forces on the Western Front." So it was to be France. Isaac's stomach churned uncomfortably. "Tomorrow you will be transported to Southampton and from there by troop ship to Le Havre in France. The entire Division will then make its way to the battle zone for training under fire..." The pompous voice continued to exhort the importance of duty and courage in the face of the enemy, but the poet was no longer listening. He was remembering his sister Annie's sad face as she stood staring at him through the wire of the camp's high perimeter fence. She had no way of knowing how close he'd come to breaking down in the face of her impassioned pleas to return home. Struggling to remain impassive, he'd eventually been forced to walk away, leaving her crying out his name until the sound faded. That was yesterday, and he was still filled with anguish and remorse. The colonel's rising warble suddenly broke through.

"...I expect, and the entire nation expects you to do your duty in the face of enemy aggression. This war will soon be over if we fight valiantly and give no quarter to the Hun. We will prevail; right will prevail. God save the King."

The men dutifully cheered and were quickly dismissed. Back in the barracks while the others smoked and played cards, Isaac assessed the impact of his recent leave.

In some respects his time in London had proved fruitful. Reuben

Cohen, as he'd expected, was greatly impressed by "Moses" and consented to produce a pamphlet of the verse play and accompanying poems, free of charge. The printer agreed that costs could be paid as a percentage of the sales and had high hopes of setting up a new press dedicated to the works of promising young Jewish writers. Isaac was more than pleased by the quality of the work and sent out copies to a number of Georgian poets recommended by Eddie Marsh. His fortunes were clearly changing and the impending tour of duty, in light of these favourable portents, seemed untimely to say the least.

His inevitable meeting with Rodker and Sonia proved a bittersweet affair. He'd hoped the pain might have abated, but found, to his dismay, that the wounds were as raw as ever. He ached for what was not possible, and experienced terrible pangs of jealousy as the pair sat snuggled up together on a dilapidated couch clasping each other's hands. There seemed little doubt, despite their obvious poverty, that love continued to burn brightly. He made a good job of concealing his despair, and sat across the tiny room apparently indifferent to their hands-on affection.

The decision not to sever ties with the couple had proved fortuitous as Jimmy was obviously working hard on his behalf. News that the influential American journal *Poetry Magazine* would most probably print "Marching", and was considering another of the "barracks" poems promoted by his friend, delighted Isaac. Also, the fact that two distinguished poets were expressing interest in his work persuaded him that things were indeed looking up.

Thoughts of his family and the lies he'd told continued to traumatise him. His mother, unaware of the imminent departure date, appeared to have reluctantly come to terms with his decision to join the army. She had chosen to believe that, because of poor health, her son had acquired a desk job and would remain in England for the remainder of the war. Convincing himself that it would be pointless to reveal the truth and therefore spoil his few remaining days at home, he actively encouraged the illusion. The knowledge that he was about to be shipped out, and the despair this would inevitably cause, gnawed away at him for the duration of the leave, making it hard for him to look any member of his family in the eye. Inevitably, he spent more and more time with his friends, allowing the accumulation of guilt and unhappiness to lift for a while. It never crossed his mind that the inevitable, explanatory letter to Annie, sent on the eve of embarkation, would have brought her rushing post-haste down to Aldershot in an effort to dissuade him. She seemed incapable of understanding that there was nothing he could do to avoid the transfer to France. The matter was out of his hands, had never been in his hands for that matter. Delaying the truth until the last possible moment, was, he now accepted, a cowardly act, designed not to spare the family unnecessary grief but himself the burden of facing up to his responsibilities.

Weary from turning the matter over and over in his mind, Isaac tried to concentrate instead on the new poem begun a few days after his return from London. He was keen to finish it before embarkation. How his writing would fare after that he had no way of knowing. The barracks was bad enough but the trenches, he guessed, would usher in an altogether new order of hardship.

The mounting racket, as the card game moved towards its climax, made work impossible. Unusually for him, he prayed for lights out.

Next day, the long eight months in training camps finally over, the troop train shunted out of the station and began its slow journey to Southampton. The crowded carriages buzzed with excitement. Isaac's grim introspection marked him out from most other soldiers on the train. Already considered a queer character, given to bouts of extreme moodiness, he was largely ignored after a few knowing nods and winks cast in his direction. Judging by the men's high spirits, it seemed they were on the verge of a great adventure. Rumour had it that the war might be over in a few weeks, and most of them fervently desired to have a go at the "bosche" before the final whistle was blown. Isaac couldn't help imagining their mutilated corpses littering some distant battlefield. He understood enough to know that stories regarding a swift end to the conflict were the result of wishful thinking and idle gossip. Marsh had made it clear in a recent letter there was no end in sight. The possibility of a breakthrough had been dashed against the wall of harsh reality; the brutality of trench warfare and the murderous efficiency of modern weaponry in particular, promised years of attrition.

His face pressed against the window, Isaac stared out at the passing countryside—its clipped hedgerows, green fields and dotted cattle bathed in warm sunlight. Notions of the ideal Arcadian past it represented left him cold. This landscape—the inspiration for so many English poets, archaic and contemporary alike—held no resonance for him. Raised in the slums of Whitechapel, and having rarely left the sooty stench of London, he felt no particular empathy or identification with rural England. The link was at best superficial and second hand.

As the miles slipped by, he became increasingly ill at ease. The prospect of death—a concept he'd once idly toyed with when the pressures of life seemed unendurable—bubbled up like storm clouds on the immediate horizon, threatening to blot out the very essence of who he was. He realised again just how desperate he was to survive this holocaust. To perish on the cusp of a major breakthrough would be a pointless end to everything he'd hoped for. As anticipated, the harsh circumstances of life in the various training camps had burned away much of the excess embedded in his pre-war poetry. Experience of the war itself might well complete the process, allowing him to realise the full potential of his expressive powers. He'd already said as much to Major Abrahams. While dreading the prospect of killing men, he simultaneously felt an intense surge of curiosity. Where would his muse lead him? Although acutely aware of the irony, he couldn't help praying to the God he'd so roundly cursed in the past to grant him the time and opportunity to make his mark.

Eventually the train pulled into a siding close to the docks. The doors were hauled open and the men sprang down. Lining up, they marched towards the waiting troop ship—a massive, rusting hulk that looked as if it had been left to rot. By now the sun had disappeared, and rain clouds crowded the sky. Some of the recruits were ordered below decks for the duration of the overnight crossing while others, including Isaac, were told to find a space on the wet, flaking deck. Even at berth the slight rocking motion of the ancient tub appeared to be having an adverse effect on a number of his companions. Despite exposure to wind and rain, he felt the men on deck were infinitely better off than those packed below in the oily darkness.

A little over an hour later, the ship edged out of the harbour towards the open sea. It was growing colder and drizzling more steadily. Initial high spirits began to diminish as wind and waves grew in intensity. Most of the men consumed their cold rations and huddled together, their heads pillowed on bulging rucksacks. Trying to twist himself into a more comfortable position, Isaac rammed his cheek hard into the heel of someone's boot. He rubbed his bruised face and swore under his breath.

Later, he woke to find one of his mates had rolled onto his left leg. At first he could feel nothing as he hauled the heavy, lifeless limb from under the sleeping body, but the pain of returning life caused him to squirm and gasp. Sleep was now impossible as the cold stealthily fingered its way through his greatcoat and the flimsy tunic below.

All through that endless night, men staggered across to the rail to urinate or throw up. Some of the waste inevitably blew back, spattering those unfortunate enough to be lying nearby. Unable to prevent themselves, they often stepped on or collided with the packed bodies littering the deck. Isaac was aware of a constant undercurrent of curses emanating from the darkness around him.

At first light, the poet found himself jammed up against the side of a lifeboat. Looking up, he noticed a jagged hole punched in its hull. God help them now if the German navy suddenly turned up to blow this wreck and its human cargo out of the water. Against the eastern skyline, a destroyer ploughed a parallel course to their own. The escort's long, dark silhouette, bristling with guns, failed to provide him with comfort.

Isaac put down his own lack of sea-sickness to the long voyages he'd undertaken almost two years ago. The trip to South Africa, indeed that entire episode of his life, seemed so distant now—somehow unreal. At times, he wondered whether he'd ever actually been there at all or had dreamed the whole thing. He clearly recalled the savage mountains stretching back into an unfathomable wilderness; the natives with their sad, downcast eyes; the huge houses where he'd wined and dined and been treated as a minor celebrity, but had difficulty placing himself there in any real sense.

Certainly, his brief affair with Marda Vanne, the *enfant terrible* of the Capetown partying set, still elicited a powerful response. The bizarre sexual encounter had fuelled his poetic output at the time and could not be easily set aside. The only other memory, which felt more than skin-deep, was watching helplessly as the bulk of his African paintings slipped from their sling while being hoisted aboard for the return journey and plunged into the blue waters of Cape Town harbour. At the time it felt like part of himself was slowly sinking into the depths.

He'd been only too glad to leave, but now, shivering with cold and fearful for the future, he wondered if the decision had been wise. Despite the rawness of the inhabitants and their ignorance of art, the lifestyle had been pleasant and the climate agreeable to his health. He'd never felt more physically healthy and active in his life. Although missing London, being away from the source of all his troubles had had its advantages. But living out a carefree existence on the fringes of civilisation was not for him. What sort of flabby, mediocre poetry would that have resulted in? The troop ship was carrying him towards his rendezvous with fate. For better or worse, he was armed with a greater purpose than he'd ever previously known.

Hours later, as they crept into port, the already foul weather took a further dip and the drizzle deteriorated into a steady downpour. Grey clouds, floating earthwards, shrouded the elongated cranes, dripping harbour walls and bleak warehouses. The soldiers, shouldering their packs and trying to shake off the after-effects of sea sickness, began to disembark. There were no bands or cheering crowds to welcome them ashore. The glamour, burgeoning in their minds over the past few days, vanished as quickly as the brown water flowing down the town's numerous drains. The wet streets were deserted as they wearily trudged along the sea front towards their temporary billet overlooking the bay.

Gradually the rain eased and the sky turned a little brighter. Just before arriving at the camp, the sun burst through the thinning clouds transforming the grey waves piling up on the beach below into a display of flashing brilliance. Isaac was greatly cheered at the sight and experienced the first, tentative tug of curiosity about his new surroundings. When the men were told later that they would be allowed to visit the town for a few hours, there was a resurgence of excitement.

Leaving the camp with its lines of tattered tents behind them, Isaac set off with Harry Jacobs and two mates to sample the delights of Le Havre. No trace of the recent downpour remained and the sun beat delightfully warm on their heads and backs. He regretted having made no attempt to learn the language, realising too late that his ignorance might prove a major disadvantage. Harry did not agree.

"Don't worry, Rosie, the frogs'll understand what we're looking for. It's not 'ard to get what you want. Where there's a will there's a way, eh? Most of 'em'll understand King's English any'ow, especially if you're willing to pay, wiv all them tourists an' all."

As they entered the town, things looked totally different than they had earlier in the day: bright coloured cafes and shops spilled out into the streets; tables, bedecked with baskets of bread and bottles of wine, beckoned to the strolling soldiers; and French sentries dressed in strange, comic uniforms, their rifles sporting extraordinarily long bayonets, proved particularly interesting to their English counterparts. Posted outside the town hall and various depots close to the docks, they drew in crowds of chortling soldiers who seemed to find them a source of inexhaustible amusement. Everything was infused with a freshness and vitality that fascinated the men, most of whom had never been out of England in their lives.

While not immune to the delights of the bustling seaside town, Isaac began to perceive something altogether different lurking in the background. The laughing soldiers, although unaware of anything unusual, were being stalked and marked out for future attention. With an apprehensive shiver, he sensed the sinister presence was in no hurry; in due time the swinging scythe would garner its human harvest. The theme for a new poem slowly started to take shape in his mind as they wandered down towards the sea front.

"I wonder if we'll get to come back tonight. I'll bet there's plenty of women for the likes of us here an' hereabouts. What do you fink?"

Harry's enquiry interrupted his dark musings. Normally irritated by such frivolity, on this occasion he experienced relief and assumed a light-hearted stance.

"I thought you said all the French whores had the p...pox, Harry."

"Well, maybe I exaggerated slightly. Any port in a storm is what I says. What about you lads? Are you game or what?"

"Chances are we'll not get leave t...tonight anyway. We better make the most of things while we can."

"For fuck sakes, Rosie, give it a rest will ya? Trust you to dwell on the gloomy side of fings all the time. Allow a man to indulge in 'is fantasies for a while. Jesus, look at the arse on 'er; I'd love to climb on board that."

As Isaac guessed, there was no more leave. Their journey to the front was scheduled to resume the following afternoon where they would join the advance party near the town of Bethune. Until then they were confined to the camp. Later that evening, while cleaning his rifle and checking his kit, he prepared to bid farewell to the old life with its endless problems and contradictions. Soon, the past would be stripped away as reality twisted itself into new and grotesque forms. The last line of the poem he'd shown to Major Abrahams flashed through his mind.

Spring! God pity your mood.

Chapter Three

1916

We made straight for the trenches, but we've had vile weather and I've been wet through for four days and nights.... We've had shells bursting two yards off, bullets whizzing all over the show but all you are aware off is the agony in your heels.
Extract from letter to Mrs Seaton: June 1916

...In spite of the most adverse weather conditions the men have kept up a remarkably cheerful spirit and have at all times done their work very well. They have been employed on patrol duty, wiring, digging, sentry duty and machine-gun work, and I trust that they will benefit from the experience gained. They have seen two mines fired, and have been shelled, trench mortared and rifle grenaded...
Extract from CO (Black Watch) describing the initiation of the 11th Battalion of the Kings Own Royal Lancasters into the trenches: June 1916

August 1914

What in our lives is burnt
In the fire of this?
The heart's dear granary?
The much we shall miss?

Three lives hath one life—
Iron, honey, gold.
The gold, the honey gone—
Left is the hard and cold.

Iron are our lives
Molten right through our youth.
A burnt space through ripe fields,
A fair mouth's broken tooth.

1916

Isaac sat hunched over a grubby sheet of paper. His efforts to protect it from the driving rain were proving less than successful.

On a break from repairing shell damage to a nearby support trench, he was endeavouring to improve the first draft of a poem completed only yesterday. The new version was so much better, he regretted having sent off the original holograph in such a hurry. He knew, however, that he had little choice in the matter. The combination of a poor memory and an alarming propensity to misplace things, forced him to despatch manuscripts almost before the ink had dried. Fear that fate might intervene and put an abrupt end to his strivings also provided a powerful incentive to act quickly.

All morning he and two companions had been shovelling gallons of mud into a massive hole in the trench wall, and forcing waterlogged sandbags back into place. The labour was heavy and unrelenting. Apart from being exhausted, soaked and covered in filth, he was convinced that the heel of his left boot was chaffing exposed bone.

His battalion had moved into this sector, north of Loos, for training "under fire" just over a week ago. Attached to a unit of the Blackwatch, the men were supposed to be acquiring survival skills from the battle-hardened veterans of Ypres, but, so far, Isaac had seen very little of them.

Approaching the front for the first time, Isaac felt as if he was crossing a spiritual as well as a physical boundary. In the ruined town of Hulluch, the low mist, hanging like a veil between two worlds, merely added to his growing sense of unreality. The rumble of distant shellfire sounded like the rumour of a storm that had passed over and moved on.

As the men marched past shell holes filled with stagnant water, and shattered buildings, pointing snaggle-toothed at the sky, Isaac felt death had shuffled significantly closer. Beyond the margin of jumbled masonry, the devastation continued: jagged tree trunks, black and branchless, seemed frozen in final twists of anguish, while the earth, churned up into a vast ocean of mud, was traversed by a network of ruptured and semi-submerged duckboards. Petrol smeared the men's boots with its sickly colours and Isaac noticed countless items of scrap scattered all around. These ranged from mountains of tins to massive fragments of artillery equipment; the rusting detritus of an army dug in for a long campaign.

His dismay was not dispelled when he noticed soldiers at the front of the line plunging off the buckled walkways into a quagmire reaching up to their thighs. They had entered the intricate network of reserve trenches which the unseasonal weather had rendered almost impassable. This was not at all what he'd imagined, although it was hard now to visualise any other possibility.

He almost lost a boot, and was forced to grope around in the stinking, yellow ooze for a few moments before locating it. Since his footwear was two sizes too big—due to the constant friction he suffered—the incident was hardly surprising. Unfortunately, the CSM, anxious to keep the soldiers moving along, failed to sympathise, and ordered the private to stumble on without retying his laces properly. Inevitably, the boot escaped again, and the purple-faced sergeant major forced him to remain pressed against the sodden sandbags while the others struggled by.

A few hours later, squeezed into a dripping dugout with three other men, Isaac wondered how he was going to survive the next few days, never mind the end of the war. It occurred to him that looking too far ahead was inadvisable—the sensible approach being to deal with problems as they arose; only by living from moment to moment could one possibly retain a fix on things out here. Like a snail stripped of its shell, its soft innards exposed to stabbing beaks, he felt terribly vulnerable. Survival would require new strategies on his part. Although only a few miles removed from civilisation, he felt as if he was on a different planet.

Suddenly aware that a soldier with three stripes on his arm was staring intently down at him, Isaac struggled to his feet and pushed the paper inside his tunic in anticipation of a roasting. A heavily accented voice put him at his ease.

"Sit where ye are, laddy. A didnae mean tae disturb ye. A wiz jist interested in what ye were doin', that's all; bein' a bit nosy a suppose ye might say. Ma name's Jim Webster; what dae they cry you?"

Isaac struggled for a moment to understand the question; the strange dialect was unfamiliar to him, but there was no mistaking the friendly tone.

"Isaac...Isaac Rosenberg."

"Well, Isaac, it's nice tae meet you." Webster smiled and stuck out a huge hand. The callused palm felt like rough bark against his skin.

The Scotsman, although only two or three inches taller than Isaac, was much broader with burly shoulders. His knees and calves, jutting out below the regulation grey kilt, looked as thick as tree trunks. In contrast to this formidable warrior, Isaac felt wholly inadequate. And yet the humour glinting in the depths of Webster's grey eyes and apparent in the quirky upturn of his thin mouth, belied the impression conveyed by the rough exterior; even the jaunty slant of an eyebrow and the intricate tracery of laughter lines suggested a rare sensitivity. It was hard to work out his age; anywhere between thirty and forty, Isaac guessed.

"I could see ye were working hard; maybe a letter home to yer folks."

Encouraged by the friendly tone, Isaac admitted to having completed the second draft of a new poem. Webster's eyes widened in amazement. He slowly eased back his helmet and massaged his forehead with the tips of his fingers.

"Well, my God, yer a poet then. Would ye mind very much giving me a wee keek at what you've written? It's just that ye don't run into poetry very often in this place."

Isaac could discern nothing disparaging or mocking in Webster's tone; he appeared to be genuinely interested. Since joining up, only Major Abrahams, back at the training camp near Aldershot, had shown any regard for his work; the response of officers, NCOs and fellow privates was normally hostile. He fished the crumpled poem back out of his pocket and handed it over, hoping the show of interest had not been a ruse to put him at his ease as a prelude to ridicule.

Webster slowly hunkered down into the shallow dugout, flattened out the paper and began to read.

Break of Day in the Trenches

The darkness crumbles away.
It is the same old druid Time as ever,
Only a live thing leaps my hand,
A queer sardonic rat,
As I pull the parapet's poppy
To stick behind my ear.
Droll rat, they would shoot you if they knew
Your cosmopolitan sympathies.
Now you have touched this English hand
You will do the same to a German
Soon, no doubt, if it be your pleasure
To cross the sleeping green between.
It seems you inwardly grin as you pass
Strong eyes, fine limbs, haughty athletes,
Less chanced than you for life,
Bonds to the whims of murder,
Sprawled in the bowels of the earth,
The torn fields of France.
What do you see in our eyes
At the shrieking iron and flame
Hurled through still heavens?
What quaver—what heart aghast?
Poppies whose roots are in man's veins
Drop, and are ever dropping;
But mine in my ear is safe—
Just a little white with the dust.

As the moments passed, Isaac experienced more than a twinge of anxiety. He desperately wanted to be understood. Already, dismay, dark as the filthy water lapping the trench walls, had seeped into him. Instead of diluting his creative juices, however, the process appeared to be having the opposite effect. This was the third poem in so many days.

"The five lines after *What d...do you see in our eyes* are new. I think they get across the p...point quite well."

The sergeant said nothing.

"Apart from that I've only made a few minor alterations..."

Tailing off into silence, he felt superfluous, and forced himself to stand still without uttering another word. Suddenly he remembered the work detail; his break had officially ended at least five minutes ago. Corporal Green would be furious. He reconciled himself to the punishment that would inevitably result from his tardiness. Perhaps it would be worth it.

Webster turned round and handed back the manuscript. Astonished, Isaac saw his rugged face was wet with tears.

"My God, laddie..." He hardly seemed able to continue. "A've never read anything quite like that before."

Although deeply flattered, Isaac felt the urgent need to excuse himself; every minute that passed would add to the severity of the retribution meted out.

"I'm s...sorry, Sergeant but I think I'd better get back to w...work now; I've overrun my break, I'm afraid."

Staring at nothing in particular, water dripping down his helmet and nose, Webster dragged himself back to the banality of the present. He smiled suddenly, his eyes twinkling.

"Don't worry yersel' about that, son. A've got a few questions tae ask ye about yer poem. Where were ye working?"

Seconds later, Isaac found himself struggling to keep up as they waded along. Turning into the support trench, he noticed his two mates hard at work, and Corporal Green staring furiously at him as they approached. Ignoring the Scot, Green started yelling.

"Where the hell do you think you've been? I'll have you on a fucking charge for this."

Webster coolly placed a hand on his shoulder.

"The lad's been wi' me, Corporal, engaged in some important work that wouldnae wait."

Eyeball to eyeball, Green began to waver. Although relishing his power, and loath to lose any opportunity to abuse the private, he felt the moment slipping away. There was something about this man that cautioned against confrontation. An over-inflated sense of his own importance, and an unwillingness to appear foolish in front of the others, however, overcame this initial reluctance.

"But, Sergeant, he was supposed to be back here ten minutes ago. I've no choice but to…"

"A've already told ye, son"—Webster's voice, although even, cut across the corporal's—"that he was helpin' me out. And, as a matter of fact, a'll be needin' his assistance with something else now, so maybe ye'd better get stuck in yersel'. That wall will need tae be repaired before the colonel makes his inspection at three o'clock. Dae ye understand what a'm sayin'?"

Thoroughly intimidated, Green gave way.

"Okay, Sarge, no bother. I'll see the job's done."

The Scotsman smiled, the underlying threat now removed.

"Right ye are, Corporal, carry on then."

He turned, signalling Isaac to follow, and started back up the trench. As they disappeared round the corner, Green muttered, "Fuckin' Jock bastard," and picked up a spare shovel. The two privates exchanged a brief wink.

Webster, still grinning, glanced round at the small soldier limping along behind him.

"I can see ye've had some trouble frae yon. Let me know if he gives ye any mair. I'm sorry tae admit that it would give me considerable pleasure tae ram ma fist down his Sassenach throat. That foot of yours looks sair; I'll have a look at it if ye like."

Just beyond the reserve line, they entered a large dugout packed with soldiers in kilts; many more than Isaac had seen since his arrival in the sector. The air was thick with smoke, and, at first, he found it difficult to breath. Many of the men shouted enthusiastic greetings as the two pushed their way through the fug; the sergeant was obviously popular and highly regarded by the rank and file.

"Sit yersel' down here, Isaac. I'm sorry about the crush, but at least we can have a chat without being disturbed. Dae ye fancy a cup of tea wi' a wee dash of something stronger maybe?"

"That would be much appreciated."

Isaac could hardly believe his luck. He'd never been treated with such consideration and kindness since joining the army over eight months ago. Thinking about the work detail, especially Corporal Green shovelling mud, brought a rare smile to his lips.

As they sipped at the petroleum-tainted tea, partially disguised by a generous splash of rum, Webster returned to the poem.

"So, tell me why ye picked on that puir wee critur, the rat." The irony in the sergeant's voice underscored a keen interest, and a passion for getting to the heart of things. "The shelling and the fear ye describe are real, God knows; and the lines about the poppies moved me deeply. I tried to memorise them." He sat back against the earth wall, a far away look in his eyes, and began to recite in a sonorous voice, catching the attention of nearby soldiers who ceased their chattering for a few seconds. "*Poppies whose roots are in man's veins/Drop and are ever dropping;' Aye that's it. 'Poppies whose roots are in man's veins.* That's some line! But getting back to that pesky rodent..."

Delighted by the compliment, Isaac, although a little embarrassed that others now appeared to be listening in, tried to explain the rat's central role in his poem.

"It occurred to me that the...the freedom rats enjoy in the trenches is entirely different to what the soldiers experience. I...I suppose they've always existed in our d...darkest nightmares—creatures we subconsciously fear. They seem to appear when...when things are at their worst. They're always around, of course, but...but...hidden."

He paused for a moment, glimpsing the hideous grey shapes bounding through his childhood. Like the trenches, the filthy Whitechapel slums seemed a fitting setting for such vermin. "I've always regarded them as representing some sort of petty evil a…alive in the world. Maybe," Isaac struggled to express himself clearly, "maybe they embody a side of our nature we conceal…even from ourselves." Again he hesitated, deep in thought. "As soon as I arrived it struck me how p…plentiful and…bold they were. It was as if we'd somehow changed places."

"How do you mean?" The sergeant leaned forward, his forehead wrinkled in concentration.

"Well, it was as if a c…c…covert evil had revealed itself. As I said, they seem so brazen, presuming the trenches belong to them…whereas the men have b…been…stripped of their power to exert any freedom of action here at all. Do you see?"

Webster looked thoughtful. Slowly easing himself upright, he stretched his arms above his head and back down again in a long swinging motion; his joints popped like small arms fire.

"I think so. Ye mean that this place and the circumstances we bide in allows the rats to prosper while we perish —that our deaths are the reason for their success? There's certainly no denying the trench rats are bigger and fatter than any I've ever seen before." He gave an involuntary shudder.

"Yes, Sarge, that's about it."

"Call me Jim. We're no on duty now."

Isaac smiled and nodded appreciatively. He felt the awakening of an intimacy denied him for so long. Encouraged by Webster's thoughtful response, his confidence grew and he endeavoured to express what lay at the very heart of the poem.

"Somehow the rats seem to realise the roles have been reversed…. . All men are the same to them whether B…British or German. They have the run of both sets of trenches, passing to and fro without hindrance, while soldiers stay put, victims of a common fate. For me, they—the rats that is—symbolise the darkness that holds us all in thrall; we're…bound and helpless while they flourish. I suppose that's…that's what I meant by *sardonic*."

"Yer maybe right. I never really thought of it like that before. This reversal in roles ye talk about suggests that something's gone far wrong."

"I...I wanted to get across how quickly our highest ideals have been...undermined. And...and men turned into the most abject of slaves."

Webster nodded.

"Aye, I see your meaning clearly enough. Ye've written some poem there, but I wouldnae put yer ideas around too much. If the CO got wind of what ye were sayin' he'd probably have ye court martialled for tryin' tae subvert the war effort. Dinnae worry about them actually seein' yer poetry, mind." Webster moved quickly to quell Isaac's rising panic. "The sensors'll no have a clue what you're on about. Fortunately, maist of our officers are no exactly endowed wi' an excess o' grey matter."

Laughter among the soldiers sitting nearby revealed an appreciation of their sergeant's brand of humour.

Webster suddenly heaved himself off the stool. Donning his helmet, he buttoned up his heavy great coat. Isaac noticed that most of the others had gone; the air was fresher and his breathing a little easier.

"Right, Isaac, I've got to go. Duty calls and all that. You stay here and finish off yer tea. Ye can take it easy for a while. As far as yon corporal's concerned, I've assigned ye to special duties. If anybody asks, refer them tae me." He stared hard at the poet for a few moments. "Maybe I can help ye learn how tae survive out here; keep the rats at bay for a while at any rate. Remember, ye must keep writing whatever happens; somebody's got tae tell things the way they really are. And, who knows, yer poetry might get through to the ignoramuses who think this war's some kind of bloody picnic. Where there's life there's hope; never forget that."

"Thanks, Sergeant...Jim, I mean."

"Yer welcome. But dinnae forget it's sergeant now I'm back on duty." Webster chuckled as he left the dugout. Isaac, lost in thought, continued to sip at his rum-enhanced tea. His teeth had stopped chattering, and he'd actually forgotten about the pain in his heel.

✳

Four nights later, Sergeant Webster dispensed some final words of warning to the assembled group of men.

"Remember what a've telt ye. Keep yer heads down at all times, keep close to the soldier in front, and if the Hun send up a flare, find cover until it's dark again, and for God's sake, don't get tangled up in the wire yer carryin'. All being well, ye'll be in no-man's-land for half an hour at the most. Whatever happens, get back to the line when ye hear the order. Is that clear?" The soldiers nodded and grunted. "Right then, stand by for the signal."

The day after Isaac's meeting with Webster, life for the recruits was racked up a notch. The Highlanders, hitherto so inconspicuous, divided the Lancasters into small groups and took charge of their training, instructing them in various aspects of trench warfare, including the hazardous task of patrolling and wiring in no-man's-land. Isaac was delighted when he found himself under the command of his new friend. This was obviously no coincidence. The sergeant had been true to his word.

Webster presented him with two pairs of thick woollen socks and a tin of soothing ointment to smear on his blisters. He also showed him how to "pop" the clusters of lice, attached to his shirt and trouser seams, using a lighted candle. Isaac regarded the tiny bloodsuckers as issuing from the same dark source as the rats; another manifestation of the petty evil allowing vermin to thrive at the expense of their human hosts.

Striving to recall what he'd learned about survival in no-man's-land, Isaac leaned against a firing step awaiting the order to advance. The rain had stopped for the first time since his arrival in the trenches, although the sky remained pitch black without sign of moon or stars. In some ways this was comforting as enemy snipers would be unable to see anything moving on the exposed terrain. Since no lamps were allowed, he didn't really understand how they would be able to locate and repair holes in the shell-damaged barbed wire, but had complete faith in Webster's judgement.

On the agreed signal, Isaac hauled himself over the parapet and, crouching low, followed the dark shape moving just ahead of him. Luckily, he wasn't carrying any wire, though he was labouring under a backpack full of steel pickets. His heart beat wildly and he felt sick with fear. Desperate not to disgrace himself, he fought to retain control and concentrate on the task ahead.

A hissed whisper halted the zigzag advance and the men sank to the ground. The pickets clanked painfully on Isaac's left shoulder as he struggled to maintain his balance. On a further command passed down the line, they continued their advance, albeit a little more cautiously.

The sky suddenly lit up as three scarlet flares burst high above the startled patrol and began their long, slow descent. The sergeant's voice erupted from the shadows ahead.

"Take cover!"

Everything lay painfully exposed in the lustre of the falling stars. The men were roughly chiselled statues rooted to the spot, and the blasted earth appeared to have sprouted sharp stakes like quills on a porcupine's back. Waterlogged shell holes glinted menacingly all around them. Isaac felt the breath smash out of his body as he hit the ground. The rattle of machine-gun fire and the pop-pop of rifles rose to a fearful crescendo in seconds; bullets whined and ricocheted among the prostrate soldiers.

Two new flares hung in the air and a strange, high-pitched wailing grew rapidly in volume.

"Incoming mortar fire—keep yer heads down."

Isaac tore frantically at the earth as the savage metal storm beat around him. When the explosions finally ceased, he began a tentative exploration for injuries, but could find nothing wrong even though his legs felt strangely weak. Aware of men rushing past him, he managed to roll over and rest on his knees before rising unsteadily to his feet. Nearby, a body had been torn into hand-size lumps of flesh, the singed and smoking hole in the grass suggesting a direct mortar hit. Only a few yard to the right and he would have been the hapless victim. The arbitrary allocation of life and death seemed to him entirely consistent with the anarchy prevailing in this infernal region.

He felt a powerful hand grab him by the scruff of his tunic and begin to drag him along. This was fortunate as his legs were barely able to support the weight of his body, despite the fact that the sack of pickets had come adrift. Perhaps he was wounded after all.

A bawled out challenge directly ahead alerted him to the fact they were close to safety. Webster shouted a password and the iron grip on Isaac's uniform loosened as willing hands drew him down into the trench. Another flare soared skywards. Men threw themselves headfirst into the arms of the waiting sentries as enemy snipers opened up once again. Bullets savaged the soggy parapets.

Propped up against a pile of sandbags, recovering from the shock which had temporarily affected his mobility, Isaac listened to Webster's preliminary report.

"I don't know what happened, sir. The Gerries must have got wind o' us somehow. Maybe somebody in a listening post heard us moving around and managed to get a message back. If that's the case, they're a lot nearer to our front line than we bargained for. I thought I heard something before the flares went up, but I wasn't sure. After that we were sitting ducks."

"Demmed bad luck, Sergeant. How many casualties were there?"

"At least four dead, including the lad I carried back with the shot-up leg. A few others sustained minor injuries but they'll live."

"Your arm looks a bit ripped up, you'd better report to the medic."

"It's nothing, sir. I just caught a bit of shrapnel."

"Nevertheless, get it seen to right away."

"Aye, sir." He bent down to Isaac. "Are ye all right, lad? How dae these legs feel?"

"Fine, Sarge. I'm sorry to have been such a nuisance."

"Don't worry yerself about that. I'll talk tae ye later after I get this arm cleaned up a bit."

"Thanks for getting me back in one piece."

"I wish I could have got everybody back safe and sound. That was a hell of a way tae experience no-man's-land for the first time."

"Sergeant!" the captain's voice interrupted. "Get yourself to the doctor now if you please; and I want your full report as quickly as possible. If there are listening posts so close to our line, there's no time to lose."

"Right ye are, sir. I'm on my way." Webster adjusted his bloody tunic and smiled at Isaac. "Maybe you'd better get the doc tae look ye over just in case. In the meantime, join up wi' the rest of the lads and get yersel' somethin' to eat and a tot of rum. Ye deserve it after that lot."

"I will, Sarge."

He noticed blood running down and dripping from the tips of his friend's outstretched fingers.

Lurching along the trench, a few minutes later, the poet was besieged by a host of nightmarish images. The whine of the mortal shells transformed itself into a shrill, demented scream of terror while the hands of a man drowning in a shell hole desperately beckoned to him. He automatically accepted a tin of bully beef and wolfed down the contents, then immediately fell into a deep sleep, his head thrown back as if in readiness for the slash of a sacrificial knife. Just before dawn it began to rain heavily again.

"So, Isaac, tell me a bit more about yerself. How did ye become a poet in the first place?"

Webster adjusted the sling on his heavily bandaged arm and tried to ease himself into a more comfortable position. According to the patient, a lot of unnecessary fuss had been made about "a daft wee flesh wound".

The two men were sitting on a battered couch in Webster's dugout. The item of furniture took up most of the available space, and even the owner didn't know how it had come to be there in the first place. Unlike most other dugouts, this one was roomy and reasonably dry. The burrow, which Isaac shared with three mates, had been flooded since their arrival and they mostly slept in niches scraped out of the trench walls.

"I'm not sure about that. I've b...been writing poetry for as long as I can remember. I used to paint, but it's hard to get hold of the materials out here."

As they talked, he glanced round frequently at Webster; his hand, grasping a pencil stub, moved rapidly over a sheet of drawing paper.

"I ken yer Jewish, but where did yer family come from? Have they always lived in London?"

"No, my father and mother came from Lithuania before I was born. They lived in Bristol and then moved to London when I was about seven years old. As a matter of fact my father was forced out. The Russians wanted to conscript him into the army and that was the worst thing that could happen to a Jew at the time."

"Why was that?"

"The life of a soldier in the Russian army was b...bad; the life of a Jewish soldier was intolerable."

"You mean due tae racial hatred?"

"Yes, and other things. That's why a lot of them fled abroad to Britain and America—to escape conscription.... . It's ironic that I've ended up in the army. It b...broke my mother's heart when I joined; probably the worst thing that could have happened to me as far as my family was concerned. But I d...didn't see I had much choice at the time."

"You mean there was a lot of pressure on you to join up?"

"In a sense, I suppose. The fact was that I couldn't find work. There seemed no way of earning a living out of selling my p...poetry and p...paintings although, God knows, I tried. I even went to South Africa to seek my fortune but couldn't stand it after a while."

Isaac sat back with a sigh, twiddling the remains of the pencil between his fingers.

"South Africa, eh. Maybe ye should have stayed there. What made ye come back anyway?"

"I felt...out of it somehow. I never thought I would miss London...I suppose I'd lived for years among p...people who were so passionate about art, that South Africa seemed like...like a sort of ...of...self-imposed exile.... . The people were practical and kind enough, although when it came to appreciating art...they were deaf and b...blind. I thought maybe I could change things—somehow make them more aware. I even gave a series of lectures on past and future trends in European art.... . B...but getting back home became the most important thing after a few months."

Webster smiled a little bleakly. "Out of the frying pan intae the fire, in a manner of speaking."

"You're right. This place is a bit like South Africa...barbaric and...sterile, although perhaps"—his tone assumed a mocking edge—"somewhat more dangerous." With a sigh, he continued his drawing.

"Were ye brought up in the Jewish faith then?"

"Yes. Before my father fled from Lithuania, he was training to be a rabbi but, of course, that came to nothing. He ended up a p...peddler, on the road for half the year selling stuff nobody really wanted. I suppose I must have been a great d...disappointment to him.... . I never took much interest in the synagogue. Fairly early on it seemed to me a way of imprisoning your soul, not freeing it."

"Aye. I can understand that right enough." Webster appeared thoughtful for a moment. "So, have ye given up on religion then?"

"No, I wouldn't say so. But my father would be shocked if he knew what I really believe... . It's hard to understand, after all that's happened, why he still clings to a god who's forsaken him and made a mockery of his entire life."

Amazed at the intensity of the response, Webster said nothing. After a long pause, Isaac continued, his voice now more calm and even:

"I do believe though, that man is capable of freeing himself. Maybe we have to hit rock-bottom before things will get b...better; it could be that this war has to be fought before people can change." He halted and stared into space. "Perhaps there is a part of us which...which is p...perfectible, but in perpetual conflict with...with contrary impulses."

The sergeant's eyes lit up as he leaned forward, thoroughly absorbed by the topic.

"Dae ye think these impulses are inside us or linked tae something beyond ourselves then?"

"Both. But the important thing is that we aspire to be more than we are and rise above the pettiness that drags us into the mud."

"That's deep, but I suppose it's all in yer poem really."

"I've tried to include it in every poem I've written."

Isaac began to recite in a slow, monotonous voice.

Moses, from whose loins I sprung,
Lit by a lamp in his blood
Ten immutable rules, a moon
For mutable lampless men.

The blonde, the bronze, the ruddy,
With the same heaving blood,
Keep to the moon of Moses,
Then why do they sneer at me?

Isaac turned round with a lop-sided smile.

"Something I wrote when life was…particularly difficult. It seems to me that our p…potential to…rise above things, is so easily lost in irrational p…prejudice. Sometimes nothing makes much sense really."

There was a profound silence before Isaac broke the spell.

"So what about you, Jim? Tell me something about your life."

The Scotsman sighed.

"It's funny, you know, but maybe we've got more in common than ye think."

Sitting back on the couch, he smiled wryly at Isaac.

"How so?"

"For a start, our faithers are similar in a way. Both of them were dispossessed and both stuck tae a strong religious point of view in spite of bein' kicked in the teeth for their pains. Ma faither lost his house and his land over forty years ago. He struggled tae feed his family on starvation wages and work a strip of soil that yielded precious little.

Until his dyin' day though, he swore by a church that had washed its hands of him."

"Why did you join up?"

"Out of necessity, lad. We've been promised land if we survive. And they're sworn tae look after our families if we don't pull through."

"Do you believe them?"

"I'm not sure, but there's nothing else for it. There's no work but at the behest of the landlords. If ye stir things up, ye'll maist likely be out of a job, and a house. The last thing ye want is tae see yer family go hungry."

Webster bowed his head unable to speak for a moment. When he resumed, his voice was uncharacteristically sombre.

"Maybe…when all this is over, we'll emigrate tae Canada. I've been trying tae save as much as I can. At least army pay is regular and, let's face it, there's no much tae spend it on out here, is there now?" A spark of humour flickered somewhere deep in his eyes. "In many ways yer right, Isaac. It's as if some power works tae the detriment of man. But, on the other hand, there's a beauty all around us, if ye can see it. Even here, there's the remains of farming land ma faither would have marvelled at. I don't know about the folk that lived near ye in London, but our neighbours wouldnae see ye go short if there was bread on their table. A ken that my ain family'll be fine unless the whole community starves. That's the way of it now, and that's the way it's always been."

"My mother's like that…. Maybe that's how it was back in Lithuania, but there's many who've taken advantage of her kindness." Again, Isaac sounded bitter. "You're lucky to be able to count on others. London's full of p…people who would cut your throat for a farthing. Mind you, I have received help from surprising sources; it would be unfair to say otherwise…although…the giving was not always…unconditional. But you're right—there is a kindness in some which almost redeems the greed and selfishness all around us."

"I believe folk have a wellspring of compassion; it's a natural impulse tae want tae help others in times o' need."

Isaac nodded.

"I admire your idealism; without it we're nothing, but sometimes it's hard to see beyond all this. Sometimes I feel so...so helpless."

Ending lamely, he gazed at his drawing for a moment, before laying the gnawed pencil on his lap.

"I think I've finished."

He handed the sheet of paper over to Webster who stared with incredulity at a face whose strength and resolution he'd long since forgotten existed.

"I'd like you to accept this as a token of my esteem and thanks for all you've done. It's clear there's still some hope left when..." Isaac suddenly faltered, emotion welling up inside at the thought of leaving his new friend behind.

Webster leaned over and patted the slight back with his good hand.

"If ye get a chance, send me some mair of yer poems. I suppose I've always valued poetry for allowing me tae see things mair clearly. Whatever happens ye must keep writin', even if people dinnae seem tae understand. When things are really bad, think about the bairns back home who deserve better. They'll need all the help they can get when this lot's over and done wi'."

Next day, in the midst of a ferocious artillery attack, the eleventh battalion of the Kings Own Royal Lancasters left the front en route for a further period of training behind the lines at Bruary. Apart from the odd sentry, the battle-hardened Gordons seemed to have gone to ground again—the winding, muddy trenches given over to the hostility of the barrage and the lashing rain. Even the rats appeared to be seeking shelter from the extremes of weather and enemy gunfire.

Attempting to escape the depressing reality of the present, Isaac focused on the miracle of meeting a man like Webster in the midst of such horror; someone who, despite the brutal nature of his existence, had retained his humanity and broad perspective on life. He feared his own efforts to surmount the terrible privations in store might prove less successful. Recording the descent of civilisation into its present sinkhole would make considerable, perhaps impossible demands on him.

A newfound determination buoyed him up as the shellfire dropped behind and the nightmare lifted to reveal some semblance of normality. He felt like a dreamer who having wakened is joyously reunited with the familiar and reassuring. He knew, though, with dreadful certainty, that the rats would return for him, dragging him back into the darkness he feared most of all.

Chapter Four

1916-17

...Since I wrote last I have been given a job behind the lines and very rarely go into the trenches. My address is c/o 40th Divisional Coy Officer. B.E.F... Pte I Rosenberg 22311. It is more healthy but not absolutely safe from shells as we get those noisy visitors a good many times a day even here.

Extract from letter to Edward Marsh; August 1916.

...That my health is undermined I feel sure of; but I have only lately been medically examined, and absolute fitness was the verdict... I have been in the trenches most of 8 months I've been here and the continual damp and exposure is whispering to my old friend consumption, and he may hear the words they say in time...

Extract from letter to Edward Marsh; January 1917.

...Ever since November, when we first started on our long marches, I have felt weak; but it seems to be some inscrutable mysterious quality of weakness that defies all doctors...

All through this winter I have felt most crotchety, all kinds of small things interfering with my fitness. My hands would get chilblains or bad boots would make my feet sore; and this

aggravating a general run-down-ness. I have not felt too happy.
I have gone less warmly clad during the winter than through the
summer, because of the increased liveliness on my clothes. I've
been stung into what we call "dumping" a great part of my
clothing, as I thought it wiser to go cold than lousy...
  Extracts from letters to Gordon Bottomley; February 1917 and
  April 1917 respectively.

Home Thoughts From France

Wan, fragile faces of joy!
Pitiful mouths that strive
To light with smiles the place
We dream we walk alive.

To you I stretch my hands,
Hands shut in pitiless trance
In the land of ruin and woe,
The desolate land of France.

Dear faces startled and shaken,
Out of wild dust and sounds
You yearn to me, lure and sadden
My heart with futile bounds.

  1916

Outside, the summer morning was perfect. The blue dome of the sky, flooded with sunlight, provided a welcome relief from the dark rain clouds belying endlessly in from the west. Although gradually heating up, the inside of the hut, where Isaac sat hunched over a small desk, was not yet uncomfortable enough to distract him from his various clerical duties.

The Salvage "Office", where he now worked, was some way behind the straggling support lines near Lens—out of range of enemy field artillery but within the compass of their heavy guns. Still, he was relatively safe here and it was a considerable relief to be away from the dangers and discomforts of the trenches. His joy at sleeping in a proper bed was only slightly diminished by the fact that he shared the tiny barracks hut with three privates and a lance corporal. For the first time since arriving in France, Isaac had free time on his hands and, although there was little to read, he was working on some new poems and catching up with correspondence.

The transfer remained something of a mystery. His health had certainly been indifferent recently, but it was unlikely this was the reason for the move. More likely his reputation as a poet had got around and the CO had decided to put his literary talents to some practical use.

Harry Jacobs dropped in to see him most days. Temporarily attached to a unit of the Royal Engineers, he was helping rebuild a nearby field hospital damaged in recent shellfire, and, like Isaac, was glad to be out of the line for a spell.

Yesterday, over a cup of tea laced with a generous helping of "medicinal" brandy, the diminutive cockney had passed on some gossip gleaned from one of his new workmates.

"Apparently this used to be a nice quiet sector until some Guards regiment moved in two months ago and fucked fings up good and proper. Accordin' to Nick, it was them that broke the truce and let loose on old Fritz. Naturally he retaliated in kind and 'asn't stopped since."

There was certainly no denying German determination to employ a range of offensive tactics. When the Lancasters first arrived, the trenches were routinely mortared, and snipers, primed to shoot at anything that moved, picked off the unwary. Dozens died before the men adjusted to the hostile conditions. Even behind the lines, roads often came under intense shelling, which could erupt at any time of the day or night.

"The hospital was meant to be out of range of the Gerry guns, but some silly bastard at Brigade got it wrong. Any'ow Nick was tellin' me that the CO is keen to get things back on the old footing, but the Hun is suspicious, of course. Maybe they'll see sense eventually— just when we're movin' out, knowin' our luck!"

Finishing the documentation, Isaac slowly rose to his feet, stretched, and stepped outside for a breath of fresh air. A fitful breeze cooled droplets of sweat on his forehead. There was no one else around and everything was unusually quiet; perhaps the Germans were beginning to ease up a little bit at long last.

He seated himself on the hut steps, now bathed in sunlight, and gave some thought to the reply he intended to pen in response to Marsh's latest harsh criticism of "Moses" and the batch of war poems his sister Annie had sent on to him. He'd been shaken by his mentor's blistering— no-holds-barred—attack. It was incredible that in the wake of Gordon Bottomley's praise, he should find himself once again confronted with outright disapproval. As usual, he was flattered by the fact that Marsh had taken time to respond to his work in such a detailed way, but it was dawning on him that the gulf between their two worlds could never be bridged. Marsh simply failed to grasp the radical shake-up in style and structure required to express something of the realities he and his fellow-soldiers faced each day In any case, Isaac, always reluctant to conform to standards dictated by literary convention, believed that circumstances now left him little choice but to jettison the remainder of this cumbersome ballast. Although things had recently improved, life remained precarious, and his yen to seize the moment eclipsed all other considerations. Yet, despite his intense irritation arising from Marsh's disapproval, he appreciated the need to remain pragmatic; links with home were vitally important to his sense of well-being; and after the war he would need all the help and support he could get.

The peace of the morning was suddenly shattered by the howl of shells passing close overhead, followed almost immediately by another flight, then another. Harry was right—things were still hot. He wondered whether the German artillery unit was targeting the busy roads, probably packed out with supply wagons at this time of day, or the hospital again. It was hard to understand why they continued to wage war on the wounded; surely the desire for revenge could not have eclipsed all moral considerations?

A hundred yards to his left, a huge pillar of earth leapt into the air and mushroomed out before crashing back to the ground. The detonation resonated painfully inside his head, while rogue stones, lethal as bullets, smashed into the hut's wooden planks and ricocheted noisily off the corrugated iron roof. He stared over at the smoking crater; either the enemy was responding to recent intelligence, or the gun's crew had made a serious miscalculation. As if in answer, shells began to rain all around. Isaac flung himself to the ground, raking desperately at the frazzled soil with his fingers. For a terrible moment he imagined himself blasted into atoms by a direct hit.

The attack was over in seconds, the air cleared, and Isaac lurched to his feet, barely able to stand at first but glad to be alive. Brushing the yellowy earth from his uniform, he spotted another eight shell holes nearby, one less than twenty yards away. The sun, almost at its zenith, lit up the pall of dust like a shimmering curtain. He noticed the office hut was still standing, although the dirty panes of glass were gone and the wooden walls were severely warped and lacerated in places. Offering up a silent prayer for his life, he staggered over and peered inside. The floor and every other surface, including his battered, old desk, were littered with glass. He sat down on the bottom step and covered his face with his hands. Some lines from the poem he was working on, ran through his mind again and again as he fought back a wave of nausea. *In the land of ruin and woe,/The desolate land of France.... Dear faces startled and shaken,/Out of wild dust and sounds...*

Almost an hour later, he started out of a thick stupor, vaguely aware that a voice was shouting from the track that meandered between the field hospital and support trenches. It was hard to know how long he'd been in this state; his head was muzzy and he still felt sick. Glancing up, he saw Harry approaching, his gnome-like face wrinkled with concern.

"Hello, Rosie. You all right?"

Isaac experienced a sudden wave of disorientation and couldn't quite remember where he was. For a moment he thought they were back in the training camp at Blackdown. The feeling passed quickly, and he managed a strained smile.

"I'm fine...I think. Just a bit shaken up. What are you doing here?"

Harry nodded and continued without answering the question.

"Gerry certainly gave you what for, didn't he! What did you do to irritate him then?"

His friend could always find an appropriate quip even in the worst of situations.

"I wish I knew. At first the shells were overhead...then one l...landed...then the rest."

"The bastards 'ave been busy this morning. Shelled the road, and the 'ospital again, didn't they! Road's full of dead 'orses and smashed-up carts; it's like a bleedin' abattoir up there right now. The CO's livid. Jesus, it's safer back in the trenches, ain't it?"

Isaac nodded in dumb agreement. He wondered if he was really any better off than before.

"You've got a cut on your fore'ead, Rosie. Not much like but we'd better clean it up. Don't want your 'ead to fall off now, do we? You're shakin' like a leaf, mate; drink some of this—it'll make you feel better."

He produced a half bottle of brandy from his inside pocket and handed it over. Not for the first time, Isaac marvelled at Harry's astonishing foraging skills.

"'Ave you got dressings 'ere?"

"Yes, inside the hut, bottom drawer of the d...desk I think. Watch out for the glass; it's covered everything in there."

He felt faint again and lay down on the dry earth. Harry continued his cheery discourse.

"You weren't fucking joking, s'cuse the French? Ah ha, 'ere we go—just where you said they'd be."

While he cleaned up the cut and applied a bandage, Harry talked non-stop. Isaac found the sound of his voice comforting.

"You'll be fine and dandy in a jif. I fink you're suffering from shock; 'ardly surprising really, when you think about it. Captain Edward's sent me down to check if you was all right. He thought some of the shells 'ad dropped short like. He wasn't wrong neither. You was lucky, Rosie. Where's the rest of your unit then?"

"They went to check a consignment of wire that GHQ are hoping to salvage. They're due back about now, I think."

Harry went quiet for a moment. When he resumed, his tone was subdued.

"How many of 'em was there?"

"Four, including a corporal."

"It's just that...there were some lads lying next to a shell 'ole up the road a bit. I didn't stop to check 'em out properly 'cause I was worried you might 'ave been..."

Isaac staggered to his feet. "That's probably them; could they still have been alive, do you think?"

"It's 'ard to tell, Rosie. They all looked dead to me. 'Ere, let me give you an 'and."

A few minutes later, shielding his eyes against the bright sun, Isaac made out four shapes sprawled near a massive crater just beyond the rutted track. Forgetting his own light-headedness for a moment, he rushed over, praying they would not be his comrades. The prayer was unavailing—it was them all right. Corporal Spence lay dead, his spine twisted out of his tunic like some strange souvenir he'd slung over his back and was carrying home. For a long moment, Isaac stared, fascinated by the rearing vertebrae gleaming red and white in the strong light. The heads and upper torsos of two others were mangled beyond recognition, any former human attributes absent; the fourth, a little further back, appeared to have escaped the worst of the blast and, pressing his ear against the man's chest, Isaac thought he could detect a faint heartbeat.

"I think Chadwick's still alive, Harry; we'll have to g…get him to a doctor. There's a handcart behind the hut. Maybe we can wheel him along in it."

"It's worth a try at any rate."

Harry rushed off to find the barrow while Isaac cradled Chadwick's head on his lap. He'd lately come to appreciate the company of the young private who'd slept in the bunk next to his. They'd enjoyed some interesting conversations, especially after discovering a mutual admiration for William Blake.

At the hospital, Harry managed to persuade a harried medic to check for vital signs. Shaking his head, the doctor turned away.

"His neck's broken, probably the impact of the explosion." Seeing Isaac's forlorn expression, he relented a little. "I suppose he might have just been alive when you found him but there was nothing you could have done. I'm sorry."

Reporting to the senior officer on duty, Isaac explained what had happened to his comrades. The captain nodded sympathetically.

"We'll get replacements sent down as soon as possible. Most likely day after tomorrow. In the meantime you hold the fort, there's a good fellow."

He was pleased when Harry managed to get permission to accompany him back and stay the night. It would have been difficult to face the silent hut on his own.

Over a meal consisting of jam mopped out of a tin with slabs of stale bread, Harry returned to a matter which had been preying on his mind for over a fortnight.

"Did you mention my…problem to your friend in London? I don't want to rush you like. It's just that…"

"Yes. I sent off the letter last week, d…directly to Whitehall so Marsh would get it quicker."

Isaac made an effort to cheer his companion up. He was beginning to feel better and was eager to show he'd not forgotten his promise.

"I'll remind him again. We should hear from him very soon. D…don't worry, he'll help out, I'm sure."

"Anything 'e can do will be appreciated. It's just that my mother'll be in a right state about fings now, and there's the kids to think about wiv Doris dead an' all."

It was a fortnight since Harry's mother had written to tell him his sister had died in childbirth. Reading between the lines, it was clear she wasn't coping well. They'd always been a close-knit family and he was desperate to get back home to help her through this hard time. The situation was worsened by the fact that she was having to care for her daughter's two orphaned children, their father having been killed at Mametz in July. The army had refused him compassionate leave so Isaac had undertaken to contact Marsh in the hope that his patron might be able to bring some pressure to bear.

It suddenly occurred him that Marsh's criticism of his poetry was trivial in comparison. Thinking about his own family and what they must be going through, he wondered how he could have become so obsessed and selfish. Weeks would pass during which he hardly spared a thought for their plight. In a recent letter, Annie had written how desperate their mother was to get him back in one piece, and the hours Barnett spent praying in the synagogue for his safe return. Apparently, Hacha begged her daughter every day to write to the authorities demanding Isaac's immediate discharge on health grounds. The war was taking its toll on everyone, not just those struggling to survive at the front.

"I'm off to get some kip. I'll see you in the morning."

Harry managed a ghost of his normal cheery grin.

"Goodnight, Harry. Th…thanks for keeping me company; I really appreciate it."

"You should get some sleep as well, Rosie—you look terrible."

"Yes, I will in a few minutes. I've just got something to finish up here first."

"For God's sake, give the bleedin' poetry a rest for a day or two, will ya."

"It's not a poem, actually. I just want to get started on that letter to Marsh while things are fresh in my mind."

Harry looked sheepish for a moment.

"Well, don't take too long about it, you needs your rest."

"Don't worry, I'll be fine, really."

"Goodnight then."

With a sigh, Isaac picked up a sheet of paper and started writing:

...By now, you must have read a letter I wrote on behalf of a friend, and sent to Whitehall to reach you during the day, as it was so pressing. I trust you have been able to do something; as it is rough luck on the poor fellow.

I was most glad to get your letter and criticism. You know the conditions I have always worked under, and particularly with this last lot of poems. You know how earnestly one must wait on ideas (you cannot coax real ones to you) and let, as it were, a skin grow naturally round and through them. If you are not free, you can only, when the ideas come hot, seize them with the skin in tatters raw, crude, in some parts beautiful in others monstrous. Why print it then? Because these rare parts must not be lost. I work more and more as I write into more depth and lucidity...

✳

Flight Lieutenant Max Schmidt leaned over the side of his Albatross D11 scanning the ground below for signs of troop movement. This was his tenth sortie since Sunday and he didn't know when there might be a let-up in the punishing routine. He was often required to fly twice a day as a result of the acute shortage of experienced pilots. Many of the raw recruits, drafted in to replace casualties, were barely able to get their planes airborne in rough weather. Engaging the enemy or carrying out useful reconnaissance missions were out of the question until they had accumulated more flying hours.

Because of the thick cloud base, he was flying well below the recommended fifteen-hundred-feet ceiling. His unease was compounded by the laboured roar of the aircraft's six-cylinder engine as he battled to maintain a level course in the face of a strong easterly head wind. Peering at his instruments, Schmidt calculated he had less than half an hour's flying time remaining. So far he'd seen nothing of note and hoped to avoid contact with enemy aircraft. Despite carving a fifteenth notch onto the fuselage of the Albatross yesterday afternoon, the prospect of aerial combat in present conditions was not a welcome one; the air was freezing, the wind choppy, and hailstones periodically rattled into the cockpit. The cold, which had begun to torture his feet half an hour ago, was now creeping up his legs.

Most of the time, it was hard to differentiate anything much on the ground; the grey sky merged with the bleak landscape, making it impossible to tell where enemy trenches ended and their own began. Sometimes, when the gradient rose a little, he could make out the distinctive white zigzag streaks facing each other across narrow sections of no-man's-land. High Command believed that enemy troops and supplies were being drafted into the sector for an imminent push, hence the increase in air reconnaissance. Schmidt and his fellow officers were convinced that campaigning would not be resumed until the spring when conditions were far more favourable. Although entirely plausible, the argument had been firmly rejected and he and his colleagues were being forced to pay the price.

The aircraft was suddenly buffeted from side to side by a fierce cross-wind, lost height and almost went into a spin. He levelled out, preparing to ascend to his previous position, but movement on the ground caught his eye and he swooped down to investigate. Squinting over the cockpit, he was amazed to see a large company of soldiers weighed down with guns, ammunition and full packs, struggling along as rapidly as the appalling ground conditions would allow. Perhaps the generals had been right after all.

He circled round and pushed the stick down, nosing the plane into a steep descent. The men threw themselves to the ground as he roared a few feet over their heads. On the spur of the moment, he decided to give the bastards something to really think about. Such an attack would validate the worth of these missions – at least in his own mind. He'd been ordered to avoid offensive tactics but the target was just too tempting to ignore.

Schmidt banked steeply and dived towards the soldiers. Some were swinging their rifles to their shoulders, kneeling and taking aim. Good luck to them; his chances in such an encounter were more than favourable. His twin Spandua machine guns barked loudly and a hail of bullets spat among the cringing puppets below. He had the intense satisfaction of seeing three or four of them throw up their hands and pitch forward into the mud. Glancing back over his shoulder, he was just in time to spot a number of tiny flashes followed by the whine of a bullet passing close to his left ear. At least one of his adversaries was a keen marksman and bent on revenge. Another bullet thudded harmlessly into the wing. He'd made his point and it was time to return to the aerodrome; the dark winter afternoon was advancing and he was running low on fuel.

He rose up into the swirling clouds, wind and sleet tearing through the wing struts. He would have to provide a convincing story to account for the used ammunition. His CO was a hard man to satisfy and invariably disapproved of any kind of foolhardy behaviour. On the other hand, engaging vulnerable troops on the ground always alleviated personal frustration without seriously jeopardising his chances of survival. He tried not to think about the average three-week lifespan of operational pilots in the war zone as his plane burst through the cloud cover and rose high into the luminous air. He gazed in awe at the vast arena of light opening below him. The sun, on its low winter trajectory, lay just above the angry grey mantle turning blood-red around the edges. Things were so different up here in this rarefied domain poised between heaven and earth. He never failed to experience inner tranquillity as fear and aggression sloughed away to be replaced by a sense of childlike wonder. Schmidt always felt he'd gained a measure of absolution before returning to the chaotic world below.

✳

As the pilot returned to base, his victims endeavoured to pick up the pieces and continue their interrupted march. Covered in filth from his headlong dive into a shell hole, Isaac experienced a surge of dizziness which left him light-headed and unsteady on his feet for a few moments. He almost envied the lot of the dead men stiffening in the mud. The plane, dropping out of the dark sky like a harpy dispatched by the gods to punish erring mankind, could just as easily be perceived as an instrument of divine deliverance. This hell on earth was not a place where one would wish to suffer indefinitely.

Within minutes the company were wading on, the wounded helped along by their comrades. The dead, left where they'd fallen, would be retrieved and buried later.

The route marches, occurring on a daily basis, whatever the weather, were designed to fool enemy observers into believing that reinforcements were being pulled into the area in preparation for a major offensive. After six weeks without a break they were taking their toll on Isaac's health, leaving him weaker than ever. Added to the freezing conditions while standing watch or sleeping out in the open, he was finding it increasingly difficult to function. The other men suffered too, of course. Even Harry, normally resilient enough in the face of harsh circumstances, was beginning to buckle under the pressure.

Conditions in the back area of the Somme, where battalions were sent to recuperate between periods of active duty on the front line, were unspeakable. Isaac wondered why the French soldiers who'd occupied the sector before being relieved by the Fortieth Division, had left the billets in such a terrible mess. Harry maintained it was all you could expect from a load of garlic-guzzling peasants and it was hard to disagree with him. The fact that no proper latrines existed and the barrack huts were falling to pieces appeared to justify the savage anti-French feeling rife among the men. The frozen or waterlogged soil, depending on conditions, proved impervious to spade work, and they were often forced to defecate into open shell holes and sleep in wet, stinking conditions. Rest periods thus turned into a further ordeal to be survived.

Struggling hard to keep up, Isaac reflected on how desperate life had become in recent months. This morning, unable to push his swollen feet into boots frozen solid during the night, he was forced to stand to in woollen socks. Only after a proper fire was lit and the boots thawed out a little, was it possible to get them on. The duty sergeant soundly upbraided him for being foolish enough to take the things off in the first place. Normally he wouldn't have, but the pain in his feet during the night had been unbearable.

The men were forced to begin their march that day without proper rations because a consignment of tinned beef couldn't be melted in time. Slices of rock-hard bread, issued instead, proved almost impossible to cut and swallow. Isaac recalled, with hopeless nostalgia, those halcyon summer days back in the Salvage Office. That beguiling season, ending abruptly with his return to front-line duties in September, now seemed like a distant dream. Beyond Lens everything blurred in his mind.

Sucked into the biggest mud bath Europe had ever known, the battalion was briefly stationed in the Hebuterne sector, before being pulled south again, eventually occupying the extreme right of the British Line at Rancourt near Bapaume. Four months later, at the start of another dreadful year on the Somme, Isaac found it hard to believe any other life was possible; the warm sun, plentiful rations and delight of hours spent in peaceful reflection, were, for him, trappings of another existence.

The track over the endless expanse of mud had disappeared. It had been there this morning he could have sworn. Maybe like the trenches themselves, it had finally sunk into the stinking grey morass without beginning or end. He tried to remember a poem completed only a few days ago, muttering the lines over and over again as he laboured to place one foot in front of another.

> *Nudes-stark and glistening,*
> *Yelling in lurid glee. Grinning faces*
> *And raging limbs*
> *Whirl over the floor one fire…*
> *…Soon like a demon's pantomime*
> *The place was raging.*
> *See the silhouettes agape,*
> *see the gibbering shadows…*
> *…See gargantuan hooked fingers*
> *Pluck in supreme flesh*
> *To smutch supreme littleness…*

He even managed a brief smile recalling the wild pleasure in stripping naked and tossing louse-infested garments onto a huge bonfire. The men had danced and yelled like savages celebrating a terrible act of revenge on their enemies. Next day, shivering disconsolately round the smoking embers in much reduced layers of clothing, he'd striven to formulate a canvas of the night's activities in his head. Recapturing the essential images, he set to work translating them into verse.

The problems of lice had proliferated since their arrival at Rancourt due to the impossibility of keeping clean. While at rest, uniforms were normally removed for delousing and the men given hot baths. The extreme weather and primitive conditions curtailed these methods of control, and the situation rapidly deteriorated forcing the majority to destroy their infested clothing. Isaac chose increased exposure to the harsh conditions rather than tolerate the plague. His body had recently become covered in open sores where he endlessly scratched to relieve the itching.

As a boy, he'd encountered lice on a number of occasions but his mother always seemed able to deal with the menace. Life was quite different out here. In common with the trench rats, these creatures seemed better "chanced" for survival than the soldiers they tormented.

The survivors arrived back at base after a further hour of heroic struggle through the thawing mud. Isaac felt so shaky and sick, he could barely touch the rations of soggy bully beef doled out along with lumps of biscuit. Later, sitting on a ledge scraped out of the side of a partially collapsed trench, he immediately slid into unconsciousness. When he woke, it was pitch dark and his greatcoat was covered in half an inch of wet snow.

Edward Marsh sat at his desk rereading the latest letter he'd received from Isaac's sister, Annie. He paused over the final paragraph before impatiently sweeping the smudged paper aside.

> *...We therefore hope you will be able to secure Isaac a desk job away from the trenches or perhaps arrange for his return to England. What to do with my mother I really don't know as she is worried to death. I'm sorry to bother you but there's no one else who can help Isaac now...*

What the hell did she think he could do? Since Asquith's fall, he'd been demoted to the Colonial office, labouring as a lowly clerk in the West African department, and there seemed little chance that anything would change in the foreseeable future. Even before his recent decline, his attempts to meddle in War Office matters had met with scant success.

For the last six months or so he'd been buried under letters from Annie beseeching him to help her unfortunate brother. Those from Isaac himself were little better. While expressing concern over his family's relentless attrition, he was not averse to applying pressure himself. Last August there had been the heartfelt appeal to assist some chap obtain compassionate leave. The situation was undoubtedly grim for the poor fellow but what could he be expected to do about it?

Predictably, his enquiries met with little success. A succinct letter from the War Office advised that any decision regarding the granting of leave was strictly a matter for GHQ, and could not be influenced by outside appeals. They ended by assuring him that all aspects of the case would most certainly have been taken into account when the request was originally submitted, and a fair decision arrived at.

And then there were the entreaties for immediate responses to poems illegibly scrawled on the backs of old envelopes and shoved in with the letters. Sometimes Isaac forwarded these first drafts to Annie for typing, but not always. The assumption that he had nothing better to do than criticise half-baked pieces irritated Marsh, especially since his recent demotion. He was now forced to accept that the subsequent humiliation had affected him more than he'd cared to admit. The knowledge that his fortunes were intrinsically linked to those of Churchill's did not make him feel any better. All a matter of thwarted ego really; he knew it was important to rise above such petty considerations and not take everything so personally. But this was much easier said than done.

Sighing, Marsh sat back and tried to think more charitably about his protégé. There was no doubting Isaac's raw talent, although his marked inconsistency and tendency to ignore established poetic technique was frustrating to say the least. He'd tried hard to help the young poet gain coherence but, while the latter always humbly accepted criticism, his next poem would exhibit similar or completely new flaws. This suggested arrogance and an infuriating propensity to fly in the face of admonition.

"Moses" had been a classic case—some truly wonderful lines buried in dross. As far as he was concerned, Gordon Bottomley had been foolish in providing such lavish praise of the piece, despite the importance he attached to encouraging fellow poets struggling to write at the front. Well-meant as Marsh knew this approach to be, it could easily result in the recipient avoiding the necessary discipline required in tempering enthusiasm with close critical scrutiny. He also believed he understood well enough, without constantly being reminded by

Isaac, the difficulties in writing while under the constraints of active duty. Aspiring poets, whatever their circumstances, must be made aware that there was no substitute for mental rigour.

Struck by a sudden impulse, he opened a drawer, rummaged through a pile of papers, and pulled out a single sheet. Rereading the lines he'd memorised and specially written out, he marvelled again at their incredible power to move him.

Ah! Koelue!
Had you embalmed your beauty, so
It could not backward go,
Or change in any way,

What were the use, if on my eyes
The embalming spices were not laid
To keep us fixed,
Two amorous sculptures passioned endlessly?
What were the use, if my sight grew,
And its far branches were cloud hung,
You, small at the roots, like grass.
While the new lips my spirit would kiss
Were not red lips of flesh,
But the huge kiss of power.
Where yesterday soft hair through my fingers fell
A shaggy mane would entwine,
And no slim form work fire to my thighs.
But human Life's inarticulate mass
Throb the pulse of a thing
Whose mountain flanks awry
Beg my mastery—mine!
Ah! I will ride the dizzy beast of the world
My road – my way.

He leaned back on the uncomfortable wooden chair, staring into space for a few moments. Surely anyone capable of such genius deserved his time. He must try to bury his irritation and empathise more fully. But how? Getting behind the diffident, rather hostile front Isaac presented to the world was no simple task. Perhaps, Marsh reflected, something to do with undue sensitivity over a lack of formal education or the circumstances of his early life. This was generally as far as he got in his efforts to fathom someone shaped by experiences so different from his own. Hailing, as he did, from a cosseted middle-class background where material needs had never been an issue and the mere mention of money a breach of social etiquette, the prospect of achieving any real insight was remote. The world of poverty and endless toil in order to earn a pitiful wage would always be a closed book to him.

Marsh recalled the anger he felt following Rupert Brooke's death when Isaac barged into his office looking to peddle a painting or two. Luckily, he hadn't actually been there or serious damage might have been done to their already tenuous relationship. As it was, he refused all contact for the next two or three weeks, only feeling inclined to relent after receiving a grudging apology. For the life of him, he still couldn't comprehend such a crass lack of sensitivity. Isaac knew how close Brooke and he had been.

He struggled hard to avoid being caught up in a renewed bout of grieving, forcing himself to return to the matter at hand. Perhaps a letter to the War Office pointing up Isaac's potential as a future poet and the desirability of finding him a desk job behind the lines might help; but there was obviously little chance of actually getting him shipped back to England as his family desired. Even light duties away from the trenches and less exposure to enemy fire and adverse weather conditions would be better than nothing. Securing the poet a new posting, however, might prove problematic. Units were understandably reluctant to take on those viewed by their officers as dead wood and he had little doubt Isaac fell into this category.

He rose to his feet and paced the narrow confines of his new office. It would be good when this war finally ended, especially in light of his current situation. Would Churchill ever come back into favour? Given the influence of the Tories in the present coalition, he doubted it. Most of these gentlemen hated Winston worse than a plague of boils. They'd probably never forgive him for his defection, or betrayal of party loyalties as they would see it. Even his own respected position within Asquith's administration hadn't saved him from the wrath of those determined to extinguish everyone and everything linked to his old boss. It was just too bad!

Of course, his reduced duties still made demands on him. There were limits to the time he could spend championing poetry, and the arts in general, these days. It was taking him forever to organise the next volume of *Georgian Poetry 1910-17*. And so many contributors were unavailable due to direct or indirect causes of war. He'd already decided that the only piece of Isaac's he was willing to include was the *Ah Koelue* speech from "Moses"; the rest—especially the war poems—were just too rough and ready for consideration. Some, he believed, had potential but were not in a fit state for publication yet. Perhaps after the war... . Their exclusion in the meantime would undoubtedly disappoint Isaac but so be it; standards must be maintained, especially at present when the arts were under fire. Hurt feelings were not a valid reason for inclusion.

So far he'd seen few poems arising from the conflict which particularly impressed him—some of Brooke's early work being the honourable exception. He stopped pacing for a moment. Now there was a poet whose pen had dripped pure gold; what a waste, what a terrible waste! When he considered their relationship, he found it virtually impossible to hold back the tears. Even after two years the pain was acute as ever. He made a desperate attempt to ease the bonds of grief a little. What had he been considering? Yes, of course, war poetry. Surely Masefield, Bottomley or even John Drinkwater would in time produce something of note. There was also the generation of talented younger poets caught up, like Isaac, in the conflict. You never knew, maybe Robert Graves or young Siegfried Sassoon would rise to the occasion.

He finally started the letter to the War Office on Isaac's behalf, his initial reluctance soon giving way as he endeavoured to utilise all the power of persuasion he was capable off. Despite their differences, he wanted to do his best and was, at heart, willing to help out in any way he could. Although accused at times of "policing" the output of his circle of intimates, and internally rebuking them for dependency on him during this particularly stressful period, he craved their survival, believing their combined vision and talent would prove invaluable to a new society tentatively rising from the ashes of the old. Without a strong focus on the arts, civilisation, he believed, was doomed to sink without trace. Too many had died already. Hot tears at last spilled over as he contemplated the long list of those who would never darken his doorway again.

Hacha Rosenberg sat quietly weeping on the sofa. This was one of her bad days and Annie knew there was little point in trying to console her. With three sons on active service, she cursed the day her husband had ever persuaded her to move to this godforsaken country. The only justification at the time was Barnett's wish to avoid conscription into the Russian Imperial Army. It now seemed particularly ironic that his timely escape had led to the sacrifice of his own sons. In the rush to blame her husband for everything that had gone wrong since their arrival in England almost thirty years ago, she was less than willing to consider any kinder interpretation of the facts, not least that Isaac had volunteered his services to King and Country.

Barnett was out on one of his long walks, and Annie hoped he would have the good sense to stay away until her mother retired to bed. This was usually the case. He was understandably reluctant to suffer Hacha's weighty silences, or the acidic comments addressed to their daughters as if he wasn't in the room but, of course, intended for his ears. Perhaps he would visit their local *chevra* and find consolation in the company of those friends whose affection and respect he could count on. There was little comfort to be derived at home these days. The rest of the family had more or less given up trying to reconcile their parents, although Annie still hoped something might be salvaged from the disaster of the marriage after the war. In the meantime, recriminations continued until she felt like quitting London and joining up herself.

At least she'd been able to assist Isaac in a practical way, which had helped sustain him during long months of training and active duty. Sorting out his correspondence and diligently typing up first drafts of poems before returning them immediately for further amendment, made her feel needed. When it came to her brother's welfare she was tireless in her efforts to make a difference and was more than willing to ignore or forgive the quirks of character that made him so difficult to deal with at times. Marsh was entirely justified in feeling under pressure to respond to her constant appeals for help.

Unable to endure her mother's dumb misery any longer, she sat down on the couch and placed an arm round the heaving shoulders.

"Getting yourself into this state isn't helping anyone you know. Things will work out for the best in the end." Annie made a valiant effort to inspire confidence, hoping she sounded more positive than she felt. "They'll all come home soon—you'll see."

Inside, she knew very well the chances of all her brothers returning unscathed from the war were remote, although, strangely enough, she still retained a shred of faith that her prayers on their behalf would be answered. She knew her father spent night after night in the synagogue beseeching God for the safe deliverance of his sons. She'd told Isaac that once. Surely He could not ignore such heartfelt devotion. An irrational hope persisted too—that her parents would come together and provide mutual comfort. At heart, each felt as strongly as the other about their children's welfare, though Hacha bitterly denied the fact. She now articulated her worst fears between deep, shuddery breaths.

"I believe they will...but...it's just that Isaac's health is so poor.... He was always such a delicate child Goodness knows what being out in the open in all weathers is doing to him."

A recent letter from her older brother had been the catalyst for this latest upset and, as usual, Annie was at a loss to know what to do. Although greatly concerned over Isaac's deteriorating health, she wished he would consider the consequences of discussing his latest setbacks in letters home. He knew well enough how fragile his mother's state of mind was. Declaring straight out that he'd come down with a bout of influenza was the surest way of upsetting her. But what appeared a selfish act to her might in reality be a desperate cry for help. How could she, or anyone else living in the relative safety and comfort of home, ever begin to understand the terrible privations suffered by front-line troops. She constantly agonised over this and other fears too numerous to identify. Bad dreams plagued her sleep, leaving her sad and exhausted each morning.

Hacha's anguished voice broke through her tortured imaginings.

"Did you write to Mr Marsh again? There must be some way of getting Isaac back home.... I don't know what I'll do if he..."

Again, she dissolved in tears unable to say the word which haunted her day and night.

"Yes, Mother, I've asked him to do what he can. He's promised to write to the War Office, but we mustn't get our hopes up too much. Maybe if he arranges for Isaac to be examined, you never know, they might consider sending him home."

She always walked a precarious tightrope, balanced between blind optimism and a less palatable but much more likely outcome. On this occasion, Hacha seemed unwilling to be comforted. As usual, she sought consolation in attacking her husband, which, if nothing else, provided a focus for her consuming bitterness.

"If only your father hadn't been so selfish. Coming to this country was a mistake. He never thought about anybody else but himself, you know. He could never face up to his responsibilities. It was his fault..."

"Please, Mother, this isn't getting us anywhere! Father is concerned for Isaac too. He prays constantly for the welfare of all his sons."

"What good are his prayers now? He should have considered the consequences of his cowardly behaviour years ago before he dragged us all over here."

"Please be reasonable. How could father have known about the war back then? He only wanted a better life for his family. What good would it have done anyone if he'd been shipped off to serve in the Russian army and killed in the process?"

"Better him than his sons."

The voice was adamant—closed to further appeals. Annie knew from experience she could never win this argument. These days her mother only saw what she wished to see. Her disappointments and fears were irrevocably bound up with the belief that Barnett was to blame for all the family's misfortunes; pursuing the matter now would only make things worse.

Against her better judgement, she decided to crank up the prospect of divine intervention. It was a dangerous gamble to involve God in such a way, but it might be the only means of allaying present anxieties and providing much needed comfort. She feared for Hacha's mental health if some method of reconciling her to present circumstances could not be found.

"You know, I sometimes feel Isaac was sent to us by God to fulfil an important destiny. He's always been so dedicated to his art at the expense of everything else in life. Do you remember the first poem he ever wrote? What was it called?"

She knew very well but was trying to redirect her mother's thoughts.

"'Ode to David's Harp'. You surely remember that!"

"Yes, of course. Wasn't that the poem that persuaded Mr Dainow, the librarian, to take an interest in Isaac?"

"Yes. Minnie spoke to Mr Dainow at the library and Isaac sent him the ode and a few other things he'd written at the time."

With a sense of relief, Annie noticed that her mother had almost stopped crying and was paying close attention.

"That was when he invited Isaac to the library for a talk. He wrote to your father to say how impressed he was with Isaac's love of art and literature. We knew then he was no ordinary son. There wasn't much we could do for him at the time; we couldn't afford to have him give up his job at Hentschels'. When he began evening classes at Birbeck College, I thought things were starting to work out but…"

"Yes, that's right," Annie hurriedly intervened to keep the memories positive. "Attending Birbeck was the beginning of Isaac's real hope of becoming a professional artist. He told me that once."

"Your father and I both believed that Isaac was marked out for greater things. Perhaps you're right; God may preserve our son's life for His greater glory."

Annie experienced a welcome surge of relief. Her plan was proving to be more successful than she'd envisaged; it had been a long time since she'd heard any positive reference to her father in relation to past events.

"I only wish we could help him somehow. It causes me such great pain to think what he's being forced to endure."

"Don't worry, Mother, I'm sure Mr Marsh will be able to do something for him."

"I hope so, Annie, I hope so. I think I'll go to bed now and offer a few prayers for his safe return to us. Our Lord's purposes are so difficult to understand at times. But I think you may be right about Isaac; he will return to us one day. The war could end sooner than any of us think."

"Some people are saying it might be over by the summer."

"I hope so, but we mustn't count our chickens before they hatch though!"

"No. We've heard these sorts of rumours before."

"Are you going to bed?"

"Not yet. I've got two of Isaac's poems still to type out and another letter to write."

"Well don't be too late. I must try to find the copy of that poem tomorrow. Mr Dainow admired it so much."

After Hacha was in bed and her muttered prayers no longer audible, Annie went through to her bedroom and wound a new sheet of paper into the rickety old typewriter. She was still hard at work when Barnett quietly closed the door just after midnight.

✳

Major Alexander was reaching the end of his morning surgery. For the last two hours he'd been subjected to the whining of the usual rag-tag collection of malingerers. So far, not one of them had come close to being excused duty, and he expected things to continue in this satisfactory manner. Proud of his reputation as scrimshanker's nemesis, Alexander made no effort to conceal a deep-rooted contempt for rank-and-file soldiers whom he believed would grasp any opportunity to evade their responsibilities.

Recently he'd cultivated a thick moustache which, along with his naturally beetling brows, conveyed the desirable impression of bristling impatience. A massive forehead, hooked nose and jutting chin completed the physical manifestation of unbending authority. Allied to his success in purging all remnants of concern for the sick and dying, the end result was impressive.

Joining the army had been a revelation, allowing him to pursue prejudices and control people in a way not possible in the general practice he'd managed in York before the war. Juniors back then had had the infuriating habit of resigning when push came to shove, and, despite efforts to browbeat patients, he was often forced to indulge their ridiculous whims. Here, at least, he was invested with enough power to ensure that few could challenge his decisions. He held that the war would have been won long ago if the men had shown more backbone and commitment. Like his paragon, Field Marshal Haig, Alexander was convinced that offensive tactics should be constantly employed to wear down the Hun and achieve final victory. The enormous sacrifices of the previous year, and the significant failure to break the stalemate on the Western Front left him unmoved. If the men were allowed any latitude whatsoever, the entire process would, in his view, be in serious danger of derailment. The fact that he had rarely come anywhere near the front line, or been subjected to the intense shelling most of his patients lived with on a daily basis, made no difference to his conviction.

232

Last week, during the trial of a corporal court-marshalled for deserting his post, he'd opposed any clemency on the grounds of shellshock. Like so many of his medical colleagues, he strenuously denied the condition existed, remaining unmoved by the fact that the accused was unable to speak during the entire proceedings and could not remember his own name or rank. Two days later, when the man was convicted and shot, Alexander heaved a sigh of relief, delighted that the authorities were resisting the infiltration of a dangerous liberal bacillus.

One way he'd discovered of deterring would-be malingerers was to provide therapy viewed as much worse than remaining on duty. For instance, he managed to put the fear of death into soldiers professing various stomach disorders by prescribing a course of painful enemas, while others, claiming cold and flu symptoms, were allotted equally appalling treatments. One of Alexander's favourites was a procedure designed to lower body temperature, which involved the patient being wrapped in wet towels and left out in the cold for several hours. Predictably, the number of men queuing up outside the clinic dropped, though a few, apparently undaunted by such unorthodox methods, persisted in their ill-fated attempts to receive a sympathetic hearing.

The last patient examined this morning appeared to be one of those poor fools who still believed the major might be persuaded to act in the interests of his patients. Shivering violently, and bent double with a racking cough, Private Williams' condition would probably have convinced most doctors that something was far wrong. Even during the examination, although fully aware that the symptoms were consistent with full-blown tuberculosis, Alexander was working out a strategy to get the man out of his surgery and back up the line. There was no question in his mind of hospitalisation. He was proud of the fact that, apart from those wounded in battle, he'd only once relieved a ranker from active duty. Considering that the latter was suffering from tertiary syphilis and could hardly stand up, never mind hold his rifle, Alexander felt he had nothing to be ashamed of.

Writing vigorously, he delivered his inevitable verdict:

"I'll give you something to control that cough and you should see a significant improvement. Your temperature is still a little high but I'm confident it will not interfere with the execution of your duties. If your condition doesn't improve, there are other treatments we might revisit."

Alexander spoke with false amiability. The message he wished to convey was that he would be perfectly willing to initiate the previous torture regime if Williams insisted on returning to his office.

Glancing through the next set of case notes, his eyes alighted on Isaac's name at the top of the sheet. If that little Jew, with his friends in high places and inflated opinion of himself, walked in here with both legs shot off, he would kick him back up the line. Colonel Ritchie might be taken in but there was no way he could be forced into collaborating with what was clearly a Yiddish conspiracy to preserve his useless existence.

Only yesterday, Ritchie phoned to tell him that some fellow at Whitehall had written to Isaac's captain enquiring after his state of health. Now he was being asked to carry out yet another examination. The outcome was already clear in his mind: no change from three weeks ago. If Ritchie wished to go easy on the bastard, he would get no help from this practitioner.

Rising, he strode over to the door, pulled it open, and walked through into the adjoining hut. Yes, there he was cowering in the corner. My God, these people were willing to sneak into the country like rats and reap the benefits, but ask them to give anything back!

"Rosenberg, come with me."

The private rose to his feet and shuffled along behind. Inside the surgery, Alexander spoke to his patient with unconcealed contempt.

"Right. Let's get this farce over with. I recently declared you fit for active duty and as far as I can see nothing has changed. However, Colonel Ritchie has requested that I look you over again. Take your clothes off."

He stood tapping his right foot impatiently while Isaac slowly removed his uniform. He found it hard to say nothing about the dirty and unkempt condition of the various garments laid one by one on the floor next to his desk. These people had no respect for the uniform whatsoever.

"So, has there been any change in the symptoms you complained about during your last visit here?"

He stared contemptuously at the thin, white body covered in lice-induced weals, some still crusted in dried blood from recent scratching.

"I have b...been coughing more, sir. I...sometimes find it difficult to breath properly while out on route marches. It's..."

"Yes, yes, I see. So there's been little change then! The doctor moved forward and sounded the pigeon chest.

"Breathe out, now in, and hold. Ah huh. Just as I told you before. There's nothing wrong with your lungs." His voice rasped with impatience. "Now cough when I tell you." He pushed two fingers into Isaac's groin. "Cough. Right, everything's fine in that department. Is there anything else you wish to tell me? Get dressed."

Isaac bent over and began to pick up his grey drawers.

"Get a move on, man; I've other patients to see this morning."

"I've been feeling very weak recently, sir. It's hard to be specific b...but... it's just that..."

"For God's sake spit it out, man!"

"I'm finding it more...more difficult to keep up. I don't really know how much longer I can..."

"As far as I'm concerned, you're perfectly fit to continue with front-line duties, Rosenberg. I'm sorry if it's not what you want to hear but that will be my recommendation to Colonel Ritchie. It must be gratifying to have so many people running around after you. In reality, however, these examinations constitute a total waste of everyone's time. Now, if you'll excuse me."

The last words were uttered with considerable venom as Isaac pulled his jacket on and left the office. Stepping outside, the fierce January wind tore viciously at the thin layers of material covering his body.

A little less than two weeks later, Major Alexander received a brief note informing him that Private Rosenberg, serial number 22311, had been reassigned to the Fortieth Division Works Battalion. Shaking his head and smiling wryly, he gazed at the sheet of paper for a few seconds more before scrunching it up and throwing it in the bin. At least his conscience was clear which was more than could said for those weaklings who allowed themselves to be influenced by so-called friends in high places. Officers like Ritchie were putting the outcome of the war in jeopardy. If only Hague could root out these soft touches and replace them with leaders who refused to pander to the disastrous lack of moral fibre among the rank and file, the Germans wouldn't last the summer.

With a sudden pang, Alexander realised that the last thing he really wanted was an end to the war. His situation had never been better. The role of army doctor afforded him a level of job satisfaction far beyond anything ever experienced in civilian life. He easily shrugged off this momentary distraction. There was a job to be done and nothing must be allowed to interfere with that.

Chapter Five

1917

...I am determined that this war, with all its powers for devastation, shall not master my poeting; that is, if I am lucky enough to come through all right. I will not leave a corner of my consciousness covered up, but saturate myself with the strange and extraordinary new conditions of this life...

Extract from letter to Laurence Binyon—Autumn 1916.

...the harsh and unlovely times have made my mistress, the flighty muse, abscond and elope with luckier rivals, but surely I shall hunt her and chase her into the summer and sweeter times...

Extract from letter to Edward Marsh—April 1917

Returning We Hear The Larks.

Sombre the night is.
And though we have our lives, we know
What sinister threat lurks there.

Dragging these anguished limbs, we only know
This poison-blasted track opens on our camp—
On a little safe sleep.

But hark! Joy— joy— strange joy.
Lo! Heights of night ringing with unseen larks.
Music showering our upturned list'ning faces.

Death could drop from the dark
As easily as song——-
But only song dropped,
Like a blind man's dreams on the sand
By dangerous tides,
Like a girl's dark hair for she dreams no ruin lies there,
Or her kisses where a serpent hides.

1917

Captain Frank Waley leaned over his desk writing yet another urgent appeal for ammunition. His consignment of mortar shells should have been here days ago, but, so far, absolutely nothing. How could he be expected to run an artillery unit without rounds?

In Waley's view, High Command had been caught completely on the hop by the recent German retreat to the heavily fortified Hindenburg line. It was typical of the crazy way this war was being run that no one appeared to have anticipated the move, hence the present shambles. Several weeks after the event, lines of communication remained unreliable. The scorched earth tactics employed by the enemy had worked only too well, and the clear-up operation was way behind schedule.

The delays he was experiencing could probably be attributed to crossed wires at Brigade HQ. Surely life was hard enough without being at the mercy of some ignorant pen-pusher billeted in a lavish chateau miles behind the lines. It was at times like these that he lost faith in a system too cumbersome and inflexible to deal effectively with rapidly changing circumstances. The bureaucrats were supposed to be helping, not hindering, the war effort. Without the means to engage the enemy, the problem of maintaining morale would become ever more pressing. There was nothing worse, he knew from experience, than trying to motivate tetchy subordinates with far too much time on their hands.

Waley laid down his pen and tried to ease the stiffness out of his neck and shoulders. Massaging the knotted neck muscles while slowly rotating his head sometimes helped avoid the headaches which followed these bouts of internalised frustration. The thud of an exploding shell almost directly overhead barely impinged on his thoughts, although he was aware of a fine dust caught in the harsh glare of the electric light.

The "dugout" where he now lived and worked, was, in reality, a spacious room, twenty feet underground, supplied with fresh air pumped through an ingenious set of interconnecting ducts and linked to various chambers by an expansive, concrete-lined corridor. It contained a large desk, two decent-size chairs, a double bunk in the corner and three wooden filing cabinets, all of which were in place when Waley arrived. Until recently, his new HQ had been part of an elaborate German structure used to house units resting from front-line duty and stockpile ammunition and rations. Considering the enemy had burned and destroyed almost everything in the wake of their planned withdrawal, he found it hard to believe they'd deliberately left this superb complex intact for the benefit of its captors. He guessed they'd not foreseen its loss and were forced out at the last minute, unable even to remove their stores of luxury rations. The officers assigned to take an inventory were delighted to find crates of superior French wine, and even a consignment of caviar.

By comparison, British trenches were perfunctory scrapes in the ground. Six weeks ago, Waley's "office" had been a cavity dug into the back wall of a disintegrating trench. He'd slept, written reports, eaten meals, issued orders and administered punishments from the leaking den he shared with a junior officer. The stench of decay had been omnipresent, saturating everything from the material of his uniform to the rations he was forced to consume; even the stewed tea contained the faint but pervasive taint of putrefaction.

It was incredible how much everyone had underestimated the resourcefulness and tenacity of the enemy. His new home provided further proof, if such was needed, of superior German engineering and organisation. No wonder the opening phase of the Battle of the Somme had failed to deliver the predicted breakthrough last summer. He still found it hard to believe that the massive artillery offensive, launched over a twenty-mile front and continuing non-stop for seven terrible days and nights, had resulted in so little damage to enemy trenches. Tens of thousands of troops climbed out of their trenches that fateful July morning, convinced their objectives would be achieved with minimal resistance.

Just as he was about to resume his written appeal to HQ, the field telephone rang loudly making him jump. He pulled up the receiver and clamped it against his head.

"Captain Waley speaking."

Colonel Ritchie's clipped voice filled his ear.

"Ah, good morning, Waley. How are you today?"

"Fine, sir, apart from being out of ammunition again."

"Brigade up to their usual tricks, are they?"

Ritchie spoke with an easy familiarity. Their association went back a long way. The colonel had served as a subaltern under Waley's uncle during the Boer War. The military credentials of both families were beyond reproach.

"Unfortunately, they are, sir."

Waley couldn't help allowing irritation to creep into his voice.

"Would it help if I gave them a call?"

"I'd appreciate anything you could do, Colonel."

"Consider it done then. I'll speak to General Sanderson and see if he can get the wheels in motion. He's not such a bad chap if you know how to handle him. We served together in 1900 you know, just after I was transferred out of your uncle's regiment."

"I didn't realise that, sir."

"Yes. It's a small world, Waley. Anyway, to get to the point, I've a small favour to ask."

"Yes, sir?"

"It's to do with one of my men —a chap called Rosenberg. He's been having various health problems —you know —hands and feet, that sort of thing. A lot to do with the sort of work we've been doing lately. He's not really up to it, I'm afraid; a completely hopeless soldier to be perfectly honest."

"Yes, sir, I think I understand."

"I'd be obliged if you could take him under your wing for a while. Some light duties perhaps, till he's recovered a bit."

"Yes, sir. I'm sure I'll manage to find something for him to do."

"Thank you, Waley. You do what you think best. It'll just be for a week or two at the most, until the weather improves a bit and we can find something more suited to his talents, if that's possible out here. He's actually a bit of a poet, you know. Showed me a piece the other day...I forget what it was called now. I thought it was really quite good. You like to read a bit of poetry now and again, don't you?"

"Yes, sir. I certainly enjoy Byron and Wordsworth."

"Ah yes, well, it's not quite in that league but get him to show you some of it anyway. He's very eager when it comes to poetry. He's also quite well connected at home, surprisingly enough."

"Oh?"

"He knows Edward Marsh—the literary chappy who put together the collection of Georgian poetry before the war, then worked for Winston Churchill at the Admiralty."

"Yes, I've heard that name before."

Waley was lying but felt disinclined to reveal his ignorance.

"Marsh actually wrote to Rosenberg's CO a few months ago enquiring after the little blighter's state of health. The captain organised a full medical examination but Alexander wasn't having any of it. You remember Major Alexander?"

"Yes, sir. Didn't he declare some chap fit for duty who later died from TB? I seem to remember that didn't go down too well at Brigade."

"Enough said about that, but you get the idea. There's nothing I can do, of course, but, in my view, Rosenberg should have been sent home long ago. I've been trying to keep him out of the front line. He's been with the works battalion for the last few weeks but, as I said, even that's proving too much for him. Anyway, I've got to dash. Thanks for helping out and I'll see what I can do about your shells."

"That would be greatly appreciated, sir."

"Right you are my boy, cheerio."

Waley slowly replaced the handset. Rosenberg sounded like a problem he could do without at the moment. It struck him that Ritchie was probably hoping he'd be sympathetic to a fellow Jew in distress. That was all very well but he was harassed enough without being saddled with what the colonel himself had dubbed a "completely hopeless soldier". COs were always looking for ways to pass on "duds" but he sensed, on this occasion at least, the request had been motivated by genuine concern; Waley even thought he'd detected affectionate regard in his superior's tone. He would just have to make the best of it. Rosenberg might prove useful in the kitchen although Corporal Higgins, the company cook, could generally be relied upon to give any new man a hard time.

He hoped Ritchie was being truthful when he said the transfer would just be for a week or two. The timescale was vague enough to concern him that he might be stuck with Rosenberg for a much longer period. On the other hand, the prospect of successfully concluding his ammunition crisis greatly relieved him. The chains binding them all to this miserable existence would rapidly disintegrate if the present impasse was not speedily resolved.

He suddenly stood up and strode out into the corridor. Where the hell was Bates with his breakfast?

Next day the rain set in again. Waley wondered if spring would ever come to this cold, muddy corner of Europe. As a young man, when he thought of France at all, he'd pictured it in a romantic light, envisaging perpetually blue skies, sun-warmed chateaux and colourful peasants in black berets. The war had disabused him of these and many other quaint notions.

At zero nine hundred hours, he led his mortar team up to the front line for the latest assault on enemy positions. These generally occurred four or five times a week—sometimes more often— depending on conditions. High Command rationalised them as a way of keeping the Germans on their toes as well as fostering the correct "offensive" spirit. A somewhat foolish notion, as all they ever seemed to do was provoke vicious retaliation, which, apart from the obvious physical dangers, led to another serious problem for Waley and his team.

The attitude of the infantry officers was becoming increasingly hostile. Last week, a furious major had ordered him to pack up his mortar equipment and return to base, insisting that the spot chosen as a firing site was unsuitable. He didn't care to explain why but threatened Waley with disciplinary action if he returned. On that occasion, under the jeering eyes of an entire company of infantrymen, he and his men had been forced to beat a humiliating retreat. Complaints to Brigade HQ failed to resolve the impasse.

Anxious to avoid further confrontations, Waley instigated a stealthy approach, arriving at a new position he hoped might prove less sensitive. Two privates on sentry duty stood by, tight-lipped, as his men set up the equipment; without an officer, there was nothing they could do to interfere. The short metal tubes were quickly positioned, trajectory calculated and adjustments made. The "plum puddings", packed with their deadly cargo of shrapnel and high explosives, were then distributed. Giving the order to fire, Waley watched the rounds arc high in the air—their passage appearing leisurely—before dropping down, with a distinctive high-pitched whine. The explosions merged into one blasting detonation, which, even at a distance of over three hundred yards, made him flinch. Private Wight, observing the German lines through a periscope, shouted that one had dropped slightly short but the other three, as far as he could tell, were on target.

After hurried readjustments, Waley resumed until his ammunition was exhausted. It was hard to know what effect they were having, but he didn't underestimate the severity of the bombardment. This was borne out a few minutes later when shells began to drop on no-man's-land only twenty yards or so in front of their own trenches. Enemy artillery had been alerted and their heavy guns were out to exact revenge. By the time Waley and his team had packed up and started moving swiftly back along the winding communication trench, the German gunners found their mark.

The hurrying group instinctively ducked as a huge missile roared close over their heads detonating five or six seconds later. Sandy soil hissed around them, covering uniforms and helmets in a fine, brown layer. Two more exploded directly ahead and another three off to the left. The buckling sensation under their feet made it feel as if the earth was coming apart at the seams.

Rushing round a corner, Waley's heart, already thumping painfully in his chest, skipped a beat when he saw the carnage ahead. One of the shells had scored a direct hit on a support trench packed with off-duty soldiers enjoying a chat and a cup of tea. He could see a smoking hole and jumbled remains littering the duckboards for yards around. A hand, its bloody fingers grasping a tin cup, lay almost under his feet while above him, someone's severed head, complete with helmet and chin-strap, was tightly jammed between two wooden support struts. Nobody appeared to have survived the blast. The nearest thing to a complete body was a pair of mangled legs and half a torso, truncated above the chest.

A childhood memory suddenly emerged of a stuffed guy he'd once seen burning on top of a bonfire. A few minutes after the fire was lit, the body had fallen apart, the bottom half sliding halfway down before becoming caught up in the charred branches. He remembered crying as the two pieces disintegrated in the crackling flames.

More shells were arriving and exploding perilously close by. One of the main infantry complaints was that mortar crews invariably escaped, leaving them to deal with the flak. This, Waley knew, was far from true. The danger to himself and his team was very real. Luck was the only thing they could hope for now.

They leapt and scrambled over the clutter. Lance Corporal Johnson, slipped and skidded face first into a pile of reeking entrails. Struggling onto his knees, he started to scream and slap hysterically at his bloody brown face. He then went limp and pitched forward for a second time. Waley directed two lads to pick him up. Although conscious, Johnson was now unable to walk and had to be dragged along. A shell landed so close Waley was blown off his feet. Desperately fighting back a wave of disorientation, he got up, gathered his men together and pushed forward once more.

Seconds later, a team of stretcher-bearers rushed past. He couldn't bring himself to tell them that they were wasting their time. Empty sandbags would be of more use than stretchers on this occasion. One of the men mouthed an obscenity through his thick, black moustache but Waley had no time to respond.

The shelling ceased abruptly. Content that honour had been satisfied, or, more likely, unwilling to expend further ammunition, the German gunners called it a day though Waley could hear the clatter of machine guns nearby. It was really little wonder that mortar units were so unpopular. The sector now resembled a hornet's nest stirred vigorously by a large stick.

Fortunately, everyone, apart from Johnson, appeared to have escaped serious injury; a few scrapes and cuts but nothing worse.

On their return to base, Waley ordered his traumatised crew to the cookhouse for a bite to eat, then arranged for the stricken corporal to be sent behind the lines for a proper examination. Back in the relative peace of his office, he settled himself down to write an account of the morning's events. The logbook had to be kept up to date and he desperately needed time and space to collect himself.

Less than a paragraph into the report, he was interrupted by a loud knock at the door. He experienced a blinding flash of irritation, barely managing to quash the impulse to order whomever it was to go to the devil. Instead, he swallowed hard and granted permission to enter. Sergeant Brooks marched in, snapping to attention and saluting smartly.

"Begging your pardon, sir, but the shells 'as just arrived from Brigade."

The surge of relief left him unable to speak for a moment. It was typical of the absurd contradictions in his life that he felt delighted about the arrival of a consignment which guaranteed further dubious attacks, exposure to enemy fire and infantry displeasure which, after this morning's events, would be running at an all time high. Pulling himself together, he tried to sound as sanguine as possible.

"Well, thank God for that, Sergeant. I was beginning to despair of ever seeing that particular consignment."

"Yessir, and that new private from the works battalion's arrived an' all. You said to bring 'im up as soon as 'e got here. If you're too busy though, I'll bring 'im back later on."

"No, that's fine. Show him through now, please."

He was tempted to put off the meeting but news of the delivery had buoyed him up.

The sergeant returned moments later with a small, hunched soldier clad in a scruffy uniform. Waley's heart sank as he ran his eyes over the dishevelled figure. At a command from Brooks, the private saluted and stood awkwardly to attention.

"P...P...Private Isaac Rosenberg, serial number 22311, reporting for d...duty, sir."

Looking closer, he realised Colonel Ritchie had not been exaggerating the man's poor condition: his hands were badly swollen and it was obvious from a chesty wheeze that he was struggling to breathe properly. Waley was therefore surprised to see that the olive-green eyes remained bright and alert, belying the first impression of someone mentally beaten down by ill-health.

"Stand easy, Private. Colonel Ritchie tells me you haven't been too well of late."

Waley leaned forward, making an effort to look concerned.

"I...I...I've had quite a bad cough sir but it...it's mainly my feet at the moment; it's hard to keep them dry. I'm...I'm looking forward to the warmer weather."

"A lot of the lads have problems of that sort, don't they?" Trying not to be over-solicitous, his voice sounded harsher than intended. "Have you been up the front line recently?"

"No, sir...I've been helping clear the roads."

"Ah yes. Keeping the supply lines open."

"Yes, sir."

Waley stood up, still unable to decide how to deal with the diminutive scarecrow shuffling nervously in front of his desk. He felt irritated while simultaneously experiencing a degree of compassion and curiosity. Without understanding why, he knew there was more to this unimpressive little man than met the eye. It was, of course, what met the eye that was so vexatious. Any lapse in dress or discipline could have serious consequences in a situation where protocols were stretched to the limit. Maintaining the balance out here was no easy matter. Life was so tenuous that officers often fluctuated between extreme measures to preserve order, and a degree of altruism which would have appeared incongruous to someone with no experience of the front. Only last week Colonel Ritchie had told him about a soldier court-martialled for falling asleep on guard duty and subsequently shot. The lieutenant who'd brought the charge was then killed several nights later attempting to rescue another of his men trapped in no-man's-land.

"To be candid, Private Rosenberg, you look a mess." Despite the criticism, he struggled to keep his voice kindly. "Try and tidy yourself up a bit, there's a good fellow. We can't have you wandering about with your shoulder strap hanging off like that, you know. And it would help if you tied up your bootlaces properly."

Encouraged by the mild tone, Isaac struggled to respond in an appropriate fashion.

"I'm s...s...sorry, sir; it's just that my boots have been giving me trouble lately. It's m...my feet as I said, sir...the chilblains, you know."

He made a feeble attempt to button up his torn shoulder strap. Irritated once more, Waley signalled him to leave it alone.

"Very well, man. Just try to make yourself a little more presentable, that's all. Maybe you could start by getting a haircut. I'm assigning you to the cookhouse; you can assist there for now. The sergeant will take you over."

"Th...th...thank you, sir."

"All right —dismissed, Private. Oh, by the way, Colonel Ritchie tells me you write poetry!"

Isaac turned quickly, looking as if he'd just wakened up.

"Yes, sir."

"Well, you must show me some of it. I enjoy reading poetry."

"I've got one here which I've been working on, if you'd like to see it."

He pulled out a dirty brown envelope from his tunic pocket and laid it on the edge of Waley's desk.

"If you c...c...could return it some time, I'd be obliged, sir; it's the only copy I've got at the moment."

The captain gazed distastefully at the discoloured object for a few seconds before picking it up between two fingers.

"I tell you what, take a few sheets of paper with you and a pen if you like. It might be of help."

He stretched out his legs beneath the desk while Isaac helped himself to some blank sheets. Almost overcome by the show of kindness, the private gulped and spluttered his thanks.

"Right, that will be all."

Backing out of the door, Isaac almost collided with Brooks.

"Steady son, steady. Watch where you're going. Wait at the bottom of the stairs."

Isaac, muttered an apology and disappeared into the corridor.

"We've got a right one 'ere, sir."

Waley studied Brooks' big, florid face for a moment before replying.

"I got a call from Colonel Ritchie yesterday. He asked me if we could look after Rosenberg for a while. He's been complaining about his breathing and the state of his feet non-stop for the past month. The doctors can't find much wrong but his CO wants him out of the way. Soldiers like Rosenberg can have a bad effect on the other lads, there's no doubt about that."

"Yes, sir." Brooks hesitated for a moment before continuing. "And that's the problem, begging your pardon, sir." He glanced down at the mass of papers littering his captain's desk. "It's just passin' the buck in a manner of speakin', isn't it, sir?"

Waley experienced another surge of impatience. He didn't need Brooks in here stating the obvious.

"That's as maybe, Sergeant, but it's up to you and me to make sure he smartens himself up a bit and at least begins to look like a soldier. Take him down to the cookhouse right away and tell Corporal Higgins to find him something to do. He'll not be with us for very long in any case—a week or two at the most. Until then, we'll just have to make the best of it." He straightened up and sighed. "Just do what you can, there's a good fellow. I'd better get on. These reports won't finish themselves."

"Very good, sir."

"Oh, by the way, has there been any news about Corporal Johnson?"

"Nothing as yet, sir, but I'll let you know as soon as I hear anything."

"Thank you kindly, Sergeant."

After Brooks' departure, Waley sat back, incapable of further effort. He hoped Johnson would recover. The man had a way with mortars; he could set the things up and calculate trajectory quicker than anyone else in the company. Although there hadn't been any physical injury, he knew well enough that a soldier's mental state had considerable bearing on his ability to function under pressure. The fact that shell shock was still not officially recognised as a medical disorder was, in his view, a deliberate attempt by the authorities to ignore overwhelming evidence to the contrary. What happened today may have been the final straw even though Johnson had exhibited no prior symptoms. Such episodes could be short-term—lasting only a few minutes—or prove severe enough to require the removal of the patient back to England for a long period of convalescence. As far as he knew, Johnson had never been granted leave; unfortunately, the rest of the unit was in much the same position.

He gazed down at his slightly trembling hands for a moment; nothing much yet maybe but you never knew where such symptoms could lead. Why was he so confused about things? While desperate to tackle the Hun at every opportunity, barely a day passed when he did not experience profound misgivings about the way the war was being conducted. The crass incompetence of politicians and generals, as well as their indifference to loss of life, were not issues he could easily put to one side. He shuddered to think what his father and grandfather, both professional soldiers, would have made of such potentially subversive notions. But they, of course, had no conception of the realities of modern warfare. The old rituals and codes of conduct had become irrelevant in the face of destructive new technologies.

The sudden clatter of dishes out in the corridor created a welcome distraction. He must work harder to avoid such moments of weakness and leave dictates of conscience to those further up the chain of command. Only by focusing on the tasks at hand—the nuts and bolts so to speak—might one pull through in the end.

Later that afternoon, Brooks and Higgins were off duty catching up on company gossip. They were sitting in what had become the unofficial NCOs' mess—an enlarged, concrete-lined dugout behind one of the reserve trenches. The Germans had used the space for storing supplies, and even now it was half filled with the newly delivered crates of mortar shells .

Higgins, a small man with thin, weasel-like features and a permanent sneer, passed over a hip flask to his friend. He was the sort who always found something to complain about. Although the extra space and equipment made his job as cook easier than it had ever been, he remained disparaging. Accepting the flask, the sergeant took a long swig. Smacking his lips, he smiled broadly.

"Thanks, Alf. So, as I was saying, I takes the little runt in an' the old man perks up. You can see 'e's not 'appy wiv the way the bugger looks, mind, but that's not the point, is it?" He paused and gazed at Higgins for a moment waiting for some sort of affirmative response. When none was forthcoming, he felt obliged to explain. "It's obvious surely. These fuckin' Jews look after their own. This Rosenberg's a sight for sore eyes; you've never seen nothing like it, but you can tell the captain's gonna go easy on 'im. That's the reason they sent 'im down 'ere in the first place. Stands to reason, don't it?"

Brooks took another drink and handed the flask back over. A little galled by the lack of feedback, he ended impatiently.

"So, that's my point. There's one rule for them and one rule for the rest of us; they stick together like fuckin' glue. Am tellin' you."

Higgins grinned, but his watery blue eyes remained hard and unsmiling.

"Yeh, I suppose you're right, Jack. Rosenberg's a useless little turd, that's for sure. Almost ruined a whole batch of potatoes las' night. Tryin' to cut out the rotten bits he says. Can you credit it? I told him I'd give him rotten bits if he didn't lay off smartish!"

"Wouldn't surprise me if the colonel wasn't a Jew-boy 'imself even if 'e is called fuckin' Ritchie. Maybe on 'is mother's side—you can never tell with these bastards."

Brooks winked and tapped his nose.

"I hope he's not going to be with us for long; there's enough problems round here, fuck knows."

"Don't worry. Looks like it's just for a fortnight or so. Even Waley can see 'e's 'opeless."

Brooks suddenly jumped up and tilted his head back, nose in the air, assuming an exaggerated pose of his CO.

"Bad for morale and all that, don't you know. We can't have you looking like a pig's breakfast, can we, Rosenberg; tidy yourself up, there's a good fellow. And, by the way, I hope you can join me for kaddish tomorrow morning."

The impersonation was passable and for the first time the cook appeared genuinely amused.

"Yeh, but as you said yourself, blood's thicker than water, ain't it?"

"I told you, don't worry." Brooks smiled, pleased at the reaction to his mimicry. " 'E'll be out of 'ere by the end of next week at the latest or I'll eat my fucking helmet."

Higgins laughed. "I'll hold you to that, Jack."

"You do that. Pass that rum, will ya?"

Brooks took a final swig. "I've got to get back. By the way, I 'ope dinner's up to scratch. Everything's got to be kosher, with all these yids around."

Higgins merely scowled in reply. The sergeant chuckled as he left the dugout and made his way towards Waley's office.

*

It was almost a week before the captain bumped into Isaac again. During an inspection of the company cookhouse he spotted the private, bent over a huge sink, peeling potatoes. He'd almost forgotten about him until yesterday when the envelope, covered in untidy handwriting, surfaced from beneath a pile of reports on his desk. Reading through the poem, he'd been singularly unimpressed. Although one of the images gave him pause for thought, the thing as a whole was incomprehensible. The worst aspect, as far as he was concerned, was the lack of traditional rhyming and metre. Recent trends in poetry left him cold.

"So, how are you settling in, Private? Everything fine, I trust."

Isaac laid down his knife and turned away from the filthy water swarming with slivers of potato skin. His face looked grey and exhausted, although the wet hands were perhaps less swollen than before. Waley also noticed his uniform was as scruffy as ever—even worse now that the fronts of the shirt and trousers were badly soiled. Why hadn't Higgins given him an apron to cover up with?

"Yes, sir...Peeling potatoes is b...b...better than filling in mine holes and carting lumps of concrete around."

"Yes. I'm sure it is."

There was an uneasy pause.

"Did you get a chance to look at the poem I gave you, sir?"

Waley, taken off guard, stared at him for a few moments before recovering himself.

"Oh yes. I've got it here somewhere." He began to rummage through his pockets as if finding the envelope was the most important thing in the world. "I know I have it with me. Ah, here it is. I wanted to return it before it got lost."

"That's all right, sir. I've written out another few c...copies of it on the paper you gave me. It makes a difference writing on real p...paper for a change. I even managed to start a new one after I'd finished up here last night." Again, there was a pause before Isaac resumed. "So, what did you think of it, sir?"

Waley, though anticipating the question, coughed and hesitated for a moment, desperately searching for something positive to say.

"Mmm...yes...I liked the bit about the larks singing actually.... . Let's see..." Peering at the envelope, he read the only three lines of the poem which had meant anything to him. *"But hark! Joy—joy— strange joy/Lo! Heights of night ringing with unseen larks/Music showering our upturned list'ning faces...* . It's strange, you know, but the birds do actually keep singing despite everything—even up on that hill behind the German lines. We've shelled the place time and time again. There's hardly a blade of grass left there, never mind a tree, but I heard a lark yesterday, high up in the air. I tried to spot it through the binoculars but I couldn't. Quite eerie really but lovely all the same."

As he spoke, Isaac felt increasingly uncomfortable. Waley had missed the point and he was desperate to explain what the lark song represented. While he fought to overcome his timidity, the captain continued his critique.

"I must say, I didn't quite see what you were getting at in the next bit. *But song only dropped,/like a blind man's dreams on the sand/by dangerous tides,/Like a girl's dark hair for she dreams no ruin lies there,/ Or her kisses where a serpent hides.* I thought the idea was that the soldiers enjoyed the birds singing. You know, they felt...uplifted for a bit. Maybe a welcome escape from the fighting, that sort of thing."

Isaac's impatience finally overcame any doubts about the wisdom of contradicting an officer.

"Yes sir, of course the song represents an escape but my point is that it's totally false: a d...deception, or mirage, if you will."

Waley tried to intervene but the private plunged on.

"D...don't you see? The song was promising something that could never be fulfilled—not out here at any rate. It's as if God is mocking us. For a moment he opens our hearts and we glimpse things— wonderful things that have been locked away for so long, and then he slams the door shut again, in a manner of speaking. Next thing we know, the shells and shrapnel are tearing us to pieces."

Waley stared at Isaac in disbelief. There was no sign of deference or indecisiveness now. The passionate green eyes were staring directly into his own, charged with a newfound confidence. He suddenly felt out of his depth and struggling to defend his corner. Seeing Higgins clumsily attempting to attract his attention, made it somehow necessary to re-establish control. He struggled to find an adequate response.

"No, frankly. I don't see. I fail to understand what a girl's dark hair, or her kisses for that matter, have to do with anything really."

Too late, he realised that his admission of ignorance had lost him the initiative.

"I was trying to suggest something of Eve in the Garden of Eden." The condescension apparent in Isaac's voice made him feel more vulnerable than ever. He hoped the cook, standing nearby, wouldn't notice anything. "The girl's sensuality is linked to the lark's song. The soldiers only hear the cascade of thrilling notes and are seduced for a while. In a sense, they're b...beguiled like the innocent girl dreaming that her beauty will bestow a future of love and delight; she doesn't consider for a moment the destructive forces at work, until it's too late of course!"

Waley needn't have worried about Higgins. The latter was too caught up in his own problems to listen to what was being said or observe the captain's discomfiture. How dare this scraggy misfit continue talking nonsense while the soup cooled and the men stood outside cursing the delay in receiving their rations! Waley was here to taste the food and inspect the kitchen. Jack had been right—these Jews were as thick as thieves. Unable to contain himself any longer, he took advantage of the charged silence.

"Beggin' your pardon, sir, but do you want to taste the soup now, sir? It's just that it's cooling down, and you said you wanted..."

Waley turned round impatiently.

"Very well, Corporal, in a minute, in a minute!"

He was desperate to demonstrate he had more insight than some jumped-up private, poet or no poet.

"Surely the point is that..."

He was amazed to be almost immediately interrupted.

"The point is, sir, that things are never what they seem. This war has made a mockery of Keat's notion that...*b*...*beauty is truth, truth beauty*. The truth out here is of an entirely different sort. Everything we once believed is gone; this is the only reality now—everything else is...is self-generated delusion. Maybe one day the world will regain its sanity, b...but not for a while yet, I fear."

Waley felt susceptible again, but this time for a different reason. He'd quite forgotten the cook fidgeting at his shoulder. The odd weakness experienced earlier—and on many previous occasions—had returned. He understood only too well the point Isaac was making. The horror and futility linked to the knowledge that nothing really made sense threatened to overwhelm him. His life was a constant struggle to keep on track; how could he continue otherwise? How could he lead his men into mortal danger each day without a rational? He attempted to pull himself together.

"Look, Rosenberg, you're missing the point. Surely we're here to preserve our way of life; to restore some sense of order and justice to the world."

At that moment, the wail of shells, passing overhead like a flight of avenging angels, seemed to mock his words. He struggled to keep his voice steady through the din.

"I know it's difficult to maintain a fix on things at times.... The war hasn't been easy on any of us, God knows! But there's still a job to be done, don't you know, and we have to see it through." As he spoke, the familiar words sounded increasingly hollow but he pressed on, desperate to convince himself at least. "One day people will look back and see something worthwhile emerging from all this—I'm sure of that."

He noted with dismay that Isaac's face had twisted into a contemptuous sneer. His thin body expanded as his arms made a huge sweeping gesture which seemed not only to encompass the mess and surrounding trenches but the entire Western Front.

"For pity's sake, sir, open your eyes! There's nothing out here but d...death and more death. Can't you see that? We're pathetic dupes stripped of our freewill and groping in the dark!"

Again, Higgins attempted to intervene.

"The soup's ready now, sir, if you'd like to..."

Isaac pushed him away, his voice suddenly loud and harsh.

"We've never been in control—that's the lie. Blake was right when he alluded to the *mind-forged manacles* chaining the human spirit. Our better nature has been locked away and our humanity perverted! We've become mere shadows of men."

For a second the entire kitchen was silent. Everyone, including Higgins, seemed to be holding their breath. Waley, realising that an immediate counter-attack was required, acted swiftly.

"Enough, Private." His voice, cutting through the hush, sounded to him as though it was issuing from another throat. "Do you realise what you are saying is treasonable? Take your poem back now." He thrust the envelope into Isaac's hands. "It's time you returned to work. And try to tidy yourself up. Your uniform's a disgrace! Hasn't cook got some sort of apron he could give you?"

He spoke, realising the argument had been lost and his retreat behind rank an act of cowardice, necessary perhaps, but ignominious all the same. He was perfectly entitled to arrest and court-martial Isaac for uttering such seditious views, but did not consider the option for a moment. He had opened the discussion and was therefore responsible for its outcome. Judging by the private's reaction, he posed no further threat to decorum. Watching him shrink back to size brought relief, but, at the same time, left Waley feeling strangely diminished. Something had happened here which he could not afford to reflect on, but yet had altered his perception for ever. He realised, for the first time in his life, that poetry could be much more than a pleasing arrangement of words on the page. Lacking the strength to face up to the truth contained within Isaac's poem, he felt a grudging admiration for the insight and courage it must have taken actually to write it down. He writhed uncomfortably beneath the calm exterior the situation now forced him to assume.

"Oh, while I remember, Colonel Ritchie phoned me yesterday to say that the Royal Engineers are looking for chaps to lay barbed wire up at the front. He thinks you'll be ideal for the job given the experience you've already had in that line of work. You're to be transferred some time next week. He promised to get back to me with more precise details later. All right?"

As Isaac mumbled his reply, Waley felt something die inside him. He swallowed what felt like a huge lump in his throat and nodded curtly.

"Very well then. Carry on."

Ignoring the cook, he turned and crossed to Sergeant Brooks who had suddenly appeared in the doorway. Glancing around to ascertain no one was listening, he addressed the NCO in a low voice:

"Have you had any trouble with Rosenberg?"

"What like, sir?"

"Has he been stirring up any of the lads at all?"

He felt guilty about asking, but knew now how potentially subversive the poet could be. Brooks' reaction demonstrated his fears were unfounded. The latter would not have dreamt of giving the benefit of the doubt, had any existed. The reply was grudging when it came.

"No, sir. Apart from the fact 'e's slovenly and in a trance 'alf the time, 'e's been no bother really. 'E's a loner though; don't mix much with the men. Stays up late, mostly scribbling away on that paper you gave 'im, sir. I told 'im last night to snuff 'is candle out and get some shut eye. Ten minutes later, 'e was still at it so I blew the bloody thing out myself and told 'im to look sharp. 'Ave you 'eard anything about his transfer yet, sir?"

Feeling more awkward than ever, Waley struggled to sound matter-of-fact.

"Indeed I have. He'll be out of here by the end of next week. Colonel Ritchie has arranged for him to join a wiring company attached to the Royal Engineers In the meantime, keep an eye on him and let me know if he says or does anything out of the ordinary."

"Don't you worry, I'll watch out, sir."

"Thank you, Sergeant."

"Very good, sir."

The captain returned the salute and addressed Higgins, who was still fussing nearby.

"Now then, Corporal, let's try that soup of yours before it gets cold."

"Thank you kindly, sir."

Turning towards the steaming tureens, he glanced over at the sink where Isaac was scrubbing unenthusiastically at a crusty pot. Somehow he must set his fears aside and concentrate on the practical issues facing him each day. Men's lives depended on his ability to think clearly without dithering. He tentatively lifted the ladle to his lips and sipped at the vile liquid.

Sergeant Brooks was lying stretched out on his bunk, shrouded in a fug of cigarette smoke, when Higgins entered, clutching a half bottle of whisky under his greatcoat. He pulled himself upright and grinned over at his friend.

"Evenin', Alf. What's that you've got concealed under your coat then? A bottle of rot gut or has Mistress Palm and her five daughters been paying you a little visit?"

He laughed uproariously at his own joke. Higgins scowled and sat down on the only chair in the small dugout.

"You can laugh, Jack, but I've had a fuckin' terrible day."

"Well, better get the cork out of that bottle and 'ave a drink then. And when you've finished, pass it over here smartish." Brooks smiled again and offered his cigarette packet. "They're not bad actually. Got them from Jackson earlier on. You remember Rob Jackson? Sergeant with the Royal Engineers—decent sort of a fella. Any'ow, 'e got hold of a box of posh Frenchy cigarettes—expensive, 'e said."

"Sorry to take it out on you, Jack, but I'm fuckin' livid."

"That's what friends is for. What's up then?"

"It's that little cunt Rosenberg, ain't it! First of all he gets the captain so riled up he says the fuckin' soup's tasteless and needs more salt. That's the word he actually used—'tasteless'! Where the fuck does he expect me to get extra salt from anyway? He's lucky I manage to get me 'ands on any at all! Everything's hard to get hold of—he knows that! It took him weeks to get his fuckin' shells, didn't it? Of course, he wouldn't normally have said anything 'cept Rosenberg got him in a lather."

"I missed most of that. What actually 'appened?"

"The old man went across to speak to the little bastard, and before you can say how's your father, they're natterin' away like old chums."

"I told you, fuckin' Jews—two sides of the same coin."

"Maybe at first, but later on I thought Waley was gonna murder 'im. Christ, you should have heard Rosenberg; he was bawlin' his head off like."

"What were they on about?"

"Well, that's the thing. I was tryin' to get the captain's attention but he wasn't having any of it. He was supposed to be tasting the soup but instead they was discussin' fucking poetry. I couldn't make head nor tail of it, to tell you the truth!"

"That's a turn up for the books. Poetry you say?" Brooks sat back and drew deeply on the remains of his cigarette. "The bastard's certainly scribbling away at something most of the time. Seems to forget there's a war on when 'e gets started. But why was Waley so worked up?"

"It beats me. Here, have a swallow, Jack—that's what it's for." Higgins, who seemed a little more cheerful now, passed the bottle across and Brooks grasped it absentmindedly.

"Yeh, thanks. I wonder why 'e got so angry though. Must 'ave been something Rosenberg said that got 'im going."

"He wasn't so bleedin' angry as me, I'll tell you that. Rosenberg actually shoved me away. Can you believe it?"

The sergeant gave a low whistle.

"Now that is 'ard to credit. He may be sloppy, but 'e wouldn't normally say boo to a goose."

"I told him afterwards that if he ever did that again, I'd fuckin' swing for him. He seemed to get the message all right. I've put him on fatigues for the rest of the week anyhow."

Looking thoughtful, Brooks raised the bottle to his lips and gulped a mouthful, gasping as the fiery liquid seared its way down to his stomach.

"Maybe they got into some sort of religious argument. These Jews takes their religion very serious, you know. Are you sure it wasn't somethin' religious they was on about?"

Feeling that his friend was showing too much interest in peripheral aspects of the incident, Higgins reacted impatiently.

"How the fuck do I know? It might have been. I think they was going on about the Garden of Eden or something."

"Well, there you go then. Stands to reason they was arguing about the bible. Maybe they 'ad a difference of opinion. That might account for them fallin' out like." He suddenly stood up and stretched. "Let's 'ave a turn down the trenches and see if anybody's fallen asleep on duty. I could do wiv a walk. And don't worry, Rosenberg's on the way out."

"Oh?"

"Yeh. A'll tell you outside."

Slowly climbing a flight of stairs, they emerged into the cool night air. The moon and stars were startlingly bright and it was so still they could hear the muffled voices of sentries almost fifty yards away. Higgins shivered and drew in his greatcoat, fastening up the buttons. He followed Brooks up the trench, their heavy boots clattering noisily on the duckboards. It was so light, they had no problem seeing where a section of the trench had been shattered by a recent shell. Stepping carefully round the hole, Brooks took out two cigarettes, lit them and handed one to Higgins. He stared at the damage, assessing how long it would take to repair.

"I don't remember this fucker landing. We'll 'ave to get it sorted out in an 'urry. If the old man sees it lookin' like this, 'e'll shit a brick. It's bleedin' still, ain't it? You could hear Fritz farting in 'is trench even back 'ere."

They walked two abreast, pausing now and again to inhale and glance up at the night sky. The Germans were largely ignoring this part of the line at the moment. Probably, the sergeant reasoned, because they wanted it back in one piece when they eventually decided to launch their counterattack. He suddenly remembered he hadn't told Higgins the good news regarding Isaac's transfer.

"Oh yeh, I was going to tell you. The old man told me Rosenberg's getting shipped over to the Royal Engineers. 'E'll probably end up in Jackson's unit. God 'elp 'im if 'e does!"

Ahead of them, a soldier wrapped in a greatcoat and sipping from a tin mug, was gazing intently at the ground near his feet. Something scuttled away as Brooks called out.

"Hey Jones, look lively. We could 'ave been the bleedin' Hun for all you know."

"Yes, Sarge. Who goes there?"

"A bit late now, son. Keep alert or I'll 'ave your guts for fuckin' garters! What was you lookin' at any'ow?"

"It was a rat, Sarge, the size of a bleedin' cat. It came right up to me, bold as you like."

"It'll soon be eating you, if you don't keep an eye out. Carry on."

They turned down a communications trench and continued towards the huge, sunken storeroom, which served as the cookhouse. Higgins led the way.

"The Fritzes certainly know how to dig trenches, you got to give 'em that. Come on in, Jack. I've got some stew left that I made special earlier on."

In the far corner, Brooks noticed someone scrubbing hard at the surface of the massive, discoloured hob.

"Okay, Rosenberg, you're finished for the night," Higgins snapped. "Get the fuck out of here and make sure you're back first thing I want that surface clean enough to eat off or you'll know about it."

Without a word, the private slowly limped out of the kitchen. Stepping into a small side room, Higgins motioned his friend to sit down.

"Here's the bottle, Jack—help yourself while I get this stew heated up." He began to busy himself, shouting various comments over his shoulder. "Rosenberg won't be writing any poetry tonight at any rate. I've had him on that cooker for three hours."

"Don't be so sure." The sergeant stretched out his legs and farted loudly. "Where there's a will there's a way. If 'e can get 'old of a candle stub 'e'll be at it for hours yet. Mark my words."

"Christ, he must be bleedin' mad."

"That's as maybe. But 'e'll soon be somebody else's problem, thank God."

Chapter Six

1917

*I am in hospital and have been here for about two months—
lucky for me—I fancy-as I got out of this late stunt by being
here...*

Extract from letter to Joseph Leftwich: 8th December 1917

*I am afraid I can do no writing or reading; I feel so restless here
and un-anchored. We have lived in such an elemental way so
long, things here don't look quite right to me somehow; or it
may be the consciousness of my so limited time for freedom-so
little time to do so many things bewilders me...*

*Extract from letter to Gordon Bottomley: on leave, 21st
September 1917*

...Frail hands gleam up through the human quagmire and lips
  of ash
Seem to wail, as in sad faded paintings
Far sunken and strange...

From "Daughters Of War": 1917

...What are the great sceptred dooms
To us, caught
In the wild wave?
We break ourselves on them,
My brother, our hearts and years.

From "In War": 1917

...Out of unthinkable torture,
Eyes kissed by death,
Won back to the world again,
Lost and won in a breath,

Cruel men are made immortal.
Out of your pain born.
They have stolen the sun's power
With their feet on your shoulders worn.

From "Soldier: Twentieth Century": 1917

Isaac stared down the trench, watching rain drops bounce on the huge, muddy puddles. It wouldn't be long, he reckoned, before the soldiers were forced to swim along the narrow channels. The glorious summer weather, usurped by equinoctial extremes, was now a fading memory. Although only halfway through, October was proving an effective harbinger of winter with temperatures fluctuating wildly and snow flakes periodically dusting the savaged landscape. He dreaded more than anything the onset of freezing conditions, recalling the hardships he'd barely survived the previous year.

Though pleased to be reunited with his mates after temporary assignment to the Royal Engineers, he realised full well that this sector, in the vicinity of Cambrai, was becoming increasing unstable—each side remorselessly harassing the other. Not a day passed without trench mortar and artillery strikes, while raids launched across no-man's-land had become regular occurrences. The steady build-up of soldiers and supplies continued, as if both sides, knowing a full-scale offensive was approaching, were determined to be fully prepared.

Isaac always felt terribly vulnerable while on sentry duty. Shivering under his saturated greatcoat, he knew from experience that the big guns could soon be targeting his own position. Even more troubling was the likelihood of a surprise attack by an enemy raiding party armed to the teeth with sharpened spades and rifle grenades. At this very moment such a force could easily be approaching, using the numerous shell-holes for cover. Trench periscopes weren't much good in the rain—the glass optics quickly blurring over; and listening posts were probably inundated with water and abandoned. The trouble was that when he had little else to think about his imagination tended to run riot, every tiny sound a prelude to disaster.

He recalled Harry Jacobs' account of a particularly vicious raid that had taken place early yesterday morning. Catching the Germans completely by surprise, the men had leapt into the enemy trench and hacked the terrified sentries to pieces. His friend had not spared him the gory details:

"One of them was just lying there lookin' up at me. I bashed 'im over the 'ead wiv me spade. I swear, Rosie, it split 'is skull in two. That'll teach 'em for Alf—the bastards."

Harry was normally less than enthusiastic about slaughtering the enemy, but the gruesome circumstances surrounding Alf Billingham's death had incensed the entire company. Wounded in the thigh while returning from a sortie in no-man's-land, Alf was caught out in the open and unable to crawl to safety. German snipers proceeded to blow him apart piece by piece until only scraps of flesh and clothing remained attached to a rusting screed of barbed wire. His mates could only grit their teeth and look on while laughter drifted across from the enemy trenches. When a revenge attack was proposed, every man in C Company volunteered his services.

Isaac tried to generate some warmth in his feet and legs by stamping up and down the few yards of trench in his immediate vicinity. His health, holding up well for the past few months, seemed to have taken a sudden downturn. At first he thought it was just a cold, but the ache in his bones and the tightness in his chest suggested something more serious. The fact that the rain hadn't stopped since his return from leave and he'd been wet through for three days in a row probably accounted for it. He wondered how much more he could take before being forced to report sick. Knowing the hostile reaction this would provoke, he was understandably reluctant to approach the battalion doctor.

The sound of a splash and muffled thump out in no-man's-land jolted him into action. Fumbling for his rifle, he yanked it round, desperately trying to get a fix on the point of the parapet where an attack would most likely come. At the same time he shouted out the set challenge with as much bravado as he could muster and demanded the day's password. His hands were trembling so violently he almost dropped the gun. A gruff voice, almost directly above his head, spat out the required words: "Tinker-fucking-bell". Isaac's relief was intense, though, as far as he knew, the middle word was not officially sanctioned. He wondered why the captain kept devising passwords so vexatious to his NCOs.

"We're coming in. Watch what you're doing with that bloody rifle, Private!"

"Advance, f...friend and be recognised."

The top of the trench suddenly swarmed with soldiers. He tried to imagine what he would have done if they'd been Germans. Several sandbags dropped heavily into the mud followed by a landslide of cursing bodies. The same angry voice shouted out again:

"Don't wreck the trench, you bastards, or I'll have you all back here repairing it in the morning. Somebody help me with Williams. Okay, son, down you go."

A groaning body was slowly lowered and Isaac laid his rifle aside to help. He noticed the man was pressing both hands hard against his stomach. Seconds later, another soldier, with sergeant's stripes, leapt down beside them gazing at the casualty now doubled up on the soggy fire-step. Isaac noted concern in the frown of his eyes as they blinked away the driving rain.

"Get a stretcher party right away, Harris." He addressed a lanky corporal whose large hands were slicked with blood—his own or that of his stricken comrade was hard to tell. "I'll wait here till it arrives."

"Right oh, Sarge."

"And make sure the men get some rations and a tot of rum."

"Will do, Sarge."

The soldiers splashed off down the winding trench.

"You," he turned to address Isaac, "keep your eyes open; we might have been followed. You couldn't see an elephant moving among these bloody craters in this weather! We certainly gave 'em something to think about though, didn't we, Williams?"

Williams wasn't listening. He was compacted into a tight ball, his groaning now transformed into harsh, throaty gasps.

The sergeant took a step towards Isaac, grimacing over his shoulder. His voice assumed a whispering confidentiality.

"A Hun bayoneted the lad in the stomach. I staved the bastard's head in but it was too late; his insides have been butchered up good."

Isaac felt sick and shaky—his physical weakness compounded by a wave of revulsion at the madness substituting for normality in this hellish place. Meanwhile, the terrible gasping accelerated.

"Where the fuck are these medics?"

Judging by the scowl of intense concentration, the sergeant appeared to be trying to conjure the stretcher-bearers out of thin air. The sound suddenly choked off followed by a massive gulping as if Williams was trying to swallow his Adam's apple. He slumped forward, at the same time releasing the grip on his abdomen. Something slithered slowly onto his lap and down the front of his legs. The stench was overpowering. Isaac recoiled in horror.

"For Christ's sake, son, I told you to hold on, didn't I?"

When help arrived a few minutes later, it was too late. Williams had stopped shaking and crouched silent, his arms hanging limply by his sides.

After the corpse was removed, the burly NCO stood glaring at the damaged trench wall as though unsure what to do next. It seemed as though an intricate carving in stone had replaced the living, breathing man. Just when Isaac began to think his silent companion might have fallen asleep on his feet, he pulled out a disintegrating packet of cigarettes from his tunic pocket and tried to light up without success. Finally, he threw the soaked fag into the mud and ground it out of sight.

"It's funny, you know, even now, after all that's happened, I've still got more respect for Gerry than these bastards who tell us what to do but never gets their own hands dirty." He turned and stared at Isaac through tormented eyes. The poet felt inadequate and awkward under the intense scrutiny. "Do you get my meaning?" Without waiting for a reply, he shrugged, apparently indifferent to the mutinous nature of his sentiments. The attitude of his audience was obviously of less importance than the need to express a profound disillusionment with the conduct of the war. "Things was totally different where we was stationed last year. We had an understanding with the Hun. You had to play the game, of course. We fired shells, they fired shells—dropping them on the same place at the same time every day. Kept HQ happy, you see; they didn't have a clue what was really going on. As long as you used up your daily quota of ammo, they was generally satisfied. Now and again somebody came down to check up on what was happening, but it was easy enough to pull the wool."

Isaac watched the ghost of a smile play around the corners of the sergeant's mouth.

"Only a couple of lads got hurt in two months! And they just happened to be in the wrong place at the wrong time; you couldn't really blame Gerry for that."

Squatting down, he slowly heaved up a displaced sandbag and pushed it back into the trench wall.

Although surprised to hear this hard-bitten soldier evincing respect for the enemy, especially after what had just occurred, Isaac was well aware that such ritualised truces were often entered into by combatants on both sides. They represented one of the few ways men could exercise any control over their lives at the front. If only, he reflected, ordinary soldiers on both sides could take the process one step further and end the slaughter.... But that was pure fantasy. The fear of retribution meted out to would-be mutineers, and the vicious anti-German propaganda disseminated by High Command to fuel aggression, were altogether too potent.

The sergeant stood up and stretched, kicking his left boot hard against the edge of a semi-submerged duckboard.

"That all stopped when we moved up here. Now we kill them and they kill us and who benefits from that?" Again, he stared blearily at Isaac. "Only boys that are happy now are them sleeping in castles fifty mile behind the lines. The Gerries are no different than us, that's the truth of it! The same shit to wade through every day; the same fuckin' awful rations and lads like Williams getting their guts torn out. Do you see?"

This time he gave the private time to reply.

"Yes. I wish we c…could…"

Unable to express the urgency of his desire to see an end to the insanity, Isaac halted mid-sentence and stared down at his feet. Like his companion, he felt more empathy for the enemy than the Hun-hating press back home, or, for that matter, the army of non-combatants vigorously promoting the conflict on the home front without sharing any of the risks or hardships involved.

With an effort, the NCO pulled himself together.

"I'd better get off. I should have reported in long ago. When are you due to be relieved, son?"

"Just under two hours, Sarge."

"Oh well, not so bad then. Things should be all right for a while. Gerry'll wait till morning to get his own back most likely. Then he'll shell the fuck out of us." He stuck out a filthy hand. "My name's Alec by the way. What's yours?"

"Er…Isaac."

"Well, I'll see you around, Isaac." He paused for a moment. "Jesus, this water'll soon be over our heads, eh!"

He managed a brief smile, but Isaac could see that the anger and pain embedded in his eyes had not diminished. Like a dog emerging from water, he shook a cascade of drops out of his hair before disappearing round the trench. Lost in thought, Isaac stared after him before resuming his lonely vigil.

His recent leave, the first since quitting English shores a little over a year ago, had generated a strange mixture of pleasure and pain. During the entire ten-day period, Isaac felt disconnected from himself and everyone else. Deep down, he found it virtually impossible to reconcile life at the front with anything experienced in London before the war. It was as if there were now two Isaacs: one, falsely exuberant, eager to scotch rumours that army life had changed him for the worse; the other, isolated and unhappy, overwhelmed by the clamour of his extrovert twin. The more he tried to make light of things, reassuring everyone that life wasn't so bad and the war would be over soon, the more he yearned to reveal the unpalatable truth.

Hacha, normally sensitive to her son's precarious mood swings, was caught up in the whirlwind of charm. Her fears fell away as Isaac displayed a bonhomie she hadn't witnessed in him before. This, coupled with having Elkon home on leave at the same time, energised a part of her that had lain dormant for years. For a time, she shed the misery accumulated as all three of her sons were gradually pulled into the conflict. To her daughter Annie's relief, she also suspended hostilities in the war with her husband. Barnett was able to walk into a room without being exposed to her withering, verbal assaults. Taking his place at the head of the table on the first night of his eldest son's leave, he even managed a pallid smile or two, although Isaac was dismayed by the prematurely ageing face, proof, if proof were needed, of the long struggle to retain a measure of dignity in a life beset by failure.

Isaac visited the people and places that had formerly provided meaning in the hope of escaping the conflict raging inside. The strange sense of dislocation persisted, however. The Slade, where his artistic skills were encouraged and honed; and the Café Royal, with its passionate debates and impromptu introductions, seemed part of a life he'd experienced vicariously.

Calling on Sonia one evening with the intention of discovering more about Rodker's recent imprisonment for evasion of conscription ordinance, he was staggered when the false buoyancy, so carefully constructed over the past few days, was almost immediately swept away by a tidal wave of emotion. He found himself expressing undying love for her through choking sobs. Life's fragility—the old patterns eroded by the war—and the need to reveal himself proved overpowering in her presence. In a strange sense, pinning his true colours to the mast brought relief, although he felt giddy as if tottering on the edge of a sheer drop. She settled herself down beside him and cradled his head between her soft breasts.

"Sssh now, sssh. You know I'll always be your friend, Isaac. I'm sorry I can't be more but I love John and there's no way that will ever change. I tried to explain how I felt years ago." Gently stroking his hair, she felt his body relax a little. "I think I understand what you've been going through. Not the war part, of course...but I do understand love and...and what it's like to ache for something you can't have...I wish there was more I could do; some way to make you feel better." She raised his head and kissed his face. "If you want we...we could...go upstairs.... Maybe you'd feel..."

Deeply moved by her compassion, he made a heroic attempt to pull himself together. It was important to retain some dignity in the face of his desperate desires. "No, n...no, I'm fine. I'm s...s...sorry this happened. It's just that..."

Sonia raised a finger to her lips and smiled. "No, don't say anything; there's nothing to explain or feel bad about."

"You've been very k...kind. I'm grateful for..."

"Ssh, Isaac. There's no need to say any more. Let's have some tea together and talk about old times. Or if you want to talk about...the...front, we can. I would like to be a good friend to you."

As he strode home through the dark streets, Isaac felt emptier than ever. It was as if another part of his soul had been siphoned off. Eager as he'd been to accept Sonia's offer, he knew the act in itself would have changed little, although her empathy had revealed to him what he'd always sought in a relationship. He didn't feel envious of Rodker any more, but glad for him. It was only love such as Sonia's that could possibly redeem mankind. While able to contemplate this greater vision in the abstract, Isaac felt more isolated than ever as if he'd been carried beyond the possibility of personal redemption. Like a swimmer struggling against powerful currents, his resources were waning. It suddenly came to him that he was probably not going to survive this war. And even if he did, something had died inside which could never be revived. Perhaps there was a point when he would cease to care. Up till now he'd persevered against the odds, but there were limits, and although his self-endurance had been tested on several occasions, these might prove trivial in light of what was to come.

The cumulative effect, he knew, was a major factor. Month after month of physical and mental strain often proved disastrous at the front. He'd seen men reach the end of their tether and openly invite death. In the trenches this was a relatively simple procedure. All you had to do was climb over the parapet in broad daylight, or walk away from the front line. The result was the same. Others attempting a "blighty" wound ran considerable risks. Trying to ensure the injury was serious enough to require immediate transfer to hospital, or better still, back home, might easily prove fatal. There was also the worry that if your superiors got wind of what you were up to, a court martial would put an abrupt end to all such efforts.

He struggled to regain his former insouciance. For his family's sake he must try to keep a tight lid on things.

Next evening, tramping the streets in the hope of achieving some peace of mind, he decided to visit Annetta Raphael, the only person who'd ever offered him the unaffected love he desired. It was impossible to gauge the welcome he would receive after the way he had treated her but Isaac was determined to put things right if he could. His conscience, coupled with a desire to resolve all conflicts in his personal life, was proving a powerful force.

As he approached Annetta's first-floor flat, perched above the blacked-out windows of a large bookshop, the drizzling rain turned into a steady downpour. Still unwilling to pull the bell stop next to the chipped door, he scouted around, trying to screw up his courage. Annetta doted on him he knew, but he'd taken advantage of her affection when it became obvious that his chances of securing Sonia's love were doomed to failure. Even now his feelings were ambiguous. Was he simply intent on using her once again, or was there something genuine behind his wish to make amends?

After ten minutes or so of internal debate, he suddenly made up his mind and tugged fiercely at the bell stop. He entered the stairwell and squinted up at the landing above; Annetta was standing there gazing down at him.

"Is that you, Isaac? I'd heard you were home on leave. How are you?"

Isaac could detect no animosity in her voice, only pleasure tinged with concern.

"Fine, thank you, Annetta—c…can I come up?"

He still believed she would most likely send him packing as soon as the surprise wore off.

"Yes, of course! You must be soaking wet. Come up and dry off."

He slowly climbed the familiar stairs and stood face to face with the lover he'd so callously deserted two years earlier. Her long, fair hair still hung loose, falling across her right shoulder just as he remembered it, although there were flecks of grey there now, and her lined, careworn face was beginning to show its age. Was she ten or twelve years older than him? He wasn't really sure. There was no doubt, though, she was pleased to see him. Her generous mouth was wreathed in smiles; it was as if she'd wiped the circumstances of their former leave-taking from her mind.

As he moved forward, she pulled his slight body into her own, curving her arm protectively around his back.

"Let me take your coat. My goodness, you are wet through. You never knew how to look after yourself."

Entering the cluttered lounge, he felt comforted by the bright fire blazing under the broad mantelpiece weighed down by the porcelain dancers she collected and loved. The place was just as he remembered it: the battered piano in the far corner, groaning under dozens of musical scripts; the rickety stand, still in the same place. It was as if he'd stepped back through time. Despite the world's descent into madness, this room remained inviolate, preserved in some sort of protective bubble. He could think of nothing so greatly contrasting the insecurity and danger left behind in France. Yet, in another sense, it highlighted his own strangeness. Standing dripping in the fire's warm glow, he felt like an intruder—an alien from a distant world.

"It's been so long, Isaac. I'd hoped for a letter or something to tell me you were still alive. When Annie told me you'd joined up I wrote, but I guess my letter never reached you."

For the first time he detected a note of regret in her voice. The letter had arrived, but he'd chosen to ignore it. In the middle of writing "Moses" and adjusting to the rigours of army life, everything else seemed increasingly irrelevant. The sense of having abused their friendship thrust back to the surface, reinforcing his awkwardness. He could find nothing adequate to say.

"Sit down next to the fire and tell me how you've been."

He eased back into a large armchair and tried to collect himself. A lump was beginning to form in the back of his throat and he felt close to tears.

"I'm s...sorry about everything. It's...it's just that I...I wanted to..."

Annetta reached for his hands and pressed them between her own.

"There's no need to say anything, Isaac, I understand."

"C...coming back after so long feels...very strange. It's hard to...to...explain...but everything's changed or...or...perhaps it's just me that's changed. I c...c...can't really decide which. It seems like I...d...don't belong here any more. I've been trying to...adjust... but... I don't... don't know what to...how to..."

He choked and began to cough, his chest feeling as if it might burst; tears sprang through the gaps between his fingers. Before he knew what was happening, Annetta had pulled him to his feet and was guiding him back through the hall towards the bedroom. He tried to protest but was cut short.

"Don't say anything, my love. Don't say anything."

On the bed she began to undress him. The faint scent of perfume and the caressing fingers aroused him in a way he'd forgotten was possible. She pulled his trousers and under-drawers over his ankles and gently eased him between the sheets. Then, hugging his thin body close to hers, she began to stroke his inner thighs and genitals. At the same time, she directed his hand between her legs against the soft parted skin. Slowly his index and second fingers felt their way inside her until they were buried up to the knuckles. She moaned and squeezed her thighs together, coming again and again. Isaac rolled on top and pushed himself into her, escaping for a time the terrible burden of his thoughts. Later, wrapped in post-coital sleep, he was unaware of the tears on his neck and shoulder.

After the first night, he returned again and again, listening to Annetta sing and play the piano, and later making love in her small, perfume-scented bedroom. The war receded a little, leaving him with a rare sense of well-being. For the first time in years his obsession with Sonia eased and he began to experience real feelings for Annetta. When they parted, he swore he'd return to her but, leaving the flat for the last time, whispering, inexorable voices were drawing him back to France and his fate.

Before boarding the train to Southampton, Isaac experienced the strongest sense of dislocation yet. As he walked arm in arm with Annie towards Victoria Railway Station, London's familiar landmark buildings and bustling streets seemed to him like a series of old, familiar paintings recapturing feelings associated with a previous existence. Similarly, the people he'd known all his life were part of this fast fading past—all dear to him but no longer part of the here and now.

Later, as the train pulled out of the station and the sad faces of family and friends blurred and receded through the dirty glass of the carriage window, he felt as though he was returning home.

✳

Three days after his encounter with the disillusioned sergeant, Isaac was ordered to report to Major Alexander for an immediate check-up. He'd collapsed on duty and was running a high temperature. Barely able to walk, he was helped to the clinic where more lectures on the evils of malingering were dispensed than medicines. On this occasion, however, having recently incurred a stinging reprimand from Brigade Headquarters for his part in returning a dying soldier to active duty, Alexander diagnosed acute influenza and reluctantly transferred his patient to the 51st military hospital for further observation and treatment.

For days Isaac was unable to distinguish between illusion and reality. He struggled in the coils of a troubling dream that rarely loosened its grip. Lost and alone in a massive forest, he walked and walked as the darkness grew ever deeper and the air harder to breathe. Reaching a moonlit glade, momentary relief was replaced with terror as he came face to face with a shining white unicorn. The fabulous creature slowly moved towards him and halted as motionless as a marble statue, its massive horn poised inches from his chest, its disturbingly human eyes holding him in a hypnotic trance. He desperately wanted to break away but couldn't move a muscle.

Isaac sweated and muttered in his sleep, at times almost jerking into consciousness before plunging back into an underworld of repressed desire.

He was kneeling behind Sonia. She lay on her front smiling round at him. Gently caressing the backs of her legs, he leaned forward to kiss her taut, upturned buttocks. The musky smell was overwhelming. At the same time he could feel her feet gently playing with his erection. Nuzzling into her warm flesh, he willingly surrendered himself to the rapture of the moment as she pressed and rubbed him with fresh urgency.

Suddenly awake, he groped around for Sonia, feeling nothing but rough sheets and heavy blankets. Gradually, reluctantly, he dragged back to reality as the vivid dream faded. He stared down the line of beds—amorphous shapes in the gritty darkness of the ward— experiencing an acute sense of loss, hard to reconcile with the fact that Sonia had never been his at any time in the past. He shivered as his sweat-soaked body began to cool, and he became aware that the front of his drawers was damp and sticky.

He rolled over and tried to wriggle onto a drier portion of the sheet. This proved tricky as the sagging springs inclined him towards the centre. His head beat uncomfortably and he felt his chest slowly tightening up again. After seven weeks in the military hospital, he seemed to be making no real progress at all. The persistent cough and chest pains convinced him that he was succumbing to TB, even though the doctors denied this was the case.

There was some comfort to be derived from the timing of his illness. The long anticipated battle was now raging near the town of Cambrai, and his own division was seriously engaged. As he lay here recovering, many of his comrades were most likely dead or injured. Lately, the hospital had been inundated with casualties shipped in from the front. Compared to these unfortunate souls, he felt like a fraud.

At first, Isaac, and those others suffering from illnesses unrelated to combat, were separated from the wounded and dying; but gradually, as the wards filled up, the segregation became impossible to maintain. The effect on his morale was marked and convalescence proved difficult. Only when asleep was he able to escape the stench and din surrounding him.

The doctors and nurses were working flat out to cope with the influx of wounded. All night long the wards resounded to shrieks and groans, while each morning several beds yawned empty awaiting their next pitiful cargo. The hospital was only a brief stopping point for the majority of injured soldiers, destined for the burgeoning cemeteries. Isaac often felt his bed to be a frail boat bobbing on a sea of death.

Many of those brought here fresh from the butcher's knife, succumbed within hours to blood loss and post-traumatic shock. Others died a little later from blood poisoning or yielded to the slow spread of gangrene. One man in the next bed, whose left leg had been amputated just above the knee, appeared to be making a good recovery at first. Isaac sketched him as he sat propped up on two pillows recounting details of the recent battle. His tales of tanks destroyed and their crews suffocated or burned alive inside, filled the poet with dread. Elkon was in the tank corps and Isaac prayed his brother was not among the casualties. The patient was particularly looking forward to being sent home. The prospect of seeing his wife and two young sons after a two-year absence filled him with joy.

A few days later, he was whisked away and returned with the remainder of the limb removed at the hip. The irresistible tide of infection could not be stemmed, and soon the bed was occupied by a young soldier whose legs had been blown off by "friendly" shells falling short of their designated target. He died screaming for his mother during the first night.

Wide awake now, any hope of getting back to sleep abandoned, Isaac contemplated the terrible state the trenches must be in. What would he find on his return to the front? News of renewed bouts of rain and the onset of freezing weather filled him with dread. Maybe, if he was lucky, the present push would deliver the *coup-de-grace* anticipated for so many long years. It was possible that the mass use of tanks might still swing the balance in the Allies' favour. In an effort to neutralise despair, he told himself how lucky he'd been not only to escape the hazards of battle, but also the equally vicious assaults launched by nature. He calculated it must be almost dawn, although, with the windows permanently closed and shuttered, it was hard to tell. The lamps, hanging from the low timber ceiling, always cast the same sallow light whatever the time of day.

A fragment from "The Unicorn" suddenly ran through his mind. *...Bestial man-shapes ride dark impulses/Through roots in the bleak blood, then hide/In shuddering light from their self-loathing.* Due to a chronic lack of paper, the redrafting process of his latest verse play necessitated a constant revision of the lines in his head. Since his memory was so notoriously unreliable, being unable to record important changes was proving to be a major problem, all the more frustrating because he felt sure this latest piece was darkly expressive in a way he'd never managed to be before.

As time went on, despite increasing weariness and despondency, Isaac believed his work was becoming much less encumbered with unnecessary baggage and growing in lucidity. His tortured vision of individuals stripped of their freewill and twisted into hideous shapes was revealed here, and he resolved to amplify and refine the rough sketch at a later time.

He often wondered how long he would be able to continue. The miracle was that he'd managed to produce so much over the summer. Apart from the obvious dangers and the fight to preserve his precarious health, petty abuse was a constant factor in the erosion of his will. Again and again, Isaac had been punished for absentmindedness and failure to adhere to army regulations—the worst of these occurring when an officer noticed he wasn't carrying the regulation gas mask. The penalty, seven days' pack drill to be completed each morning between shifts up the line, had fuelled deep resentment at the time. He recalled the effort and boredom involved, and a growing suspicion that the authorities, in league with higher forces, were out to silence him once and for all. Gritting his teeth, he'd persevered, determined that nothing would be allowed to interfere with his writing. One day the true nature of this slaughter would emerge. Burying the past was not an option as far as he was concerned. If anything was to be salvaged, he must somehow prevail.

More lines returned to him as some poor soul, further up the ward, began to moan in his sleep. The waves of sound, increasing gradually in volume, conveyed a terrible sense of despair.

Mere human travail never broke my spirit
Only my throat to impatient blasphemies.
But God's unthinkable imagination
Invents new tortures for nature
Whose wisdom falters here.
No used experience can make aware
The imminent unknowable.
Sudden destruction
Till the stricken soul wails in anguish
Torn here and there.

As he picked a tentative path through his internal no-man's-land, sleep finally ambushed him. When he came to, the weeping had stopped and the nurses were beginning to serve breakfast. Pulling himself up into a sitting position, he noticed two more beds were empty. The mummified patient directly opposite was gone. Strange, given his restlessness, he hadn't witnessed the nocturnal departure.

Deposited here three days ago, the body, completely swathed in bandages, had instantly intrigued him. As far as he knew, it hadn't moved or uttered a sound during its entire time on the ward. Isaac wondered, at first, if someone had mistaken the hospital for a mortuary. He'd noticed that the arms and legs were unnaturally stunted, and the face, beneath its white covering, was strangely flat.

Overcome with curiosity, he'd eventually plucked up courage to ask one of the nurses about the case. She appeared strangely willing to tell him what she knew. Perhaps, like everyone else on the ward, her growing obsession with what lay behind the anonymous bandages required an outlet.

Known to his comrades as a hell-raiser and fanatical Bosch-hater, the soldier had seemingly slipped into a shell hole and broken his leg while returning from a raid on enemy trenches. Sustained sniper and machine-gun fire had forced his comrades back, frustrating any immediate chance of rescue. The following night, during the cover of darkness, an attempt was made to recover the body. Incredibly, he was still alive, but after having been immersed for long hours in freezing water up to the waist and exposed to sub-zero air temperatures, his face, feet and hands were so severely frostbitten the doctors amputated almost everything, in a desperate attempt to circumvent gangrene. Recovery was theoretically possible, though, as far as the nurse knew, he'd so far refused to eat anything offered, and was simply fading away.

As he contemplated the empty bed, Isaac considered once more the full extent of the dehumanising forces at work in the trenches. This sad creature symbolised naked aggression stripped of all restraint and pity. Transformed into an efficient killing machine conditioned to destroy the enemy, a swift reversal of fortunes had turned the aggressor into victim, tortured by an equally merciless foe and, in a final ironic twist, hacked to pieces by the knives of those trying to save his life. The case highlighted, more clearly than anything else Isaac could think of, the terrible damage inflicted by the war. And now, like so many before him, he was filling a hole in the ground—another wretched victim of a conflict devoid of meaning or purpose.

Isaac sometimes wondered if the psychological wounds perpetrated on the living would ever heal. Could words torn from the souls of poets, caught up like himself in the violence, have any real effect? Would anyone ever be able to assuage the fear that bred such savagery? He understood more clearly than ever how war could beget war— one conflict moving easily to the next—each generation carrying the hidden contagion. The present catastrophe was the logical progression of all wars that had gone before it. Mankind, especially in the light of recent technological advances, would surely soon be extinct or damaged beyond repair. Maybe this was the fate God had planned all along for his children—everything beyond malevolence and the consuming lust for power, pure illusion, fashioned to snare gullible fools like himself. The wrecking power he envisaged at the heart of civilisation appalled him more than anything else.

In his present mood, Isaac found himself questioning everything that had provided meaning in the past. There was little doubt he'd altered beyond recognition. Edward Marsh's latest collection of the "best" in contemporary poetry frankly bored him. Many of the well crafted lines in *Georgian Poetry 1910-1917* seemed incredibly shallow in light of recent events. Even the fact that Marsh had included a tiny fragment of "Moses" left him unmoved. A few short months ago he would have been delighted at any such recognition, however desultory, but now felt it to be insulting and meaningless.

Trevelyan's latest volume, given him by the author in London, also failed to generate much enthusiasm. The philosophy and noble sentiments at the heart of the verse—ingredients which he'd long believed to be the life-blood of art—were rapidly disappearing down a black hole of cynicism. Isaac wrote to his fellow poet from hospital expressing appreciation even though the gesture was as superficial as the bonhomie exhibited during his recent leave.

Feeling feverish and disinclined to eat anything, he lay down, striving to blot the world out. The day passed slowly. Isaac's chest was sounded in the afternoon by a thin, ascetic doctor who merely frowned and said nothing to his patient. He moved quickly on to the next bed occupied by a soldier whose buttocks and upper thighs had been lacerated by an exploding mine.

Unable to restrain himself, the poet watched as the light gauze dressings were carefully removed. The man appeared to have no skin remaining from the waist down, only a mangled mess of angry red flesh closely resembling the heaps of fatty beef Isaac had often seen displayed in the windows of butchers' shops in Whitechapel. He lay on his front, denied movement by a box-like apparatus mounted round his upper torso, while the doctor, with the help of two nurses, began to gently swab the exposed area with wads of cotton wool and pick away pieces of blackened flesh with steel forceps. Despite the delicacy of the operation, the mutilated back quivered in agony as he bit hard into a chunk of wood. Although two inches thick, the wedge was almost completely bitten through after days of grinding pressure. Isaac wished the staff would pull screens around the bed, thus denying him the dreadful temptation to observe the procedure.

After half an hour, the dressings were finally replaced, and despite the continuing noise on the ward, Isaac was able to return to "The Unicorn". His persistence through the remainder of another endless day was finally rewarded by the emergence of three perfect lines.

The roots of a torn universe are wrenched,
See the bent trees like masts of derelicts in ocean
That beats upon this house this ark.

Chapter Seven

1918

...there is no chance whatsoever for seclusion or any hope of writing poetry now. Sometimes I give way and am appalled at the devastation this life seems to have made in my nature. It seems to have blunted me. I seem to be powerless to compel my will to any direction, and all I do is without energy and interest.

Excerpt from letter to Miss Seaton: February 14th, 1918

...I suppose I could write a bit if I tried to work at a letter as an idea—but sitting down to it here after a day's dull stupefying labour-I feel stupefied. When will we go on with things that endure?

Excerpt from letter to John Rodker: February 23rd, 1918

...since I left the hospital all the poetry has gone quite out of me. I seem even to forget words, and I believe if I met anybody with ideas I'd be dumb. No drug could be more stupefying than our work (to me anyway) and this goes on like that old torture of water trickling, drop by drop unendingly, on one's helplessness.

Excerpt from letter to Gordon Bottomley: February 26th, 1918

*...I've seen no poetry for ages now so you mustn't be too
critical—My vocabulary small enough before is impoverished
and bare.*
Excerpt from final letter written to Edward Marsh: March 1918

...Pallid days arid and wan
Tied your soul fast.
Babel cities' smoky tops
Pressed upon your growth
From: "Girl To Soldier On Leave" 1917

Through These Pale Cold Days

Through these pale cold days
What dark faces burn
Out of three thousand years,
And their wild eyes yearn,

While underneath their brows
Like waifs their spirits grope
For the pools of Hebron again—
For Lebanon's summer slope.

They leave these blond still days
In dust behind their tread
They see with living eyes
How long they have been dead.
1918

Aching and weary, Isaac sat slumped on an old wooden box wondering how he was going to survive the second half of a ten-hour shift. The physical labour involved in loading endless crates of ammunition onto motorised vehicles was back-breaking, and every muscle in his body protested against further abuse.

Each morning, as daylight picked its way over the horizon, 8th Platoon, B Company, 1st Battalion of the Kings Own Royal Lancasters assembled outside the arms depot ready for work. A vast amount of freight was moving slowly south east from the coast toward the front line where rumour had it the Germans were planning a major offensive. Years of propaganda suggesting the enemy had been broken and demoralised seemed absurd in the light of recent intelligence.

In addition to transporting equipment and creating an effective supply line, the weakened British Expeditionary Force was hastily developing a new defensive strategy aimed at reducing the overall number of battalions while bringing key units up to full, fighting strength. In the wake of this rationalisation, Isaac's old battalion was broken up, and he found himself transferred north to the 4th Division stationed in the village of Bernaville near Arras.

He prayed for a change in tempo, even viewing a return to active duty as preferable to the mind-numbing labour he was now engaged in. Formerly able to craft a few lines of poetry between tea and lights out, even writing a letter these days proved extraordinarily difficult. Years of battling ill-health and surviving appalling conditions were finally taking their toll. His creative powers, so formerly adept at transfiguring harsh experience, appeared to be on the wane, and, like a mourner at his own funeral, he could only lament their passing.

In an attempt to eschew reality, he applied for a transfer to the Jewish

Battalion, stationed in Palestine. So far there had been no response. At the back of his mind, he'd never really believed anything would come of it, but an unrealistic optimism persisted. Perhaps the warm sun of his ancestral homeland and the camaraderie of brothers-in-arms would regenerate his spirit. The prospect of writing a proud battle hymn for dispossessed Jews around the world was the only thing that kept him sane. In the meantime, he remained a pack animal passively anticipating another bout of back-breaking toil.

The squabbling of his mates, engaged in a bout of gambling with three cups and a stone, diverted him for a moment. Why not join them in their mindless games? Being able to forget, even for a short time, was a tempting prospect. He pulled out a scrap of paper containing the only poem he'd written since arriving in Bernaville. A precious jewel, hewn from the strata of memory, had fired his imagination and briefly restored his former potency. He now struggled to draw inspiration from the terse lines:

> *Fierce wrath of Solomon*
> *Where sleepest thou? Oh see*
> *The fabric which thou won*
> *Earth and ocean to give thee—*
> *O look at the red skies.*

He suddenly scrunched it up in his fist, unwilling to read on. Why must he always undermine such life-affirming imagery, especially when in desperate need of a lift? Could poetry never simply be a balm? Must it always wither the reader with its freezing breath? Reluctantly, he unclenched his fingers and flattened the paper out.

> *Or hath the sun plunged down?*
> *What is this molten gold—*
> *Those thundering fires blown*
> *Through heaven—where the smoke rolled?*
> *Again the great king dies.*

His dreams go out in smoke,
His days he let not pass
And sculptured here are broke
Are charred as the burnt grass
Gone as his mouth's last sighs.

The final stanza was more about himself than Solomon. His will was a forest devastated by war; in the place of tall trees, once hardy and supple, there remained only a wilderness of smouldering stumps. In a moment of rare clarity he knew that only a return to hospital, or a swift end to the war itself could save him now; he remained unwilling, as yet, to consider the release death offered.

A harsh voice, embodying the forces besieging Solomon's temple, returned him to earth with a jolt.

"Right, you lot, break it up. I want this consignment loaded up by five o'clock, and no excuses."

"But, we've still got five minutes left, Sarge." One of the gamblers unwisely voiced his frustration.

"You've got what I say you've got. Get off your arses or you'll all be here an extra hour tonight. Move it!"

Muttering and grumbling, the men began to line up. Isaac, barely able to straighten his aching back, joined them as they marched towards the open doors of the depot. He could already see the enormous stack of boxes piled on the raised platform ready for loading. At this distance they looked like the high wall of a prison, cutting him off from life and liberty. The roar of reversing lorries and the blue exhaust fumes filling the air, merely added to his impression of some infernal region from which there was no conceivable escape.

The weight of each crate meant that two men were required to shift it the few yards from warehouse to vehicle; it wasn't so much the effort of lifting one crate that Isaac found so taxing, but the number they were expected to move in a relatively short period of time. Sergeant Maxwell and his corporals ensured that no one slacked. Only after an hour or so were they allowed a few minutes' respite, and this at

Maxwell's discretion.

Harry Jacobs, observing his companion's listlessness, experienced more than a twinge of concern. Clearly, something had gone badly wrong. Unlike most soldiers, Isaac had always kept himself apart, preferring isolation to intimacy; but in recent weeks communication appeared to have been severed completely. It could be the prelude to some sort of breakdown; he'd seen it before. Although they'd been together for almost three years, Harry couldn't honestly say he knew much more about Isaac than when they'd first met. He was certainly an odd character, constantly scribbling on scraps of paper or old envelopes, unerringly clumsy, habitually forgetful and invariably the victim of bullying NCOs. Most soldiers, especially those who'd survived this long, were able to avoid or deflect the punishments of over-zealous superiors, but not Isaac. He remained a magnet, exerting a vexatious pulling power. Fearing his friend's capacity to attract unwanted attention, Harry had attempted to distance himself over the years, but his efforts were always in vain. He couldn't help feeling anxious and responsible when things went wrong, as they so often did. This stemmed, not only from their long service together, but his admiration for Isaac's remarkable tenacity. Perhaps it was this quality that was missing now.

Not knowing what else to do, he attempted to draw the private out of his shell.

"You look as though you lost ten bob and found threepence. A penny for your thoughts, Rosie."

Not even the flicker of a smile. Harry felt somewhat miffed; in his view the pun had been worth at least a chuckle. Maybe he was losing his touch. To his surprise, Isaac suddenly spoke:

"I'll be fine. Let's get started."

As these were the first words Harry had heard his friend utter in almost two days, Harry felt a little more hopeful.

"Yeh. We'd better start loadin' before that bastard Maxwell notices anything."

For the rest of the afternoon, Harry maintained a cheery banter, designed to raise his companion's spirits. He cracked endless jokes and constantly reiterated how lucky they were to have such a cushy job away from the fighting.

"God, when you think 'ow bad it was back in the trenches last year. Remember when you got ill and went to 'ospital? I never thought we'd ever see you again, but back you popped. Of course, you was jammy. A whole bleedin' battle fought and you tucked up in a nice ward wiv all them nurses an' all. I thought at the time, you lucky little bleeder. But that's the luck of the draw, ain't it? Anyway, 'ere we are, 'umping a few cases around; fings couldn't be much better really. Do you fink Gerry'll 'ave a go then? Can't see it myself after what the brass was sayin' about 'aving destroyed their will to fight an' all. Mind you, Bill Carter, you know, that big fucker what works in the mess? He finks wiv the Ruskies beat an' all, Gerry'll be able to get reinforcements down 'ere. But I told 'im, the yanks'll make up for any shortfall like. He says that the yanks is all talk an'll probably run off when fings get tough. Just shows how bloody lucky we are not to be up at the front, doesn't it?"

Although Isaac contributed nothing to the monologue, Harry's efforts were not totally in vain. He forgot the pain in his arms for a while, and experienced a temporary diminution in the weight pressing down on his spirits. Even if he heard nothing more about his transfer to the Jewish battalion, there was a possibility the war might end. Like most of the other men, he'd heard about the Russian capitulation but was cheered by talk of American involvement. If nothing else, perhaps a further period of leave was in the offing. Even a week or so back home would be better than nothing. He knew there was still a great deal inside him waiting to be written if only he could escape this mind-numbing existence for a while and recoup his powers.

Marching back to their billets, several hours later, Isaac struggled to keep some hope alive, but already the darkness was beginning to press close in around the little fire Harry had lit. Deep down, he knew that nothing had really changed; the underlying spiritual malaise persisted, and talk of the war ending was spurious. Even if it did, how

would he ever manage back in the real world? Recalling the confusion
and feeling of insubstantiality he'd experienced during his last leave
in London, any prospect of reintegration seemed unlikely. Perhaps
he would always remain cut off from the places and people he'd known
during those far off pre-army days. Despite everything, it was only
on his return to the front that he'd actually felt grounded again.
Whichever way he turned, the walls of the temple were crumbling;
how much longer he could hold out was hard to predict.

The shelling was relentless. For six hours, Isaac and his fellow Lancasters
lay in reserve trenches cowering under the solid mass of metal shrieking
over their heads. The second phase of the huge enemy offensive was
well underway. Hardly touched by the massive onslaught which the
week before had overrun British positions around St Quentin, the
fourth Division was fully engaged in an urgent bid to prevent the
Germans capturing Arras and pushing the Third Army back into the
sea.

The initial strike, two days ago, had proved to be something of an
anti-climax. More than anything else it appeared to be a means of testing
British fire power – the initial bombardment lasting less than an hour
before the German soldiers spilled out of their trenches and pressed
forward. For the first time in the war, Isaac experienced a full-scale
battle. Like everyone else, he was ordered onto the parapets and emptied
round after round into the anonymous grey mass until his rifle became
almost too hot to hold. He knew his bullets must be killing and maiming,
but fear of the enemy rushing the trenches and the vicious hand-to-
hand fighting which would inevitably ensue, subdued any doubts. When
the advancing lines disintegrated well short of their objective and fell
back, the relief was palpable. The men cheered even though they knew
this must only be the beginning.

The battalion was relieved later that afternoon and moved into
reserve, less than two miles behind the lines. Next morning, Isaac's
company was ordered to stand to at four-thirty, and, apart from short

breaks for meals and sleep, remained on high alert. Supposedly resting, after a prolonged tour of duty at the front, they were ready to support forward positions.

Crouched now in the heart of the storm, Isaac waited for the explosion that would rip him to pieces. Only fifty yards to his right, a direct hit had blasted open an entire section of trench; mud, splintered wood and wrecked sandbags jumbled with the pulped remains of men. He secretly prayed for such a swift end; it was the screams of the wounded being stretchered out that most unnerved him.

Retreats into a dim inner world, where a coalescence of dreams and memories blunted the sharp edge of fear, had become more frequent of late. Even when wide awake and engaged in the simplest of tasks, he would often lapse into a kind of trance. So far, no one, apart from Harry Jacobs, had noticed anything unusual in this behaviour. Isaac's reputation as an absent-minded ditherer effectively obscured the deterioration in his condition. These evasions were only partially successful, however. Too often, it felt as if he was tapping into someone else's rose-coloured impressions of life before the war, shallow and second-hand. When the walls separating the two finally caved in, he feared for his sanity.

Without warning, the shelling ceased. Isaac found the resulting hiatus hard to bear. The silence, swarming in his ears, created a seal of deafness. Rotating his jaw and trying to yawn failed to relieve the sensation. A strident voice, cutting through the thick air like a knife, quickly convinced him he was not so badly affected as he'd thought.

"Right, men, on your feet. Be ready to move forward on the command."

Isaac rose unsteadily. Ahead of him lay uneven ground pock-marked with smoking shell holes. To his left and right the land rose, offering ideal positions for enemy snipers to target exposed troops. There was little doubt the Germans were at this very moment advancing over no-man's-land, hoping to achieve the decisive breach previously denied them. The only chance of stemming a full-scale rout lay with the battered defenders up ahead who might just manage to hold on until reinforcements arrived.

Already, the distant stutter of small arms fire and the thump of mortar shells indicated what they might soon expect. The fact that the German artillery had ceased shelling, even back here, suggested the enemy were anticipating a rapid breakthrough. He shivered as his fear, barely contained during the bombardment, began to trickle back.

Seconds later, a soldier a few yards ahead of him and a little to his right, suddenly clutched his throat and toppled forward—the crack of the sniper's rifle audible before he hit the ground. From a small copse, three or four hundred yards beyond the advancing line, Isaac spotted tiny bursts of light followed by the distinctive rattle of machine-gun fire. More men fell as bullets tore into the front ranks. The storm troops had arrived quicker than anticipated; the only hope now was that the breakthrough was limited to a few enemy platoons ordered to push ahead without stopping while the next wave swept round to mop up remaining pockets of resistance. It was quite possible they hadn't expected such strong reinforcements to be on hand so quickly. If the trenches had already fallen, however, and this merely the advance guard of a much larger attack force, Isaac's battalion would never reach the old front line.

Orders to find cover and return fire were rapidly issued as field artillery opened up on enemy positions. Soon the copse was reduced to a mass of splintered trunks. Units were then assembled and pushed out onto the flanks with orders to seek and destroy the bands of snipers subjecting the men to a withering cross-fire. Isaac crawled into a nearby shell hole with six of his mates. The stones and scorched earth inside remained hot to the touch. Above, bullets whined and ricocheted. He wondered if this was the end. Would they be given a chance to surrender, or would the Germans simply shoot them out of hand? Rumours of remorseless cruelty were rife, but who could tell?

Gradually the firing tailed off and one of his bolder companions climbed up to take a look. Glancing back, he grinned broadly.

"Looks like the Hun haven't broke through properly yet. Let's get to fuck out of here. Watch them stones when you climb out; some of them is bloody sharp."

He held up a gashed palm.

Standing up top, tentatively glancing around, it seemed to Isaac the man was correct. The breach must have been contained, at least for now. Sporadic shooting up ahead revealed that things were still hot, although the main fire-power of marauding units had obviously been silenced. He spotted at least thirty bodies slumped within a hundred yards radius. Caught up in a waking dream, he felt as if he were floating along, somehow immune to surrounding dangers. Harry Jacobs found him, a few minutes later, beginning to drift off the line of advance.

"You all right, Rosie? Where do you fink you're going? Orders is to get up to the front wivout delay."

Isaac swung back into consciousness.

"Oh hello, Harry. How are you?"

"Fine at the moment, thanks, but ask me again this evening. If any of us gets through this mess, we should be sent 'ome with a chest full o' bleedin' medals, that's what I say. The sooner we gets up to the front, the quicker we gets clear of this open ground."

"Yes, Harry; you're right. It's just that I'm finding it hard to...to concentrate. I thought I was lost for a while. Then Annie, my sister, was begging me to come home, just like at Blackdown, b...before we shipped out. Do you remember?"

"Yeh, Rosie. I remember fine. But we need to keep moving now, okay?"

A lieutenant suddenly stepped out in front of them.

"Are you men all right? What's wrong with you, Private?"

The officer approached Isaac who, by this time, was smiling vacantly, his eyes tightly shut. Harry quickly intervened.

"He's fine sir. Just a bit shell-shocked, that's all. I'll look after 'im; 'e'll be right as rain in a minute or two, sir."

"He'd better be! Keep moving. We've got to get up to the line before the next wave arrives. Our lads are holding on, but only just."

"Yessir. Don't worry, we'll be up there in a jiff. No problem, sir."

"See that you are!"

Not wholly convinced, he watched as the pair stumbled forward. By now, Hacha's tired, sad face was materialising out of thin air. Isaac reached out to touch her cheek, desperately wanting to reassure her that things would be fine and he'd be back home soon, but the tear-stained eyes seemed to be focused elsewhere.

As they entered the forward zone, the disorientation suddenly lifted and Isaac glanced curiously around him.

"Where are we, Harry?"

"Good to 'ave you back, Rosie. We're 'ome, that's where we bleedin' are!" His voice sounded unusually strained. "The whole place 'as been shelled to fuck. God knows how long we can 'old onto this!"

His friend was not exaggerating. It was almost impossible to negotiate the shattered trench. Old bones, dislodged from the pulverised walls, mingled with the remains of soldiers recently blown to pieces. He steeled himself as heavy artillery fire began to build slowly—the undoubted prelude to yet another infantry assault.

For the next twenty-four hours, the Germans hammered the defenders without pause—an hour of shelling invariably followed by a rush of storm troops across no-man's-land. Stubbornly, the men returned to their guns again and again, fighting off successive attacks. It was as though there was no end to the bobbing spiked helmets pushing forward over the heaped bodies of their fallen comrades.

Eventually, the inevitable occurred: after a particularly sustained push, the German masses reached the line and spilled over the battered parapets. Desperate hand-to-hand fighting broke out, but the inexorable tide gradually undermined the defenders' capacity to resist. Slowly but surely, the first battalion was driven back, trying in vain to maintain an orderly retreat.

Taken completely by surprise, Isaac instinctively plunged his bayonet into an enemy soldier who rushed full pelt round the corner of a support trench he was guarding. The gun was almost wrenched out of his hands, and in a desperate attempt to retrieve it, he inadvertently butchered the man's stomach. Under normal circumstances, he would have been no match for the highly trained assault trooper, but in the unpredictable world of rubble and narrow, winding passages, the odds were evened out. Horrified at what he'd done, and by the high-pitched screaming, he dropped to his knees.

A fellow Lancaster, appearing round the same corner several seconds later, turned swiftly and discharged a round in the direction he'd come. Isaac heard the thump of a body hitting the ground. Another man, close on the heels of his stricken comrade, tripped and sprawled over the corpse. A swift bayonet thrust to the neck put an abrupt end to his efforts to regain his feet. His killer grinned at the poet through clenched teeth, his eyes bright with blood lust.

"By Christ, you fairly did for him." Although no longer screaming, Isaac's victim continued to gasp and squirm, face down in the mud. "He's like a fish out of fucking water. I'll bet he wished he hadn't got out of his trench this morning—just like these other two Hun bastards." He grinned again, and motioned with his head. "Come on! Let's get the hell out of here before we end up the same way. There's a lot more where they came from." Dragging Isaac to his feet, he pulled him along for a few yards into a wider communications trench. "Right my son, keep going down there. We're done for the time being so take my advice and don't hang around."

Locked in the grip of a living nightmare, Isaac gazed into the eyes of what he believed must be a demon incarnate. The maniacal face, streaked with filth and dried blood, was suddenly removed, and he heard the thump of boots on duckboards fading into the distance.

Hardly capable of independent thought or action, he tried to keep moving in the direction he'd been told. At one stage he registered the spatter of gunfire, and men all around him. The next thing he was properly aware of was sitting back in reserve with a mug of hot tea clasped in his hand.

Time lost all meaning as the battle continued to rage. After two endless days and nights struggling to stem the German advance, the men were reaching the end of their tether. Former reserves had become the new front line, and, without further reinforcements, defeat seemed inevitable. Twice Isaac almost lost his grip on sanity, but that part of his stubborn will which had sustained him for so long remained intact. Like an exhausted climber watching the strands of his rope fray and separate one by one, he was acutely aware of the gulf yawning below him. Although the act of falling backwards seemed incredibly appealing at times, his toes and fingers continued to grope for precarious holds in the sheer rock face.

Stumbling back behind the line for a few hours sleep during a temporary lull in the fighting, the few remaining members of 8th Company were aware of nothing but the effort involved in placing one weary foot in front of another. The prospect of reaching billets where they could lie down and sink into oblivion was the only thing that kept them moving. Forced into the village of Fampoux, the new reserves were located in the rooms and cellars of houses rising gently up from the banks of a winding canal.

The men barely noticed the renewed crackle of gunfire; a fresh assault would have to be dealt with by those left behind. Human endurance was a finite resource, and those deprived of sleep for almost forty-eight hours had become more of a hindrance than a help.

As they crossed the canal via a narrow, metal bridge almost within sight of the billets, a runner suddenly burst through and blocked their way forward.

"Hold up a minute, will ya!" The man, grasping the rail just where it began to curve down onto a narrow stairway, tried to catch his breath. "Jesus, didn't you hear the gunfire? Major Collins is askin' for volunteers. The Hun's broken through again."

Harry Jacobs looked up at him through bleary, red-rimmed eyes. His unshaven cheeks had shrunk inwards, the sharp contours of his skull looking ready to pierce the tight skin. He struggled to express himself through a parched mouth, with a tongue which felt as though it had swollen to twice its normal size. His words, when they came, were slurred and hesitant as if uttered by a drunkard:

"Is Collins giving us an order, or what?"

"No. He said volunteers only."

Harry nodded. "Then get to fuck out of here, and leave us alone. Surely, it's obvious we're fit for nuffink but sleep. That's why we're 'ere now and not back where you just came from."

Incapable of further speech, Harry pushed past, trying to focus on negotiating the steep metal steps. The sound of a familiar voice halted him, and he swung round, unable to believe what he was hearing.

"I'll go with you, b...but I'll need your help."

"What the fuck do you think you're doing, Rosie? You're not going with him, are you?"

"I'll be fine, Harry. You get some rest."

"But, you'll never make it, man; don't be so bloody stupid!"

He made to grab Isaac's arm, but the runner intervened.

"Look, mate, if he wants to come back, that's his affair—nothing to do with you!"

"Fuck off, you bastard! What the 'ell do you know? Leave us alone. Rosie's comin' back wiv us."

"Don't worry, Harry; it's for the best. I got some sleep earlier. I'll see you soon."

"Don't be a fool. You know what'll 'appen if you..."

Looking around, Harry saw he was on his own. The remainder of the platoon, unmoved by the major's appeal, had already shambled past and were descending the stairs. He stood still, undecided for a moment. It occurred to him that he should have tried harder to discourage his friend, but it was too late; he'd never catch them up in his present state. Isaac had obviously cracked and there was nothing he or anyone else could do. Clutching the handrail, he eased himself down towards the dark towpath below.

In a sense Harry was right. Isaac knew very well what would happen and welcomed the prospect. Living was a burden he no longer felt able to endure. Moreover, memories of his bayonet piercing human flesh and the screaming of the dying man were becoming unbearable. What use was poetry in the face of this? People protected from the horrors of the war could never understand the colossal barbarity, and yet to those exposed to horrific injury and slaughter on a daily basis, there was no denying its capacity to blunt all but the most basic survival instincts. Isaac felt nothing but pity for those dreamers, who, like his former self, believed their work could make a difference. Bottomley's finely crafted lines and Marsh's studied idealism would all be finally extinguished in the face of encroaching darkness. The world was what it was—art a mere palliative, perhaps capable of diverting one's attention for a while but ultimately illusory. Why would he want to survive in the face of a renunciation of everything he'd once held dear? What meaning could life hold for him now? And the fate of his fellow Jews struggling to forge a homeland in the face of implacable hostility? If successful, he doubted whether they'd ever be able to live in peace. Like the flawed god they worshipped, desire for vengeance and the accumulation of power would ultimately blacken their hearts. The answers were clear to him and he wanted no part of it.

The runner's excited babble and the sound of approaching gunfire barely impinged on his consciousness. The only thing he desired now was a swift end to his misery—a cessation of life itself.

Then he was suddenly alone in a strange subterranean world where sounds from beyond its blurry limits were muffled and unthreatening. A face swam close up and stared at him for a moment before retreating into darkness. He found it hard to move, like a diver encumbered by a heavily weighted suit. Lines of poetry entered his mind before quickly passing out like bubbles through an air tube. Maybe he was dying. A clamour, distant at first but becoming progressively louder, filled him with terror. His immediate surroundings were sucked down as if into some huge, invisible hole, and he was back in the midst of battle.

He noticed a group of soldiers standing a few yards up the trench and stumbled towards them.

"Glad you're here, Private." A wiry sergeant stepped forward, his intense, blue eyes fixed on Isaac's face. "I've been ordered to take some prisoners. The brass is keen to know what the Hun are going to do next."

This, Isaac reasoned, must be utter nonsense but it didn't really matter; trying to capture prisoners in the midst of a full-scale enemy assault seemed a sure way of bringing things to a satisfactory conclusion.

"I'd like to volunteer, Sergeant."

"Very good, Private…?"

"Private Rosenberg."

"I think it best if we try to capture two or three of them over towards their own lines. That way we'll have the element of surprise."

The man sounded plausible despite having clearly lost his mind. No one could possibly have ordered him to commit suicide in this way. Under present chaotic circumstances nothing was expected beyond resisting the enemy as long as humanly possible. Isaac wondered if the others, now preparing to leave the relative safety of the trench, were equally insane. It was reasonable to assume they were. The question was, how much pressure could any man endure before cracking up completely? Everyone gathered here, including himself, must have reached their individual breaking points. Some, like the sergeant, might still be going through the motions, desperately trying to rationalise what was happening, without the slightest chance of success.

"Right then. The quicker we get going, the quicker we're back." The men nodded dumbly and began to climb the firing steps. "Keep your heads down and move to the right."

As they set off across no-man's-land trying to avoid sprawled bodies and gaping shell holes, renewed machine-gun fire and the yells of charging soldiers, off to the left, alerted them to the fact that yet another assault had begun. The hiss of the sergeant's voice sounded just behind him.

"We're almost there. Only another hundred yards or so."

Suddenly, the ground ahead began to move. A German raiding party, at least a hundred strong, perhaps hoping to flank British positions engaged in beating off the main force, was advancing swiftly and silently over the battered terrain. As luck would have it, Isaac and his six comrades were directly in their path. Pulling his rifle to his shoulder, the sergeant fired into their midst. For a second his hooked nose and thick moustache were illuminated in the blackness.

"Fuck taking prisoners. We've got to stop this lot. Fire at will."

Isaac, with no intention of killing anyone else, dropped to his knees and pushed his rifle away. A volley of shots filled the air. The sergeant, a few yards to his right, pitched forward, his chest smashed open by a spray of bullets. The others, engaging in a last act of defiance, or turning to run, were shot at point-blank range.

A storm trooper viciously chopped the sharpened edge of his spade into the base of Isaac's bowed neck, the force of the blow almost separating the head from the torso. Raising the improvised weapon again, he brought it crashing down full force on the back of the poet's skull; shattered bone and brain mingled with the flow of blood from severed arteries. The burly German grimaced and muttered something to a nearby comrade, before moving swiftly on, leaving Isaac's corpse crushed in the mud.

Then the darkness before dawn, and, at last, silence.

Epilogue 1918

My sisters have their males
From the doomed earth, from the doomed glee
And hankering of hearts...

From "Daughters of War": 1917

So, he went back up the line. There was nuffink I could say or do to stop 'im. 'E didn't really seem to care any more."

Harry was sitting in the front parlour of the Rosenberg household in Stepney, the day after his return from France. Although somewhat reluctant, he felt he owed it to his friend's family to tell them what he knew as soon as he arrived home. The situation had weighed heavily on his mind since that fateful night, bridging March and April. He stared at the chipped fireplace as he spoke, unwilling to catch anyone's eye. Barnett sat slumped in the corner as if asleep, his head bowed and his grey beard spilling over his chest. Hacha wept quietly, still unwilling to accept that her son was never coming back. For the past few months she'd been hoarding tiny fragments of hope, mainly derived from the fact that Isaac's body had never been officially identified. Part of her still believed that one day he would walk through the door, returned to the bosom of his family by some powerful providence. Every so often, she stole a hostile glance at the man who seemed bent on unravelling the remaining threads of her cherished illusions. She bitterly resented the fact that he was here while Isaac remained somewhere in the killing fields of northern France.

In the meantime, Annie was finding it hard to focus on the here and now. As Harry spoke, she clearly envisaged her brother, exhausted and terrified, stumbling back up the line to die. She felt his inner emptiness and his life force ebbing away, replaced by an intense desire for death.

Long before word arrived declaring him missing in action, she knew he'd lost his internal battle for survival. That vast reservoir of creativity, representing so much more than the sum total of his failures in life, had at last run dry. He'd sent her virtually nothing since the turn of the year—the trickle of poems finally freezing in the depths of another winter on the Western Front.

"I fink 'e wanted to die. 'E knew what would 'appen if 'e went back."

Harry's words echoed her own thoughts.

Annie understood very well what he was getting at and was desperate to learn as much as possible about the circumstances of Isaac's death. Hacha, on the other hand, fought hard to control the urge to throw the little Jew out of her house.

"We'd been fighting all day and most of the night. It's funny but that was only the beginning. We got reinforcements next morning, and the whole battalion—what was left of it, that is—was pulled out. Day after, Gerry broke through, proper like this time, and we was brought back to try and 'old them just outside Arras. Then, for some reason, they fell back again and we moved right up to the old front line. It went on like that for the next few days until they finally gave up. By then the brass seemed to 'ave got their act together."

"Did you hear anything about what might have happened to Isaac?" Annie, intent on uncovering any snippet of information, forgot for a moment how sensitive her mother was on this issue.

"Annie, I don't think Mr Jacobs knows…"

"It's all right, Mrs Rosenberg. I did actually 'ear a few rumours but nuffink definite. Some fellow told me 'e saw Isaac wiv a sergeant by the name of 'Arkins. Apparently, 'e was a bit of a fire-eater; wanted the Hun for breakfast, dinner and supper, if you take my meaning."

"Did my son go out on patrol with this sergeant, Mr Jacobs?"

Barnett's sudden intervention took everyone by surprise. Hacha glared over the room as if she was seeing her husband for the first time.

"Well, the man I was talkin' to seemed to fink 'e may 'ave done, Mr Rosenberg, but nothing's certain, you understand. There was too much 'appening at the time to be sure. 'Arkins, 'ad a bit of a reputation, as I said, but…according to a few of 'is mates 'ed started to get carried away. Any'ow, he disappeared the same night as Isaac and they never found 'im neither."

"Would Isaac have got a... decent burial if he'd been...?" Hacha couldn't finish the question. Annie looked over at her mother in amazement. This was the first time she'd come near to admitting that her eldest son might actually be dead.

"Most likely, Mrs Rosenberg. When Gerry retreated our lads went out and buried as many of the dead as they could. Unless it was obvious who was who, they probably wouldn't 'ave been reported dead like. You've got to understand, that ground shifted from one side to the other over the next few days. I was told it might be years before everybody gets put in a proper cemetery, but the lads would 'ave shown respect and made sure they was out of 'arm's way for the time being."

"Thank you, Mr Jacobs, you'll have to excuse me now."

Hacha rose ponderously and left the room, failing to look either at her husband or her daughter. Annie knew she was deeply upset, but at least there were signs that the process of mourning Isaac's death might soon begin.

"I'm sorry if I upset your..."

"Don't worry, Mr Jacobs. I think what you said will do my mother good in the long run. She's not really been able to accept the possibility of Isaac's death. We all appreciate what a good friend you were to him."

"I wish I could've done more. 'E was a very...private man you've got to understand, but 'e was kind; 'e tried 'ard to get me some 'ome leave when my sister died. I wanted to 'elp my mother get through an 'ard spell what wiv Dora's young uns and all. Anyway, it wasn't to be, but Isaac kept at it like. I'll never forget 'im for that, and other fings an' all."

Annie found herself unable to reply for a few moments; tears crowded her eyes as she envisaged her brother's last few moments of life.

As Harry was leaving, he turned and looked Annie straight in the eye.

"There was a lot I didn't understand about your brother; 'e was an 'ard man to read if you take my meaning. But, I've never seen anyone braver than 'e was . 'E was scared all the time like, but that didn't seem to make no difference. They couldn't break 'im. Isaac wasn't the best soldier in the world, but they couldn't break 'im. I don't know what he was about; never really did. Whatever it was though, he stuck to it like bleedin' glue, 'scuse the language, but 'e was 'is own man. That's all I've got to say. Goodnight then."

"Good night and thank you again, Mr Jacobs."

Annie stood staring up the dark street long after Harry had disappeared from sight. Eventually she stepped back inside, quietly closed the door and began to climb the stairs to her mother's bedroom.

The End

Author's note

While *Beating for Light* is primarily a work of fiction, much of the novel's factual information was drawn from the four excellent biographies of Isaac Rosenberg. I therefore gratefully acknowledge:

Journey To The Trenches by Joseph Cohen.
A Half Used Life by Jean Liddiard.
Isaac Rosenberg: Poet And Painter by Jean Moorcroft Wilson.
God Made Blind by Deborah Maccoby.

I also wish to express gratitude to Ian Parsons for his introduction and notes to *The Collected Works Of Isaac Rosenberg* published by the New York Oxford University Press; and thanks to Jane Tatam, Peter Cowlam and Trevor Lockwood for their insights and perseverance.